TO HAVE AND TO HOLD

*They dreamed of a wedding day filled with
satin and lace, champagne and caviar.*

*But for Sunny, Kathi, Kate and Shelly, the
road to "I do" is filled with surprises, mishaps
and adventures.*

TO HAVE AND TO HOLD

*Written by four of your favorite Harlequin
authors, these stories will make you laugh,
cry—and believe in the power of love.*

*If you thought getting married was easy, wait
until you meet these four brides...*

TO HAVE AND TO HOLD

About the Authors

BARBARA BRETTON—One of Harlequin American Romance's most loved authors, Barbara has written over twenty novels. She is the recipient of numerous writing awards, including Best Series Writer from *Romantic Times,* and is listed in *The Foremost Women in the Twentieth Century.* Barbara lives with her husband in New Jersey.

RITA CLAY ESTRADA—This Waldenbooks bestselling author has penned eleven novels for Harlequin Temptation, including the popular *The Ivory Key.* She is a cofounder of Romance Writers of America and served as its first president. The mother of four, Rita makes her home in Texas.

SANDRA JAMES—One of Superromance's most popular writers, Sandra is the author of nine books for the series. A "typical American housewife," as she labels herself, she worked as a secretary and a military personnel clerk for the U.S. Army before turning to writing ten years ago. Along with her husband and three daughters, Sandra lives in Oregon.

DEBBIE MACOMBER—This prolific novelist has authored over forty novels, including a dozen for Harlequin Romance, as well as a short story in Harlequin's MY VALENTINE 1991 collection. She makes her home in Washington State, with her husband and their four children.

BARBARA BRETTON
RITA CLAY ESTRADA
SANDRA JAMES
DEBBIE MACOMBER

TO HAVE AND TO HOLD

Harlequin Books

TORONTO • NEW YORK • LONDON
AMSTERDAM • PARIS • SYDNEY • HAMBURG
STOCKHOLM • ATHENS • TOKYO • MILAN
MADRID • WARSAW • BUDAPEST • AUCKLAND

TO HAVE AND TO HOLD
Copyright © 1992 by Harlequin Enterprises Limited

ISBN 0-373-83238-9

TO HAVE AND TO HOLD first printing April 1992

The publisher acknowledges the copyright holders of the individual works as follows:

I DO, I DO
Copyright © 1992 by Barbara Bretton

BRIDE ON THE RUN
Copyright © 1992 by Rita Clay Estrada

BRIDE IN BLUE
Copyright © 1992 by Sandra Kleinschmit

THE FIRST MAN YOU MEET
Copyright © 1992 by Debbie Macomber

CONTENTS

I Do, I Do

BARBARA BRETTON

A Note from Barbara Bretton

I never played "bride" as a little girl, never planned an imaginary wedding.

So what happened two months after my eighteenth birthday? You guessed it. I got married.

The kind of married that has everything to do with love and not one blessed thing to do with organ music, china patterns or engraved invitations.

Roy and I were married on a sunny Sunday morning in September 1968 in the front room of a judge's home in Yonkers, New York. I wore a short white dress. Roy wore his air-force blues. My parents chauffeured us in their lime-green car and, after the ceremony, the entire wedding party shared a celebratory breakfast in a four-star diner before the afternoon reception.

There was lots of laughter—and some happy tears—and I doubt if a fancy orchestra and reception line could have made the day any more splendid than it was.

In the past twenty-three years, Roy and I have argued, worried, laughed, cried, struggled and sometimes wondered if every dark cloud really did have a silver lining. But through it all one thing has been constant: love. He's my best friend, my favorite person in the world, and I can only shake my head in wonder that two teenagers had been smart enough (and lucky enough) to know what was really important in life.

Weddings, elaborate or simple, last just one day. Marriage, if you're lucky, is forever.

I wish you all many happy endings of your own.

Barbara

Chapter One

THEY SAID a man never forgot his first love, the first woman to claim his heart. Maybe that was why the sign in the art gallery window caught Robert's eye on that bright April afternoon. *Grand Opening*, it read in bold deco print. *Sunny invites you to a wine-and-cheese open house to celebrate the opening of Gallery One.*

Sunny. The name alone was enough to summon up the memory of warm summer nights and youthful dreams. Lately he'd found himself thinking about her—the woman he'd once loved and married—at the oddest of times. The scent of Shalimar... a woman with eyes the color of a green meadow... the nagging feeling that if they'd tried harder or loved each other more their marriage might have worked out.

The odds of bumping into his ex-wife after fifteen years were probably a million to one. There had to be more than one woman named Sunny in the state of Pennsylvania, he reasoned as he opened the door, then stepped inside the gallery.

"Hi," said a middle-aged woman dressed in white. "Help yourself to some wine and cheese." He was about to thank her when she gave him a closer look. "Are you the guy from the bank? Mr. Daniels said he was—"

"That's what I get for wearing a suit to an art gallery," he said with an easy laugh. "I'm just taking a look around."

She shrugged. "Well, enjoy yourself. And make sure you have some wine."

He glanced around the crowded gallery. The women in the room were either too old, too young, too tall or too average to be Sunny.

Unless she'd changed. He'd been looking for a curvy slip of a woman with a fiery personality to match her wild mane of red curls. She could be a blonde now. She could have tamed both her disposition and her hair and turned into someone he wouldn't recognize without a name tag. The thought of Sunny trading in her dreams for a stock portfolio was enough to ruin his day.

A man's first love was meant to live on in his memory forever, beautiful and perfect, untouched by time. This had been a lousy idea, and the thing to do now was get out while the getting was good and his memories were still intact.

And then he saw her.

He would have recognized her anywhere. She was standing near a Chinese screen, looking as beautiful as she had the last time he'd seen her. She wore a spandex miniskirt, an oversize silver-and-gold sweater and sheer black stockings with patent-leather ankle boots. A Technicolor tumble of red curls fell halfway to her waist and he wanted to plunge his hands into the silky mass and—

Whoa!

Ex-wives weren't supposed to get a man's heart pumping hard inside his chest. He had no business noticing the way the glittery sweater clung to her rounded breasts or the shapely length of leg revealed by her mini. He'd known her back when breasts like that were a fervent dream, not a luscious reality. He'd seen her with her hair in rollers, with makeup and without. Happy, sad and every mood in between.

A big guy with a shock of ice-blond hair whispered something in her ear and she laughed. Husky. Low. Sexy.

He'd never heard her laugh like that before, and the sound sizzled its way to all of his major body parts. Who did that bozo think he was, whispering to her that way? *Back off,* an inner voice warned. *That bozo could be her husband.*

"No," he said out loud. "No way in hell."

She was his.

SUNNY WAS STILL LAUGHING at Vladimir's joke when she saw him. Suddenly she stopped.

"It can't be," she whispered, oblivious to everything but the man approaching her.

Was it possible that the one man she'd loved enough to marry was about to step back into her life? Impossible. Absolutely, positively impossible.

The man stopped a few feet away from her. "It's been a long time, Sunny." That voice. Deep. Rich. Vibrant. The kind of voice that could talk a woman into bed before she knew what was happening. Dear God, it was . . .

"Robert?" She stared at him, openmouthed. He was bigger than she'd remembered, and older, but he was still the most beautiful man she'd ever known and she wondered how it was they had ever said goodbye. "Robby!" She threw herself into his arms, tears and laughter erupting simultaneously. "My God! I can't believe this!"

He swept her up into an exuberant bear hug that lifted her from the ground and made her feel fragile and feminine and infinitely desirable. He smelled faintly of soap, and his cheek was still warm from the sun. His thick dark brown hair grazed his collar, the same as it had years ago, and she found herself wondering if it would feel as silky as it looked. He was broad across the chest and still narrow of hip and he was still the sexiest man she had ever seen.

He released her from his hug, and she found herself reluctant to let go. It had been so long since she'd been close to him and, right or wrong, it felt so wonderful in his arms.

He gave her a long and appreciative look. "Only you could get away with an outfit like that."

She tugged at the tie that hung loosely about his neck. "And only you could get away with this and still look sexy."

"You look great, Sunny."

"So do you." Age was always kind to men, and in this case, it had been extremely generous. Was it possible for a man's eyes to grow bluer with time? She doubted it, but still . . .

"When did you—"

"What brought you—"

They met each other's eyes and laughed again.

"You first," he said.

She felt as if she were caught somewhere between the past and the present, suspended on a cloud of bitter-sweet memory.

We can make it, Sunny, I know we can. I'll work part-time at McDonald's and after the baby comes, you can—

She shook her head to banish the memory. "What on earth are you doing here?"

"Business meeting just outside of town. I was hunting around for a place to grab some dinner."

"You're the last person I expected to see."

"I'm kind of surprised myself."

She made a show of inspecting his attire. "Judging by the suit, I'd say you became an attorney, after all."

He favored her with a wry smile. "Judging by the gallery, I'd say you found your career in art."

"I'm not going to be the next Picasso, but I'm happy."

"I'm glad."

She tilted her head, looking at him with open and unabashed curiosity. "You're telling me you just happened to walk by my gallery?"

He motioned toward the sign in the front window. "I saw the poster. You know what a sucker I am for wine-and-cheese parties."

"This from the man who once told me he'd rather be trapped in a locked basement with Godzilla than go to a party with my artsy friends?"

"I'm never going to live that down, am I?" He shook his head. "I was eighteen. I've mellowed."

Impulsively she reached out and took his hand. "You don't know how wonderful it is to see you again, Robby. I'd hoped to see you at our tenth reunion." *Idiot! Why don't you just pin your heart to your sleeve and be done with it?* It wasn't as if she'd spent the past fifteen years pining after her ex-husband. She had a successful career, a happy life, friends and family who loved her. She had no right to want more. "I mean, the old gang really missed you."

An odd look drifted across his face and he glanced away for a moment. Just long enough for her to sense the gulf time had placed between them.

"You didn't miss much of anything," she continued, trying to fill the silence with chatter about the last reunion of the class of 1976. "Lisa was pregnant with her fourth baby. John lost weight. Kenny is cornering the market on Minoxidil and Karen still loves Paul."

"And what about you?" *Who do you love, Sunny? Who claimed your heart?*

"Still a free spirit," she said, feeling anything but. The sweet yoke of their common history tugged gently. "Drifting through life, wondering what's around the next corner."

"People who drift through life don't open their own art galleries."

"Oh, I land from time to time," she said, trying to figure out a way to release his hand without seeming rude. "I'm not a total flake, Robby. I just look like one."

"I never said you were."

"That's right," she said softly, remembering. "You never did." Everyone else had laughed at her dreams, told her to put aside her visions of glory and study business like the rest of them, but not Robert. He had been behind her all the way, even though her dreams must have seemed as formless and bizarre as a Dali painting to him.

"Excuse me." Her assistant, Joi, bustled up to them. "No more champagne. No more pâté. No more crackers." Her glance flickered to Robert, then back to Sunny again. "What now?"

"No more party, I suppose." She glanced at her watch. "Actually we've run an hour later than I'd planned."

"The painters called and they're itching to finish up in the back. Can I give them the go-ahead?"

"Another half hour," said Sunny. "I'd hate to give our guests the bum's rush." *Especially you,* she thought, stealing a look at Robert. It had been so long—and there was so much she wanted to know about him.

Her assistant hurried away to give the painters the go-ahead, and Sunny turned back to Robert. She had already noticed there was no ring on the appropriate finger, but that in itself meant little. One of her most persistent would-be suitors had been a ringless married man. *Ask him if he's married, you coward! It's a perfectly normal question.*

"Are you married?" asked Robert.

She blinked. "I was about to ask you the same thing."

"Are you?"

"No." She took a shaky breath, remembering something about a wife and children. "Are you?"

He shook his head. "Widowed."

"I'm sorry."

"And I have two kids."

She took another deep breath. "Two?"

"A six-year-old boy and a twelve-year-old girl."

"Oh."

"Do you like kids?"

"I like them just fine." She'd given him children, whoever his wife had been. A sharp stab of envy knifed at her heart. "It must be difficult, being a single father and all."

"I'm luckier than a lot of people," he said, eyes locked with hers. "I can afford help at home."

She tried to imagine him driving a car pool or fixing school lunches, but failed miserably. He had everything they'd ever wanted . . . everything they'd ever dreamed they would one day have together.

"Sunny!" Her assistant's voice rang out. "Roscoe needs some help over here."

"Go help Roscoe," said Robert with an easy smile. "I'll still be here when you're finished."

Her heart did a strange little dance inside her chest. "You will?"

"I'm taking you to dinner."

"That sounds wonderful."

"Know where we can get some good food?"

"Oh, yes," she said with a pleased smile. "I know just the place."

SUNNY HADN'T BEEN his wife since Jimmy Carter was in office and the Bee Gees ruled the airwaves, yet the minute Robert stepped inside her house overlooking the river, he instantly recognized her personal touch in every corner of every room. From the floor-to-ceiling wall of cuckoo clocks in the foyer to the lemon-yellow hammock suspended from the exposed beams in the living room, the place was pure Sunny.

"Help yourself to some wine," she said, heading toward the narrow staircase to the left of the foyer. "I'm going to change into something more culinary."

"Nothing wrong with what you have on." Covering up those legs of hers would be a capital offense.

To his amazement color flooded her cheeks as if she had read his mind. "The glasses are in the kitchen. Second cabinet to the left of the sink. Pour me some chardonnay," she said, running a hand through her tousled curls with a quick, yet graceful, motion. "I'll be right down."

He stood at the foot of the stairs, blatantly watching her until she disappeared through the door at the top of the landing. Her slender hips still swayed gently when she walked, like a provocative metronome. It was nice to know some things didn't change. He'd spent the better part of four years of high school enjoying the way the back pockets of her jeans moved to the syncopated rhythm of her walk. You wouldn't think a man would remember something like that after all this time. He'd finished law school, remarried and fathered two children, but still the memory of Sunny in her jeans lingered.

Sunny was the first girl he'd ever kissed, the first girl he took to bed, the first to share his name. It was only logical he'd feel something toward her, a tug of emotion over what they'd once shared. They'd loved with the intensity of youth, the fire of innocence. They'd believed in the sanctity of marriage, that the vows they'd taken with such hope for the future would last a lifetime.

For an instant he caught the scent of roses and orange blossoms in the air and he glanced about the room, looking for a potpourri hidden away somewhere. He couldn't find one, but that didn't mean it wasn't there. Nobody imagined the scent of orange blossoms.

SUNNY PRAYED he didn't notice the way her hand was shaking as she accepted a glass of chardonnay a few minutes later.

"To old friends," he said.

She smiled. "To old friends."

They clinked glasses. Sunlight streamed in from the stained-glass window on the far wall, casting shadows of sapphire and ruby across the polished-oak floor of her living room. She wished she'd turned on the radio, anything to mask the thundering of her heart. What had she been thinking of, inviting him back to her house like this? They should have gone to a restaurant, some nice, innocuous place in the center of town where she knew everyone and everyone knew her.

She felt painfully aware of his presence, the faint citrusy smell of his skin—the way she longed to run her hands through his thick, silky hair. *Get a grip on yourself, Sunny. This isn't a date. This is your ex-husband.* Ex-husbands didn't make your hands tremble or your pulse beat faster. And they certainly didn't make a woman dream of slow kisses in the moonlight.

Or of second chances.

The thing to do was put some space between them.

"There's a beautiful view of the river from my back porch," she said after taking a sip of wine for courage. "Why don't we take our drinks outside?" Space and fresh air would help her recover her equilibrium.

But sitting outside didn't help. The scent of orange blossoms followed Robert, and the world itself seemed too small to contain the emotions in Sunny's heart. For an endless time neither one spoke. Sunny made no effort to excuse herself to prepare the lunch she'd promised him. Robert made no attempt to leave. After a while he reached for her hand, lacing his fingers through hers. They'd held hands like that back in high school, enraptured by the way their fingers meshed so perfectly. Everything had seemed miraculous back then, as if a benevolent God watched over them, making sure no harm could ever come their way.

They watched as the sun began to disappear behind the trees, blushing the sky with the pink-and-orange flames of evening.

But it was always you, Robby. From the very beginning, it was you and you alone, Sunny thought.

I loved Christine, but no woman ever touched my soul the way you did, Robert thought.

The night breeze off the river grew chilly. Still holding hands, they rose and went back inside.

The house seemed to reach out and embrace Robert.

To Sunny it felt like a home for the very first time.

He built a fire in the hearth while she prepared a simple dinner. The domestic intimacy between them felt simultaneously familiar and exciting and terrifying—a wild combination of emotions that charged the cottage with electricity. There was a sense of destiny about them, as if the fates had conspired to bring them together once again . . . to give them one last chance at happiness.

Robert pulled a bridge table close to the fireplace in the living room, and Sunny set the table with cherry-red water glasses shaped like tulips and plates painted to resemble giant cabbage leaves.

"Chopsticks?" he asked as she laid the ivory utensils across the lime-green linen napkins.

"Live dangerously." She took her seat opposite him. "Chopsticks improve the taste of everything."

"Of potato salad?"

"You'd be surprised."

"You haven't changed," he said, refilling their wine-glasses from the half-empty bottle of chardonnay on the red lacquered butler's table. "Still taking the road less travelled."

She took a sip of wine. "That's where you find the best scenery."

He started to say something flip about the scenery being just fine from where he sat, but the words stayed locked inside his throat. This was the real thing. Not dinner with some friend of a friend who's dying to meet you. Not just a way to pass a lonely spring evening while the kids were out of town.

This was Sunny.

His Sunny.

"It looks great," he said, gesturing toward the food on his plate, "but I'm not hungry."

She pushed her own plate away. "Neither am I."

The look in his eyes was as hot and dangerous as the fire burning in the hearth. "Do you still believe in love at first sight?"

Her eyes fluttered closed for an instant as the impact of his words ignited an answering flame deep inside. "Robby, I—"

Her words ended abruptly as he pushed back his chair and stood up. He reached for her, and as if in a dream, she placed her hand in his and rose from her chair. She felt his touch on every part of her body, and she wondered how it was she had managed to live without the other half of her heart. The feeling was dangerous and mad and totally irresistible.

Slowly, deliberately, he drew her into his arms, pulling her so close that her body seemed to melt against his.

"Put your arms around me, Sunny."

Lifting her chin, she met his eyes. The look in them was smoky. Unmistakable. The boy she had married years ago was gone. He was a man now in every way. Taller. Broader. More self-confident. She shivered with pleasure as he threaded his fingers through her hair. *More demanding.* She placed her hands on his shoulders.

"You've been lifting weights," she murmured. He ran his thumb over the swell of her lower lip. "I always imagined you'd play squash or something. Don't all successful lawyers play squash?"

He placed his hand beneath her chin and tilted her face up toward him. "I don't want to talk about sports, Sunny."

"You don't?"

"And I don't want to talk about the law firm."

Her laughter was low, her excitement deeply female. "What do you want to talk about?"

"Nothing," he said, dipping his head toward hers. "Not one damn thing."

And then he drew her closer still until the last of the emotional barriers between them incinerated before the primal rush of passion their first kiss brought to life. His mouth was hard and demanding, her lips, soft and yielding. She answered his need with a fierce need of her own, and he didn't leave her wanting.

All they had shared was in that kiss and in the dozen kisses that followed.

"Robby...oh, God..." Her voice drifted away on a wave of pleasure. "This is crazy."

"Yes," he said, his lips hot against the curve of her breast. "Crazy."

"The sofa," she said as her knees grew weak. That soft and welcoming sofa before the fireplace where she'd watched television alone.

Moments later they lay together, greedy for the feel of skin against skin. He cupped her breasts beneath her T-shirt, letting his palms tease her nipples until they grew taut and hard. She felt that touch in the deepest, most secret part of her body. She fumbled with the buttons of his shirt. Robert moved her hands away, then ripped it open, scattering buttons across the floor. In the space of a heartbeat he stripped her of her T-shirt, then eased her jeans and panties over her hips and legs. The night breeze rippled over her heated skin. He devoured her with his eyes, as if he owned her, body and soul.

She reached for his belt buckle, and he laughed deep in his throat. Moments later they were both naked, so ravenous for the sight and sound and smell of each other that they had no time for preliminaries.

Only a raw and primitive mating could satisfy their need.

Their lovemaking was sweet and savage, as swift as the river flowing beyond the open window, and when it was over and she lay in his arms with her cheek resting against his chest, Robert knew without a doubt that he'd never let her go.

"Sunny."

She burrowed closer to him. "Hmm?"

"We're getting married."

Chapter Two

SUNNY SAT STRAIGHT UP and stared at him. "What was that?"

"Marry me," he repeated in a tone as maddeningly calm as before.

"You're proposing to me?" She had to be dreaming. Things like this didn't happen in the light of day.

He swung his legs from the sofa. "I know what's missing," he said, dropping to one knee. "You want an official, old-fashioned proposal of marriage."

"You're naked, Robby," she pointed out, starting to giggle.

"Good. That way you'll know I'm serious."

"You can't possibly be. We barely know each other."

"We've known each other since we were thirteen years old."

"And we haven't seen each other since we were teenagers."

"Can you tell me you don't feel what I'm feeling?"

"Of course I do, Robby, it's just . . ."

"You're afraid."

"I'm not afraid of anything."

"Maybe not," he said, settling back onto the sofa next to her, "but you're afraid of this." He placed her hand against his heart. "You're afraid of failing a second time."

How terrible—and wonderful—it was to be with a man who knew you so well. "And you're not?"

"We're older this time. Fate's brought us together and I can't believe it's not for a reason."

"That's all very New Age, Robby, but there's more at stake than our feelings—your children, for instance."

"They'll love you as much as I do."

"You can't be sure of that."

"How could they help it?"

Sunny wasn't worried about his little boy, but the notion of a preteen daughter gave her pause. "Daughters are notoriously possessive of their fathers."

"Jessi's a good kid. She needs a mother as much as I need a wife."

Sunny bridled at the implication. "If you're just looking for a housekeeper, then—"

"I love you, Sunny."

She stared at him, his words echoing inside her heart. "You can't."

He shrugged eloquently. "I do."

"That's crazy."

"You won't get any argument from me."

"Love at first sight doesn't happen twice with the same person."

"It just has." He met her gaze and held her fast. "Hasn't it?"

It was one of those moments that defined the rest of your life. One second she was Sunny Talbot, a fiercely independent art-gallery owner; the next second she was a woman head-over-heels in love who could think of nothing beyond how badly she wanted Robert to kiss her. She knew that the smart thing would be to turn away from him and chalk up this interlude to one of life's stranger moments.

But this was Robert. She'd grown up with him. Despite the fact that their marriage hadn't survived, she wouldn't have missed those years with him for the world.

And she still loved him. Dear God, it was true. She still loved him. All of the pain and sweetness of first love was there inside her heart, ready to deepen into the kind of love that could last a lifetime.

"The road less travelled," she said softly. "I pick it every time."

"I can't guarantee the scenery."

"There's only one guarantee I want." She moved into his embrace. "That no matter what happens, we'll face it together."

"We can't rewrite history, but we might have a good shot at the future."

The past rushed back at her in all its heartbreaking glory. "I loved you so much," she murmured, her lips brushing against his. "With my heart and soul."

He stroked her hair, and she heard the way his breath caught for a moment. "I would have done anything for you, Sunny... laid down my life for you if it would have made things different."

"Why didn't it work?" Her voice was a whisper.

"Because we were young," he said after a moment. "So damn young..."

All through high school they had been the golden couple, beautiful, blessed with brains and talent and the certainty that life would always be as perfect as it was the day they met.

"We gave up so easily, Robby. We should have fought for our marriage."

"We didn't know how."

"We could have learned."

"Maybe we didn't want to."

His words stung because she sensed the truth in them. The miscarriage had been their first failure, and they had turned away from each other as if that tragedy had somehow put "finished" to their marriage. Golden couples didn't fail at anything. Any teenager could tell you that.

And that's all they had been. Teenagers still wet behind the ears, with about as much understanding of the real world as they had of quantum physics.

Sunny leaped the sofa and rummaged in the cedar chest that rested beneath the window.

"Look at this." She handed Robert a framed photo, then curled up next to him again.

"Our prom picture," he said, chuckling. "Will you look at those sideburns?"

"Our wedding picture," she corrected, "and I happen to think those sideburns were adorable."

Robert shook his head as he met her eyes. "Were we ever that young?"

Sunny's eyes misted over with sentimental tears. "The wonder of it is that anyone thought we were old enough to get married. We look like children playing dress-up." Her thoughts drifted back toward the night of the senior prom when they'd realized that in a few short months they would be in college, thrown into a brand-new world where anything could happen. "I couldn't imagine a life without you," she said. "There wasn't anything on earth more important than being together."

And so while their friends had gone on to an all-night postprom bash, Sunny and Robert had pooled their money, then climbed into his Chevy for the trip down to Maryland where they were married by a justice of the peace.

"Do you remember the way they looked at us in that diner near the Delaware border?" Robert asked. "There we were, looking like Ken and Barbie in our prom clothes, surrounded by Hell's Angels."

"They did look rough," Sunny conceded, "but they paid for our wedding breakfast."

"We're lucky we got out of there alive."

"We were young and in love and they thought we were adorable."

They laughed about their first apartment, the one with the hot plate and the cranky landlord and how their parents shuddered each time they came for dinner.

"My folks thought we needed an armed guard to pick up the mail," Robert said.

"And my mother was convinced the landlord was a Peeping Tom."

Despite everything, the Talbots and the Hollands had stuck by their kids through thick and thin.

"They're not going to believe this," said Robert.

"I know," said Sunny. "They'll say we're crazy."

"Considering what's happened in the past few hours, I can't say I'd blame them."

"Once she gets over the shock, my mother will be ecstatic," said Sunny. "She thought you were the greatest catch since Prince Charles."

"Just as long as she doesn't expect us to get married at Westminster Abbey."

"They're going to hate the idea of a small wedding," said Sunny.

"You don't—"

"Good grief, no! Big weddings are absurd."

"A waste of time and money."

"I'd rather be surrounded by the people who love us the most."

"Just family," said Robert. "Small and simple."

"In my yard, overlooking the river. The view is beautiful and no reservations are necessary."

"How about next week?'

"Sounds perfect," said Sunny with a contented sigh. "Our families won't have time to kick up a fuss."

"So now that we've got the wedding plans ironed out," said Robert, "we can start enjoying the honeymoon."

"I have a few ideas that might interest you."

Moving swiftly, he pinned her beneath him on the bed. "Anything you can show me?"

She gasped as he found her center. "You might be able to persuade me."

"Like that?"

"Oh, God . . . Robby, I—"

The honeymoon was a smashing success. Now all they had to worry about was the wedding.

"WE HAVE TO BE STRONG," Sunny said as they pulled into the restaurant parking lot the next evening. "They're going to be tough on us."

"We're in this together," said Robert, turning off the engine. "United we stand."

"Don't bet on it. Divide and conquer is more like it. I'll bet they're inside, planning our downfall."

They'd broken the news of their engagement earlier in the day. Both sets of parents had been surprised and thrilled by the unexpected turn of events and had eagerly accepted the dinner invitation and the chance to renew an old friendship.

"All we have to do," said Robert, helping her from the car, "is tell them we want a small wedding."

"You make it sound so easy," said Sunny, shaking her head. "It isn't."

"Sure it is," said Robert as they entered the restaurant. "We're adults. We can have the wedding we want."

"Right," said Sunny, waving to her father across the room. "I bet you still believe in Santa Claus and the Tooth Fairy."

"Sunny! Rob!" Her father Stan Talbot embraced them both in a bear hug. "It's about time. George and I have a toast ready and waiting."

"Buckle your seat belt," Sunny murmured to Robert as they took their seats. "The roller coaster ride's about to begin."

The wine flowed. The toasts were loving and hopeful and filled with genuine emotion. Sunny's mother, Millie, and Robert's mother, Olivia, cried happy tears while the two fathers congratulated themselves on having such exceptionally clever and attractive children. Olivia passed around pictures of her grandchildren, Jessi and Michael, and Sunny watched as a kaleidoscope of expressions passed across her mother's face. *I know exactly how you feel, Mom,* she thought. *I'm as amazed as you are.*

They made it through the soup and salad courses on a wave of high spirits.

"See," Robert whispered in her ear as the main course was served. "I told you we wouldn't have a problem."

Sunny remained unconvinced. "Two more courses to go," she whispered back. "We're not out of the woods yet."

They were halfway through their fettucine when it happened. Sunny was lifting a forkful of noodles to her mouth when she noticed a look passing between her mother and Olivia. Her heart dropped to her feet.

"We've been doing some thinking..." Millie began.

"And we've come up with some great ideas," Olivia continued.

"You're going to love them,' Millie said, pulling a stack of cocktail napkins from her purse.

"We've written them all down for you," said Olivia, withdrawing a similar stack from her own purse.

"Mom," said Sunny cautiously, resting her fork on her plate, "I thought I told you we wanted a small wedding."

"Of course you did, dear," said Millie. "We've just drawn up a guest list."

Robert eyed them with suspicion. "On the cocktail napkins?"

"We wanted to get a head start," said his mother, the ultimate organizer. "One works with the materials one has on hand."

Robert started to say something but Sunny kicked his leg beneath the table.

"How many names are on that list?" she asked, as calmly as she could manage.

Neither woman said a word. Stan and George rose from their seats and beat a hasty retreat to the bar. Robert reached across the table and grabbed the cocktail napkins.

"Don't crumple them, Robert!" his mother warned. "That's our master list."

Sunny studied the "master list" with a growing sense of horror. "There must be three hundred names here."

"Westminster Abbey," Robert said, throwing up his hands in disgust. "I told you they'd want Westminster Abbey."

"Mother," said Sunny strongly, "we don't *know* three hundred people."

Millie and Olivia exchanged amused glances.

"Honey," said Millie "you're *related* to three hundred people."

"And so are you, dear," said Olivia to her son. "We've done our best to prune the list, but I'm sure you don't wish to insult anyone."

"The hell I don't," said Robert. He turned to Sunny. "And quit kicking me under the table."

Sunny's face flamed. "I'm sure we can discuss this rationally."

"Of course we can," said Millie, sensing victory. "Just leave the whole thing to us and don't worry about a thing."

Sunny took a deep breath and marshaled her forces. "Mother, Olivia, we need to talk."

The two women met her eyes as if they were as innocent as lambs, but Sunny knew she caught the glint of wolf's teeth behind the ingenuous smiles. "Yes, dear?" they said in stereo.

She looked toward Robert for support. "We want a small wedding."

"Of course you do, dear," said her mother, patting her hand, "but this happy occasion would mean so much to the people who love you."

"A wedding is a celebration," said Olivia, gathering speed. "The opportunity to share your happiness with others. It's one of the oldest ceremonies in civilization."

"They've done their homework," Sunny said to Robert. "We're in trouble."

Robert waved the cocktail napkins in the air. "There's nobody on this list you can cut?"

Both women shook their perfectly coiffed heads. "Not a soul."

Sunny took a peek at the list of names. "You forgot my assistant, Joi," she said. "I could never get married without Joi present."

Robert took a second look. "If you invite Kyle Pruitt you have to ask Derek Andersen."

His mother brightened. "How could I make such a foolish mistake?" She started a supplementary list on another cocktail napkin. "And if we have the Andersens, we can't forget the Giffords."

"Traitor," said Sunny to Robert. "I can see Westminster Abbey in our future."

"Look at their faces," said Robert, pointing to their mothers, once again engrossed in major-league list-making. "They're on Cloud Nine."

"I suppose we could have the ceremony in my backyard and the reception someplace else," she said. It *was* hard to ignore the glow of happiness emanating from the two women. "As long as we don't have to wait."

"Of course you won't have to wait, dear," said Millie. "We can arrange a beautiful winter wedding."

"Winter!" Sunny and Robert yelped. "We can't wait until winter."

"Autumn, then," said Olivia, the peacemaker. She looked at Millie. "I'm certain we can arrange an autumn wedding."

Millie pursed her lips. "Well, I—"

"Next week," said Robert in his most authoritative courtroom voice.

It was Millie and Olivia's turn to yelp in stereo. "Next week! Impossible."

"Next week or no wedding," said Robert as Sunny gained a new appreciation of his legal-eagle expertise.

"We need at least six months," said Olivia, meeting her son's eyes.

"Out of the question."

Millie looked toward Sunny. "You understand, don't you, honey?"

"Next week," said Sunny. "It's nonnegotiable."

Robert grinned. "Good going. We could use you at the firm."

"*L.A. Law,*" she said modestly. "Three years' worth."

"September," said Millie, tossing them a bone.

"Two weeks from today," said Sunny.

"A June wedding," said Olivia. "The roses will be in bloom."

"April," said Robert. "Before the end of the month. We'll live without the roses."

The two women whispered frantically.

"Six weeks," said Millie, jaw set.

"The second weekend in May," Olivia elaborated.

Robert looked at Sunny.

Sunny looked at their mothers.

"I suppose six weeks is reasonable," she said slowly. "There *is* a lot to be done."

Olivia and Millie conferred one last time.

"Done," said Olivia. "Six weeks from today, you'll be man and wife for the second time."

She and Millie looked at each other and broke into triumphant smiles.

Sunny and Robert met each other's eyes.

"We won, didn't we?" Sunny asked.

"I'm not sure," he said.

"You won't regret this." Millie leaped up to hug her daughter and future son-in-law. "I promise you won't have to worry about a single thing between now and the big day."

"Absolutely!" said Olivia, leaping up to do the same. "This will be the wedding of your dreams."

Chapter Three

FROM THE OUTSIDE, Letitia's Bridal Salon looked a great deal like the other shops scattered along the tree-lined street. With its stone facade and Williamsburg-blue shutters, Letitia's blended in perfectly with the air of countrified gentility common to the rolling hillsides of Bucks County, Pennsylvania. Slender mannequins, faces forever frozen in expressions of sublime happiness, graced the window display, their bridal finery adding a touch of romantic splendor to the quiet street.

You'd never suspect it was a torture chamber.

"Now I remember why Robert and I eloped the first time," said Sunny as Madame Letitia closed the fitting-room door behind her. "Weddings are exhausting."

"Exhausting?" Millie stared at her daughter as if she'd never seen her before. "I'm not exhausted." She turned toward Olivia. "Are you exhausted?"

Olivia threw back her head and laughed. "I don't know what's the matter with the younger generation," she said with an affectionate glance toward Sunny, who was slumped on a boudoir chair near the mirror, her crinolines piled high on her lap. "I think you need vitamins."

"I think I need my head examined." Sunny struggled to hold back a yawn. "Why we ever let you two talk us into this three-ring circus is beyond me."

"Because you and Robert deserve the very best, that's why," declared Millie.

"And because we got cheated out of it the first time around," added Olivia. "If you think we're going to let our children run off somewhere and elope, you are sadly mistaken."

"We weren't going to elope," Sunny explained once again. "You know we were planning to have a nice, quiet ceremony in my backyard."

Olivia looked as if she were about to faint, while her mother's lips pursed so tightly that it was a wonder she didn't swallow them.

"Your father and I have been saving up for this occasion since the day you were born," said Millie. "Grandma Talbot says she'll die happy once she sees you walk down the aisle wearing her mother's veil."

"That's hardly a pleasant thought, Mom."

"Oh, dear. You already have a veil." Olivia's feathery brows drew together in a genteel frown. "Robert's father and I had so hoped Sunny would wear Mother Holland's veil."

Was their no detail these women left to chance? Sunny took a deep breath and faced the opposing team. "To tell you the truth," she began carefully, "I wasn't planning on wearing a veil at all."

"No veil!" Stereo maternal outrage. It was enough to make Sunny hightail it for the nearest bunker.

In for a penny, in for a pound, she thought. "I was thinking of wreath of flowers."

"This isn't the sixties, Sunny," warned her mother in her most stern tone of voice. "Formal weddings are all the rage again."

"So is frugality," her daughter shot back. "You and Dad aren't getting any younger, and it seems to me that with retirement on the horizon and Liz still single, you should—"

The door swung open and a chirpy bridal consultant bustled in. "Madame Letitia told me of Mrs. Talbot's concerns," she said, marching confidently into the line of battle, "and Madame said we can most assuredly add more pearls to the bodice for you." She batted her false eyelashes at the assembled women. "For a small additional price."

Sunny groaned and buried her face in her hands. She didn't know whether to laugh or cry. Her mother's obsession with seed pearls would be the death of her yet.

"Prewedding jitters," said Olivia, patting Sunny on the head. "She'll be fine in a moment."

"I wouldn't bet on that," mumbled Sunny.

The three women ignored her.

"Now, if you ladies will excuse us," said the consultant, "I'll help Ms. Talbot into the gown and take another fitting."

"Another fitting?" asked Sunny. "I doubt if Princess Di had so many fittings."

"This is the last time," said the consultant.

"You said that two weeks ago."

"You have my word," said the consultant, crossing her heart. She waggled a finger in Sunny's direction. "Just don't lose any more weight and we'll be fine."

"I'll see to that," said Millie Talbot, although how she would manage that feat with her daughter living three towns away was beyond Sunny. She could imagine her mother showing up on her doorstep each morning with a picnic basket of bagels and cream cheese.

Millie and Olivia reluctantly retired to the front of the salon while Sunny gave herself over to the ministrations of the consultant and the seamstress who joined them.

From the moment she and Robert had announced their engagement a few weeks ago, it seemed to Sunny that life as she'd known it had ceased to exist. It had been easier to open an art gallery than it was to buy a wedding dress.

"Ouch!" Sunny grimaced as a pin grazed her left breast.

"You mustn't squirm, dear," muttered the seamstress through a mouthful of said pins. "I'm almost finished."

Sunny shuddered as the woman whipped out a wicked-looking pair of shears.

"Now don't breathe."

"I wouldn't think of it," said Sunny.

Battenberg lace. Illusion veils. Sweetheart necklines and fingertip sleeves. The world of weddings had its own rules—and its own language. Ushers were now called groomsmen. The best man could be a woman. Children played a larger part in formal ceremonies than ever before—thanks, no doubt, to second marriages and blended families.

Which brought Sunny back to the problem she'd been wrestling with since that fateful day when she and Robert fell in love all over again.

Family.

Hers. His. *Theirs*.

Sunny glanced down at the seamstress. "Do you have kids?" she asked.

"Three," the woman said around the pins. "Two girls and a boy." She visibly beamed with pride. "My oldest girl served in Desert Storm."

"You must have been a nervous wreck," said Sunny, trying to imagine her offspring going off to fight a war. She could barely imagine how it would feel to see Robert's little boy cross the street by himself.

"We stayed glued to the television for three weeks," said the woman, leaning back on her heels to inspect the hem of the wedding gown. "I don't think I slept a wink until she came home for the Fourth of July." The seamstress looked up at Sunny. "I take it your intended has kids."

"Two," said Sunny. "A boy and a girl."

"From the sound of your voice, it isn't going well."

Sunny sighed. "Everything with Michael is as easy and natural as can be."

"But the girl?"

"Difficult. Robby and I had one of those whirlwind romances and we took everyone by surprise. I think she's afraid I'm going to try to take her mother's place." There was a sadness about Jessi that touched Sunny's heart, but try as she might, she found it impossible to reach the girl.

"Divorce?"

Sunny shook her head. "Death."

"That makes it rough. Nothing's tougher to fight than memories."

"Tell me about it." Even as she said the words, Sunny wasn't entirely convinced of them. In truth, she had the feeling the problem was more complex than that. Jessi had been the woman of the house for so long that it seemed to Sunny the girl even resented the house-keeper's authority. More often than not, Sunny found Mrs. Maxwell reading the newspaper at the kitchen table while Jessi prepared one of the health foods she loved to foist on her unsuspecting father and brother. "Everyone tells me it gets easier," she said with a sigh. "I just hope it happens sooner rather than later."

"Don't you look so down, Ms. Talbot. All it takes is common sense," said the seamstress, sounding suspiciously like Sunny's own mother. "Follow your instincts. Nothing's more natural than being a mother."

AN HOUR LATER, Sunny burst into the jewelry store in Lahaska where she was to meet Robert to choose their wedding rings.

"Look at you," she said, after they shared a kiss. "Mr. Big Shot Attorney in his Savile Row duds." She made a show of checking him out. "Whatever happened to the boy who wore faded jeans and sweats?"

"He became a partner in a law firm," Robert said dryly. "Jeans are for weekends."

"I'd go crazy if I had to adhere to a dress code."

He tugged gently at one of her peacock-feather earrings. "Somehow I can't imagine you dressing for corporate America."

She glanced down at her biking shorts and tank top. "Maybe I should have borrowed one of Madame Letitia's crinolines."

"I like you the way you are," he said, sweeping her into his arms in a decidedly un-corporate-America way. "Feather earrings and all."

"I knew you were a renegade at heart," she said, laughing as he set her down atop the jewelry counter. "What would your partners say if they saw you now?"

"They'd say I was a damn lucky man. I—"

"Good afternoon, friends," intoned a parchment-paper voice to their right. "And how may I help you?"

Robert and Sunny turned to see a dapper man of indeterminate age coming toward them from the back room. The man's professional smile faded when he looked from Robert's impeccable business attire to Sunny's funky gear. Sunny offered up her friendliest smile.

"We'd like to see some wedding rings," she said, sliding off the counter, to the man's obvious relief. "A friend of mine says Bentley's has the finest selection in Bucks County."

The salesman visibly preened. "And that we do." His gaze slid from the peacock feathers in her ears to the expensive watch on Robert's left wrist. "And who is the lucky couple?"

Sunny's eyes widened. "Well, *we* are."

"Of course," said the man, covering up his embarrassment with a cough. It was plain to see he felt they were the most mismatched pair since Felix and Oscar. "If you'll come this way, I'll show you my best."

"Don't laugh," Sunny warned as she and Robert followed the man to a counter on the opposite side of the luxurious store. "If you laugh, then I'll start laughing and the poor man will end up calling the police!"

Robert's shoulders heaved with suppressed mirth. "The guy doesn't know whether to show us rings for our fingers or our noses," he said too loudly for Sunny's comfort. "I can't wait to see his first choice."

"Diamonds," Sunny whispered, wrinkling her nose. "He saw that fancy suit of yours and figures you're good for it."

Robert gave her a surreptitious pinch on the bottom. "Puzzle rings," he said, eyes twinkling with amusement, "because he can't figure out how we ever got together."

The salesman, however, was a sophisticated man, and by the time Sunny and Robert sat down in the chairs offered, he had recovered his equilibrium. He reached into the jewelry case and withdrew a pair of plain gold bands. No diamonds. No fancy scrollwork. Traditional, old-fashioned. "Perfect for all occasions," the salesman said smoothly. "Don't you agree?"

"A little ... plain, don't you think?" asked Robert dubiously.

Sunny held the rings in the palm of her hand. The gold was warm, solid, an endless circle of hopes and dreams. To her amazement, her eyes brimmed. "How did you know?" she asked, looking at the salesman through a haze of tears. "These rings couldn't be more perfect." They represented everything that was real and enduring and wonderful about the love she had for Robert and the plans they had for their future together.

The salesman looked from Sunny to Robert then back again, and a big smile creased his oh-so-proper face. "Practice, my dear," he said with a nod. "Practice."

SUNNY AND ROBERT reluctantly parted company a little while later. He had a meeting with an important client while Sunny had to at least pretend the gallery was the most important thing in her life. In truth, the wonder of falling in love—and the chaos of planning a wedding— had steamrolled over everything in its path, leaving Sunny apologetic but still falling rapidly behind.

She went back to the gallery and was instantly engulfed in more chaos.

By the time she pulled up in front of Robert's house a few hours later, she was frazzled, rumpled and ready to crawl into bed and sleep for a week. There had been a mix-up at the gallery while Sunny was entangled in crinolines at Madame Letitia's, and by the time she returned a full-scale disaster was well under way. It seemed to take forever to soothe ruffled feathers, flatter dented egos and redirect the delivery of an art deco statue that a state senator thought resembled his mistress.

Frowning, she peered into the rearview mirror. The circles under her eyes had multiplied. She had enough bags to pack for a month's stay in Europe. The blushing bride-to-be looked ready for an extended sojourn at Leisure Village, and there were still three weeks to go until the Big Day.

"Thank you, Mom and Olivia," she mumbled as she climbed out of her car. If only the two women had listened to her and Robert in the first place, they would be happily married by now and all of this craziness would be behind them.

"Hey, guys!" she called as the front door closed behind her. "First call for Chinese food. Last one to the chopsticks does the dishes."

She heard a whoop of excitement from the den, followed by the thud of kid-size sneakers heading in her direction.

"Sunny!" Michael threw himself at her legs like a high-impact cannonball. "Did you get fortune cookies?"

She ruffled his hair affectionately. "Would I forget fortune cookies? They're your favorite thing."

He peeked into the shopping bag from the Magic Wok. "Fried rice?"

"Fried rice and the soup you like."

"C'mon!" Michael tugged at her sleeve impatiently. "Jessi's in the kitchen."

"Is your daddy in there, too?"

Michael shook his head. "Daddy had to work late."

"Did he say when he'd be home?"

"I don't remember."

"That's okay," she said, following the boy down the hall and into the kitchen. "I'm sure he'll be here before too long. Your dad loves Chinese food as much as we do."

Jessi's high, clear voice floated across the kitchen. "My father doesn't eat Chinese food."

Sunny's stomach knotted. So it was going to be one of those days, was it? Well, she was prepared. "I also brought a meatball hero from Luigi's. That should hold him until breakfast."

Jessi, a slip of a girl with big blue eyes and silky brown hair, pointed toward a pot simmering on the stove. "Daddy's watching his cholesterol. I made him a vegetable stew."

Vegetable stew, thought Sunny. Since when did Robert eat vegetable stew for dinner? In the weeks they'd

been together she'd seen him eat Szechuan beef, pep-
peroni pizza and fried chicken but she'd never once seen
him eat vegetable stew.

"Won't the stew hold until tomorrow?" asked Sunny,
unpacking the cartons of Chinese food. "Moo shu pork
doesn't reheat real well."

Jessi wrinkled her nose but said nothing.

Sunny gave Michael the task of opening cans of soda
to go with their dinner, then ladled generous portions of
food onto the plates she'd found in the cupboard. "I
thought you guys could help me with something while
we eat," she said, gesturing for Jessi to help herself to a
bowl of hot and sour soup. "Your dad and I have until
tomorrow morning to choose a band for the wedding and
I brought the audition tapes along."

"Old people in tuxedos," Jessi said. "That's as bad as
listening to the Bee Gees or Barry Manilow."

Sunny started to laugh. "I don't know how to tell you
this, Jessi, but there was a time when your dad and I
thought the Bee Gees were hot stuff."

"Gross," said Jessi, looking at her as if Sunny had
suddenly sprouted platform shoes and a shag haircut.

"Come on," said Sunny, inclining her head in the direction of the den. "Let's go watch the tapes."

"I have math homework to do."

"But you have to eat," Sunny protested.

"I ate at Marcy's house."

Sunny arched an eyebrow. "I hope you're not dieting,
Jessi. You're as petite as can be already. You looked like
a dream in the junior bridesmaid's dress last week."

Jessi mumbled something about hoping none of her
friends saw her in that outfit, but Sunny chose to ignore
it. Part of motherhood, she'd already learned, was
knowing when to be selectively deaf.

"Will you join us for ice cream after your dad gets home?"

Jessi shrugged as if she had many more important invitations to consider before she could commit herself. "I dunno. Maybe."

"Well, you know where to find us," she said easily. "I'd better go join Michael."

Walking away was one of the harder things Sunny had had to do, but she managed it. Her instinct was to throw her arms about the child and wear down the girl's defenses with love and affection, but Jessi had made it clear that she maintained a hands-off policy when it came to her future stepmother.

And it was a shame, thought Sunny, as she curled up on the couch next to Michael and dived into her moo shu pork. She'd discovered she thoroughly enjoyed being around kids. Last week she had even attended her first parent/teacher meeting at Michael's school. She'd dressed up in a knock-off designer suit, pale hose and a pair of sedate black pumps like the perfect suburban matron, only to have Michael burst into tears at the sight of her. "Not like that," he'd said. "I want you to look like you."

Nobody had ever said anything sweeter to her.

She'd changed back into hot pink shorts, a crocheted white sweater and ballet flats and off they'd gone to Parents' Night.

If only she could find the way to Jessi's heart as easily.

IT WAS TEN-THIRTY when Robert pulled into his driveway. He was tired, hungry and generally in a lousy mood, but the moment he saw Sunny's VW parked next to him, his lousy mood vanished. That was all it took. That ridiculous twenty-year-old Beetle with 200,000 miles under the hood was enough to make him forget everything but the woman he loved.

And the best thing about it, he thought as he walked up the path to the front door, was that this was only the beginning. With Sunny back in his life, he felt as if he were eighteen again when everything was possible as long as she was by his side.

She was dozing in the family room, curled up on the sofa with her head pillowed on one of his old sweaters. Her wild mane of red hair was spread out across her face and shoulders, the curls tumbling across her cheeks like living fire. She wore faded jeans and a baggy kelly green sweater with Elvis Presley's face emblazoned front and back. If someone had told him a year ago that he'd fall in love with a woman who wore Elvis sweaters, he would have laughed out loud. But this was Sunny. It didn't matter if she papered her walls with pictures of the King or believed he was alive and well and living in the White House.

He sat down on the arm of the sofa and touched her cheek. She stirred, her body arching with almost feline grace. Her brow furrowed slightly, then her lids fluttered open.

"Robby." She sat up, tugging at the edge of her sweater where it had ridden up over her flat stomach. "Those band videos would cure the worst case of insomnia. How long have you been home?"

"Not long." He leaned over and kissed her mouth, still warm from sleep. "Szechuan?"

Her chuckle was sleepy and unbearably sexy. "I could never love a man who didn't love Chinese food."

He glanced around the room. "Is Michael asleep?"

"I tucked him in around eight."

"Where's Jessi?"

"Upstairs." Sunny paused a moment. "She had to study."

He gave her what he hoped was a wicked grin. "So we're all alone."

The look she gave him could raise the dead. "We're all alone."

He held out his hand and she stood up. "Come here," he said gruffly. "We haven't had a hell of a lot of time for this lately."

An instant later she was in his arms. Her fingers worked the buttons on his shirt until it fell open. She trailed her fingernails gently across his bare chest, then raised up on tiptoe to press her lips to his skin. A shudder rocketed through him as her tongue found his flat nipple. Hot. Wet. Incredibly—

"Daddy!" They leaped apart at the sound of Jessi's voice behind them. Sunny felt her face flame with embarrassment. "You must be starving."

"Hi, sweetheart." Robert winked at her, then turned to greet his daughter with a kiss on the forehead. "Sunny said you were doing your homework."

"Oh, I finished that ages ago. I was listening to a tape."

Score one for you, Jessi, Sunny thought.

"I can heat up the vegetable stew for you in two seconds," Jessi went on, pretending Sunny was back in New Hope.

"That sounds great, sweetheart, but I picked up something on the way home." He pointed toward a brown paper bag sitting on the foyer table. "Meatball hero."

Jessi turned and ran back upstairs, slamming her bedroom door behind her.

Robert started after her. "Did I say something wrong?"

"It's a long story," said Sunny, torn between laughter and tears for the second time that day. "Eat first. I'll tell you about it later."

Robert made short work of both meatball heroes, then ate a bowl of vegetable stew to make Jessi happy. Sunny nursed a mug of tea and nibbled at a fortune cookie. "Good things come to those who wait," the white paper slip read. She could only hope that fortune cookies knew more about stepdaughters than she did.

Robert had wanted to go upstairs and read Jessi the riot act for running from the room before, but Sunny had convinced him that that would only make things worse. Their whirlwind engagement had taken everyone by surprise—his children most of all. Michael was young enough to welcome Sunny with open arms. Jessi, however, was almost an adolescent, and her memories of her mother were still fresh and clear. Besides, Jessi considered the house as her domain and the thought of an interloper on her domestic territory must be frightening. There was little enough in life that you could control when you were twelve years old. Sunny's heart went out to the girl, but that didn't mean the situation was any less puzzling.

After he finished dinner, they loaded the dishwasher, then settled back in the den on the sofa.

"Believe it or not, we had another wedding emergency this afternoon," she said, drawing her legs up under her and nestling close.

"Your mother hates our wedding rings and decided to pan for gold herself," Robby guessed.

She was too tired to laugh. "Battling florists." She kissed his shoulder, then rested her head against him. "Mother is on a quest for the fanciest buds in the western hemisphere, and she refuses to let common sense enter into it. If she could import them from Mars, she would." She lifted her head to look at him. "Do you have any idea what stephanotis looks like?"

"I'm still working on freesia."

"Even I know freesia. I have until tomorrow morning to decide if I want a nosegay, a loose cascade or a cluster."

"How about a bouquet?"

"Those *are* bouquets."

"How about a dozen long-stemmed roses with a ribbon tied around them?"

"Higher education wasn't wasted on you, Mr. Holland," she said dryly.

"I think I have something that'll make this whole thing easier on us." He reached for his briefcase and extracted a floppy disk in its paper jacket. "One of the paralegals gave me this. It's a checklist program designed specifically for weddings. It claims to make it categorically impossible for anyone to forget anything from engagement to honeymoon."

"A tad anal retentive, don't you think?"

"It's no worse than sticking notes on every available surface."

"I resent that. At least you don't need electricity and a machine to use them." Sunny had a particular affinity for self-sticking notes. "Besides, I'm not computer literate."

"Jessi is."

Sunny's face lit up. "Maybe that's not such a bad idea, after all. It might make Jessi feel more like a part of things." She leaped to her feet. "Why don't I see if she's awake. We could—"

"No, we couldn't." He pulled her down onto his lap and held her fast.

"It's not that late, Robby. She'd probably get a kick out of showing us how to use the software."

He kissed her quiet. "I don't want to talk about software anymore."

"Oh, really? What do you want to talk about?"

His answer was earthy.

Her response was immediate. She dipped her mouth to his. Her lips were soft, pliable, surprisingly demanding.

For a long, delicious moment they forgot all about fittings and flowers and blended families—they forgot everything but the sense of wonder that had brought them to this time and this place.

"Let's lock the door," he growled into her ear. "You be quiet and I guarantee I'll be fast."

She was tempted but held her ground. "Not until we get married," she said, touching his mouth with the tip of her index finger. "At least, not here."

"You expect to wait three weeks, four days, ten hours and fifty-five minutes?" he asked. "Not that I'm counting."

"There are other ways to pass the time," Sunny said, wishing the wedding were tomorrow.

"Name one."

She ticked them off on her fingers. "Choosing a band for the reception. Deciding on what style bouquet I should carry. Buying gifts for the ushers and bridesmaids." She met his eyes. "Shall I go on?"

"Is romance anywhere on that list?"

"Romance?" She laughed. "That's the one thing engaged couples don't have time for. I thought you knew that."

"We should have eloped again."

"Once we're married, we'll have all the time for romance that we could possibly want."

"I'm going to hold you to that."

"You'd better." She reached for the remote control and switched on the VCR. The strains of the Jack B. Quick Dance Band playing the "Hawaiian Wedding Song" on accordions filled the air.

"You're kidding," said Robert. He paused. "Aren't you?"

"It gets better." She winced as the lead singer hit a sour note. "Trust me."

"How many more bands are there?"

"Six, if you don't count Maeve McLaughlin's Irish Rovers."

"What's wrong with Maeve's Irish Rovers?"

"They play bagpipes on roller skates while singing 'Endless Love.'"

It was going to be a long night.

Chapter Four

A MAN AND WOMAN MEET. They fall in love. They get married.

What could be easier?

By the time the wedding was one week away, Sunny was thoroughly convinced that the plans for D-Day had been simpler.

"The Pentagon missed out on a natural resource when they let you two slip through their fingers," said Sunny over lunch Saturday afternoon with Robert and their respective mothers.

"I don't know why organization amazes everyone the way it does." Millie's smile was exceedingly self-satisfied. "Do you, Olivia?"

Olivia Holland flipped through the pages of her jam-packed notebook. "I haven't a clue. Orderliness is the sign of a superior intellect."

Sunny would have laughed at the hubris displayed by both her mother and her future mother-in-law, but there was something terribly impressive about their twin notebooks with duplicate information neatly filed under headings like "Florist," "Videographer," "Seating Arrangements" and "Fabric Samples." The two women had color-coded their calendars, photocopied floor plans of the church and obtained sheet music for the "Trumpet Voluntary." They would probably choreograph the honeymoon if Sunny and Robert would let them.

"And you said the wedding software was anal retentive?" Robert muttered under his breath. She kicked him lightly in the shin.

"Who's picking Aunt Carol up at the airport?" Sunny asked, nibbling at her chef's salad, eyes wide and innocent.

"Your brother Jack," said Millie.

"Is she bringing Angela?"

"Who's Angela?" Robert asked Sunny.

"My ancient aunt's extremely ancient Siamese cat."

Robert looked up from his cheeseburger. "She's bringing a cat to the wedding?"

"Of course she's not bringing a cat to the wedding." Millie Talbot looked at him as if she wondered how he'd got through law school.

"Everyone else seems to be coming to this wedding," Sunny remarked. "Why shouldn't Angela?"

"Carol's neighbor is going to watch Angela," Millie said tartly with a pointed glance at Olivia, her partner in crime.

"Thank God for that," muttered Sunny. "Otherwise you'd need a section in your notebook for cat sitters."

Millie shot her a look that would have sent Sunny running to her room twenty years ago. Robert, however, laughed so hard that other diners turned to stare.

"Robert!" Olivia slapped him on the forearm with her napkin. "Stop that this instant."

"Where's your sense of humor, Mom?" he asked, still laughing. "You know as well as we do that this whole thing has gotten out of hand."

Olivia turned to Millie. "Have you any idea what on earth the boy is talking about?"

Millie shook her head. "Not the slightest."

The two matrons leveled their best maternal looks on their recalcitrant children, but to no avail.

"Come on, Mom!" said Sunny, winking at Robert. "You know darned well you'd categorize my trousseau lingerie if I let you get your hands on it."

"She's right about that," Olivia conceded, to their surprise. "I've seen her making copies of copies of the dinner menu."

"You can't be too careful," said Millie with apologies to no one. "I've waited thirty-three years to plan a wedding for my oldest daughter. It's going to be perfect or I'll know the reason why."

"It would serve you right if Robert and I eloped."

Millie's gasp could be heard in Ohio. "Over my dead body!"

Sunny felt instantly chastened by her mother's vehement response. "I'm only kidding, Mom," she said, hugging the shaken woman. "I promise you we won't elope again."

Millie struggled to regain her composure. "Your brother's a policeman," she said sternly. "I have a good mind to ask him to put you in protective custody until your dad walks you down the aisle."

Sunny didn't dare admit that there had been the tiniest nugget of truth in her teasing threat to elope. In the past few days she had felt overwhelmed by the avalanche of details surrounding the nuptials. RSVPs. Logging wedding presents. Fielding telephone calls from cousins and friends and business associates, all of whom were eager to set up a lunch or dinner with "the happy couple." She found herself longing for a moment to stop and catch her breath—or to spend alone with Robert without one single wedding-related task to be accomplished.

Olivia withdrew her gold compact from her handbag and checked her lipstick in the mirror. "Would you two do me a favor?"

Sunny looked at Robert, then nodded. "If it doesn't require licking postage stamps." Sending out the invitations, announcements and thank-you notes had been a monumental undertaking. "Glue is beginning to taste like mother's milk."

Olivia clicked shut her compact and slid it back into her handbag. "Would you run by Robert's house and pick up the sheet music for the organist? I believe it's in the living room near the piano. Mrs. DeBenedetto must have it by tonight so she can practice."

A HALF HOUR LATER Robert pulled into the driveway and stopped the car. Why he'd found it necessary to explore every side road between the restaurant and home was beyond her. She'd forgotten how stubborn men could be about admitting they were lost. He'd turned a five-minute drive into an excursion. "You go get the sheet music," he said, an odd smile playing at the corners of his mouth. "I want to check the oil."

"Check the oil?" She felt his forehead. "You must be running a fever. I haven't seen you check the oil since you were in high school."

"Just get the sheet music," he said, leaning over and opening the passenger door.

Strange, she thought, glancing about as she walked up the path to the front door. Usually she had to step over a tangle of bicycles and assorted toys, but today the yard was immaculately neat. Michael must be spending the afternoon with his pal Seth, turning the Petersons' front yard into a toy store.

She let herself in the front door with the key Robert had given her the night they'd become engaged. "Jessi! Are you home? I—"

"Surprise!"

She stopped dead in the doorway and stared at the crowd of happy, smiling people adrift in a cloud of pastel balloons and crepe paper. "I can't believe it," she said, starting to laugh. "A shower! You're giving me a bridal shower!" She heard the merry beep of the horn as Robert beat a rapid retreat to higher ground.

Marcy, her younger sister, stepped forward wearing a pair of wide-legged pants, platform shoes and a polyester blouse. "Welcome back to the 1970s," she said, patting her Farrah Fawcett hairdo. "You cheated us out of all the fun last time, but this time you're not going to escape. We're giving you the shower of your teenage dreams!"

That was putting it mildly. From the wishing well covered in white tissue paper to the organdy lace umbrella fastened to the back of the bride's throne, her family and friends had managed to recreate every bridal shower Sunny had attended in the past fifteen years. Even the presents were a trip back in time: plastic lettuce savers, two toasters, one hand-crocheted toilet-paper cover. The lacy lingerie, however, was timeless.

"Not the bonnet," she said, laughing as Olivia—the height of blue-blooded propriety—sat on the floor attaching discarded ribbons and bows to a white paper plate.

"You know I'm a stickler for tradition," said Olivia, her eyes dancing with laughter.

Sunny turned to Jessi who was seated on the far end of the sofa, a stiff smile on her face.

"Did you ever think you'd see your elegant grandmother pinning ribbons to a plate?"

"No." One word. No expression. Dead end.

Sunny, however, was as stubborn as her future stepdaughter. She rose from her throne and approached the girl. "I could use some help with all those presents," she said softly. "Maybe if you would sit next to me, we could—"

"I like it here," said Jessi.

Sunny reached out to touch the girl's shoulder, then caught herself. Everything about Jessi's body language said *don't touch*. This wasn't the time to push the issue, not with both families there watching.

"Well, thank heavens the shower was here. At least we don't have to lug all of this loot back home again."

Jessi forced a smile that stopped short of her eyes.

TWO HOURS LATER the last of the presents had been opened and duly admired, the wishing-well gifts had been giggled over and Sunny had been subjected to the embarrassment of wearing the bonnet of bows her soon-to-be-mother-in-law had labored over. Her own mother seemed to be everywhere, darting from living room to kitchen to dining room, seeing that each of the guests was having as much fun as she was. The look of happiness on her mother's face made the paper-plate bonnet almost bearable.

After coffee and dessert, Sunny's sister Liz produced a big fat family photo album and everyone crowded around.

"First picture ever of the bride and groom," said Liz, pointing to a photo of Sunny and Robert dressed for a junior high Halloween party.

"Frankenstein and his bride," said her cousin Ronnie. "Even then they knew—"

Sunny tossed a pillow at her. "Unfair," she protested. "What we didn't know was that those pictures would be passed on for posterity." Out of the corner of her eye she noticed Jessi moving closer to the center of activity. Her heart did a flutter inside her chest as she realized Jessi was interested in the photo album. Olivia put an arm about the girl's slender shoulders. "Doesn't your dad look young?"

Jessi nodded, her eyes not straying from the photo album. "Daddy knew Sunny in junior high?"

Olivia glanced at Sunny, who fielded the question. "We met in chem lab the very first day." She thought for a second. "We were just about your age."

Jessi looked as if she found that idea too farfetched to believe.

Sunny launched into a funny story about the junior high prom and Robert's struggle with a bow tie. The corners of Jessi's mouth twitched, but she managed to suppress her smile. *Oh, honey, don't fight so hard,* thought Sunny. *You may not want me for your mother, but I might not be so bad as a friend.*

Sunny casually moved over, making room for the girl to sit down next to her. There were times she felt as if she were trying to gentle a nervous pony. Well, at least Jessi was still in the room with them. A few weeks ago that would have been too much to even dream about. She held her breath as Jessi perched on the arm of the sofa. "Take a look at this one," Sunny said casually, pointing toward a picture of Robert and herself taken in front of a tiny brick office building. "That's our wedding picture."

Jessi's eyes widened. "You got married in your prom gown?"

Sunny nodded. "Other kids went to the lake after the prom. We went to Maryland to get married." She laughed softly, remembering. "At least your dad had mastered the bow tie by that time."

"Didn't you want to go to college?" Jessi asked.

"Sure I did," said Sunny, trying to act as if this friendly conversation with Jessi was an everyday occurrence. "We had it all planned."

"We didn't," said Olivia and Millie in unison.

"Were you mad at Dad and Sunny?" asked Jessi.

Millie yielded to Jessi's biological grandmother. "Not that they loved each other or wanted to be married," Olivia said, smoothing her granddaughter's hair off her forehead. "But we wished they had decided to wait. It didn't have to be as difficult as it was."

Jessi turned to Sunny. "Where did you live? Did you go to work?" Her tone made it obvious that she couldn't possibly imagine how two teenagers could make enough money to pay rent and buy groceries.

Sunny told the girl the truth. "We had a little studio apartment in South Philly with a shower stall and a hot plate. It was very difficult," she said, "but we loved each other so much that we didn't mind."

"Then what made you get a divorce?" Jessi persisted. "If two people love each other, don't they want to stay together forever?"

"Sometimes life gets in the way," Sunny said quietly.

"You don't have to tell me," Jessi said, that stiff smile appearing once again on her face. "I mean, it's not like I have a right to know or anything."

Olivia and Millie excused themselves and headed for the kitchen to make coffee. The other guests busied themselves admiring the myriad gifts.

"I'd like to tell you, Jessi." Sunny met the girl's eyes. "You see, not long after we married your dad and I found out we were going to have a baby."

"You weren't pregnant when you got married?"

Sunny shook her head. "Despite popular opinion, no. The baby was a surprise—a wonderful surprise." Her voice caught on the last word. "Unfortunately, it wasn't to be. I miscarried and your dad and I..." She let the words fade away.

Bright patches of color appeared on Jessi's cheeks as she looked at Sunny. "A baby," she said, as if she'd never considered that possibility.

"We didn't know how to handle sorrow," Sunny said after a moment. "We broke up not long after." She turned her hands palms up in a gesture of finality. "You know the rest." Robert went to law school where he ultimately met Christine, while Sunny threw herself headlong into the pursuit of the art career she'd always wanted.

Sunny watched as Jessi struggled with her thoughts. The girl's emotions were so close to the surface that Sunny could almost reach out and touch them. It had to be hard to imagine your father in love with somebody else—or that if things had been different, you might never have been born at all. *Talk to me, Jessi. We could be such good friends....*

"Can I be excused?" Jessi asked. "I have my math final tomorrow and I have to study."

Sunny suppressed a sigh. "Go ahead," she said, feeling another opportunity slip through her fingers. "I wouldn't want your math final on my conscience." Try as she might she couldn't keep the disappointment from her voice.

"Sunny, I—" Jessi stopped.

This is it! thought Sunny. *She wants to talk to me.*

"Sunny!" Her sister Liz popped up next to her. "Mom needs you to check the final seating for the rehearsal dinner."

"I'll be there in a few minutes," Sunny snapped. What rotten timing. She looked back at Jessi. "What were you about to say?"

Jessi hesitated.

Sunny held her breath.

In the doorway Liz tapped her foot impatiently.

"Nothing," Jessi said after a moment. "I guess I'll go to my room."

"WE WERE *THIS* CLOSE to becoming friends," said Sunny to Robert over dinner later that night in a lovely French restaurant in New Hope. "For the first time I think Jessi really saw me as a person."

Robert refilled her wineglass. "I hadn't told her about the baby."

"I figured that much."

"I'm surprised you told her."

"I want to be honest with her, Robby. At that age there's nothing harder to deal with than half-truths."

"You're going to make a terrific mother," he said, eyes glittering in the candlelight.

"If I get the chance."

"Michael is crazy about you already."

"Michael is a great little boy." She sipped her wine, then smiled. "He wants to know if he can call me Mom after we're married."

"And what did you say?"

She started to laugh. "Are you kidding? Mom, Mommy, Mother—take your pick." She gave Robert a wry glance. "Now if Jessi liked me half as much, I'd be home free."

"She likes you. It's the idea of 'us' that's giving her trouble."

"This is all happening so fast," she said, gesturing with her salad fork. "Maybe we should have waited awhile longer, given her a chance to adjust to everything."

"How long is long enough?" Robert countered. "What if she takes a year to adjust to our wedding? Life doesn't come with guarantees, Sunny. It can be over before you know it."

"You must do well in the courtroom."

"This has nothing to do with the courtroom." He reached for her hand and held it tightly. "This has to do with the rest of our lives. We'll work on it together, Sunny. As her parents."

She thought of Jessi's mother and of how the future could be over in the blink of an eye. "I want so much for us," she whispered. "For all of us. We're so lucky to be given this second chance, Robby. I want everything to be perfect."

Music drifted toward them from the next room. "Do you remember the last time we danced together?"

"The senior prom?" she asked.

He nodded. "It's been a long time."

"What if we make a spectacle of ourselves at the reception?"

"Couldn't let that happen." He pushed back his chair and stood up. "We used to be pretty good."

She grinned and rose to join him. "We were a lot younger."

He took her hand and led her toward the dance floor in the next room. "Some things get better with age."

"You were right," she said a few moments later. "Some things definitely improve with age."

If possible, they fitted together even more wonderfully than they had as teenagers. The music was slow, dreamy. They stood together on the floor with their arms around each other and swayed with the rhythm. With her head nestled against his shoulder and his hand warm against her back, Sunny felt as if she understood what heaven was all about.

"Don't dip," she murmured into his ear. "I'm too tired to be dipped."

"Don't worry," he said. "I don't intend to let you go long enough to dip."

"The next time we dance will probably be at our wedding."

"And the next time we make love . . ."

"Seven days," she whispered, pressing closer to him. The one good thing about a wedding was the fact that the wedding night was guaranteed. Lately there hadn't been time for much in the way of romance. "Do you realize that this time next week I'll be a mother?"

She sensed a certain tension in the way he held her.

"Robert?"

He stopped dancing and led her back to their table. "We need to talk."

Her stomach knotted. "You look serious."

"There's one thing we haven't talked about," he said, holding her chair out for her.

"What type of champagne to serve at the reception? The first song? Stuffed cabbage or pepper steak on the buffet table?"

"A baby."

"A baby?"

"Our child," he said, his voice low and intimate. "Part of us both."

"Oh."

"How do you feel about that idea?"

"Elated . . . scared . . ." Her eyes brimmed with tears. "Hopeful."

They were quiet while a busboy cleared the table and the waiter served coffee and dessert.

"It won't be like the last time," Robert said, linking her fingers with his across the table.

"You said life came with no guarantees," she pointed out. "What happened that time might happen again." Her miscarriage had not been the result of an underlying physical problem, yet she knew anything was possible.

"No." His voice was strong, firm. "Not this time."

"You can't be certain."

"The hell I can't. *Whatever* happens, this time the marriage is for keeps."

Tears of happiness spilled down her cheeks. "I love you, Robby," she said.

"Care to show me how much?"

She started to laugh. "Here? I don't think the staff of Chez Ondine would appreciate it."

He threw down a pile of bills on the table and stood up. "I know someplace better."

Ten minutes later, he angled his car on a rise overlooking a valley and doused the headlights.

"Inspiration Point," Sunny breathed, glancing toward the other cars scattered about. "When was the last time—"

"The night of the prom," said Robert, unsnapping his seat belt.

There was something about the look in his eyes that made her blood run quick and hot as he unsnapped her belt. "The night we decided to get married."

"You're sexier today than you were as a girl."

"Smart man," she said, sliding closer to him. "If we were in the back seat, I'd prove it to you."

Moments later that was exactly where she found herself.

"You're incorrigible," she giggled as he reached beneath her silky top and deftly opened her bra. "You haven't lost your touch."

"Come here, woman," he said, pulling her onto his lap. "You talk too much. This might be our last chance until the wedding night."

"Yeah?" she said, bringing her mouth close to his.

"Yeah." His mouth covered hers, and she felt as if she were standing in the middle of a raging fire. She pitied the adolescents they'd once been. Teenage lust was nothing compared to adult passion.

And passion combined with love was a potent mixture, designed to bring a man and woman to the flash point in an instant.

"This is crazy, Robby."

"No, it's not. It's the only sane thing we've done since the day we met at the gallery."

"Someone might see us."

"The windows are fogged over." His low laugh thrilled her. "Besides, they're all too busy to worry about us."

He moved a little to the right, she slid over a tad to the left and the next moment they agreed that nothing was impossible if the man was inventive enough—and the woman limber.

THEY WALKED UP the steps to Sunny's front door a little before 2:00 a.m.

"A policeman," Sunny said, shaking her head in bemusement. "How embarrassing!"

"He didn't take our names," Robert pointed out.

"It doesn't matter. I almost died when he pointed that flashlight in the window."

"I thought you were the unconventional one."

"About some things." She fished around inside her purse for her house keys. "What if we'd been arrested? Our mothers would have publicly disowned us."

"Not before the wedding," he said dryly.

He watched as she unlocked the door. No woman had the right to look so beautiful by moonlight. He wanted to toss her over his shoulder and spirit her upstairs to her bedroom and have his way with her again.

"I'm worried about you," Sunny said after they stepped into the dimly lighted foyer. "That long drive home..."

He pulled her into his arms. "I can think of a way around that long drive."

"Oh, no," she said, laughing. "I think that policeman was an omen. Maybe we should wait for our wedding night."

"Bad idea."

She laughed and placed a hand on his chest. "What would the kids say if you stayed out all night?"

"I'd be home before anyone knew I was missing."

"Kids know more than you think," Sunny chided, shooting him a sharp look. "I hope you haven't been shortchanging them, with all the wedding fuss going on."

"I've been shortchanging everything: kids, work, you."

"I know what you mean." Sunny sighed. "With all the wedding hoopla, I feel like a hamster on a wheel." Keeping her mind on gallery business had required Herculean effort. She thanked God every day for her assistant, Joi, who managed to keep things running through the chaos Sunny's sudden engagement had brought about.

He followed her into the living room, waiting while she switched on the Elvis desk lamp she was so fond of. "You planning on bringing that with you when you move in?"

"You don't like my Elvis lamp?"

He bypassed the question and gestured toward the bright yellow hammock swinging from the exposed beams. "That might end up in the backyard."

She put her hands on her hips and glared at him. "Are you telling me you hate my furniture?"

"I'm saying we might have a problem fitting everything in."

"You look like the cat that ate the canary," she said. "What are you up to, Robby?"

He grinned at her and gave Elvis a playful sock on the jaw. "You'll find out soon enough."

Chapter Five

"THERE," said the seamstress, adjusting one of the hundreds of tiny seed pearls on the bodice of the gown. "You're a vision!"

Sunny, in wedding gown and running shoes, looked toward the women assembled in the doorway. "What do you think?"

"Spectacular," said Olivia, hands pressed together in rapture. "You *are* a vision."

"Wow!" said Jessi. "You look like a princess in that dress."

Sunny's mother didn't say a word. Millie's tears of joy spoke for her.

"Take a look, Ms. Talbot," the seamstress urged. "This is your last chance before the wedding." Today was Wednesday. The rehearsal dinner was just seven hours away—if Sunny's nerves held out that long.

Slowly Sunny turned to face the three-way mirror. She'd never considered herself the traditional type. Her own sense of fashion was decidedly funky and imaginative. The thought of being decked out in a fairy-tale princess wedding gown was as foreign to her as the thought of wearing a navy blue business suit. *Just keep cool,* she warned herself as she opened her eyes. *Even if you hate it, don't let anyone know.* This wedding meant so much to everyone that she wouldn't do anything to upset things at this late date.

At first she didn't recognize herself. The dress was a confection of satin, lace and pearls, and not even the running shoes peeping beneath the hem could dilute the effect.

"Oh!"

"You like?" asked the seamstress.

"I don't like," she breathed. "I *love*!" She pirouetted before the mirror, shamelessly entranced with the romantic loveliness of her reflection. "I never dreamed I could look like this."

"Just you wait until you walk down the aisle on Saturday," said her mother who had recovered her voice, "and Robert sees you for the first time."

"Did I hear my name?" A male voice floated through the half-closed door to the main dressing room.

Sunny shrieked. "Robert! Don't you dare come in here!" She spun around and looked at her mother and Olivia. "Stop him!"

"You're superstitious," Robert laughed a few minutes later when, back in jeans and T-shirt, she read him the riot act.

"I'm not superstitious," she lied, fingers crossed behind her back. "I'm cautious, that's all."

"I'm going to see you in your wedding gown in three days. Why not a preview?"

"Over my dead body," said his mother, glaring up at him in her most patrician manner.

He turned to Jessi. "What do you think about it, sweetheart?"

The girl visibly beamed. "I think you should wait until Saturday."

Sunny clapped her hands together. "Female solidarity is a wonder to behold."

Robert looked bemused and somewhat bewildered. "I hate to break this up, but we have something to do."

Jessi stepped forward, looking expectant. "Lunch at the Happy Sprout."

He ruffled her bangs. "Not that carrot juice and tofu place outside of town?"

Jessi's face drooped and Sunny immediately stepped in. "I'm in favor of lunch at the Happy Sprout. It wouldn't hurt any of us to try eating healthily for a change." She looked at her mother and Olivia. "You'll join us, won't you?"

Millie reached for her notebook and flipped to her daily calendar. "Today we have a run-through with the caterer."

"Not the caterer," said Olivia, opening her own to the appropriate page. "We have to review the florist's sketches."

"I'm sure it's the caterer." Millie trailed a finger down the items on her To Do list. "We have to sample the dessert crepes and make a final decision."

"But the florist is expecting us," Olivia pointed out. "He found a source for stephanotis and—"

Sunny moved closer to Robert. "I think this is our chance to escape."

"Yeah," said Jessi. "We could be at the Happy Sprout before anyone knows we're missing."

"Sounds good to me," said Robert. "Why don't we—"

"Not so fast, you three." Millie, the General Patton of wedding preparations, swung on them with all guns blazing. "We're not through with you yet."

"Us?" Sunny stared at her mother. "Since when do we have anything to do with this wedding? So far the only thing you've let us do is choose our wedding rings."

"The license," said Millie, checking her list. "We need the license for Reverend Davies."

"We applied for it weeks ago," said Sunny. She turned to Robert. "Did you pick it up?"

He shook his head. "I thought you did."

"Me? When would I have time? You said you'd get it next time you were at the courthouse."

"I don't know where you got that idea. You told me you'd swing by there next time you went to see one of your artist friends."

Olivia looked to be on the verge of swooning. "Do you mean to tell us you *don't have your marriage license?*"

"There's no need to yell, Ma," said Robert, wincing.

Elegant Olivia, however, was beyond decorum. "The wedding is in *three days* and you *don't have a marriage license?*"

"Grandma," said Jessi, staring wide-eyed at the woman. "Your face is turning all red."

Millie gave the future bride and groom her sternest look. "I can't believe you two could be so irresponsible! We ask you to do one thing and you can't manage that."

"Like we have nothing else on our minds, Mother?" Sunny's own temper flared to life. "I'm trying to get my art gallery off the ground, Robby has a law practice and we'd like to find time to have a life."

"And I suppose you think planning a wedding has been easy on Olivia and me?" Millie was a match for her daughter. "We're working our fingers to the bone, trying to make this the most wonderful day of your life."

Sunny refused to back down. "Sometimes I wish Robby and I had eloped again and simply presented you with a fait accompli."

Bingo.

The word *elope* brought both mothers up short.

"Sunny!" they said in unison. "You wouldn't."

Robert, bless him, stepped into the fray. "She wouldn't," he said.

"I always said he was a good boy," Millie remarked, gazing at her future son-in-law with devotion. "He understands."

"He doesn't understand anything," said Olivia with a sniff. "He just knows when he's in more trouble than he can handle."

"I think we'd better get that marriage license," Sunny said to Robert.

"If we want to escape with our lives," he mumbled under his breath. He pulled some money out of his pocket and handed it to his daughter. "Lunch is on me."

Jessi looked crestfallen. "You're not coming with us?"

"We can't, Jess. By the time we get the license, the afternoon will be shot."

Sunny gave Jessi an apologetic smile. "Just a few more days of this craziness and we'll be back to normal."

"You'll sit with us at the rehearsal dinner tonight," Robert promised. "Place of honor."

Millie rested a hand on the girl's shoulder. "Are you hungry, Jessi?"

Jessi shrugged. "I guess."

"We'll go to the florist first and then the caterer's," said Olivia, jotting an entry in her notebook, "and then the Happy Sprout."

"We'll make it up to you, sweetheart," said Robert. "We promise."

Sunny only hoped Jessi would let them.

FROM THERE the day slid from bad to worse. Two of the bridesmaids were late for the rehearsal, Millie lost her contact lenses, and Sunny's grandmother flatly stated she wouldn't drink champagne no matter who was getting married.

And now Michael had decided to play hide-and-seek.

"Michael!" Robert's voice rang out through the small church. "If you don't come out by the time I count to three, I'll—"

Sunny grabbed his forearm and squeezed hard. "You're in church," she reminded, her voice a frantic whisper.

Robert glanced toward the minister standing at the foot of the altar. Sunny wasn't entirely sure her intended registered the man's presence.

"Stay here," she urged. *Stay quiet!* "I'll look for Michael."

And while she was at it, she'd look for the exit. So far, the entire wedding rehearsal had been an unmitigated disaster and they'd yet to get past their arrival at the church. One of the ushers had tripped in the vestibule and sprained his ankle, necessitating a trip to the emergency room. "I'll be back even if my foot's in a cast," he'd promised cheerfully, sending her sister Liz into tears. "I can't walk down the aisle alone," she'd wailed. "I'll look ridiculous."

Sunny snorted in disgust. "No more ridiculous than I look right now," she muttered as she crawled around the organ in the balcony, looking for Robert's errant son. "Michael, if you're anywhere in earshot, come out. You don't want your dad to find you."

She heard the rustle of clothing somewhere near the choir loft. "This isn't funny, Michael," she warned. "We can't get married if we don't have a ring bearer." A stifled giggle sounded from nearby. "It's late, we're all tired and hungry and I'm not in the mood for games."

He popped up, face streaked with dirt, eyes dancing with pure mischief. He looked adorable but she wasn't about to tell him so. "Bet you thought I'd run away, didn't you?"

"No, I didn't," she said, pulling a tissue from her pocket and trying to wipe away the worst of the grime. "I thought you were hiding."

"Were you scared?"

She shook her head. "Your daddy and I were annoyed. We need you downstairs, Michael, not up here playing games."

He didn't look terribly contrite. What was there about this wedding rehearsal that was bringing out the worst in people? She felt like throwing a tantrum herself.

"Come on," she said, offering Michael her hand. "Let's go downstairs and practice."

Michael stuck out his lower lip. "Don't want to."

"Well, I don't much want to myself, Michael, but that doesn't matter. Reverend Davies expects us to."

It was a little like leading a recalcitrant water buffalo to higher ground. Sunny wouldn't have believed that someone so small could be so stubborn. She'd have to remember never to underestimate the willpower of a six-year-old boy.

"I found him," Sunny said as Robert stormed up the aisle to where she and Michael waited in the vestibule. "He was in the choir loft."

"We'll talk about this later, young man," Robert barked. "Now let's get this show on the road."

Hardly the stuff of romance.

But then there wasn't much about the wedding rehearsal that had anything to do with romance.

Two of the ushers got into an argument about who was the taller. There was something almost comical about a pair of thirtysomething six-footers asking a minister to referee their heated debate. The bridesmaids, however, weren't about to be outdone. Sunny's sisters battled over which one of them would adjust the bridal train before Sunny walked down the aisle. Even her uncles had teetered on the verge of mayhem.

Sunny's father escorted her down the aisle, beaming with pride although this was only a rehearsal. He handed her over to Robert, who looked as if he'd been catnapping on his feet.

Sunny stifled a yawn as they turned to face the waiting minister. "Two days from today," said Reverend Davies with a big smile, "and you'll be husband and wife."

"If we live that long," said the happy couple in unison.

THEY SURVIVED the rehearsal and the dinner afterward—but not by much. Robert's habit of questioning friends as if they were courtroom witnesses got on her nerves and she had reason to suspect he'd be a lot happier if she hadn't chosen to spike her hair for the event. *This is normal*, she told herself as they drove back to Robert's house. He'd insisted they stop there before he took her home. *All couples fight*. The miracle was that they hadn't squabbled long before this. Certainly the first time around their relationship had been as fiery as it had been romantic.

Sunny flipped on Robert's answering machine. "Broken!" Sunny shrieked. "Ed's ankle can't be broken! What on earth are we going to do?"

"I don't suppose Liz would be willing to walk down the aisle alone."

"You heard her before. She'll get hysterical." At the best of times her sister was prone to melodramatic outbursts. She could only imagine what histrionics this development would produce.

"Ed said he still wants to be in the wedding. He could always use a cane."

"With our luck he'd trip over the white runner Mother insisted on." She thought for a second. "How about a wheelchair?"

"Sounds good to me," said Robert. "We could drape it with flowers and Liz could hitch a ride on his lap."

Sunny had to laugh at the idea. "Wouldn't she just love that." Jessi popped up in the doorway to the kitchen. "I'm going upstairs," she announced. "Want me to put Michael to bed?"

"Not yet."

"There you go again," said Sunny, glancing at him. "You look like the cat that ate the canary. What gives?" She'd seen the same expression on his face the night of her bridal shower.

"As soon as I get the whole group of you in the den, I'll tell you."

"Fair warning, Robby," she said darkly. "I'm not up for any more surprises." She turned to Jessi. "Do you have any idea what your dad is up to?"

Jessi shrugged her narrow shoulders. "Maybe we're going to get a dog."

That was all Michael had to hear. He forgot all about the chocolate milk he was drinking and started running around the kitchen pretending he was a golden retriever. Even Jessi looked excited.

"Those kids are expecting nothing less than Lassie," she said sotto voce as they entered the den.

"Better than Lassie," he stage-whispered back.

"Bigger?"

"That, too."

"A horse!" Sunny brought her hands together in glee. "You remembered how much I'd always wanted a horse."

Apparently a horse was even better than a dog to Michael, because he stopped barking and started whinnying at the top of his lungs.

"What's the surprise, Dad?" Jessi sat on the edge of the sofa, her blue eyes expectant. "*Is* it a horse?"

Robert no longer had the cat-and-canary look about him. "It's not a horse."

"Then it has to be a dog," said Sunny, wondering how she'd like living with a canine who weighed more than she did.

"It's not a dog," said Robert.

Michael's lower lip trembled. "I want a dog."

Sunny reached out and gave him a hug. "When your dad and I come back from our honeymoon we can talk about getting a dog."

"This isn't going exactly the way I had it planned." Robert was looking more befuddled by the minute. It was nice to know that family matters could undo even the best of men. He reached into his pocket and withdrew a key on a red satin ribbon, then handed it to Sunny.

"A car?" she asked, puzzled.

"A truck!" said Michael, ecstatic.

"A minivan," said Jessi, wrinkling her nose.

"A house," said Robert.

"What?!" Three voices in unison. Then Sunny's rose over the pack. "You bought a house?"

"Five bedrooms, three and a half baths. The kitchen is as big as your entire cottage."

She stared at him, unable to comprehend his words. A house! People didn't just go out and buy houses for other people, no matter how much money they had. Houses were something you worked for, struggled over, dreamed about with the one you loved.

"I haven't exactly bought it yet," Robert went on, feeling the way he had during his worst days in law school. Where were the jubilant cheers and the looks of adoration? "I put down a deposit last week."

"I want a dog!" Michael cried, bursting into tears.

"Where is this house?" Sunny asked. "I thought we'd decided this location was perfect."

"Two towns west of here. This place is better than perfect, Sunny. You can have your own studio, complete with north light."

The artist in Sunny was tempted. The woman, however, was not. Jessi remained ominously silent. Robert produced pictures of an exceptionally handsome ranch house. They all stared at him. "The studio is over there," he said, pointing, "and the kids' rooms are on the opposite side."

"I don't want a new room," said Michael. "I want my old room."

"Jessi?" He turned toward his daughter. "What do you think?"

Her face was streaked with tears. "What do you care?" she threw back at him. "You just do whatever you want, anyway. You don't care what I think anymore about anything."

"Jessi." Sunny stepped forward. "I don't think your dad wanted to upset you. He meant well."

"What the hell do you mean, 'he meant well'?" Robert exploded. "A man buys a great house for his family and instead of thanking him, you're all looking at me like I'm a mass murderer. What in hell is going on around here?"

Sunny wheeled toward him. "You don't spring houses on people, Robert. You spring dogs on people, or horses, but houses usually require a bit more communication."

"So do weddings," he shot back. "For the past two months you've been calling all the shots there."

"Me? If you remember, I didn't want anything to do with a big wedding. It was your mother's idea."

"Yeah, right," he said with a snort of laughter. "Like your mother wasn't calling the caterers before we finished announcing our engagement. They don't call her the Terminator for nothing."

"Oh, yeah? Your mom makes mine seem like Mary Sunshine by comparison."

They glared at each other across the floor plans.

"You're awful!" Jessi cried, breaking the silence. "I hate you both." Turning, she ran from the room and seconds later they heard the sound of her bedroom door slamming shut.

"I'm going up to talk to her." Robert started for the stairs.

"Leave her alone," Sunny snapped. "We've made big enough fools of ourselves already."

Michael's head swiveled from one to the other as if he were a spectator at Wimbledon. Sunny didn't dare imagine how ridiculous grownups must seem from his vantage point.

"I would like to go back to my parents' house," Sunny said quietly. She was spending the week before her wedding with the Talbots.

"Fine."

He didn't have to sound so eager.

She helped Michael on with his sweater. "What about Jessi?"

Robert stood at the foot of the stairway. "I'm taking Sunny home," he bellowed. "Do you hear me, Jess?"

Amazing how much emotion could be contained in the simple word "Yes."

They drove back to the Talbots' house in silence. Michael was dozing in the back seat and Sunny kept her gaze on the road. What a disaster this whole terrible day had been. Ed's broken ankle, Liz's tears, her uncles practically coming to blows over a Cuban cigar . . . She tried to console herself with the fact that even Princess Di had messed up her wedding vows.

It gave her hope.

MICHAEL HAD SOMEHOW managed to sleep during the ride to the Talbots' house and back, blissfully oblivious of the icy undercurrents. There was something to be said for being six years old, Robert thought as he lifted his sleeping son out of the car and carried him into the house. He wouldn't have minded sleeping through that ride from hell himself.

"Wait," he'd said as he stopped the car in her parents' driveway. "I'll walk you to the door."

"Don't bother," she'd snapped. "I'll see you at the church on Saturday."

Ten minutes later he and Michael were back home. He started up the staircase with his sleeping son draped over his shoulder. Sure it had been a lousy night. That wedding rehearsal had only served to remind him that you get older, but you don't necessarily get smarter. He and Sunny had been right the first time. Too bad the wedding was only three days away, otherwise he'd grab Sunny and drag her off to a justice of the peace.

Jessi's door was closed but the light filtered out through the bottom crack. How in hell the house of a family's dreams could throw them all into chaos was beyond him. Maybe Jessi'd be able to explain it to him. He rapped on the door with his elbow.

"Jess? Open up. We need to talk." He waited, but no response. He rapped on the door again. "Jessi, give your old man a break. Something's bothering you. I want to know what it is." Still nothing. Beads of sweat broke out on the back of his neck. He shifted Michael's position, then reached for the doorknob.

The bed lamp was lighted. The radio was tuned to one of those stations that made him understand how his parents had felt twenty years ago. Everything looked normal. The only problem was Jessi was nowhere in sight. He laid Michael down on the bed and knocked on the bathroom door. She wasn't in there, either. He slid open the doors to her walk-in closet. If she'd packed, she hadn't taken much. Her favorite denim knapsack was gone and her wallet and the locket Grandma Holland had given her for her twelfth birthday and the picture of her mother.

Apprehension turned to fear.

His daughter was gone.

Chapter Six

SUNNY WAS SITTING on her parents' front porch feeling sorry for herself when she saw Robert's car turn into the driveway and all of her fears vanished in a burst of elation. He'd come to make up with her! She leaped up from the glider and hurried down the steps to meet him.

"Oh, Robby!" She ran to fling herself into his arms. "I'm so glad you—"

"Jessi's gone."

She stopped a few feet away from him. "What?"

"She's gone. Her light was on, the radio was blaring—" He stopped and she saw him swallow hard.

She felt as if someone had literally knocked the breath from her body.

"I'd been hoping she was here, but..." His words died away as he turned his head to hide the glitter of tears.

"Her friends," Sunny said, struggling for their names.

Robert shook his head. "I tried them."

He'd called movie theaters, the skating rink, even Reverend Davies at church.

"Where's Michael?" Sunny asked, glancing around.

"Asleep in the back seat."

"Does Olivia know Jessi's missing?"

"Not yet. I figured there was a good chance Jess'd be here, so why worry her?" He'd called his mother with some lame question, hoping against hope Jessi would be sitting at the kitchen table complaining about him.

"Have you called the police?"

"No accidents."

Sunny's knees went weak with momentary relief. "Thank God."

"I'm going to check the parks," he said, racing toward the car.

"I'm coming with you." Sunny was close behind.

They got to the school yard in record time. A splash of moonlight silvered the grassy soccer field. No sign of Jessi anywhere. They drove to the town park where Sunny, a sleepy Michael in tow, checked the playground while Robert searched the bushes and other hiding places. Jessi was nowhere to be found.

"The bus station," Sunny said, her heart thudding with fear. "Maybe she . . ." Her words faded away in the darkness. She couldn't finish the sentence, not when Robert seemed to be aging right in front of her eyes.

The bus station was at the far end of town. The ticket clerk was dozing over his newspaper. He yawned and stretched as Sunny and Robert, with a sleepy Michael in his arms, approached.

"I'm looking for my daughter." Robert pushed a photo of Jessi toward the clerk. "Have you seen her?"

The clerk seemed only mildly interested. "No kids here today." He gave Sunny a look. "Would she hitch?"

Sunny looked toward Robert who shook his head. "No way. That's the one thing I'm sure of."

Back at the car, Sunny settled Michael in the back, then buckled herself into her own seat. Robert's fingers drummed against the steering wheel. His jaw was locked tight.

She struggled to find something—anything—that might comfort him. "She's probably with the one friend we forgot to call," she offered, trying to control the quaver in her voice. "She probably didn't run away at all. She never has before, has she?"

He shook his head. "She's threatened a time or two." He chuckled grimly. "Last time I told her she couldn't stay up late for *Saturday Night Live* she said she was going to run away to live with Christine's parents in Florida, but—" He looked over at Sunny as he stopped for a red light. "That's it. Florida."

Sunny frowned. "How on earth could she get to the airport?"

"She's a smart kid. She'd call for a cab. When she and Michael went to Florida last month, they took one of the radio cabs we use at work."

"How would she pay the cab fare?"

"Kids today have bigger allowances than your take-home pay when we were first married. She could scare up enough money to get to Philly International." The light changed and he stomped on the gas. "She knows the airport drill as well as I do. With that damn frequent-flyer card, she could go just about anywhere."

"But she wouldn't, would she?" The pieces of the puzzle were beginning to fall into place. "Florida is probably the only place where she can escape the wedding," she said. "With her mother's family."

THE TERMINAL at Philadelphia International was practically deserted. A maintenance crew desultorily went about their business, cleaning and waxing the floors, while two security guards laughed with a pretty female colleague.

"Come on," said Robert, taking Michael's hand. "This way."

"Daddy!" Michael stopped dead in his tracks. "I have to go."

Sunny knew a father's job when she saw it. "I'll run down to the gate. You take Michael."

"Careful, ma'am," called out one of the cleaning crew. "These floors are slippery. Don't want to break a leg or anything."

Sunny was beyond caring. All she could think of was Jessi alone somewhere, feeling scared and abandoned. She raced down the endless corridor, heedless of the way her feet slid on the linoleum. The next plane to Florida was due to board in five minutes. *Please let me be on time,* she prayed. *Please, please, please . . .*

Gate 3 loomed up ahead. The waiting room was crowded with travelers, clutching cameras and carry-on luggage. Babies in their mothers' arms. Toddlers. Servicemen in uniform and elderly couples and everything in between. *Jessi . . . where are you . . .*

If she lived to be one thousand, Sunny was certain she would never know another moment of such pure, mindless relief. The sight of Jessi sitting on the bench, clutching her bag, was more beautiful to her than a Hawaiian sunset. Did she run up to the girl and envelop her in a hug? Did she act casual and pretend Jessi ran away every day? Did she ground her for life and consign their future to the dustbin?

Fortunately, she heard Robert's footsteps, and smiling through her tears, she pointed toward the forlorn child. "Over there," she said. "Your daughter's over there."

A moment later Robert was castigating Jessi—but hugging her while he did it. The look of relief on his face was profound.

I love her, Sunny thought, in amazement. *I love her as if she were my own!* Loving Michael had been easy. She looked down at the little boy running circles around the small waiting room. She defied anyone to resist a six-year-old's charm. Jessi had been something else entirely. Prickly, self-conscious, protective of her place in the world, a little girl on the brink of adolescence, Jessi had made it hard for Sunny to get close to her—and Sunny had allowed it all to happen.

Until now.

Suddenly Jessi was no longer Robert's daughter but a vital part of Sunny's own family. Not flesh of her flesh but something equally precious: a child of her heart.

And so she did what she should have done two months ago—what she had wanted to do all along. She opened her arms to her daughter.

Jessi hesitated—but only for a second.

A moment later she was in Sunny's arms.

"Don't you ever do that to us again!" Sunny admonished, letting Jessi see how much she cared. "You scared the daylights out of us."

Jessi hung her head. "I'm sorry," she mumbled.

"Was it the wedding?"

"Sort of."

Sunny tilted her chin up so their eyes met. "And the house?"

Jessi nodded. "I don't want to move."

"...don't wanna move," repeated Michael as he stared longingly at the snack bar across the corridor.

"But it's a great house," said Robert, looking befuddled.

"We know it is," said Sunny, meaning it. "And maybe someday we'll be ready to appreciate it, but for now I think we should stay where we are."

"You, too?"

"Afraid so. The house you have feels right to me."

"It's home, Daddy," said Jessi, "and we want to stay there."

Sunny reached for Robert's hand. "We'll have plenty of time later on to go house-hunting." She looked down at the kids and grinned. "As a family."

He ruffled his daughter's hair. "So you left because of the house?"

"I didn't think anyone would notice," Jessi said. "All anyone thinks about is the wedding."

"Wedding, wedding, wedding," Michael piped up.

Sunny met Robert's eye over the girl's head. "There hasn't been a lot of time for anything else, has there?"

"All you do is try on dresses and plan menus and fool around with computer programs," Jessi continued. "What does that have to do with love?"

Robert didn't take his eyes from Sunny. "I've been asking myself the same thing."

"Ice cream," said Michael, jumping up and down as he pointed toward the snack bar. "Can I, Daddy? Please!"

Jessi met Sunny's eyes and they exchanged a look that only a woman would understand.

"I think we can bend the rules this once, don't you?" asked Sunny.

Jessi nodded and smiled up at her father. "I think I'd like some ice cream, too."

Robert knew when he'd been bested. He shrugged and handed them a five-dollar bill. "The snack bar and no place else. Understood?"

Jessi raised up on tiptoe and kissed his cheek. "Understood." Shyly she turned to Sunny. "I'm glad you found me."

Sunny gave her another hug. "Me too."

They watched as Jessi and Michael ran to the snack bar.

"Out of the mouths of babes," said Sunny.

"The house?" asked Robert.

"The wedding," said Sunny. "They said everything we've been thinking for weeks now. I haven't had time to breathe since the night you asked me to marry you." Fittings and menus were the least of it. She'd been eating, breathing and sleeping weddings for more than two months and not once had she she stopped long enough to appreciate the miracle that had happened that first afternoon in her art gallery when Robert walked in the door and changed her life.

It wasn't about flowers or "The Wedding March" or a white lace dress with a cathedral train. Lost in the thousands of details surrounding the wedding was the reason for the celebration, the miracle that had brought them together in the first place: the renewal of love. The commitment to be a family.

The certainty that the future was theirs for the asking.

"Too late to back out on it now," said Robert, his expression grave.

"It would break our mothers' hearts," said Sunny.

"Not to mention your dad's bank account."

Sunny chuckled grimly. "There's that, too. Sometimes it feels as if the wedding has nothing to do with either one of us."

A grin began to play at the corners of Robert's mouth. "There is something we can do that would mean a lot to us." The woman he loved looked up at him, realization dawning.

"We couldn't," said Sunny slowly. Then: "Could we?"

"They wouldn't have to know."

"You mean . . . ?"

"You got it."

A ripple of excitement moved along Sunny's spine. "History repeating itself?"

He kissed her mouth. "More like getting it right the second time."

"That's crazy!"

"No, it's not. It's the first sane thing I've come up with since I proposed to you."

"I have the license at home," said Sunny.

"And I have the rings."

"Could we find a judge on such short notice?"

"I'm a hotshot lawyer," Robert said, his grin widening. "I guarantee I can find us a judge before daybreak."

"What about the kids?"

He took her hand. "Let's ask them."

Jessi and Michael looked up from their hot fudge sundaes as Robert and Sunny approached.

"I asked for tofu ice cream," said Jessi sheepishly, "but they didn't have any."

"You only live once," said Sunny. "You can splurge now and then."

"We have something we want to tell you," said Robert, eyes twinkling.

"You see, there's something we can do as a family that would mean a lot to your dad and me," Sunny chimed in.

Robert's eyes met hers and she nodded. "What would you guys think of going to a wedding tonight?" she asked.

"A wedding?" Jessi looked from her father to Sunny then back again. "Tonight?" The happiness in the girl's voice warmed Sunny's heart. "Just for us?"

"Just for us," said Sunny.

"Can you?" asked Jessi, wide-eyed.

"We have the license," he said, smiling broadly. "We have the rings. We have our two favorite people to share it with us. What more do we need?"

"Not one thing," Sunny said, her heart filled with joy. "If you ask me, this time we have it all."

Epilogue

JUDGE HANSELL was a friendly sort, one who understood that love and romance didn't always follow a timetable.

"Damned irregular," he said, knotting the belt on his red plaid robe as he inspected the marriage license, "but everything seems to be in order."

"You're going to marry my daddy?" Michael asked.

The judge laughed and patted the boy on his head. "No, I'm going to marry your dad and Sunny to each other. I'm just the middleman."

"They were married before," said Jessi, clutching the nosegay of daisies the judge's wife and daughter had plucked from their backyard garden for the occasion.

"Lots of second marriages these days," said the judge.

"We were married to each other," Sunny explained. "When we were teenagers."

Poor Judge Hansell looked terribly confused. "Well," he said. "Well, well, well."

"They fell in love when they were about my age," Jessi confided, "but it didn't work out that time."

"We made a lot of mistakes," said Robert, taking Sunny's hand in his, "but we're older and wiser this time around."

"Not every couple is lucky enough to be given a second chance," said Sunny. "We intend to make the most of it."

The judge's brow furrowed. "Wouldn't you like a big fancy wedding with all the trimmings?"

"Saturday," said Robert, anxious to get on with the ceremony. "White carpets, limos and weeping relatives. The whole shebang."

"That one is for our families," said Sunny. She looked over at Jessi and Michael and felt a rush of emotion unlike anything she'd ever known. "This one is for us."

"Modern life," said the judge with a shake of his head. "I don't know if I'll ever understand it...."

They took their places in front of the fireplace. The judge's wife stood next to Robert while his eldest daughter stood next to Sunny. Jessi and Michael flanked the judge, their eyes wide with excitement. Sunny closed her eyes for an instant, trying to imprint the scene on her heart forever.

Later on, both Sunny and Robert swore that they'd caught the scent of orange blossoms in the air, but they were the only ones in the room who noticed it. Judge Hansell intoned the sweetly familiar words of the wedding ceremony, words that held special meaning now that they understood how miraculous a thing happily-ever-after truly was.

"What are you waiting for, man?" Judge Hansell boomed as his wife and daughter applauded. "Kiss your bride!"

"Ugh," said Michael, his voice high and piping. "They're kissing!"

"Of course they are, silly," Jessi said through happy years. "That's what newlyweds do."

"I love you," said Robert to his brand-new bride. "More than I thought possible."

"You've always been the one," Sunny said, her voice clear and strong. "My only love."

"Are we a family now?" asked Michael, tugging at his father's sleeve.

Robert scooped him up into his arms then looked at Sunny. "What do you think, Mrs. Holland?"

"Almost," she said, "but not quite." She looked at the man she'd always loved, at the little boy who made the sun shine. Jessi stood a few feet away from them, her eyes wet. Sunny smiled. The girl grinned. Sunny opened her arms wide and Jessi ran to her, and the four of them stood there laughing and hugging and talking all at once.

"Now," said Sunny, looking at her husband and children. "Now we're a family."

"Forever?" asked Jessi as Michael looked on.

Robert met Sunny's eyes and in them she saw their past, present and future intertwined, each link forging a chain of love and commitment that nothing could ever break.

"Forever," said Robert.

"Yes," said Sunny, heart soaring with love. "This time it's for keeps."

Bride on the Run

RITA
CLAY ESTRADA

A Note from Rita Clay Estrada

Weddings have always held a very important place in my life, first as a bride and then as the mother of the bride. I have three daughters and a son. My last unmarried daughter, Rita, got married this past year. It marked the end of a household full of children and the beginning of a very different kind of life.

Despite all the work and the hectic pace before one of my daughter's weddings, I wanted that day to be special, for my daughter to have memories that she would cherish for the rest of her life—just as I did.

Of course, in between the constant worrying that everything would go wrong, I often said aloud that an elopement sounded better and better. Since I don't have to plan my son's wedding, I'm looking forward to it. A day I can fully enjoy without all the work. But now I worry that I grumbled so much that he might decide eloping sounds good!

Rita

Chapter One

It was Kathi Rebecca Baylor's wedding day.

The announcer on the car radio reported that in Miami it was the hottest day of the year. Somehow, it seemed appropriate. Kathi was marrying her old friend, Timothy, in less than six hours and would probably faint from heat instead of passion.

She was sitting on the proverbial hot seat—all because her sister hadn't turned her back on temptation. Vivian had gambled away everything she owned and then went through Kathi's savings . . . and more. Much more.

When the gambling debts hit fifty thousand dollars, she'd come to Kathi begging for help. In turn, Kathi went to Timothy and begged for a solution. Timothy, being the best friend he was and having the wealth of Donald Trump on a good day, helped. But everything had its price. Kathi was just beginning to come out of her despair and recognize his. When he proposed, she had accepted—for all the wrong reasons. What Timothy had always wanted was a family. Family never asked questions and always gave support. If Kathi married him, the three of them—Kathi, Timothy and Vivian—would be that family. Instantly. So she'd said yes. It had seemed logical at the time. It was only now that she realized gratitude was *not* a good basis for marriage.

It was a tough realization to come to on her wedding day. She'd racked her brain but had found no answer to the dilemma. So she would marry Timothy and pray it all worked out.

The sleek maroon Fifth Avenue car wheezed, then coughed, then spurted. With alarm, Kathi watched the needle on the mileage indicator make its way to zero. The car barely reached the side entrance ramp to one of Miami's main highways. Then it jerked, clanked and sputtered to a halt. Judging from the steam escaping from under the hood, something major had happened to the engine.

"Great! Just great," she fumed, hitting the steering wheel in frustration. Here she was, stuck on a major highway ramp outside of Miami's airport.

And it wasn't even her car.

After taking the key from the ignition, she opened the door and stepped onto the pavement. A blast of heat slammed into her, taking away her breath. It was so hot that she could cook pancakes on the road surface.

But it didn't matter. A broken car wouldn't keep her from her wedding in Orlando. This was a delay, not a reprieve. *Damn*.

No matter how many excuses Kathi created—and she'd thought of a thousand in the past three days—there was no way to get out of the debt she owed her fiancé and still *not* marry him. And now she'd probably just slaughtered his car. It was one more sin to add to the growing list. But she was the one keeping the list. Timothy couldn't have cared less what her sins were.

Instead of feeling sorry for herself, she ought to have been thanking her fairy godmother for Timothy. He was a wonderful, forgiving man who was more than eager to give her everything she'd ever wanted—except the love she craved to feel for the man she married.

A horn honked and Kathi jumped out of the path of a speeding car, then shook her fist at the driver. She opened the trunk and pulled out the only item in the car that mattered—a clear plastic dress bag holding her mother's ivory wedding dress and headpiece. Sharp bulges of plastic at one corner revealed her shoes and other accoutrements were still in the bottom of the bag.

Hot sun beat down on her blond head. The car popped, then continued hissing as she wondered what the next step was. Given time, Timothy's mechanic could pick up the car and fix whatever was wrong. But she didn't have enough time to fool with that nonsense right now. Her wedding party—her bridegroom and sister—were waiting for her in Orlando. Kathi had suggested having the wedding there, where they could all laugh and play the week away. Visiting Walt Disney World would leave no time for tears. However, two of her best clients had called with last-minute appointments. Truth to tell, she hadn't minded sending Timothy and Vivian ahead. Disney World was their idea of a fun vacation, not hers. She liked sipping a drink and looking at the sea with nothing but the breeze and an occasional bird for sound effects. So she'd made her apologies, promised to be there in time for the wedding and waved them both off. It had given her some much-needed time last night to see if she could find a way out of the marriage. She hadn't come up with an answer.

And now she needed to get there. Pronto.

Scrabbling in the bottom of her purse, she found a pen and an old grocery list. She turned it over and wrote a note to the police saying that the car wasn't abandoned, just broken, and that a tow truck was on its way. Then she slipped it under the windshield and considered what to do.

Of course! If the ticket didn't cost more than fifty dollars, she could go by bus. That was all the cash she had with her—that and Timothy's gas credit card. She couldn't afford a plane to Orlando, and her own car was in her driveway, minus a starter.

The major thoroughfare light turned green and traffic poured out of the wide airport drive toward the highway. Certainly one of those cars could stop and offer her a ride. She put on her brightest smile.

Half an hour and what felt like three buckets of sweat later, someone did, even though it might not have been strictly voluntary. Kathi acknowledged that the huge, shiny black truck with pink and blue neon striping might not have stopped if she hadn't stepped out in front of it. She made it almost impossible for the big wheeled thing to go around her. It was one of those monster trucks that towered high above the street by at least a mile.

With relief, Kathi opened the door and hoisted herself up into the cab. The air conditioning felt so good. Closing her eyes, she murmured, "Ahh."

"Has it dawned on you that you're lucky to be alive? I could have run you down."

She didn't need to open her eyes to confirm it was a male voice—a very deep and sexy male voice. A slight exasperated, maybe even angry, male voice. Her nerve endings told her that. She readjusted the dress bag, her eyes still closed. "Give me a minute and I'll think about it," she said, her nerves on alert. Not only was the voice low and sexy, but there was something familiar about it.

"I'd love to, but we're stopping traffic. I need to know what you're doing in my vehicle and where you think I'm supposed to be going."

She opened her eyes and turned her head to stare at him. "I'm sorry! But, you see, my car broke down, or my fiancée's car broke down, and now I need to get to the bus station. I've got to be in Orlando in six hours." He was huge, and very well built, if the well-tailored, light-weight beige jacket and matching slacks were any indication.

"Wouldn't a taxi have done better than hitching a ride?"

"If I'd seen an empty taxi in the past half hour, I would have grabbed it," she answered.

"So it's *my* privilege," he retorted softly.

"Right." Already liking his dry wit, she continued to study him.

His hair was sandy colored with sun-toned strands. Judging from the expert cut, he had money. He had a strong jawline and a wide, strong forehead. His eyes were hidden by the mirrored sunglasses.

"Are you through?" His smile was magic.

"Through what?" she asked, still staring at him.

"Through ogling me as if I'm the fat lady in a freak show."

Her cheeks reddened, but she refused to back down. It would be a sign of weakness. "You're obviously not that, but I *was* wondering if you have your clothes hand tailored or you buy them off the rack."

His smile was still there, but his gaze wasn't laughing. "And your conclusion?"

"Hand tailored." Then she looked away, relieved she'd carried that off without backing down. That way it didn't look as if she was too chicken to look him in the eye. It was a trick she'd learned in her old neighborhood at an early age. Boys were always bullies, and the only way a female could deal with a bully was never to show fear.

"You're right." He slipped the truck into gear. "I just arrived in town. Where's the bus station?"

Kathi sat up in surprise. "You'll *really* take me?"

He looked straight ahead, his hands tight on the wheel as the vehicle slowly entered the freeway ramp. "You're here now. I might as well."

Kathi hesitated, afraid he might change his mind, but it was only fair to let him know his options. "You could drop me off at a gas station. After all, you weren't going to stop until I flagged you down."

"Until you stood in front of the truck," he corrected. "Is that what you want? To be dropped off somewhere else?"

"No!" She leaned forward, placing her dress bag neatly on the wide expanse of the floor. "I mean, I appreciate your help."

The radio played a jazzy, light-hearted tune and Kathi began to relax. But the handsome man beside her wouldn't let her lower her guard too much. Long ago she'd learned to be careful in a handsome man's presence. Every handsome man she ever met always seem to think that everything—especially women—should fall into his lap like ripe plums.

"Well?" he asked. "Are you going to tell me how to get there?"

"Just stay on this freeway until I tell you differently." She didn't know which was worse—being stuck without transportation or marrying a man you didn't love. Both were pretty bad, although, she supposed wryly, the latter was a lifetime trouble.

The radio tune ended and the fake, resonant voice of a disc jockey prattled, announcing the lottery's Fantasy Five numbers.

Before bed last night, she'd gone to the nearest corner store and bought a cold drink—and a Fantasy Five ticket. She'd been down about the wedding and unable to figure out a way out of marrying Timothy without hurting his feelings and her pocketbook. She'd been so down that she'd even ignored the fact that playing the lottery was gambling. She wasn't the one with the addiction, she was the one with the problem.

"Once more, those winning numbers are fifteen, twenty-one, seven . . .

Kathi's heart pounded. She had chosen those numbers. *She had chosen those numbers!* With shaking hands, Kathi reached inside her purse and pulled out her wallet. Opening it, she glanced down at the colorful Florida lottery ticket with a conch shell and Florida written in pink across the top.

She was right. She *had* chosen those numbers! The ticket didn't lie.

". . . thirty-two and . . ."

Her heart stopped completely. That number, too, was on her ticket. She had four out of five numbers. Four out of five! That meant she'd won some money for sure. But if she could get just one more, she'd win the grand prize. . . . She stared hard at the last number, praying number twelve would be called, but knowing the chances were astronomical.

". . . the last number in the Fantasy Five number series is . . ."

"Twelve," she prayed in a whisper.

"Twelve," the disc jockey repeated.

It took a minute to realize that he'd *really* said the number. Still, she didn't *really* believe it. "Did he say twelve?" she croaked.

"I don't know. I wasn't listening." He glanced in her direction, for a moment distracted from driving. "Why?"

Excitement bubbled inside her as she clenched the wallet tighter. Kathi opened her mouth then clamped it shut. She wasn't the winner, the ticket was. As long as she held the ticket, it was possible to have it stolen or taken or torn or lost. And then her fortune—however much it was—would be lost.

"So whoever you are," the deejay went on as if in answer to her unasked question, "if you chose all the right numbers, you've just won $302,918.91." He went on to describe what four out of five correct numbers would bring in, but Kathi barely heard him. She couldn't hear anything. Suddenly, she was the winner of more money than she could earn in a lifetime. In *two* lifetimes! She could open her own beauty shop instead of working in someone else's for the rest of her life! She could afford the expensive support panty hose so she wouldn't get those ugly blue veins so many of her coworkers got from standing on their feet all day long! She could ...

Kathi turned toward the voice that was practically shouting in her ear. "Wha ... ?"

"Sorry to interrupt your daydreaming, but I'm trying to figure out how to get to the bus station and you're not helping." His voice was deep with sarcasm and impatience.

"I'm sorry, but—" Again she stopped. She needed time to think what she was going to do next. Her mind was buzzing with incomplete thoughts. She was close to being a very rich lady. Very rich. But she needed a course of action.

Kathi remembered a TV news report on what-to-do-in-case-you-win scenario. She had two options. She could validate her ticket in a store that sold lottery tickets and wait two to four weeks for her prize money. Or she could go directly to Tallahassee and collect her winnings in a matter of hours.

The choice was obvious.

She turned to her chauffeur, refusing to acknowledge his good looks and irritated attitude. "You aren't by any chance heading toward Tallahassee, are you?"

"Why?" he asked cautiously.

She gave a deep sigh. Why couldn't he just answer the question? "Because I need to get there as soon as possible."

He looked puzzled. "I thought you said you needed to be in Orlando in six hours?"

Kathi bit her lip. She'd forgotten about that. In fact, she'd forgotten about her wedding completely! Timothy and Vivian were waiting for her.

Suddenly, she grinned, then laughed aloud at the sheer pleasure of her thought. Now she didn't have to marry Timothy! She didn't have to do anything, except collect her money and pay off the bills that hung over her head like a well-baited wedding trap. Years from now, Timothy would thank her for this. Besides, he really wanted Vivian. She was more his type than Kathi was. He was just too stubborn to admit it—especially since Vivian had turned him down once. In fact, Timothy might thank her in a month or so, just as soon as he realized that having his way wasn't always good for him....

Even to Kathi it sounded a little weak, but she grinned widely to show how happy she was over the decision she'd just made. "My mother needs me."

"Your mother?" he repeated, the emphasis on the last word. "She lives in Tallahassee?"

So it was a bigger white lie than she was used to telling. Her mother had died more than ten years ago when Kathi was a sophomore in high school. She continued to smile. "Yes."

"I see," he said slowly. "Are you going to tell the groom-to-be that you're not showing up?"

"Of course I am!" Kathi answered indignantly, realizing she hadn't really given a thought to that side of the problem.

"In *this* lifetime?"

"In this hour," Kathi corrected stiffly. "Just as soon as I figure out how I'm getting to Tallahassee."

"You still haven't told me how to get to the bus station. Does your figuring out how to get to Tallahassee mean you no longer need a bus?"

"No. Yes. No." Kathi couldn't think quickly enough. The Fantasy Five lottery ticket in her purse was so all-consuming that her thoughts jumbled around it. "Just a minute," she ordered crossly. "I need time to think!"

"Obviously," the man agreed tiredly. "And I need to get something to help combat this horrible heat from hell. Can I treat you to a soft drink?" He pulled into a fast-food chain and parked—very carefully—in what seemed like the farthest spot away from the door.

"I'd love an iced tea, but why don't we just go through the drive-in?"

"Because this damn thing might be too high and knock something off its perch" was his answer as he flipped off the engine and opened the door to let in a blast of heat that slammed into her. It was a potent reminder that the temperature was probably just a degree or two lower than hell. Walking to Tallahassee was out of the question.

"Where are you going?" she asked, panic lacing her voice.

"I'm going to the rest room and then to get a soft drink." He pocketed the truck keys and stared at her a moment, one very sexy brow arched in inquiry. "Is there anything else I can answer before I disappear into the air-conditioned confines of the restaurant?"

"Sorry." She should feel herself blush, but she couldn't afford to lose him. This man—or rather this truck—was the only form of transportation she had available to her at the moment, and she needed it. "Could I get your drink while you're, uh, busy?"

"No, thank you. But I would appreciate it if you'd let me know your intentions. Are you going inside or staying out here?"

"Oh, I'm staying right here."

"Are you sure? It's frying outside."

"The heat feels good," she lied.

"Suit yourself," he stated, as if he knew she'd be contrary. He stepped onto the running board, then down. Kathi noticed that even though he was standing on the ground, he was still able to see clearly into the cab. He was obviously very, very tall. And very muscular. And very handsome. "If you change your mind and decide to go inside, please lock up."

"Yes, sir!" She saluted smartly, a smile tilting her lips.

He stared hard at her for a moment, his gaze fathomless. Then he turned away, shutting the cab door before striding across the tarmac to the orange-and-green building beyond.

Kathi watched his retreating steps in the rearview mirror and wondered where she'd seen someone walk like him before. She searched her memory but came up blank. Come to think of it, that look he'd given her just before he left touched a memory, too. Try as she might, nothing came to mind.

With a fatalistic shrug, she placed the elusive memory in the back of her mind for consideration at a later date.

She had other problems on hand to deal with *now*. She pulled the winning ticket out of her purse, kissed it and then tucked it into her shoe. A girl had to be careful and a purse was just begging to be robbed.

The winning lottery ticket was the answer to all her prayers.

Three years ago, Timothy had been her best friend instead of her fiancé. He was also in love with her sister, Vivian, and not her. But neither she nor Timothy had known that Vivian was sick. Oh, not the ordinary illness that affects the body, but the illness that could affect the soul, the spirit, the emotional gut level. Unknown to either Timothy or Kathi, Vivian was gambling on everything and anything. She'd even bet whether or not the gas pump would automatically stop on an even or odd number. They didn't find out about it until she tried to commit suicide by taking an overdose of pills. It was then that the truth came out. She was in debt over fifty thousand dollars—and some of it at such a high rate that the interest alone could feed the world's hungry for years to come.

After her suicide attempt Vivian had agreed to counseling. Timothy, bless his heart, had stood by Kathi while she tried to make sense out of the mess her sister was in. The more she found out, the more she realized that she couldn't pay anyone off, let alone stop the interest from piling up.

Kathi was a hairdresser. She made good money, but it certainly didn't bring in enough to cope with more than the average bills of living. And as Vivian moved in with Kathi, having lost her job as a retail window dresser, money was even tighter. What little savings her sister had accumulated was long gone.

That was where Timothy came in. His father, an emotionally stingy man who had abandoned Timothy and his mother years earlier, had died, leaving Timothy a fortune as well as a well-respected car dealership.

Timothy knew how to survive. He'd been raised in a neighborhood where tough and mean gangs had slowly transplanted the original hardworking blue-collar laborers. As kids, he and Kathi had protected her younger sister. Kathi had protected herself, too. She had no choice. As the only female in a six-block radius, she had bluffed her way into being tough. It was either that or get pushed around or beaten up. Once Timothy had moved in, they'd stood united—for two years. Then Timothy had moved away, and she stood alone. When Timothy took over his father's business, he'd found his real niche. Most of his time was spent making a profitable business even more profitable. His protectiveness of her sister had turned to love for a while, and he asked Vivian to marry him. She'd never answered, but she *did* string him along. His free time was usually spent with Kathi waiting for Vivian to come home from her roaming. When they found out about her problem, each felt guilty for not realizing sooner that something was wrong.

Just like when they were kids, they'd united forces and drawn together in mutual support. Timothy settled all her sister's debts, then paid for the intensive counseling that had helped get Vivian back on the right track again.

While Vivian still had more counseling treatment to undergo, an important step was working at Timothy's office. She was at the threshold of a new life and needed the backing of her family to gain her stride again.

Timothy's unspoken price for all he had done was that Kathi marry him and give him the family he'd always craved. Feeling guilty for borrowing the money, realizing it would take her a lifetime to pay him back, and knowing that in some crazy, friendly way, she loved him, too, Kathi had said yes. She hadn't known what else to do.

Now she did. She had the answer to her prayers in her shoe. She'd pay Timothy back and be free to enjoy his friendship once more. She'd make sure that enough money was set aside for the rest of Vivian's counseling. Then she'd open her own beauty shop and be independently wealthy. Well, at least independent.

Kathi would explain it all to him and Timothy would understand. But it would have to be later. Right now, she needed to get to Tallahassee.

Kathi wiped more perspiration from her forehead and thought of the wedding dress encased in plastic at her feet. Her parents would be so glad she wasn't wearing it when she really wasn't in love—not the way she should be. Her mother had designed and made it herself, creating a tangible expression of love that most women only dream of. Her parents had such a wonderful marriage and everyone she'd ever lent the dress to had had that kind of happiness, too. Kathi wasn't sure if her mother screened the potential partners well, or if it was really as her mother used to say—that the dress itself was a good-luck beginning.

Who knew? But it had been worn by fourteen brides— all still married. She'd like to find a minister who could claim the same record.

Back to her problem. She had to get to Tallahassee so she could make *her* dreams come true for a change. The driver's door opened again, and Kathi gave a relieved sigh in spite of the heat that poured through the opening. The big bad driver of the big black truck was back.

Now all she had to do was convince him to drive her to Tallahassee.

"Hold these," he ordered, handing her two paper cups.

She did as she was told and watched as he climbed up to sit behind the wheel. Her heart did a triple somersault as he turned and took his soda away from her, giving her a smile as a thank-you.

"Okay," he said after taking a long sip. "Where do you need to go?"

"Tallahassee," she answered promptly.

His head turned toward her as he stared for a long, silent moment. "Impossible."

His gaze dried her mouth. She wet her lips and tried to ignore her body's response to his sex appeal. She'd known he'd turn her down, but it had been worth a try. "Why? Do you have something better to do on a hot weekend?"

"Almost anything is better than driving eight hours in a truck down the middle of Florida, Kathi."

He knew her name. He knew her. Even his demeanor had announced it, but she'd been too preoccupied to pay attention. Lottery tickets were all she could think of.

"Excuse me," she began. "But do I know you?"

This time the corners of his mouth turned down, matching the frown between his dark brows. "I'm afraid so."

Quickly, she took in his haircut and decided she hadn't seen him in the shop. She never forgot a cut. "Have we met recently?"

He shook his head. "Not for a long time."

She was at the end of her rope and she didn't feel like dangling there. This was no time for games, and she'd be *damned* if she'd ask his name. Her pride dictated that he had to volunteer the information or she would die biting her tongue. "Is this Twenty Questions?"

He shrugged. "Why not? I've asked twice and haven't received a clue where I'm supposed to drop you off. Why should I give you an answer?"

That commonsense approach. That nerdish commonsense approach. She knew it. *She knew it.* All she had to do was concentrate and it would come to her. . . .

HANNIBAL SAUNDERS slipped the key in the ignition and revved the powerful engine as if he knew what he was doing in this truck. He wanted to grin in satisfaction, but kept himself in check. For once, Kathi didn't have the upper hand. For once, Hannibal was in charge and Kathi was at *his* mercy.

If his memory served him right, she was used to controlling everything around her. Especially the opposite sex. Kathi Rebecca Baylor, his nemesis from middle and high school, was sitting next to him and didn't know his name. That thought produced a mixed bag of emotions. He felt good about having her wonder, but he also felt insulted that he wasn't more memorable. After all, he'd had a secret crush on her as they grew up.

When his parents divorced, he'd been shipped to Miami to live with his grandmother. Kathi was their next-door neighbor. In those days he'd cringed at the sound of her voice. He'd wait for something sarcastic to roll out of her pursed mouth and punch him in the emotional stomach. Yet he was always surprised when it did. She had always *looked* so angelically sweet and kind and nice. But her sharp tongue had always packed such a wallop!

Kathi leaned forward just enough to catch some of the chilled air blasting from the vents. She stared at him as if memorizing his face. Apparently, nothing in his adult features gave him away.

She leaned back and sighed heavily. "Since you obviously know my name, then you must know I don't usually ask favors."

Hannibal slipped the truck into gear and cautiously backed it out of its parking space. "No quarter asked, none given."

She barely hid her surprise. That used to be the line Timothy and she quoted just before taking on the "enemy," whoever it might have been at the time. "Then will you please think about taking a detour to Tallahassee?"

"No."

He drove out of the parking lot and turned toward the highway.

Kathi sat quietly next to him—probably plotting the overthrow of the nearest bus or airline president. Or maybe she'd graduated to stealing cars by now? The neighborhood they had lived in as kids had certainly been a terrific training ground for occupations like that. For all he knew, the old gang could be blowing up banks now. He didn't have much to thank his father for, but at least the old man had gotten him out of that neighborhood. In turn Hannibal had helped his stubborn grandmother financially, but she had refused to move and lived there until her death five years ago.

Hannibal checked the highway signs and carefully pulled onto the cloverleaf. A quick glance told him that his "guest" hadn't noticed. She was still deep in thought. He'd give his next winning case to know what was going on in her mind. He knew it had to do with him.

He shifted in his seat. He never should have looked at her. Ever since she'd climbed into his borrowed truck, he had been much too aware of how beautiful she'd become. She looked like the woman he'd fantasized she'd grow into. Damn. All those looks and a wicked tongue with a devious mind to boot. How lucky could he get? He could have picked up anyone—but he picked up the one woman who could slice his ego apart without effort. She could also get a rise out of him, he thought ruefully, shifting again to accommodate the problem.

Thank God she was getting married. Despite his reluctance to tell her who he was, he was more than willing to help her reach her original destination of Orlando. He had time to burn and was bored as hell. This way his conscience would be clear and he would still relish having the upper hand with Kathi Rebecca Baylor.

He leaned back, prepared to enjoy the ride and anonymity.

"Where are we?" Kathi asked suddenly, looking around as if coming out of a dream.

"We're on our way to Orlando. I can get you close enough for you to call your fiancé and have him worry about getting you the rest of the way." He wished he hadn't looked at her again. Her long blond hair was a perfect complement to her peaches-and-cream complexion. Bright blue eyes were wide with disbelief right now, but he remembered times when they were narrowed in diabolical planning. "It's the best I can do." Damn! That old expression sounded too much like an apology. Give her an inch...

"The best you can do?" Kathi repeated slowly, then swung her body sideways to face him. A look of disbelief graced her face. "It *can't* be! Hannibal Saunders always announced that sentence as if it were a pronouncement from God. You can't be *him!*"

She leaned forward as if searching his face for a tattooed birth certificate. "You are. Good grief, you are!" She laughed, and what would have probably sounded like water dancing on rocks to others, resembled a witch's cackle to Hannibal.

"My goodness, I don't believe it. Hannibal Saunders is driving me to my wedding!"

"Not if you don't watch your tongue, woman," he growled, surprising both of them with his aggressiveness. His hands clamped the steering wheel of the truck and edged from the fast lane into the middle lane. "So sit back and say your please and thank-yous or you'll be sitting alone on the side of the road in no time flat."

For one long moment, the truck cab was silent. Hannibal should have known it wouldn't last.

Chapter Two

KATHI STARED at the man seated next to her as if he held the answer to a puzzle—which he did.

"You can't be Hannibal Saunders!"

"Okay," he answered calmly. "But just a minute ago, you said I was. Which is it?"

"I don't know."

"That's unusual, Kathi. As I recall, you always knew everything. Even when you didn't know a damn thing." His voice was dry, his words a drawl hinting of the South, but not Florida.

"What's your grandmother's name?" she asked suspiciously.

He made a sound that resembled a strangled moose. "If you've classified me as a spy, all I have to give is my name, rank and serial number."

She swore she wouldn't ask. She'd promised herself not to give him that satisfaction. Then she did it, anyway. "What's your name, your real name?"

"Hannibal Saunders."

"I knew it!" she crowed. She stared at him again, trying not to be too obvious about it. It was impossible to do since they were the only two in the cab.

His choice of words was familiar, but the man seated next to her looked nothing like the Hannibal she'd known as a child. The teenage boy next door had been tall, but very thin. A Florida spring breeze could blow right through him.

But his eyes—they were still the same piercing blue probes that never failed to make her uncomfortable. As a child, she'd been certain he could see right through her. As she grew older she'd made every effort to stay as far away from him as possible. On those occasions when they'd been thrown together, she'd tried to hold her own by staring him down, giving as good as she got. In that neighborhood, it was the only way to treat the guys on her block.

But deep down, she'd always admired the way Hannibal dissected a problem and answered in questions order of importance. No moaning and groaning for him. Every problem deserved a thoughtful solution. Although the other boys didn't like to admit it, they had respected his brain.

"Look at me," she demanded, reverting to her childhood way of ordering instead of asking. In the old neighborhood, manners weren't used unless adults were within earshot.

His hands tightened on the wheel, but he stared straight ahead, guiding the big truck through town traffic. He refused to remove his sunglasses. "Do you still get your way when you make demands?"

"I do. Especially when I'm speaking to Hannibal Saunders."

"Obviously your old method doesn't work anymore. If it did this truck would be a wreck."

Kathi waited. Maybe if she stared at him long enough, he'd take off those mirrored sunglasses and do as she asked. Then she'd know...

His hands never left the steering wheel. He continued to stare straight ahead.

Kathi leaned back, shoulders drooping as she smoothed out the frown between her brows. "You can't be Hannibal Saunders. He'd be flinching by now," she stated firmly.

"You never stop trying, do you? Even in youth, you could have given lessons in the art of intimidation."

"I didn't have much choice in those days," Kathi defended. "If you recall, I was the only girl my age in a six-block area, and all the guys—present company excepted—were trying for the honor of being the youngest to earn room and board in federal prison."

"That's your excuse?"

"That's my *reason*," she corrected. "If I was going to survive and pave the way for my little sister to do the same."

She remembered those days all to vividly. "Some things don't change. I still have to be twice as smart and twice as tough just to hold my own in the business world. Most men mistakenly believe that brawn is directly connected to brain cells. Women know that it's not true, but in order to prove it we have to be twice as good."

"If this is the 'I'm-a-female-and-need-a-break' line, I'm not interested. My sister comes up with new statistics every day and is more than thrilled to repeat them to me on a regular basis."

Kathi stared at him. "Your sister! That's right! There *was* a little girl who used to visit on occasion. She lived with your mom, right?"

Before Hannibal could answer, she continued. "She always wore darling pinafore dresses, tights and patent-leather shoes. And she wouldn't step off the front porch. Every time one of the guys talked to her, she'd stare at the ground and nod."

Hannibal's usually full lips thinned. "She hated that place even more than I did. Finally, she was allowed to move back in with mother. I had to stay with Grandma."

"Why?"

He shrugged uncomfortably. "Because I was 'too much boy' for my mother to handle."

Kathi gave him a startled look. *"You?"*

She didn't have the courage to voice her real thoughts—that he hadn't even come close to being what the neighborhood considered a "boy," let alone the "too much." The best description of Hannibal in those days was nerd—the kind she now knew frontiered the development of the personal computers. But nerd definitely didn't fit the man sitting next to her. "And so your grandmother inherited you? That doesn't seem logical. I mean, your grandmother worked hard at the shirt factory all day, kept her house as clean as a hospital and cooked you nourishing meals as well as helped you with your homework. How could she do all that and your much younger mother wasn't able to cope?"

"Mother was high-strung, as they used to say. She was lucky enough to marry wealthy and was smart enough to be kept that way in divorce. Having me live with my grandmother meant that my dad had to send money for my support. My mother said it was giving money to Grandma. Everyone else knew it made my mother's life easier."

"How nice for your mother," Kathi stated dryly. "But then your grandmother didn't seem to mind. After you went off to college, I used to sit on the porch with her occasionally. No matter how late at night I came home, I'd find her sitting on the swing in the shadows, watching people."

"I tried to tell her it was dangerous but she wouldn't listen. She said she'd sat on that porch since she was a young bride, and she'd sit there until she died."

116   *Bride on the Run*

"I remember," Kathi said softly. "I used to perch on her step, stare at the stars and tell her what was going on in my life. She was always so easy to talk to." Kathi stared at her hands, seeing instead the old hands of a woman who had worked hard for her daily bread. Those crippled hands had sewn shirts on every shift the factory had to offer. "And sometimes she would talk about you, and how much she missed you. Every time she talked about how big and strong you'd grown, I could only imagine you as I knew you."

Hannibal laughed. "I was eighteen and living in my dad's house in Sumpter, South Carolina, before I began to fill out. The first year in college, I grew three inches and gained more than twenty pounds."

Kathi ran an appreciative eye over his long legs and well-fitted suit coat. "Looks like you didn't stop there."

Hannibal pretended to be shocked, but there was a twinkle in his smile. "Is that a compliment?"

"Just an observation, Bull."

His humor left. "Don't call me that."

It was her turn to be surprised. "Why? We always called you Bull!"

"That's why I don't allow it now. Bull was a derogatory nickname. I'm not that person anymore."

Kathi understood. She had a few bad memories of her own concerning the old neighborhood. Since she was one of those who had teased him, she was embarrassed and wasn't sure what to say.

"Hannibal?" She asked, and he nodded to tell her he was listening. "Does your wife call you by your full name?"

"I don't have a wife."

"Did you ever?"

"Nosy, aren't you?"

She nodded, smiling. "You bet."

"Okay." He gave a mock sigh. "I never married. My sister is an attorney married to another attorney. I like playing with my computers, long sunsets, light beer and good wine. I enjoy rare steaks, women who are well rounded and tropical vacations."

"Except for the last part, you sound like a personal ad."

"It was an ad. Before you ask, it was not mine, I just recited it. Anything else?"

She shook her head, unwilling to voice the other questions his answers had spawned.

The road stretched ahead. Kathi eyed the traffic around them. Was anyone else as excited as she was? Did they lead wonderful, exotic lives that took them around the world? Or did they get to go home to a beautiful palace on the water, or at least a big home on the intercoastal canal?

Did the rich really own boats that moved so quickly in the water that wakes were seen after they passed out of sight? Did they drink champagne all day and eat caviar for snacks? Was silk really something they slept on as well as something they wore?

"What's going through your mind?" Hannibal interrupted her thoughts.

She smiled at her own flight of fancy. "Have you ever had lots of money, Hannibal? I mean lots and lots."

"As in being a millionaire?"

Kathi nodded, watching him closely. Millionaire, thousandaire: both solved the problems only money could.

"No."

Kathi leaned back. "Do you ever wonder what you'd do with it if you had it?"

"I *know* what I'd do with it."

"Oh? What?"

"I've been trying to find backers. I want to buy a small electronics firm in Mobile. If I had private money, I wouldn't have to worry about sharing the profits with partners. I'd be the only one involved. Right now, I've almost got the backers covered and the deal's done, but I still need just a little more."

"What kind of electronics?"

He glanced quickly at her, then trained his gaze back on the road. "Guess."

"Computers?" She said the first word that popped into her mind.

He nodded. "I thought I was going to grow up in the industry. I didn't. But I still enjoy them."

Kathi laughed. "Even when you were a kid, you were a computer buff. In fact, I learned a lot when you explained computer functions to your grandmother."

His brows rose. "You eavesdropped?"

"You bet."

"That's not fair. I never eavesdropped on you."

"Sure you did. You just didn't learn anything."

He didn't deny it. "And what did you learn?"

"That if more businesses used computers, they'd have an up-to-date inventory, balanced books and an idea of where their money was coming from—as well as going to." She wouldn't admit how much of that advice she'd clung to over the years. She'd used it in almost every beauty-shop business she could persuade to listen, including the last shop she worked for. It had certainly increased their productivity.

"For a kid, I did better than I thought," he murmured thoughtfully. "And so did you, if you got all that out of a teenaged boy's ramblings."

"It wasn't rambling, Bull—I mean Hannibal," she corrected quickly. "You were so patient with your grandmother. You always found ways to help her understand what you were talking about. You never did that with the rest of us."

"The 'rest of us' weren't around much. You never knocked on my door or shouted at me to come out and play. You never even invited me to sit on your porch when all the other kids were there."

"I did once," Kathi defended, compelled to set the record straight but unwilling to remember the incident in detail.

But Hannibal wasn't as shy. "If I were you, I wouldn't bother remembering how you tricked me into playing the fool for you and your friends. I haven't been that stupid since."

Silence hung in the air like dirty laundry. Kathi's imagination relived every moment of that night.

A summer storm had been approaching, electricity sizzling in the hot, damp air. Pretending she was younger than her fourteen years, she'd been playing dolls with Vivian. A neighborhood bully and his buddy had called her out, waiting in the shadows until she appeared. Once she was far from grown-up ears, they had plied her with questions about Hannibal's sister, wanting to know when she would visit, and if she was moving in with her grandmother. The bully was obviously smitten with the young girl and unwilling to wait to make his move. It was one of several times Kathi had been scared because her little sister had called out for her. At seven years old, Vivian was tiny and dependent. She couldn't do anything without Kathi's help and guidance. The teenage Handle, known for his methods of "handling" people, got right to the point. If Kathi didn't want Vivian's little butt kicked, she'd get the information he wanted.

Kathi had three strikes against her because she was a girl. Most of the guys treated girls as if they were trash or treasure—neither being equal to a male.

That was when Kathi devised a quick plan to get the heat off herself and onto someone else: Hannibal. At the time, she thought he could take their pressure better than she could.

She was almost right. Hannibal could handle the pressure all right. But he chose not to.

She'd invited him to sit on her porch. For a fleeting moment, guilt at using him overcame her own fear of the bullies hurting Vivian. It didn't last long enough, just enough time for him to saunter over from his porch to hers. He was grinning in anticipation.

Moments later he'd realized he was being used to get to his sister. He had glared at Kathi, but there was nothing she could do. She'd stared back, shrugged and strolled into the house, letting him fight it out with the bullies. She didn't want to witness, but she couldn't leave the side of the dining room window, listening to the conversation.

Once Hannibal had realized what they wanted, he told them off in a low, disgusted tone that had Kathi shivering.

She'd wondered how it would feel to have a man stand up for her the way Hannibal had for his sister. She'd been jealous.

With a spit of disgust, he stepped off the porch and into the darkness between their clapboard homes. "You're all a bunch of creeps and jerks if you think I'd give you any information."

Then he stepped into the shadows. That had been his big mistake. As long as he was on the porch, they wouldn't touch him. Once he was in the dark, however, they could gang up on him. And they did.

That night, Hannibal Saunders got beaten to a pulp. When it was over, he had two black eyes, a cracked rib and a lost tooth. And all because of Kathi.

"You never accepted my apology." It was her only defense.

"You never meant it then. Looking back, I realized why you reacted the way you did. I can understand now, Kathi. I guess I would have made the same choice. Hell, I did make the same choice. I just got the beating for it."

She released her breath slowly. "Thank you."

His brows rose. "For what? Telling the truth?"

"No, for exonerating me. You could have held a grudge."

"I could have. But there are so many other things I could be angry with you about. That one incident seems small in comparison."

She smiled sadly. "Was I that bad?"

"You are."

"Don't change tenses," she ordered. "You don't know me well enough to make that a statement."

Now he was the defensive one. "I know you well enough. I had enough experience with you to last a lifetime."

"Then why did you pick me up?"

He cocked a brow. "Because you stood in the middle of the road."

"Oh." Kathi felt her skin flush. She sat back and stared straight ahead at the traffic in front of them.

But something else occurred to her. She glanced at Hannibal, distracted for a moment by a frown marring his brow. He was no longer an adolescent boy. Apparently his hormones had kicked in late—but when they did, they packed quite a wallop. He was the most masculine man she'd ever seen.

"What's going through that mind of yours?" he asked, startling her.

"Not a thing." She would not blush again. She would not!

"Something is, I can tell."

"I was thinking that I used to wonder what happened to you after your grandmother died. I never heard what you were doing."

"I'm an attorney."

She wasn't surprised. "What made you go into law? I imagined you'd be knee-deep in computers."

"Obviously your imagination was awry."

Kathi smiled. He hadn't lost his ability for sharp repartee. If he thought her tongue was honed, he should be subjected to his own brand of rapier wit.

But today, that was all right. Today, she was an almost millionaire. She could afford to be generous—if not with money, at least with kindness.

"I bet you're fair and detail-oriented," she said, remembering that one of her clients who was in business always used those phrases. Kathi liked those official-type terms. They summed up what she admired: a sharp mind. She was in awe of people like that. After all, they were *successful*. And Hannibal had to be successful, because here he was, taking a vacation when her only time off in years was the three days she was taking now—for a honeymoon she didn't want.

Her honeymoon! In four hours, she was supposed to be in Orlando, slipping into a wedding dress and looking forward to saying her vows with a dear, sweet friend.

Hannibal looked at her. He couldn't quite figure her out. She smiled as if she didn't have a care in the world. "What are you thinking?"

Her smile widened. She was torn between indulging in her fantasies like flying around the world or dealing with the guilt of breaking up with Timothy—practically dumping him at the altar. There might be a better way to do it, she admonished herself, but she didn't have time to find out what it was.

"Would you mind pulling over and letting me use the phone?" she asked.

Hannibal glanced down at his wrist and Kathi spotted the gleam of gold and an *R* at the beginning of the watch name. After she claimed her money, she could buy one, as well.

"I have to make a phone call, too," he muttered, easing into the far right lane, preparing to exit.

Within minutes, they were parked in a coffee shop parking lot. Kathi checked the corners of her purse for quarters, finding only two. "Damn," she mumbled.

But Hannibal had guessed her problem. "Use your telephone credit card."

"I would if I had one. The average working woman doesn't have those little luxuries, you know."

Hannibal shrugged as he locked up the car. "Then reverse the charges or try charging it to your home phone."

"Thanks," she retorted dryly. "I don't know what I'd have done without your sage advice."

He grinned all the way to the phones. Kathi tried to ignore his broad shoulders as he turned his back to her, almost hunching over the phone to dial. She felt miffed that he thought she'd be interested—which she was.

"I need to charge this to my home phone," she said quietly to the operator, feeling odd knowing that Hannibal was standing not two feet away. When the operator connected her, she told Timothy's mechanic where he could pick up the car. She then called the hotel where Timothy and Vivian were staying.

The phone rang several times in the hotel room before Timothy answered. His tone was laced with irritation and anger as he barked. "Suite 412."

"Having a wonderful time and wishing I was there to run interference?" Kathi asked sweetly. She knew that if Timothy was upset, it had something to do with her sister, Vivian.

"She has as much common sense as a hothouse flower," Timothy said. He didn't have to say who he was speaking about.

"What is it this time?"

"She decided to eat an ice-cream cone dipped in sprinkles, and bought one in the lobby yogurt store. She then proceeded to leave a trail of colored sprinkles all the way across the lobby, up the elevator and to our suite. If the establishment chooses to charge me for an extensive carpet cleaning, I can't argue—the path leads straight into this room."

"And don't forget . . . to your bed!" Vivian loudly reminded him, a giggle in her voice.

Kathi sighed wearily. If she hadn't won the lottery, she'd be with them. The thought of acting as referee wore her out. Their voices drained all buoyancy from her. For once in her life she didn't have to deal with them.

"Where are you?" Timothy asked petulantly. "I still don't understand why you couldn't come up here with us. It doesn't matter whether or not your boss has enough employees to cover a rush, you won't be working after we're married."

"Timothy, listen to me," Kathi began patiently. This wasn't going to be easy. "First, your beautiful car is being hauled into the mechanic's shop."

Instantly his tone changed to one of concern. "How are you getting here? Do you need my credit card?" As he spoke those words, Vivian stopped her loud humming. Obviously they were now both concerned.

"No," Kathi said gently. "Timothy, you know I think you're the dearest, sweetest friend a woman ever had. I appreciate you more than you'll ever know. You've always been there for me..." The unspoken *but* hung between them.

"What's going on, Kathi? We're due to be married within the next four hours. The judge called a little while ago to remind us to be on time. Are you going to be late?"

She was sure Timothy knew what she was leading up to. He just didn't want to hear it. "Timothy," she began again.

"Well, that's okay," he continued as if she hadn't spoken. "We'll just set it up for the morning." She heard his deep breath. "Now, I'll pick you up, wherever you are. Where are you?"

"Timothy, I'm not going through with the wedding. You deserve better. You deserve more. You deserve..." *someone who loves you.*

Kathi heard Vivian groan. She must have understood the gist of the conversation. "Just tell me where you are and I'll pick you up," Timothy repeated.

"I'm going away for the weekend," she prevaricated. "I need to think." She had already thought. Now she was implementing. "I'll call you again on Monday or Tuesday."

"Wait!" Timothy shouted. "You can't cancel out on our wedding!"

Kathi blinked the tears from her eyes. "Yes, I can, Timothy. And I am. It's the right thing to do. You'll see. Meanwhile, please know that I promise I'll pay you back real soon."

Vivian's whine echoed through the receiver, then Timothy expelled an oath. "Kathi," he said hurriedly. "Stay with the car. I'll charter a plane and be with you within an hour. Do you hear me?"

"I'm not with the car, Timothy. I'm already several miles away. Please understand. I love you, but not as a husband. Not the way I need to love. I'll talk to you more about this when we all get back home. Meanwhile, take care of Vivian and tell her I'll call her later tonight."

"But, Kathi . . ." Timothy began.

Quietly, sadly, but with resolution, Kathi hung up.

She stared at the hot, gray concrete and silently ordered her salty tears to dry up.

Two strong arms wrapped around her waist, bringing her slim body closer to a brick wall of a chest.

She hiccupped and squeezed her eyes shut, burrowing even deeper into the hard muscled body. Hannibal's scent was light, yet masculine, his arms comforting.

Her heart stirred, and she wrapped her arms around his slim middle.

"Are you all right?" His breath touched her hair and caused another reaction—one that had nothing to do with tears.

She nodded.

"I'll take you to Tallahassee."

She wanted to cry again, this time with happiness. "Are you sure?" she murmured into his chest.

"I'm sure," he said, expelling a breath. "I'll commit myself later for this decision. But right now, I'm game if you are."

Reluctantly, she raised her head and stared into his eyes. This was Hannibal, all right. No one else could have that beautiful, clear sky-to-primrose-blue-eyed gaze. Then she noticed his sexy, rueful grin. "You won't be sorry."

His gaze dropped to her mouth. "Dear sweet heaven, I am insane," he stated. Dropping his hands from the softness of her body, he strode toward the truck. "Let's go before I change my mind."

Kathi followed, grinning all the while.

They pulled out of the parking lot and into traffic. She silently admired his handling of the big truck. It wasn't until later that she realized how quickly her tears were forgotten. She'd dismissed her former fiancé and her troublesome sister as if she believed they could truly take care of themselves without her intervention.

And Hannibal's arms had felt just right around her body. Amazing . . .

Chapter Three

DRIVING AS IF the demons of hell were tailgating him, Hannibal clutched the wheel and stared straight ahead. He was afraid to look at Kathi. He was afraid of Kathi. Every masculine inch of him needed to make love to her. Every masculine inch craved to touch her when she was within holding distance. Every masculine inch of him had gone slightly berserk, promising things like taking her all the way to Tallahassee.

He just didn't understand himself. Her tongue used to cut his ego to ribbons, not playfully tease him. Her body used to edge away from him, not call him like a siren from heaven.

Sitting next to her now, he found it was hard to hold on to those bad memories. Instead, he remembered her smiling sweetly at him. Laughing with him instead of at him—talking to him over the backyard fence one night when the stars shone like silver lights on a dark velvet curtain.

He only hoped Kathi was as confused as he was.

"Hannibal?" Her voice was soft, liquid sweet and slightly perplexed. "Why did you volunteer to take me to Tallahassee?"

Damn. This wasn't going to be easy. "I don't know."

"Are you heading that way?"

"No."

"Did you always want to visit there?"

"No."

"Do you want to spend time with me?" Even she sounded incredulous.

"No." He sighed. "Not exactly," he amended.

Kathi leaned back. "Oh."

He knew what she was thinking. And she was right. She must have known that when he had held her, he'd wanted to go on holding her. He hadn't wanted to let go. But her assumption must have been that he wanted to make love to her. That was wrong.

No it wasn't, a little voice said.

"Look. I couldn't help hearing that you were having a hard time on the phone. I felt sorry for you. No one should marry because they feel obligated." He gave a snort of disgust. "But then, what the hell do I know? You agreed to marry him. It's really none of my business."

Her hand came to rest on his arm and he clamped the steering wheel tighter.

"I've put you in an awkward spot and I'm sorry. But if I say I'll find some way to get there myself, I'd be stranded. So I'm going to be selfish and say thank you for taking me, no matter what your reasons. I promise, Hannibal, I'll repay you for your time and trouble."

"How?"

"What?"

"How can you repay me?" he asked calmly, knowing she thought he'd already worked out a form of payment. "You don't have enough money to buy a bus ticket, let alone food for the trip."

Her full lips formed a straight, stubborn line. "I'll do it. Don't worry."

"I'm not worried, Kathi." He softened his tone. "I'm concerned that you're running away from a tense situation. There are other—better—ways to handle it. Marriage is a big decision, but running away isn't the solution. You might as well deal with it now."

His glance caught her smile. With great difficulty he forced himself to look at the road again. The late-afternoon sun now headed for Gulf water, turning orange in protest. It was going to be a beautiful sunset. And though he really was concerned about her, Kathi made this sunset even better.

"Hannibal," she said thoughtfully. "Are you trustworthy? *Really* trustworthy."

"My daddy thinks so. Why?"

"How much money do you have in the bank?"

"Which bank?"

She thought for another moment. He couldn't figure out where this was leading, but he was intrigued.

"Your checking account."

Reaching inside his coat pocket, he pulled out a leather-encased checkbook and tossed it onto the seat between them. "Add a thousand."

"Why?"

"In case I need it." He shifted into another lane. "Besides, it keeps the bank from charging service fees."

"You can do that?"

"Sure, if you keep your balance over a certain amount." He hesitated a moment. "Don't you have a checking account?"

"I used to, but I don't anymore."

He knew there was a story there, but it was obviously upsetting to discuss, so he left it alone.

"So you know what it's like to have money."

"Everyone knows what it's like, Kathi. It's just the amounts that are different."

"Oh, no." She shook her head vehemently. Then she leaned toward him, her arm brushing his. Every muscle in his body tightened. "Only someone who always knows where the next meal is coming from could have that attitude," she said earnestly. "It shows that you've never really been down to your last penny, with the landlord threatening to throw you out and keep your possessions."

He grinned. "No. I've never been there. But like most people, I've been caught short between paychecks. That's why I have a thousand dollars in checking."

"And a savings?"

He nodded.

"IRA?"

He nodded.

"Stocks and bonds?"

He nodded again. "Are you the Internal Revenue Service?"

"No." She leaned forward even more, her face lit with excitement. "Just a poor working girl with lots more outgoing problems than incoming solutions. Until now."

"What happened? Are you going to rob me?" His words were said jokingly but a small part of him was serious.

"Of course not!" Turning in the seat, she tilted her head and a wave of thick luxuriant hair fell over her shoulder. Hannibal's fingers itched to touch it. "You don't really think that, do you?"

"No. But that little statement you made is leading. Why is everything different now?"

Her impish grin looked as if it could barely contain the happiness she felt. "Because my luck has changed. Because I'm a rich woman. Because I get a chance to do it all over again, and this time do it with money."

"Excuse me if I repeat myself. What has changed?"

"I won the lottery." She took a deep breath. "That's why we're on our way to Tallahassee. That's why I can call off the wedding and still know that my sister will be able to continue her therapy."

"Lottery? As in ticket?"

Her laughter was heady. "Yes. As in over three hundred thousand dollars, even if I have to share it with others."

"Did you just find out?" He stared at her. The big truck glided to a stop on the shoulder of the freeway.

Kathi looked around. "What are you doing?"

"Talking to you. I can't seem to concentrate on both you and the road at the same time, so one of them has to go." He turned toward her. "I repeat. Did you just find out?"

She nodded and the late sun glinted off her taffy-colored hair, making a halo. "Yes. After Timothy's car broke down and I got into yours, I heard the disc jockey announce the numbers. They match the ticket I bought yesterday."

"Is that why you called off your wedding?"

Kathi stared down at her hands. Suddenly her expression was sad. "Yes. Timothy's been my friend all through high school. He even took me to the prom. And when my sister gambled away all her money and mine, plus more money than we could make in a lifetime, Timothy came through and paid off her debts. I owe him a lot."

Anger welled in him. Anger and jealousy. He didn't know where either emotion came from. "But not your life."

"Almost."

"No."

Kathi looked as startled by his emphatic statement as he felt.

"No one owes another his life, Kathi," He stated more calmly. He ached to touch her, to make her understand, and he gave in to the urge. His large hands wrapped around her shoulders. He wasn't sure whether he was holding her away from him or trying to pull her toward his own body. Instead, he kept her where she was—at a tantalizing distance. "You don't owe a man more than friendship, even when he's loaned you money."

Her wide eyes looked as if they held the sorrow of the ages. "You've always had a choice, Hannibal. You didn't really belong in the neighborhood. Your grandmother did, but you didn't."

"We all have choices."

"Not really. You never had to choose between belonging and surviving. I did. My parents were blue-collar workers. My mom worked with your grandmother in the shirt factory. My dad worked on the docks. All they ever wanted was to make sure that Vivian and I wouldn't have to lead that kind of hand-to-mouth existence."

His thumb outlined the fragile, sparrow bone of her collar. "And you do?"

Kathi nodded, her gaze never leaving his. "Yes. After Dad died, Vivian fell apart. What little he left us went toward paying off Vivian's gambling debts."

He felt her pain behind the brief words that summed up a lifetime. "Does she still gamble?"

"She says not, but I'm never sure."

"It's still not a good enough excuse to marry someone, Kathi. Nothing less than love is a good enough reason to spend a lifetime with someone." He took a sigh. "My mother married for money instead of love, and she was unhappy the rest of her life."

"Like your parents, most people don't last a lifetime. Most people spend a few years together and then move on."

"Not you. Not me. We're too damn stubborn to do anything less than a complete commitment."

Her eyes widened. "How did you know?"

"I remember you as a kid. Whatever your adolescent tendencies were then, they're written in stone now."

"And they are?" she prodded gently.

"Tenacity. Stubbornness. Loyalty to a fault."

"I'd use those same words to identify you."

His grin widened. "See? I knew if we tried hard enough, we could find something in common."

Her lips parted. Her pink tongue peeked out. He thought he'd groan with the effort it took to keep him exactly where he was instead of falling on top of her and ravishing her body. "Hannibal?"

He grunted, unable to move, to form a word.

"Why did you offer to take me to Tallahassee?"

He cleared his throat. "I don't know."

Her eyes crinkled in the corners. "An honest answer, even though it's not satisfying."

"I think because I knew you needed help even though you never seem to ask for it. As a kid you tried to bluff when you were in the weakest position."

"Sometimes it worked."

"Most of the time it didn't."

"At least I didn't lose my bluff all the time."

"Like now?"

She hesitated before answering. "I'm not bluffing."

His voice felt as if it was coming from his toes. "Am I?"

She stared up at him with blue eyes big enough to dive into. "You want to kiss me. I want you to kiss me. There are no bluffs."

It was the best invitation he'd ever had. He took it. With the need to touch her making his hands tremble, he bent his head and brushed her parted mouth. She felt so soft. She tasted so sweet. Her fingers lightly grazed the side of his cheek and his hands tightened.

He sipped her lips, intoxicated at being this close to her. Wanting her. Then, when restraint refused to be leashed any longer, he plundered the soft sweetness of her, giving no quarter to her response. Her answer was as strong and needful as his and Hannibal was elated. His arms circled her back, resting gently against her waist as he shook from the hunger.

Her muted sigh caught in his mouth. His arms tightened in response to the primitive need, she provoked. Kathi responded by circling his neck with her slim arms, silently telling him she needed this kiss as much as he did.

When he pulled away, he wasn't sure his feet were still on the floorboard. All his life, Hannibal had heard about fireworks that appeared when you kissed someone you were in love with—or lusted after. But Kathi was his first experience with these legendary fireworks, and it scared the hell out of him.

From the amazed look on her pale face, he could tell she felt the same. Protective urges flowed through him, erasing his own fear. He brushed a lock of hair behind her ear. "Are you all right?"

Kathi nodded. She was stunned by the depth of her response and didn't quite know what to say.

"Are you sure?" He looked so worried that she knew she had to reassure him that everything was fine. And she would, as soon as she found her footing.

His hands cupped her face. "Kathi?"

She knew what he was asking—the question was in his eyes. He needed as much reassurance as she did. She covered his hands with hers, giving his palm a light kiss. "It was a bit of a shocker to kiss my nemesis, but it was even more startling to realize how much I enjoyed it."

"*Enjoyed it* wasn't quite the description that came to my mind," he stated dryly. "Explosive, maybe."

She reached up and touched her lips to his for a light, quick kiss. "That sounds too dangerous."

"It is," he growled before turning her quick kiss into a longer one. Just one more, his head told him, but his heart wanted more. So did his body. What was the matter with him? Was he so stupid that he didn't know danger when he held it in his arms?

Her honest response was enough to bury those thoughts and just let the moment flow through him. This time she led the way into sensuality, holding him closer and teasing his senses with her touch around his neck, circling his ear with a light fingertip. He was drowning in the sensations she evoked.

He sought her waist and dragged her even closer, then his hands slid under her blouse and up the satin-softness of her skin until he held a breast in his palm. It was a perfect fit. Perfect.

Kathi's hand slid over his, stopping his movements but not removing his touch. She pulled back and leaned her forehead against his chest. He felt her pounding heart, satisfied that he wasn't the only one who had almost lost control.

"I'm sorry." Her voice was muffled against his chest, but he heard the words plain and clear.

"For what?"

"For leading you into thinking…" She stopped, then began again. "For letting you . . ."

"For kissing me back without completing the promise you thought you were giving me."

"I won't go any further."

"I didn't ask you to."

She shook her head and he watched the last light of day glint off her hair. "You didn't have to."

"Yes, I do. We're not kids anymore, and don't have to play by silly teenage rules." He lifted her chin. "You gave me a kiss. That didn't imply anything other than a kiss."
Damn!

Her bottom lip trembled as she valiantly tried to smile. "I know. I was just testing to see if you knew that."

"I know."

An eighteen-wheeled truck passed closely by, lightly rocking their vehicle. It also reminded Hannibal that they were supposed to be on their way to Tallahassee. "Why Tallahassee?"

"It's the headquarters for the Florida Lottery."

"Can't you just go where you bought it and cash it in?" He didn't want to spend time traveling. He wanted to spend time wooing her, showing her what a great guy he was. How wonderful it could be for both of them . . .

"Only if I want to wait four to six weeks to receive a check in the mail. Not me. I can't wait that long."

"If it's money you need, I can lend you some," he offered. He didn't even feel bad because of his ulterior motives.

"No. I want my own money, not someone else's. Or else I would have married Timothy."

Good point, he thought, both cursing and praising her value system.

With great reluctance, he released his hold on her and turned to face the front of the cab. It was time to get back to the business of driving.

Slipping the large truck in gear, he edged his way back on the road and sped up. He was getting used to this vehicle. It was amazing, but he was honestly enjoying driving the big bulky thing. In fact, he almost felt macho—and unconventional. That's why he'd borrowed the truck from his friend Nick. He'd had an overpowering urge to arrive at his business dinner in it, shocking his clients. But by picking up Kathi, he'd gotten more than he'd bargained for.

Once the truck was in traffic, Hannibal reached for Kathi's hand, bringing it back to rest on his thigh. He might have to do without her kisses, but he damn well didn't have to put up with a lack of her touch.

She never said a word, but he caught the smile that dimpled her cheeks, and felt her tantalizingly stroke his leg.

Once the shadows began to grow, darkness descended quickly. Hannibal flipped on the headlights, then covered Kathi's hand with his own again. "Tell me about your life."

"Why? It's not half as exciting as yours. You're probably a wonder to watch in court, you're so big and strong and handsome."

"Am I?" He'd heard it before and it had always made him feel as if the woman was patronizing him. But not this time.

"I'm sure a hundred women a day tell you that. You don't need me to repeat it."

"Right now, I need to hear it from you."

She cleared her throat as if she were getting ready to recite. "Hannibal Saunders, you're really one of the most handsome men I've ever had the privilege to meet. You're not only handsome but charming and gallant to boot. I know this because so far you've offered to drive me to Tallahassee, and you haven't killed me and left my body by the side of the road after stealing my lottery ticket.''

His brows rose. "Did you think I would?"

"No. Well, maybe."

"Then why did you tell me?"

She shrugged. "I don't know. Probably for the same reason you offered to take me to Tallahassee. I trusted you enough to take the chance. Besides, I had to tell someone before I burst with joy!''

Her laughter was infectious and Hannibal joined in. Her zest and romance with life came through her every movement, every word. Even when she was down, she never seemed to completely bury that enthusiasm.

His large fingers gently circled her wrist. "You've turned into a very special person.''

"I was *always* a very special person, just like you," she corrected. "The sad thing was that we were never special together. As a child, I always felt alone. What about you?"

"I *was* alone. You had a neighborhood of kids who talked to you. I'd sit upstairs by my open window and listen to everyone laugh and wonder what was wrong with me.''

"That's simple. You had an opinion and you shared it. Bullies don't want any opinion other than their own." Her hand tightened. "I learned quickly and at a very early age that in order to survive in tight spots, keep your mouth shut and smile a lot. It works in adult life as well, only lately I found I'm having a harder time keeping my mouth closed. Instead, I want to state an opinion."

She stared delightedly as he gave a deep, delicious chuckle. "You've always stated opinions, Kathi, you just phrased them so they didn't hurt anyone's feelings."

"Thank you."

"And I didn't learn that little trick until much later. In fact, I still don't think I've learned it."

"You're doing pretty good," she teased.

He gave her hand a squeeze.

Nighttime wrapped around the truck, isolating them in a cocoon of velvet. Kathi's hand resting on his thigh filled his head with thoughts and ideas that came to mind with the darkness. The air in their close quarters was permeated with her light scent.

"We have to stop somewhere tonight. What about Gainsville?"

His heartbeat accelerated with the thought. "Don't you want to drive through?"

He felt her gaze. "No. I'm not into suffering more than necessary. Besides, the lottery office is open tomorrow, and if we keep driving, we'll get there tonight and be dead tired. Might as well pace the driving time."

Hannibal checked the next mileage sign. They had less than a hundred miles to go before they saw the Gainsville city limits.

"Dinner." He imagined a gourmet feast in posh surroundings with wine and candlelight and low, sexy music playing softly in the background—and Kathi sitting across from him.

"Right," she answered in a businesslike tone. "There should be a fast-food restaurant close by. Maybe we can pick up a hamburger or something."

He wasn't about to let his imagination down. "How about waiting until we get to Gainsville and having a nice dinner?"

"Don't worry," she reassured him. "I've got enough cash for both of us."

"I have cash, too."

"I wouldn't want to put you out. Besides, I can't afford a 'nice dinner' in Gainsville. I won't have enough to pay for a room tonight if I do that."

"The hotel and meal are my treat, to help celebrate your good fortune." He sounded much more definite than he usually did.

"Thank you, but I can't let you do that. It's taking advantage of you."

"Kathi," Hannibal sighed. "Look at me. Do I look as if people readily take advantage of me? Do I look as if I can be manipulated?"

"Of course not, but—"

"No buts. I'm not the skinny little kid next door with no muscles and all brain. Everything has evened out now. I can make decisions and articulate my wants and needs very adequately."

"I never meant otherwise, I just didn't think it was right that you pay for me. After all, if I hadn't stepped in front of you, you'd be somewhere else right now, enjoying a beautiful sunset, a drink and good company."

"Hardly," he stated dryly, remembering the business dinner he was missing. Seven men and women wishing they were somewhere else. He'd decided not to bring a date; in fact, he'd almost decided not to attend at all. But since these were his top clients he couldn't back out diplomatically without a good excuse.

Kathi was that excuse. He'd run into an old friend. Let them make of it what they wanted. He didn't care. He didn't even care that he had to drive this bigger-than-a-dinosaur truck. In fact, it was growing on him.

That worried him, too.

Chapter Four

"THERE'S A MOTEL right off the highway, if I remember correctly," Kathi volunteered.

"From visiting your mother?" He called her lie.

She ignored it. "From years ago when Mom and Dad took us to my grandmother's funeral."

Hannibal nodded without saying anything, even though this was his opportunity to rub her own words in her face. He wasn't the least vindictive. She liked that. "Hannibal, it should be coming up anytime now."

He didn't answer.

"It should be reasonably priced."

They passed the outskirts of Gainsville with alarming speed. Two motels, three motels, four motels sped by her window.

"We can stop anytime," Kathi stated dryly. Had he decided to drive all the way through to Tallahassee?

Just as she was about to object to his new plans he slowed down, then pulled under the porte cochere of an obviously exclusive hotel. Her mouth opened but she was too astonished to form the words.

Hannibal had ignored her other remarks, but now he decided to answer her unasked question. "This is my treat. I'm not going to stay in a highway chain motel when I can sleep in a hotel with thick towels and central air conditioning instead of a window unit."

"Poor baby," she soothed. "No telling what might have happened to you if I had subjected you to such grossly inadequate surroundings."

"Be nice, Kathi. You don't really know me well enough to ridicule me." He parked the truck and opened his door, stepping down to the pavement.

Kathi was ready to tell him what he could do with his "treat" when the doorman opened her door and stared up at her. She clamped her mouth shut. Normally she would have objected to spending money like a wastrel. But now that she had money, she could chalk this up to experience. After all, she should know what it was she was thumbing her peasant nose at.

The lobby was graced with richly patinated antique furniture set in cozy, conversation arrangements. Bellhops walked on plush carpeting from lobby to elevator banks, doing whatever it was bellhops did.

Hannibal strode to the desk. By the time Kathi reached his side, Hannibal had already registered and his credit card was handed back to him. She clutched her dress bag, unwilling to hand it over to a disgruntled bellboy standing behind her with Hannibal's small case in his hand. She still held tightly to it as the elevator took them all the way to the top of the hotel to their suite. The bellhop dropped the luggage, palmed his tip and was gone.

She'd made up her mind not to jump to conclusions. Just because they had kissed, just because she tingled all over when Hannibal was near—well, that didn't mean he could take her for granted. He obviously expected them to sleep in the same suite together. She waited for her conscience to agree with her logic. Nothing happened.

When they were finally alone, she turned to confront him. He was smiling down at her. All her accusations flew out of her head.

"What?" she asked warily.

"You're beautiful when you're confused."

Her eyes narrowed. Her heartbeat accelerated. All her well-trained defenses came to the fore. "If you think I'm confused, you're wrong. I'm not. I'm just not ready for the cozy little setup you have in mind, Hannibal Saunders."

He gazed pointedly at the garment bag she still clutched in front of her. "You're holding that dress as if it's the only armor you have. Let me put your mind at rest. There's a door behind you and a door behind me. Both are bedrooms. This is a suite with a living area between the rooms."

She refused to look at either door. She tried not to allow her eyes to wander. But they did. "I knew that."

"Right." He grinned again. "Each bedroom has a separate bath. Why don't we freshen up and go downstairs to the restaurant for dinner? I'm so hungry that my stomach is growling."

His words eased her apprehension. She smiled. "That invitation beats a hamburger with secret sauce any day. Meet you back here in five minutes."

"Three," he fired back. "You take that room, I'll use this one."

With a light-hearted salute, Kathi hurried into her portion of the suite. Now that her fears had been put to rest, she could relax and enjoy the ambiance of a fine hotel. Her room was huge, with a king-size bed occupying one wall and a mirror covering the wall opposite. The other two walls were upholstered in a deep rose-and-blue paisley, matching the spread and pillow shams. Deeply padded rose carpeting extended all the way into the bath area.

She stopped at the entrance to the bath. Obviously this wasn't just an ordinary suite. This one room was as large as the dining and living area of her home, and held all the wonders of modern living, from the hairdryer built into the wall to the step-down tub with jets. The largest towels she'd ever seen were folded on a rack by the door.

So this was how the rich lived. The really rich. Even after winning the lottery, she'd never live like this. She wouldn't waste this much money when there were bills to pay, psychologists to hire, a shop to run and security to think of. This was—luxury. Things this luxurious and rich weren't in Kathi Rebecca Baylor's diet.

"Damn," she muttered, half in awe and half in regret that this stay in a luxury hotel would probably be her last. She told herself if she'd wanted this life-style she would have gone through with her marriage to Timothy. Instead, her sister, Vivian, was with him. Maybe they would console each other and come to their senses.

Now that the wedding was off and the worst was behind her, Kathi knew for certain that Timothy and Vivian belonged together. Because of Kathi's problems, she hadn't really seen the situation before, and the hotter the water had became, the more she'd tried jumping out of it. Now the answer seemed crystal clear. Timothy and Vivian loved each other, but they just hadn't been mature enough to deal with that fact. Vivian wanted to act the child forever and not make any decision harder than what to wear or to eat. And Timothy wanted to be taken care of at home, after a hard day of slaying dragons. Neither of them gave emotional support—they demanded it.

Silently, she blessed Hannibal for coming along that busy highway just when she needed him the most. His silent strength, quiet manners and knowledge of her own roots made him the security blanket she desperately needed right now.

So why wasn't she relaxed? Every nerve in her body danced and swayed to his nearness.

Hannibal Saunders was the sexiest man she'd ever met. In fact, if her body's reaction was anything to go by, it was dying of thirst and he was an oasis of clear spring water.

"Ready?"

Kathi jumped and looked over her shoulder guiltily, as if Hannibal could see the erotic images in her mind. Her face flamed.

Hannibal walked toward her, his smile becoming a look of concern. "Are you all right?"

"I'm fine." She backed up until her legs hit the commode. "Are you?"

Hannibal stopped, concern replaced by a knowledgeable look. "Come here," he said quietly. "Please."

"Why?"

"I want to kiss you and see if the sparks still fly. If they do, then we know it wasn't an accident. If they don't, then we can relax and enjoy the rest of the evening in friendly companionship."

"No."

"Chicken?"

"No."

One dark brow rose intimidatingly. "What do you have to lose besides a minute in my arms?"

More than you know! she wanted to say, but refused to give him that satisfaction. With his looks, he must have women all over him all the time. She wouldn't— couldn't—be one of the gang. "It's okay to say no."

He nodded. "You're right. I wouldn't want it any other way. But for old times' sake, can't you tell me why?"

Her whole body cried out to him. She felt her muscles tighten, heat, loosen, melt in anticipation of turning dream to deed. So why was she balking? For an obscure set of rules and regulations that only she made and kept? If she *did* kiss him, would he remember her in the bevy of women in his life? Of course. No matter what she did, he'd probably always remember her as the pest next door all grown up.

"I changed my mind," she said, stepping toward him. She placed her hands atop his broad shoulders.

His expression showed surprise at the turn of events. Then his blue-eyed gaze narrowed. Her blood raced as he focused on her parted mouth. His lips took hers in a kiss that began spinning the world in a different direction. She clung to his shoulders and a soft, kittenish moan escaped her.

He pulled her into the hard planes of his larger body, urging her to yield her softness, to mold herself to him. Kathi's hands slid up past his shirt collar to feel the strength of his neck and the dark, rough texture of his hair.

His mouth was firm and sure, and she followed his direction, marveling at her own reaction. She'd never reacted more than pleasantly to a kiss before, but now a thousand wonderful feelings inundated her.

Hannibal pulled away. With heavy-lidded eyes, she gazed at him.

"Open your mouth, Kathi. Give me all of you." His voice was hoarse and low—golden, warm, honey spiked with strong, dark spirits.

Her reaction was instant. She cradled his head and stood on tiptoe as she blended her own lips into his kiss.

His hungry groan was his answer. Fingers ate into her flesh as he held her even closer, almost absorbing her into his own body.

Jubilation at his reaction echoed through her own spirit. Then it was lost in a tingling, falling, vertigo as he took over. Her hair tangled in his fingers, her body heated and became pliant in his warmth. Breath mingled, was shared, then lost in sighs.

This time, when he pulled away, Kathi didn't look at him. She didn't have the energy to open her eyes. Instead, she burrowed her face in his chest, her pounding heart beating in unison to his own erratic beat.

"The first kiss wasn't an accident," he said.

Kathi shook her head, denying what was so evident. "It was just a fluke, that's all," she mumbled into his chest.

A low rumble, vaguely resembling a chuckle, echoed in her ear. "Like hell, lady. I can be fooled once but I can't be fooled twice. Dynamite just exploded."

She shook her head, still denying it.

"Your shallow breathing says it exploded in you, too."

Why did he want a confession? They both had to walk away from this encounter. She preferred to be whole when she did so. Getting involved with Hannibal Saunders wasn't the way do to it.

But the little devil in her told her to enjoy their time together. Next week Hannibal Saunders would be back in his world and she would be...well, she'd be busy paying old debts, looking at beauty salons to buy, carrying on with her life.

Maybe the gods owed her these wonderful two days....

She opened her eyes and stared at him. Her fingers traced the strong, clean line of his jaw. "You're right," she breathed. "Dynamite exploded."

"Was that hard to admit?"

She nodded. "It's the supreme sacrifice to confess my own feelings."

His lips brushed hers again. "The hard-bitten bully, Kathi Rebecca Baylor, admits to tender and vulnerable feelings."

She couldn't let that go by. "No, I didn't. I admitted to having sexual fantasies and sensual images for the length of a kiss."

"That's all?"

She nodded, unwilling to expose her feelings more. "Besides, I haven't heard any admissions of tender, vulnerable, sexual fantasies or sensual images from you."

"Yes, you did. I admitted that dynamite went off in my head and other more private parts of my anatomy."

"Not enough," she goaded softly, her fingers now busy combing through his thick hair.

"Then, I'll have to admit it all. I look at you and my body notices the way you sway when you walk, your sweet Southern drawl and the coy way you glance at me through your lashes."

Her breath caught in her throat.

"I tell my body to behave, but it doesn't listen. I tell myself to ignore your smile, the shy tilt of your head, the sweet shape of your breasts. When you cross your legs, they look like they're a mile long. Your own special scent fills the air until I think I'll go crazy with it."

She covered his lips with her fingertips. "Enough," she begged, knowing that if he said more, she'd seduce him then and there. And that wouldn't do. Not at all, she told herself, willing her heartbeat to slow down from its frantic beat.

Closing his eyes, Hannibal sighed heavily. When he opened them again, his gaze was filled with regret.

Kathi felt more dismay than she could have believed. Questions flew through her mind. Had he not meant those wonderful things he said? Were they just a line? Was he playing with her because she was a woman out of his class? From his clothes and taste in hotels, she'd bet beauticians were pretty far down the list for him to socialize with.

"Ready?"

She became leery. "For what?"

"Dinner."

She felt herself blush. "Yes," she admitted, dropping her hands and taking a step back.

But when his arms left her, she felt a chill. Then he took her hand in his and, suddenly nothing else seemed as important as being with Hannibal.

She smiled and he stared down at her, mesmerized. "We'd better get out of here while I still have an ounce of control," he muttered, leading her out of the bedroom and toward the hallway.

"You may be dressed for this type of dining, but I'm in jeans," Kathi whispered in the formal dining room.

"So you are," he answered. "And looking beautiful." Then he nodded his approval to the maître d' as they were ushered to a secluded table in the corner of the room. Crystal chandeliers gleamed softly.

Kathi tried to act as if restaurants like this were an everyday thing to her. But her eyes darted everywhere, from the formal-jacketed waiters to the pristine, blue-and-white napkins and tablecloths. When the menu was handed to her, she didn't blink an eye at the fact that there were no prices on her side of the menu. But Hannibal noticed that her eyes narrowed dangerously.

"Something wrong?"

"They obviously don't think a woman needs to know fundamental things like prices."

"It's so women will order without regard to price."

"It's sexist, and I don't like it."

Hannibal handed her his menu. "Then use mine."

When she saw the prices, Kathi wished she hadn't been quite so determined to know. Hannibal's treat or not, it was a lot of money for a meal when she'd spotted a cafeteria down the street two blocks earlier.

"No, we're not going someplace cheaper," Hannibal murmured as he quietly looked over the menu. "There are things other than price that make a meal."

"Name one." Kathi wished he wasn't so quick to read her mind.

"Decor, space between tables, the presentation of food and service."

"Well, shut my mouth and call me a big bass," she teased, realizing he was probably right but aware of her ignorance about the subtleties of those differences. Apparently, Hannibal wanted her to find out.

The waiter took their order, then brought the requested bottle of chilled white wine. When it came, its taste was crisp and clean. It definitely didn't come with a screw cap, Kathi observed dryly.

Hannibal lifted his glass to her. "To old friends and new acquaintances, especially when they're one and the same."

She raised her crystal glass and it tinkled against his. "Especially when they've grown into such handsome devils," she added.

"Thanks." He grinned. "Now, tell me what my beautiful neighbor has been doing with her life. Besides getting engaged to friends instead of lovers."

Her skin flushed at the compliment, but she answered.

And answered. And answered.

She told him the whole story of her engagement to Timothy. And for the first time, she opened up enough to tell someone her dream. Someday soon, she'd own her own beauty salon. In fact, she might build it into a chain of salons. Then she could take care of herself and her sister and help Timothy in case he ever needed it. After all, he'd been there for Kathi.

Hannibal's voice was low but firm. "No, he was there for Vivian. That's not quite the same."

"It is in this family. If you help her, you help me."

"And if I help you?"

"Then you've helped her."

"One for all and all for Vivian?"

She heard the ring of truth in his voice but she couldn't allow him to think badly of her sister. "Yes, because she deserves it."

"So do you."

She grinned, but it was wobbly. "You didn't think so when we began this trip."

"I was wrong." His strong tone brooked no argument. "But now that I'm right, I won't make the same mistake again."

The mischievous twinkle in his blue eyes kept her from taking him seriously. "You're kidding."

"Yes."

"I get the feeling you don't get playful very often."

"Only when I'm lured into the future of possibilities by blue-eyed sirens who also let me see the past."

"What does that mean?"

"It means that you brought back the past, and with it, reminded me how it was for all of us, not just me. It's a different perspective."

"You helped me see the past, too."

His laugh, warm and deep and highly erotic, skimmed down her spine like light fingers feeling every ridge. Her breath caught in her throat.

"Me?" he scoffed. "How could I help you with the past? I thought you had it made. People talked to you, played with you, enjoyed your company. You *made* the past, you didn't drift through it."

"No, I . . ." She began apologizing for her part in his past. But something in his eyes prevented her from finishing. The look was there; he was a man who saw something he not only liked, but coveted. He wanted her. Kathi wasn't mistaken about that. The problem was that she wanted him, too.

That wouldn't do.

A little demon on her shoulder told her to worry about that later. Now it was time to enjoy. Tomorrow, she would apologize for her part in his past. Tonight, however, should be enjoyed.

As if reading her mind, he leaned forward and refilled her glass with wine. "Tell me about your wedding dress."

"It was my mother's."

Hannibal nodded thoughtfully. "I remember now. There was a rumor that it was a very special dress." He smiled.

"It *is* a very special dress. Out of all the brides who wore it, not one has been divorced. That alone makes it special."

"How many have worn it?"

"Fourteen now."

"Too bad there weren't more. We might have been able to change the statistics on divorce."

"I doubt it, but at least it's a start in the right direction."

"Have you tried it on yet?"

She shook her head. "Not yet, but I know it will fit just fine. Mother was my size when she married."

"You should try it on, to be certain it's right for you. After all, no one can really predict the future of a marriage unless the gown doesn't fit—then you know your wedding won't be the way you dreamed it to be."

"Don't make fun of it, Hannibal Saunders, or you'll be sorry."

"Good grief, you sound the same way you did in high school," he finally answered. "How will you make me sorry?"

"I don't know yet, but I'll think of something."

His grin expanded. "I'm sure you will."

They spent the rest of the meal in small talk. Kathi was surprised at how much they had in common. Jazz, comedies, old "M.A.S.H." television programs, Western and romance novels—all were beloved and familiar.

By the time dinner was finished, Kathi had polished off her share of strawberries and cheesecake with three cups of coffee and some liqueur.

They left the restaurant, Hannibal's arm wrapped proprietorially around Kathi's back as he led her out of the elevator, then down the hall to their suite. She tried to remind herself that it was just a gallant gesture— something a gentleman like Hannibal would do. But his warm palm against the small of her back sent waves of a different nature to her senses.

Her imagination ran wild. She imagined them clasped in each other's arms, their naked bodies touching. She imagined his lips claiming hers....

Her breath came short. She glanced his way and saw that he looked as intent as she felt.

He unlocked the door and led her down the hall. "A drink?" he asked, not looking at her.

"I don't think so. I had enough wine at dinner. Besides," she added, watching him fix one for himself. "I'm sleepy." *Please come over here and kiss me,* she begged silently. *Make me know you want me as much as I want you!*

Hannibal's back was turned toward her and she wished she could see his face. His expression usually gave him away. But he didn't move.

"Hannibal?"

"Hmmm?" He still didn't turn around.

"Are you tired?"

"No. You go on to bed."

"Are you sure?"

"I'm sure." His voice was rough, his back still turned to her.

Dejectedly, Kathi walked into her bedroom, wishing she was walking toward Hannibal instead of away from him. He didn't want her or he would have tried to convince her to keep him company.

"Good night." She waited at her bedroom door for an answer. It was long in coming.

"Good night, Kathi."

She closed the door. Her body cried out to be held by Hannibal Saunders, but her mind was still in control. She wished she had some excuse to go to him, but there was nothing she could do unless she wanted a dose of rejection. The thought of Hannibal rejecting her was painful. The reality would kill her.

What was the matter with her? This was supposed to have been her wedding night with Timothy. Instead, she was pining away for someone else!

Her mother's wedding dress, still encased in plastic, lay across the bottom of the bed. She lifted the bag, smoothed it, then hung it in the closet. Someday she would wear this dress for all the right reasons. She would be in love with the man standing at her side, and he would vow to cherish her for the rest of their lives. Until then, she had to be content to just look at it.

Unzipping the plastic, she carefully lifted the dress from its padded hanger. Holding it against her, she looked in the closet-door mirrors. The temptation became too great. With deft movements, she stepped out of her clothes and slipped on the dress.

The overhead light created shadows on the planes of her face, making her look as sad as she felt. With a deft movement, she tried to push her hair over her shoulders, but the errant curls bounced back.

The dress was antique ivory satin, the tightly woven material forming a light-catching sheen that gathered around her. A lacy V-neck and sleeves accentuated the bride's face and throat. Form-fitting, it hugged Kathi's body to the hips, where it flared, then fell in a circle to the floor.

The tinkle of ice against crystal echoed through the door. Kathi smoothed the satiny material over her hips and stared at her reflection in the mirror.

She looked beautiful.

Trying to quell the nervousness of the silent invitation she was delivering, Kathi opened the door.

Her breath caught in her throat at the sight of him. He was facing her, his gaze on the drink in his hand. In the light of the single lamp, she noticed he'd taken off his tie, pulled out his shirttail and unbuttoned his white dress shirt all the way down. It hung straight, showing off a strong chest lightly covered in dark blond hair. His abdomen looked strong and well chiseled.

He knew she was there. He looked up and this time he caught his breath on a sigh. His eyes widened. "Dear sweet heaven." It was a prayer. It was a plea.

Nothing ever meant as much to Kathi as his opinion did now. Nothing. She needed to know he thought she was beautiful. She needed it badly.

"What do you think?" Her voice sounded shy.

He was silent as he set down his drink and walked toward her.

Her nerves stretched to a thin, tight wire. Instead of looking beautiful, she must look ludicrous. Stupid. Sexless. She'd used bad judgment.... She shouldn't have come to him dressed in a wedding gown...

He didn't stop until he reached her. He stared down, his warm breath caressing her cheek. Tears pricked her eyes as his narrowed gaze went from her stockinged toes to the top of her head, hesitating only briefly at the full roundness of her breasts.

"You're probably the most beautiful thing I'll ever see in my whole life," he finally said.

Her eyes widened. "Really?"

"Really." His hands tightened into fists. "In fact, beauty like yours deserves to be rewarded."

His voice was low and so sexy; it played against every nerve she had. She leaned toward him, unconsciously seductive as she wet her dry lips. "How?"

"How do most princesses get rewarded?"

"With a kiss."

He smiled, but his smile was as tightly wound as her body. "Then a kiss it is."

When he wrapped his arms around her, she gave a sigh of relief. *Now* she felt complete. *Now* she felt safe. *Now* she felt *alive!*

His lips claimed hers with both determination and command. His touch was firm yet gentle. His large hands splayed across the small of her back, bringing her into the solid warmth of his body.

Kathi wound her arms around his neck and held on for dear life. If she was going to ride the roller coaster, she wasn't going to ride alone. Dear, sweet, strong and sexy Hannibal Saunders would be with her all the way.

Chapter Five

KATHI'S BODY hummed under the sensuous touch of Hannibal's hands. He grazed her shoulders, and she stroked his. He cradled her head in his large palms, she ran her fingers through his vibrant hair. He sipped at her neck as if there was nectar hiding in the shadows, and she breathed deeply of his chest, reveling in the male scent and feel of his skin.

Leg tangled with leg. The cool wall was against Kathi's back, Hannibal's heated body leaning on her breasts. She loved the feel of both.

His kisses were heady elixir, his touch an aphrodisiac, his barely leashed strength exciting.

Light breath collected in the air. When Hannibal drew away, Kathi felt bereft. His hands sought hers, and they clasped, twining fingers with fingers. He pulled her arms up and against the wall, leaning into her as he lightly kissed her forehead. Her hands were pinned, but she wasn't afraid. It was Hannibal, her very gentle, very sensual giant.

He took a deep breath and opened his eyes to stare deeply into hers. "You're incredible."

She was caught in his sensuous web. Worse, she didn't care. "So are you."

"You're beautiful beyond belief." His voice was a mere whisper, his intense gaze speaking loudly.

She stared up at him, loving the way he sounded, the words he chose. He cared. "So are you."

His grin was boyish. "I doubt it, darlin'." With a deep, shaky breath, he closed his eyes and tilted his head back.

She wanted to reassure him that they were supposed to be together like this. She had no doubts. But she couldn't find the right words. "Hannibal?"

He opened his eyes and stared down at her. His blue gaze was so hot that it melted her insides. "I want you so damn bad it hurts."

Slowly, she smiled. "I want you, too."

It took a minute for her answer to sink in. "But?" he queried, as if he couldn't believe all he had to do was ask.

Her head arced from side to side, a small smile lifting the corners of her mouth. "No buts."

He leaned toward her, letting a low moan escape as he buried his face in her loose hair. "You have a very special scent that is all yours. Did you know that?"

With a hum, she closed her eyes, trusting in him completely.

His fingers stroked the back of her hands rhythmically. "Will you let me make love to you?"

"Yes."

His lips brushed her neck, the outer shell of her ear. "My little bride on the run. You're so beautiful and so willing. I'd be crazy to turn down an invitation like this."

"Then don't," she said recklessly, needing, wanting, craving to touch him—all of him. She'd never felt this reckless and abandoned, and she wanted the feeling to continue forever. She could climb mountains, swing from stars, tell Hannibal to love her.

His mouth captured hers and she went spinning out of control. Shaken to her core, she brought his hands to her body, cupping her own breasts with both their hands. Breath hissed sharply between his teeth.

Unlocking her hands from his, he stroked the soft flesh beneath the ivory satin, running his fingers over sensitive, budding nipples. Sheer pleasure zinged through her body and Kathi arched to receive his ministrations more fully. She reached for his shoulders, resting instead on his biceps.

With a touch as light as a dove's wing, he slowly undid the tiny satin buttons that ran down the front of her dress. She watched his large hands, tanned, strong and yet so capable as they manipulated each buttonhole.

Once he reached the waist, he stopped. The fabric gaped open, exposing the swelling roundness of her breasts. One finger traced the indentation of her cleavage. "So smooth," he murmured.

Without reservation, her fingers traced the arrowed line of hair from his chest to his navel. "So rough," she murmured.

Hannibal slipped the slick material off her shoulders, holding her arms captive by the fabric. Time stood still, as if there was no need to hurry ever again. With quiet deliberation, he began the torture of touching her breasts the way he had before, only this time there was no barrier of clothing to separate his lightly callused fingers from her already sensitive nipples.

With a rough growl, he bent and took one swollen bud into his mouth, teasing its tip with his tongue. Kathi clasped his head in her hands, holding him as her world narrowed into just the intimate space surrounding the two of them.

He nuzzled one breast, then favored the other. Kathi's breath was so light that she wasn't sure she was breathing. He stroked the material down her arms, waist and over her hips, until they both stood in a puddle of white satin.

"My God," he muttered in a voice so low and gravely that it rasped. "You're even more beautiful than I imagined. I knew you'd grow into the woman I would be mightily tempted by. That's why I ran so fast and so far away from you."

Her chuckle was breathless. "I didn't know I was a siren."

"You always were. I heard your call as a teenager."

Kathi reached for his belt buckle and within seconds had undone the clasp on his pants. Soon they were both naked.

In all her life she'd never have imagined the gangling teenage Hannibal Saunders and this specimen of manhood being the same man. He was as sturdy and strong as a chestnut tree, in both mind and body. Yet he was gentle and kind. He was gorgeous.

Before she could form a thought, he picked her straight up in the air and held her high against his chest. As she looked down at him, her hair fell over her shoulders, allowing only the tips of her breasts to peek through the lustrous strands.

She held on to his broad shoulders for balance, but she wasn't afraid. Her body heated to the melting point as he devoured her with his gaze. Then suddenly his teeth flashed in a grin, and the sound of deep, rumbling laughter echoed through the suite. Joyfully, she joined him.

With sure hands, he lowered her against him; tough, tanned skin touching soft vanilla skin every inch of the way. With a light kiss, his tongue honored her navel before he lowered her farther. When her breast reached Hannibal's mouth, he held her suspended there. His tongue circled the darkened areola, warm breath sensuously stimulating every nerve ending. Her moan was so low that it resembled a whisper. But he heard her. Wrapping his tongue around the bud, he gently teased until she thought she would faint from the exquisite pleasure.

"More?" he asked, his voice gravelly.

"Please," she managed.

When he lowered her, Kathi's feet still didn't touch the carpet. Face-to-face, they stared at each other. There were no walls, no barriers to their innermost emotions. For just a split second of eternity, they saw the vulnerability in each other.

Kathi's eyes widened as she realized that he wanted her even more than she craved him. Then the wall was there again. Hannibal narrowed his eyes, tightened his grasp on her and strode into her bedroom, carrying her like a prize from war. Placing her on the king-size bed with extreme tenderness, he stood by the side, staring down, eyes gleaming.

"Hannibal," she began, but the fire in his eyes quelled whatever she was about to say.

One hand reached out to trail down her cheek and follow an imaginary line to her throat. "You're so damn beautiful, it hurts to look at you. I can't believe you're really here, with me."

She swallowed hard to erase the lump in her throat. For all her pretended worldliness, most of it was bluff. And the few who knew her also knew she never thought she was special or beautiful. Far from it. She usually thought of herself as undesirable and pretty ordinary.

But the look in Hannibal's eyes told her he truly believed what he said. It didn't matter that she knew better—*he* believed.

"Please," she began.

And he did.

Enfolded in his arms, she touched the spots he touched. Kissed him where he kissed her. Her heart beat so quickly that she thought she'd almost stopped breathing.

When he pulled her on top of him and showed her his rhythm, she flowed with it. And when her body stiffened with ecstasy, he pulled her down and kissed her into even greater delight. As she slowly floated on a cloud, his own ecstasy began.

Later, in the dark of night, she watched the sleeping giant beside her. His tousled hair reminded her of when he was young and too absorbed in a project to care whether his hair was combed. In those days he studied in the shade of his porch, working for hours until something clicked inside his head, and he'd smile until his smile enveloped his whole being.

Kathi knew that smile. It meant victory was at hand. As a teenager, she'd been jealous of that smile. It meant he had accomplished something—underlining that she hadn't. After seeing whatever that project was, she wouldn't talk to him for a day or two because it brought home her every inadequacy. She had no goals other than to survive, so his smile also told her that she had not accomplished anything to cause someone to say, "Look, isn't that wonderful?"

It was apparent from the time he moved in with his grandmother that he wouldn't stay in the neighborhood. She was jealous of that, too. He smelled of success instead of reeking of the failure that seemed to permeate everyone else. She wanted to leave with him. She wanted to be with him. She wanted *him* to want to be with her. But he never did more than tease her, ignore her and occasionally—very occasionally—smile at her.

So most of the time she remained distant. When they were brought into contact, she teased him, taunted him, tried to drive a wedge between them. It wasn't just keeping the neighborhood at bay that isolated her from Hannibal. It was her own feelings of inadequacy.

For those same reasons she would leave him tomorrow and not ever see him again.

Money was many things to Kathi. Her winnings would enable her to cover a multitude of deficiencies. But when it came to Hannibal Saunders, money was not an equalizer. She would never be quite good enough for the social stratum that she was sure he moved in. No one had to tell her that—she knew it. Hannibal had even realized that as a kid and had steered clear of her as much as possible. So, much as she wanted to continue this relationship, there was no way. Everyone, including Hannibal, would know she wasn't worthy of a man like him.

That thought was hard to bear, but it was the deep-down truth she knew in her gut. She propped her head in her hand to study his face. It was a strong, gentle face. A face to love, just like the man.

Tears formed in the corners of her eyes, but she closed them and tried not to cry. Hannibal groaned, turned toward her and flung an arm across her hip. She snuggled against him, pretending this night would last forever.

HANNIBAL SAUNDERS opened one eye and stared at the woman lying next to him. He could hardly believe it. He opened both eyes and studied her.

If someone had told him that someday he'd be lying next to the woman who had haunted his dreams—and nightmares—he would have laughed. But not now. Now he realized that those immature childhood fantasies had grown into desires that had the capacity to come true.

He'd always been interested in taking things apart and putting them back together again, sometimes in better order, sometimes they didn't work at all. Because he had never fitted into the neighborhood gangs, he thumbed his nose at them by excluding himself from their activities before they could do it for him. Instead, he found things to do that were one-man jobs. It had been the loneliest time in Hannibal's life. There was no one to show off his accomplishments to, no one to share them with. His grandmother was proud of him, but she wasn't a peer. She loved him regardless of whether he could invent, replace or rebuild.

There was really only one person he wanted to show off to: Kathi. If he mentioned what he was doing or showed her a piece of his lonely work, she grew distant, finally turning away from him and not talking to him for days. Some of the others who found out what he was doing in his spare time ridiculed him, knowing just what buttons to push to make him feel inadequate. He learned to keep those idle, solitary activities to himself.

Now, here he was. Kathi was next to him and they had made wild, wonderful love. He finally understood the words, making love. What a far cry from having sex. The emotions involved were so much more complicated, but added everything meaningful to the experience. And he was in love all over again with the girl who had once stolen his heart at the tender age of thirteen.

"Damn," he breathed.

This path could lead nowhere but to heartbreak. Now that she had money, what could he possibly offer to entice her to stay with him? Marriage? As beautiful as she was, she could have anyone she wanted. In fact, she was running away from a marriage now. And Timothy was probably as wealthy as Hannibal.

Okay, so that wouldn't work. What would?

He couldn't come up with a solution, but neither would he back off from seeking one. His logical side told him that there was always a way, and all he had to do was find it. His emotions told him he'd better find a way or he'd be miserable the rest of his life.

Now that Kathi was with him, he remembered and re-lived all those pent-up feelings he'd squelched and tried to forget so long ago. He was going to marry Kathi if he had to kidnap and hog-tie her until she agreed. It was the best he could do.

"ROOM SERVICE for breakfast or hotel restaurant?" Hannibal held her in his arms, his fingers tangled in her hair. As dawn had peeped in through the curtains, they had made wild, passionate love. Hannibal was sated—for the moment.

"I think I'd like to go downstairs." Her eyes were still closed, a small, secret smile on her lips.

He kissed her smile, then shared it. "Then that's what we'll do," he stated, throwing off the sheet and standing to stretch. Sun poured in the sheet curtains covering the floor-to-ceiling window, gilding the room and Hannibal with gold.

Kathi's actions were quick. She jumped from bed and ran to the bathroom. "Last one in the shower pays for breakfast!"

Hannibal bounded over the bed and joined her, his grin wide as he stepped into the shower while she adjusted the water.

"It's your treat."

"That's not fair!" she exclaimed. "You wouldn't be showering if it weren't for me. I had to turn on the water!"

His grin widened. "Don't be a sore loser. Come join me instead." His gaze narrowed with obvious intent. "I'll wash your back if you wash mine."

"Nothing else?"

"Whatever else you think you're big enough to handle," he answered.

Kathi stepped in front of him, allowing the water to sluice over both their bodies. Her gaze glistened with intent as she picked up the soap and rubbed it in her hands. Then she held the soap against his chest and lathered. Trailing the soap flow, she followed the arrowing of his chest hair. "I'm a big girl now, Hannibal Saunders. You always *did* underestimate me."

He watched her hand, fascinated. "Did I? I don't remember."

Hannibal also forgot he was supposed to be sated by their lovemaking earlier. He forgot breakfast. He forgot everything except the luscious and determined woman who stood in front of him in the confined space.

It was an hour later when they walked into the garden dining area for breakfast.

Hannibal escorted her into the dining area, glaring at every man who looked her way. Even in her well-worn shirt and jeans she was beautiful.

A waitress led them to a table by the window overlooking a garden and pond, then handed them menus and promised to return quickly. As far as Hannibal was concerned, the waitress could have taken a month before returning.

The glow of Kathi's skin, the sparkle in her eyes and her softly swaying body as she walked were manna to Hannibal. And now that she was sitting next to him, he could bask in her smile. Even more satisfying was the thought that he might have put it there.

She looked up at him. "I'm starved!"

"For anything in particular?"

Dimples graced her cheeks as her gaze lit with mischievousness. "Don't fish for compliments. You already know how I feel about that hunger."

Hannibal couldn't look at the menu. All his attention was focused on Kathi Rebecca Baylor. "Come back to Boca Raton with me."

Her delightfully open expression became guarded. "I don't think I'd fit in very well with your friends."

"Why not?"

"Because I don't hobnob well with the rich. And they can usually spot a phony a mile away."

"You're not phony. They are."

"We all are."

"Then join me."

"No." She placed her hand on his, stilling his impatience. "I won't lie to you and I won't go. But please don't ruin this time we have together now."

"All I want is for us to have more time."

"We'll see," she sighed, withdrawing her hand from his arm and opening her menu. "Right now, all I can think about is rich, fat-laden food."

According to Kathi, the conversation was over. Hannibal recognized the signs. He'd pressed her too hard and she'd backed off. His mother used to say those same words before she changed the subject. "We'll see" usually meant no, but it was a softer, less argumentative answer.

He began to tell her not to humor him or treat him like a child when a voice called Kathi's name.

Standing at the doorway was a well-dressed couple. Hannibal recognized Timothy and what looked like a grown-up version of Kathi's little sister, Vivian.

"How did they know where we were?" Hannibal wondered aloud.

"I called Vivian last night to let her know everything was all right." Kathi looked worried. "I didn't mean for her to tell Timothy, or for either of them to come looking for me."

"Don't worry. You're tough," Hannibal said, more for something to say than to believe. Since she hadn't called Timothy, Hannibal could relax. "Besides, I'm here if you need me."

The fun was just beginning.

Timothy held tight to Vivian's arm as she walked through the long room to their table. Timothy paid no attention to Hannibal's presence.

"I knew you'd still be here." Timothy crowed as Vivian sat down next to Hannibal while he took the chair next to Kathi. "Vivian thought you'd be gone by now, but I told her that since you didn't get a chance to sleep in too often, you'd still be here."

Kathi sighed and gave her sister an exasperated look. "Timothy, there's a reason Vivian wasn't supposed to tell you where I was. I wanted this time alone. I was going to explain everything once I got back home."

Timothy grinned, revealing an excellent capping job some dentist had been paid handsomely for. "I saved you some time. You can explain now."

The waitress interrupted by taking everyone's order, then poured a round of steaming coffee. Timothy continued to ignore Hannibal. Hannibal understood that it was the poor guy's way of postponing an out-and-out fight.

Hannibal decided to play along. He sat back and waited to see what would happen next. Whatever it was, Kathi was in charge—until she needed help. He wouldn't let

Kathi go through this without his help and support, whether she wanted it or not.

"I'll explain when I return home," she promised after the waitress left. "You know I'd never hurt you if I could help it—either one of you. So you understand that changing my mind was a hard decision for me to make. Right?"

Timothy and Vivian both began speaking, "Yes, but—" and "I know, however—"

Kathi held up her hands. "Please. Listen to me. I love you both very much. I'd do—and will do—almost anything for you. But, Timothy, I won't marry you when it isn't me that you love like a wife and helpmate. You don't need to marry your mother. You love Vivian, and as soon as her life is back on track, you'll both realize it."

Timothy looked furious. Vivian didn't look all that happy, either.

"You don't know that," her sister said with a pout.

"And we both know that if Timothy didn't care for you, he wouldn't have taken you along on our honeymoon," Kathi replied.

"I can speak for myself, Kathi," Timothy finally said, and Hannibal wanted to rush in and tell him to do it, then. He bit his tongue with the effort to remain quiet. Timothy went on. "And I still want to marry you. We could fly to Vegas this afternoon."

The waitress returned to serve breakfast, never speaking a word. But her bright-eyed gaze gave away the fact that she'd been listening. Hannibal waited impatiently for the woman to leave. He was about to rush in where fools dared to tread.

Kathi gave the woman a frozen stare, then returned her attention to Timothy. "I love you, you know that, Timothy." She took his hand in hers. "But's it's not the kind

of love that you want or need. It's not the kind of love *I*
need to give, either." She leaned forward and kissed him
on the cheek. "We all deserve more."

Feeling satisfied that Kathi had handled it well so far,
Hannibal bit into his Eggs Benedict. Kathi continued to
chide Timothy and Vivian for their foolishness. Great.
And most important, she had not told them of her winning ticket, but she *had* confided in Hannibal. There was
more between them than a one-night stand.

Neither Timothy nor Vivian recognized him, although Vivian kept glancing at him with a question in her
eyes. Timothy's lack of speculation about Hannibal's
place in Kathi's new life was what had kept Hannibal silent this far.

Timothy rubbed a spot between his brows. Finally,
with as much distance as an iceberg to a South Seas is-
land, he stared at Hannibal. "Is it because of him?"

Kathi didn't bother with introductions or explana-
tions. She wasn't going to prolong this agony. "No. I'd
made my decision before." Odd, thought Hannibal. She
still didn't mention his name.

Vivian still looked furious. "Now what happens?
Timothy won't have me and I've just lost my two best
friends."

Hannibal thought her statement sounded more like a
whine. He recognized the sound—his mother used that
same tone when things didn't go her way. It meant *poor
little me, no one will continue to spoil me the way I want to
be spoiled*.

Kathi sighed heavily and he tensed, wondering if it was
time to step in so she wouldn't give in to these two.
"Timothy and I haven't *died*, Vivian. You'll still have
both of us."

Timothy sipped the last of his coffee and stood. "Come on, Vivian, we'll drive Kathi home."

Hannibal stiffened. If this guy thought for a moment that he was taking Kathi from him, he could think again. In anticipation of a fight, he laid his fork carefully on his plate and prepared to stand.

Once more, Kathi beat him to the punch. "I'm staying. You two are going back alone." Before either could argue, she finished. "There will be no more arguments. Wait until I get home."

"When will that be?"

"In two or three days." Kathi stood and hugged both of them. "Have a good trip and don't think badly of me. I promise this will all work out."

With great reluctance, they walked out of the restaurant. Kathi's parting smile broke Hannibal's heart. Vivian got to the restaurant door, and turned to give her older sister one last pleading look.

Kathi waved goodbye.

Once they were gone, she sat down and played with her pancakes, pretending she was eating and nothing unusual had happened.

But now he knew better. "They're going to do just fine."

"Yes." She sipped her milk.

"You made the right decision."

"Yes."

"Sometimes, Kathi, what's good for other people isn't always what they want. We all have to grow up and learn to rely on ourselves."

"You're right."

He reached over and tilted her chin toward him so he could see her eyes. "Then why are you so sad?"

Big fat tears rolled down her cheeks. "Because I love them so much and I hate to hurt them. I want to be there for them."

"You are," Hannibal said, wiping away another tear with his thumb. "They just didn't understand that no is a good answer, too. Someday they will."

She smiled uncertainly. "Think so?"

His heart felt her pain. "Definitely." Unable to resist, he leaned forward and breathed a light kiss on her lips. "Now eat so we can leave. The sooner you get your money, the sooner you can straighten out your life."

"Right." She smiled but the sadness was still in her eyes.

"Kathi—" He stopped. What the hell was the matter with him? He was just about to say *I love you* to a woman who was in the throes of despair because of a broken engagement. He had to let her bounce back from that decision before he forced her into making another.

He silently promised himself that he would make this hurt up to her—he just wasn't sure how.

Chapter Six

BACK IN THE TRUCK, Hannibal wondered what he could do to persuade Kathi to come to Boca Raton with him. He needed time to convince her that he was the man for her. He needed time to show her they were perfect for each other. He needed time to let her fall in love with him. He needed time to convince her that together they were a rare combination.

He needed time, dammit!

Kathi sat in the center of the seat, knees primly together, her hands clasped in her lap. What hurt was her blank stare at the road ahead.

On the cab floor, right at her feet, was the plastic bag that held her wedding dress. If Hannibal lived to be a thousand, he'd never forget her standing in the doorway of her bedroom, wearing that dress. He'd never before seen anything so beautiful that it hurt to look. But then, his reaction to Kathi had always been extreme.

She had also been open and honest and direct. He loved that. Or she *had* been, he amended, until this morning. Except for the small bout with tears during breakfast, Kathi had built a wall. Hannibal had tried to start a conversation several times, but to no avail. Instead, she gave two- or three-word answers, then was quiet again. He couldn't reach her.

Frustration was killing him.

Normally, he would have allowed it to continue killing him. But for some reason when he was in this truck, he spoke in a way he didn't usually speak, drove in a more aggressive manner and even became more forthright in his questions. But he didn't have time to think about it now. Now, all he had to deal with was Kathi. That was enough.

Finally, he confronted the problem. "Kathi, tell me what's on your mind so I know how to help you."

She turned wide, blank eyes to him. "Why, nothing. I'm just thinking of all the things I need to do when I get my money."

That was the longest sentence she'd spoken since they had eaten this morning. He was encouraged. "Like what?"

"Oh, you know...." she said, her voice trailing off as she turned back to stare out the window.

"No, I don't. Tell me." He was trying to coax her, but instead he sounded demanding. And he didn't care. He had to get her to talk because he felt shut out and afraid he'd lose her once they reached Tallahassee.

"The usual things. Open a bank account. Pay Timothy back. Buy a car that won't fall apart when the ninety-day warranty is up."

Weren't those things already done? He was beginning to remember how it was to be poor. Not broke for the week, but downright *poor*. "I didn't know there was a ninety-day warranty. Why don't you just buy a *new* car? Then you won't have to worry for several years."

"I could, couldn't I?"

"Kathi, when we get to Tallahassee, I'm checking in to a hotel. I'll send you over to the lottery office in a taxi so you won't have to worry. Then, when you're done, we'll meet at the hotel."

"That's kind of you, but you don't have to do that. You can just let me off at the office and I can figure out a way home from there." Kathi continued to stare out the front window. "I know you need to get back to your party."

"I don't *need* to do a damn thing I don't want to." He took a deep breath, trying to calm himself. "Look, all I want to do is let you do your thing, then come back to me at the hotel."

"Why?"

"Isn't it obvious?" Dammit, was she going to make him say it?

"No." She turned her head, staring at him. "Why would you want me to meet you at the hotel? Unless you want to make love?"

"Is that what you think?"

For the first time since they'd gotten into the car, she looked at him. Really looked at him. "No. I don't really think that."

"Good." He reached for her hand, bringing it to his thigh. "I would love to make love to you. Anywhere. Anytime. But I also thought that by the time you finish with the photographers and the attorneys, you'd be exhausted or on a high. Either way, I want to be with you to celebrate."

Kathi knew that. Her comment had been an off-the-top-of-her-head response to his order. She turned her hand over and clasped his. Forcing herself to think of Hannibal instead of the absolutely wonderful relief, and consequently the guilt she felt at cutting the apron strings with Timothy and Vivian, she focused on their entwined hands.

She felt as if they'd been together all their lives, instead of just the past day. It hurt to think that, at most, they would have one more day together before Hannibal went back to his world and Kathi to hers. How quickly twenty-four hours would speed by!

"Thank you for this time," she admitted softly. "It means a great deal to me." *It means I love you and I can't let you know.*

Hannibal didn't say anything, but his anxiety eased.

When they reached the outskirts of Tallahassee, Kathi sat up straighter. Hannibal stopped at a gas station to ask directions, and she listened as carefully as he did.

They drove to the center of town. Once Hannibal found the hotel he wanted—Kathi should have known it was going to be another expensive one—he pulled up to let the valet parking take over. She clutched her wedding dress in one hand while he helped her out of the truck and toward the taxis waiting at the curb.

With a firm but gentle grasp, Hannibal took her plastic bag and opened the taxi door. "I promise this will be safe with me." He placed a light kiss on her mouth. Then one more. With a groan, he pulled her into his arms and gave her a kiss that made her head spin. With great reluctance, Hannibal finally released his hold and helped her into the back seat of the taxi.

He slipped several bills through the side window to the driver. "Take good care of her and wait until she's ready to return. The doorman will pay your cab rate and tip."

"Hannibal," Kathi began, only to remember she had little money and the lottery was probably not going to pay her taxi fare. Unused to anyone paying her way, she promised she would reimburse him as soon as she cashed her check.

The driver had a chance to glance at the bills. He nodded at Hannibal and grinned. "Yes, sir!"

"Thanks."

Kathi watched Hannibal as the cab pulled away. Her precious dress was over his arms. She knew he'd take care of it.

Why hadn't she realized how wonderful he was when they were younger? She could have been building a teenage relationship with him if she'd known earlier that he was what she was looking for. Youth obviously didn't have the sense to be discriminating.

When the cab pulled up in front of the lottery office, Kathi forced a smile on her face. She'd just won the Fantasy Five Lottery and she shouldn't look as if she'd just lost her best friend.

A glance at her watch told her it was only one o'clock. She hoped this wouldn't take long—she didn't want to waste a minute of what little time she had left with Hannibal.

It was four-thirty by the time she left the building. Kathi had no idea so many things had to be done. She hadn't even thought of having to deal with the Internal Revenue Service! Anyway, with a check equaling a little over half her yearly earnings, she was on her way back to the hotel for the last time.

HANNIBAL WAS stretched out on the bed and staring at the ceiling. The bed was empty without Kathi. It was unbelievable that he could miss her so much when she'd only been back in his life for twenty-four hours.

He wanted her.

Oh, that thought wasn't new, but this time his motivations were based on getting to know her as she was now, not the terror of his youth. And this morning at breakfast when Timothy and Vivian showed up, he realized how important she was to him. How important she had always been to him.

She'd been his first love, and then he'd unconsciously used her as a measuring stick for all other women in his life. No wonder a few of his dates had thought he was boring—he hadn't bothered to keep up the pretence of interest once he'd found them lacking. Those women weren't sharp enough or witty enough or beautiful enough.

They weren't Kathi Rebecca Baylor.

The suite door opened but Hannibal remained where he was, eyes closed.

He heard her tiptoe in. He could feel her gaze on him and wondered what she would do. He wished she would crawl into bed with him.

He heard the closet door roll back, then the crinkle of plastic. It took him a minute to realize that she was going to leave without saying goodbye. *She was actually going to leave!* His heart pounded hard as he listened to her footsteps cross the carpet, then quietly shut the bedroom door behind her. He was too stunned to call out.

He sat up and listened, wondering what to do next. When the outer door didn't open and close, he knew she was still in the suite. But doing what?

He walked to the door and opened it. Kathi stood at the desk, busily scribbling a note on the hotel letterhead. His heart sank to his toes. Then, very slowly, his dejection turned to anger. "Were you going to say goodbye or just sneak out?"

Her head popped up, blue eyes wide. "I wasn't sneaking out. I was writing you a note thanking you."

"No one can say your manners aren't impeccable," he sneered. "And then what?"

"And *then* I was leaving." She stood straight, her gaze holding as much anger as he felt. "It won't work, you know. You couldn't live in my world any more than I could live in yours."

"We don't belong in different worlds. Look around, Kathi. We're together *now*."

"You know what I mean."

He knew. She wouldn't let their relationship work. "How the hell do you know what will work or not? You're on the run again. You don't stick around long enough to see if it will work."

Her face turned white. "That's not fair."

"Right now, lady, it's as fair as you're going to get. And it's a damn sight more fair than I got from you. You won't even discuss it. To you it's a closed case and I didn't even get a trial."

Disgusted and hurt, he strode back into her bedroom, lying down on the bed again and staring at the ceiling. If she was going to leave, he couldn't watch. He promised himself that he would not lose his temper. He was that thirteen-year-old boy again, with hurt in his eyes and a lump as big as a lemon in his throat.

He didn't need to see her. It would only bring home the fact that now she had money and didn't need him anymore. She didn't need anything.

But Hannibal did. He needed Kathi. His entire body called out to her.

She stood in the bedroom doorway, staring at him with tears in her eyes. "Please don't fight with me," she said softly. "But we both know this could lead nowhere."

"I don't know a damn thing," he stated stubbornly.

"Let's start again. Maybe we can talk this out," she said.

"Is this a 'we'll see' kind of answer where I'm going to regret thinking there was any hope?"

"I don't know yet. Want to try and see where this leads us?"

"What the hell," he stated bitterly. "You're going to do what you want, anyway. I might as well play along."

"Very well," she said. "Pretend I just came in." She hesitated. "Hi."

"Hi."

Kathi dropped her purse and slipped out of her shoes, then walked to the end of the bed and slithered up to where Hannibal's head lay on the pillow. "How was your afternoon?" she asked as she brushed a lock of hair away from his forehead.

Against his will, he felt the anger ebb. With a heavy sigh, he gave in and played the game her way. He rubbed her spine, feeling the tension there. "Fine. Do you feel rich now?"

"Yes, even though the IRS got almost half." She leaned over and brushed her lips against his.

"It's the penalty you pay for having money. Pretend you're Robin Hood, taking from yourself to give to the welfare recipients."

She leaned her head on his shoulder. "I think I paid for half the interstate highways in America all by myself."

"You don't sound very upset about it."

Her laughter was soft and feminine, delighting him. "I'm not upset. I'm rich. Richer than I ever dreamed of being."

His hand ran down her spine to her buttocks. "And do you have to go back tomorrow and fill out more papers?"

She caressed the pulse point at his temple. "No. I'm finished. All I have to do is figure out how to cash the darn check."

"Never mind. I'll take you back home."

She tensed.

He went on. "I'm going in that direction, anyway."

Some of the stress eased from her body. "Thank you, but you need to get on with your life and I need to get my life together."

With lazy movements, Hannibal took the pins from her hair, letting riotous curls fall to her breast, teasing his shoulder and chest. "Stay with me." Damn! He hadn't meant to say that yet. He'd meant to wait . . . at least until they'd made love and she was all soft and mellow.

"I'll stay with you. Until tomorrow."

"Don't play games. You know what I mean."

Kathi pulled back and sat up. She pushed her thick hair behind her shoulders and stared down at him. Deep in thought, she let her fingers trail down his chest to the waistband of his slacks. But as sensual as her movements were, her frown verified how hard she was trying to speak her mind. "You live in another world. You know where I come from, and my life is nothing like yours. My world is full of women who work hard all day, then drag home to look after their children and cook and clean. Women in my world aren't pampered princesses."

Hannibal stared up at her, realizing again just how smart this woman he loved was. She might not have a degree, but she was just as sharp as any psychologist. Even though he agreed with several of her ideas, that didn't make her right on all of them. But he had to know what she was leading up to, so he allowed her to continue without interruption.

Her frown deepened. "I want to be in the best of both worlds. I want the man I marry to be proud to be with me, but I also want him to realize that I'm a person just as important and as productive as he is. I want a career, a helpmate and to be allowed to be myself."

"That's a lot to put on anyone's plate," Hannibal suggested.

"Not when it's shared."

Unable to resist the temptation of her loosened hair, he played with the golden strands that fell over one breast, his fingers teasing each lock, twisting it around his finger. "And does this man have to know your qualifications immediately or are you going to break the news of this kind of compromise gently?"

Her gaze narrowed. "You're making fun of me."

"No. I'm telling you that relationships have to be worked on. The man has a say, too, Kathi. And getting to know someone is important, more important than setting ground rules right away."

"That piece of philosophy, Hannibal Saunders, depends on where you're coming from."

"Meaning?"

"Meaning that you're a man, and the world expects different things from you than it does from a woman like me. In fact, on occasion I'm patronizingly patted on the head as if I'm a faithful dog instead of a capable, intelligent woman."

"Kathi..."

"Shhh." Her fingers lightly grazed his mouth. Her own lips followed, brushing his lips into submission. "I want you."

He steeled himself not to react instantly to her invitation. "Not enough."

"Too much." Her words were warm against his jaw.

"Right here," he said, pointing to the other side of his face. She followed the movement. "And here." He pointed to his forehead. "And here," he said, pointing to his chin.

When he couldn't stand it anymore, he encircled her body with his arms and held her to him. "I want you, too." He was confessing more than his desire.

"It's about time." Her voice was whispered honey. Her kiss was determined, demanding, selfish. He loved it more than breathing.

Using every ounce of his strength, he pulled away. "Nothing happens until we talk this out."

Kathi's eyes lost their dreamy look. "Is this a bribe or a threat?"

"Neither," Hannibal said, running a hand through his hair. "We've got a problem communicating and I want to solve it...."

Kathi sat up and stared down at him. "Okay. What exactly is it that you want from me?"

His grin was contagious. "Your body, for one thing."

But she wasn't smiling. "You turned my body down."

"Only for the moment, and only because of your ability to withhold what I want the most." His determination was clear. "And I won't guarantee how long I'll be able to withhold myself from you."

"Hannibal," she began, but he covered her lips with his fingers.

"For once, Kathi, please don't stop the confrontation. This time, stay with me and battle it out."

She began to argue with him, only to realize how right he was. With every confrontation, she tried to distance herself from the hurt. She'd always run when she could, but not this time. This time she would say what she had to say and the devil be damned.

"All right, Hannibal, but don't tell me later that you didn't ask for all this honesty. I'm more ready for this than you are. I have something to prove—something that needs to be proved not only to you, but to me."

"Tell me." His voice was a whisper.

"You want me to be with you. I'm not even sure what that means, but I do know what it doesn't mean. It sounds like the future is still as uneven and rough with you as without you. The answer is no."

"That's not—"

This time she covered his lips. "Let me finish." It was an order. "Also, no matter what you might have in mind, you and I don't have the same background. Not really. We were just acquaintances who met and then moved on into their own orbits. I don't fit in your world. You certainly don't fit into mine."

"So you think we ought to part here, and be thankful that we brushed shoulders in the same crowd for a while?"

"Yes."

His gaze hardened. "You're a snob, you know that? You're willing to give up anything that might bring happiness just in case you have to ask more of yourself than you're willing to give."

"That's not true!"

"Yes, it is and you know it. You're afraid of reaching out and grabbing happiness. If you weren't, you'd be taking advantage of the emotions we're feeling, trying to see if there is a chance for us instead of running away so you won't get hurt." His hands slid down her arms to her waist. "Take a chance, Kathi. Gamble with me the way you did with the lottery. Who knows? You might win the prize again."

She swallowed hard to dislodge the lump in her throat. "You're the prize?"

"No. *We're* the prize. Together we could have a relationship that would rival your parents'. It's worth a try."

She stared down at him, tears flowing from her eyes. He knew exactly what to say to make her cave in. But didn't he see the problems ahead? Couldn't he tell she wasn't the type to sit back and play a grateful Cinderella to his Prince Charming? She needed to be busy, to own a business. She wasn't a glamorous woman who dabbled in real estate or financial matters—she was a hairdresser.

His hand brushed her wet cheek.

"Tell me, Kathi," he softly urged. "What do you want to be when you grow up?"

It was the easiest question she'd answered so far. "I want to own a string of beauty shops. Maybe someday, I'll even open a beauty school."

"And you can't do that if you're married?"

Her eyes widened. "Who said anything about marriage?"

"I did."

"I didn't hear it."

"Answer my question."

"Of course I can do that married." She knew her tone was defensive but she couldn't help it. She'd fought too long and too hard. "I can do anything a career man can do—and probably better."

"Then why would you be willing to dump me and go find someone else to spend your life with, when I'm willing to help you and our family succeed?"

"I…" She didn't know what to say. His words stunned her and all the excuses she'd used to keep them apart disappeared.

"Unless you *don't* love me."

"Love?" she repeated, her own emotions in turmoil over his insight. "Of course I love you."

"Then why won't you be with me?"

She'd already admitted more than she should have. She didn't need to lose any more dignity—or pieces of her heart. Ignoring her quickening heartbeat, she plunged ahead. "Wait a minute. Just what do you mean, 'be with' you? Is this a proposal or a proposition?"

"A proposal. Unless you want the other. Everything's negotiable except your leaving me. That's not even a thought." He looked at her sternly. "Now answer my question, Kathi. What do you want that I can't give you?"

A smile tugged at the corners of her mouth. She tried to keep it at bay, but continued to grin. "I want a marriage where the two people are equal. Where the male is as responsible for the house and the children as the woman."

"I will be." His voice lowered. "I am."

"I want to be able to be in my own business and not have my husband patronize me by calling me the 'little woman' or consider my work just a pastime to keep me occupied."

He ran a hand up and down her arm, his touch so light that it was a butterfly's kiss. "I'll always take whatever you do seriously as long as you take whatever I do seriously."

"I want a working knowledge of all the money we spend and where it goes. I want to be part of the decision-making process about our bills, savings and businesses."

"Scout's honor," he said, his fingers against her heart—and breast.

She couldn't think of another thing to say. Her thoughts were muddled as her body felt his intimate touch. "I want a man—"

"—who loves you," he finished for her. She couldn't do anything but nod in agreement. "And you want him to cherish you and take care of you and allow you to take care of him, too. You want a man who fantasizes about you by day and turns those fantasies into reality by night."

He stared up at her. Without thinking, she reached to touch him, to feel the heat of his skin against the palm of her hand. That way she would be certain that he was real and not a figment of her imagination.

Her gaze locked with his. "Promise?"

"Promise."

"And what do you expect from a marriage, Hannibal?"

"A wife who looks to me to share her life, not expect me to be her source of entertainment. A wife who has other interests to bring to the marriage. A wife who wants me to be her fantasy as much as I want to be it." His hand touched her heart again. "I want you."

"Anything else?"

"A truck with tractor tires." He couldn't keep the mischievous look from his eyes.

"Oh, no you don't." She looked as stern as he had earlier. "I don't know if you've noticed it or not, but every time you get behind the wheel of that thing, you turn macho and bossy. You can have anything else you want, but that's a joint decision, and my side says no."

"I think it's grown on me."

"Life is a compromise," she retorted. "And if you want me, you have to give up the truck."

"What a sacrifice."

Kathi Rebecca Baylor laughed. "I'll tell you what. For being so wonderful about it, I'll let you rent one of those trucks on an occasional weekend—not to exceed four weekends a year."

His fingers curled possessively around her neck and pulled her down to just above his mouth. "You drive a hard bargain, lady. What do I get in return?"

"A woman who has more dreams than you could believe, and with them, the imagination to carry them out."

His expression changed, tightening with the thought. "Care to try one out?"

"Now or after the marriage?" she asked innocently, reminding him that they still had a piece of unfinished business.

Hannibal stared at her a moment, then dropped his hand from her neck. "You're right," he stated as he stood. "We should wait. We'll fly to Las Vegas right now."

Kathi stared up at him, dismayed. He didn't have to take her words to heart. Not this instant, anyway. "Now?"

"Right."

"It's almost dinner," she protested. "Can't we wait until tomorrow?"

Hannibal stood, hands on hips. "Are you sure you can trust me?"

Kathi smiled slowly. "I have this fantasy about the night before my wedding..."

Hannibal's eyes narrowed. "Unless you can talk about it, it's only a thought."

Patting the bed, she smiled slowly. "Come sit down and let's discuss it."

"Is this another negotiation?"

"You bet."

Hannibal sighed, then reached for her and they fell across the bed, his arms holding her tightly against him as if she would disappear. "Okay, if you must. But this time I have a price."

She kissed the tip of his nose. "And it is?"

"You. For always."

"Paid," she said, just before he claimed her mouth in a kiss full of meaning. Kathi was where she wanted to be, doing what she wanted to do with the man she loved.

She was no longer an in-debt bride on the run. Thanks to Lady Luck and Hannibal Saunders, she was a wealthy woman on her way to becoming the happiest bride in the world....

Bride in
Blue

SANDRA
JAMES

A Note from Sandra James

You've probably already guessed that I'm the sentimental sort. I cried the first time my family and I watched the movie, *E.T.*—and the second and third time, as well. Whether they're tears of happiness, tears of empathy or tears of pride, it doesn't take much to bring a lump to my throat and a sheen to my eyes. I guess that's why I like to put readers through an emotional wringer—but only after I've been there myself.

So did I cry at my own wedding? Of course. I was so choked up I could hardly say "I do." And forgive the cliché, but I was also busy pinching myself, feeling as if I were the luckiest woman on earth and brimming with joy.

To this day, I'm still counting my blessings. My husband and I have three beautiful daughters whom I hope will be as fortunate as their father and I. It takes a great deal of time and effort to build a successful marriage, and maybe even a little luck....

Most of all, it takes a whole lot of love.

Weddings come in all shapes and sizes—old-fashioned and traditional, fancy and elaborate. Some are simple and small, and others are anything *but* traditional. So when it came time to write Kate and Grant's story, I had to figure out what kind of wedding these two should have. As always when I'm writing, the characters become very dear to my heart, and it was no different with Kate and Grant. Here were two very special people who deserved a very special wedding.

It wasn't long before I realized...any wedding, no matter how big or small, is special.

I think Kate and Grant would agree.

Wishing you all the best,

Sandra

Chapter One

THIS WAS NOT how she'd planned to spend her first full day of summer break.

Standing in the dressing area of Mary Ellen's Bridal Salon, Kate Harrison wiggled her pinched toes and prayed for salvation. Fifteen minutes of being stuffed into satin pumps was fifteen minutes too long—which was one of the reasons why the librarian at Gold Beach Elementary School had never worn heels in the twelve years she'd worked there.

The other had something to do with being five foot nine in her bare feet and a lifetime of wishing she wasn't.

"Kate, don't move or you'll end up getting stuck!" intoned a female voice in the vicinity of her waistline. *I already am,* Kate thought grimly. "Let's see. One more tuck at the waist…there, I think that should do it." Mary Ellen's voice sang out gaily. She gave Kate a gentle shove toward the angled mirrors. "All right, Kate, tell me what you think."

Kate gingerly edged forward to examine her wide-eyed reflection. The dress was simple yet elegant, with gracefully sweeping folds of satin and lace. Beneath a dainty flowered coronet atop her crown, layers of sheer nylon framed gleaming shoulder-length hair the color of mahogany. It was truly an exquisite gown, Kate decided wistfully….

But she couldn't shake the feeling she was staring at a stranger.

At last she cleared her throat. "Looks ... nice," she ventured weakly.

"Nice!" Mary Ellen let out a gusty laugh. "Honey, that's not the word for it!"

Behind her, Kate's younger sister, Ann, clapped her hands. "She's right, Kate," Ann cried. "I've never seen you look so ... so stunning!"

Stunning. *Oh, brother,* thought Kate. Ann had always had a flair for the dramatic, from the time she was a child—and her three-year-old niece Stacy had inherited it, as well.

Kate's mother, Rose, simply beamed. Kate took advantage of the lull to duck into the dressing room again, knowing the silence wouldn't last long.

Both her mother and Ann had stationed themselves in the front of the salon when Kate emerged from the dressing room, dressed in slacks and a light cotton sweater, her feet blessedly free from their pinched confinement. Neither noticed her reappearance. Her mother was talking, gesturing with both hands, while Ann's head was bobbing up and down in agreement.

That was not a good sign—not a good sign at all.

"Oh, and I nearly forgot! I didn't tell the florist to put violets in the table centerpieces at the reception—they're Kate's favorite, you know."

Kate nearly groaned. Her mother and Ann had had her in tow since this morning. First they'd checked in with the florist to review the arrangements they'd made weeks ago; the caterer and photographer had come next. Between her mother and sister, Kate wasn't certain she would survive the next few weeks.

She stepped forward. "Mother," she said gently. "There's no need to make such a fuss over every little thing."

"No need to— Why, Katie, of course there is! Honey, a woman's wedding is the biggest day of her life. I want you to have a wedding you'll always remember!"

The beaming smile was back in place again, and so was Ann's dreamy look. She turned to her older sister eagerly. "Kate, you know, I've been thinking. Why don't you wear the diamond teardrop necklace Mom and Dad gave me when Steve and I were married? You can wear it and someday Stacy can, too. And who knows? Maybe you and Derek will have a daughter, too—soon, I hope!—and she'll wear it, too. Why, just think. This could be the start of a whole new family tradition!" She threw her arms around Kate and hugged her fiercely. "Oh, Kate, I'm so excited! I don't know how you can be so calm!"

Outwardly Kate was smiling, but inside she winced. She was as patient as a saint with the five-year-olds who rummaged through the library bookshelves, but her patience was in short supply these days. Whenever she was home, it seemed the phone was constantly ringing off the hook. If it wasn't her mother, then it was Ann.... *What color scheme do you prefer, Kate? ... I've heard black and white is a popular theme again this year...But the silver and rose is so eye-catching...And what about the reception dinner? ...Sit-down or buffet? ...And the flowers? ...Lilies or mums...*

To Kate, this wedding was more chore than pleasure, more duty than joy. If this had been the first time she had gone through this, she would have enjoyed it, treasured every moment of planning her wedding to the most minute detail.

But it wasn't, and the knowledge was like a sliver beneath her skin. The memory of that long-ago day had dimmed, but not the hurt... never the hurt.

For the span of a heartbeat, an elusive pain tugged at her heart. Kate hadn't been entirely jesting last night when she suggested to Derek that they run off for a quickie wedding in Reno this weekend. From the moment they'd learned of her engagement, her mother and Ann were determined that she have a lavish, traditional wedding with all the trimmings—the wedding she'd been cheated of a dozen years earlier.

Kate simply didn't have the heart to let them down. She loved them both too much to disappoint either.

And maybe some perverse little devil inside demanded justice for her wounded pride—maybe she wanted to show the entire populace of Gold Beach, Oregon, that spinster librarian Kate Harrison hadn't ended up an old maid, after all.

But try as she might, Kate simply couldn't match her mother and Ann's enthusiasm for her impending nuptials. When Mary Ellen joined them, the trio strayed toward the salon's front counter. Kate remained where she was. Her mother was counting off on her fingers, no doubt reciting the entire guest list to Mary Ellen.

With a weary sigh, Kate gazed through the shop window. A short distance away, a solitary figure stood atop the bridge, gazing down where the waters of the Rogue River flowed into the Pacific. A pang of guilt knifed through her—right now she'd give just about anything to trade places with the loner.

A tap on the window distracted her. Her eyes widened as Kate's best friend and maid of honor, Joanne Simms, rushed inside.

"Oh, Kate, you'll never guess what happened!"

Kate pulled her over to where two chairs nestled along the far wall. Her mother, Kate noted dryly, took no notice of the newcomer. Her animated conversation didn't miss a beat. Joanne, however, was both excited and distraught, as Kate soon discovered.

"Oh, Kate, I—I don't know what to do! You know that this weekend is our fifteenth anniversary?"

Joanne had married Bill when he was just out of college, while she'd been nineteen, like Kate. Bill was the industrial shop teacher at the local junior high; they had two boys, ten and twelve. During the summers, they operated an overnight river inn, fifty miles upriver on the Rogue.

Kate scarcely had a chance to nod before Joanne hurried on. "Last night Bill told me he made reservations for a surprise two-week fling in Acapulco this weekend, just the two of us. I was thrilled because he's never done anything so extravagant . . . he timed it so we'd be back a couple of days before your wedding, thank heaven, but . . . oh, Kate, we're supposed to fly out from Medford this Saturday!"

Her voice trailed off to a wail; all at once she looked ready to cry. Kate blinked. "If it's the boys," she murmured, "I'd be glad to have them stay with me—"

"They left for camp this morning, and they'll be there for the next month. The problem is the inn—we have a guest due in Saturday for two weeks! Bill arranged for his parents to stay there while we're gone, but we found out this morning that his mother broke her ankle. She's on crutches and there's no way she can negotiate the stairs!"

Kate had a good idea where the conversation was leading. Her mind was already churning. The inn was quiet and secluded, unreachable by car since the nearest road extended only as far as Agnes, twenty miles west of the inn; the only access was by boat. One thought led to another. . . . Her mother couldn't pop over to fuss about the menu. Ann's sprightly chatter wouldn't drive her up the wall. It was a certainty she could find a little peace and quiet....

Joanne moaned. "Our trip to Mexico is off unless we can find someone to man the inn for us. But we'll never find someone at this late date—never!"

Kate took a deep, fortifying breath. "Joanne," she said slowly, "I think you've just found your rescuer."

HER MOTHER was horrified, her sister aghast. But as Kate patiently explained to Ann, all of the details had been seen to, so it wasn't as if her wedding couldn't go on exactly as planned. Besides, Kate had been feeling rather superfluous anyway. And Derek—dear, sweet Derek—had kissed her on the cheek and said he understood; she could hardly forsake her best friend at such a time.

Three days later, Kate stood on the wide redwood deck of the Riverbend Inn. Giant Douglas fir trees stretched skyward, arching over an elbow in the river. The river's fury had taken a breather here; the surface was smooth and placid. A profusion of wildflowers spiked the opposite hillside.

Oh, yes, she decided with a satisfied smile she couldn't withhold. This was just what she needed. She braced her hands on the railing and closed her eyes, letting nature's peace wash over her. For a long blissful moment, there was only the keening sigh of the wind sweeping through the treetops, the gentle swish of water on the riverbank...

...the strident summons of the telephone.

Kate's eyes flew open. It rang once—twice and then again—hatefully insistent. With a scowl she stalked through the open French doors and across the inn's living room. There she snatched up the receiver. If it was her mother or Ann . . .

"Riverbend Inn," she said into the mouthpiece. She only barely managed to keep the brusqueness from her tone.

There was a long pause, and then a rather stilted male voice. "This is Grant Richards."

Kate snapped to attention. Grant Richards was the guest who was due to check in today. "Yes, Mr. Richards. What can I do for you?"

"I'm here at the airport. I was told someone would be waiting to take me to the inn, but the only other person here appears to be a janitor."

He sounded just as disgruntled as she had a moment earlier. *My, but we're testy today, aren't we,* she thought, mildly irritated.

"Mr. Richards," she said sweetly. "Does this janitor happen to be wearing a faded brown shirt and a fire-engine red baseball cap? And does his shirt have Rogue River Tours and the name Charlie printed just above the front pocket?"

Footsteps could be heard, and then an instant's silence. "It does," came the disembodied male voice, sterner than ever. "Look here, Ms. . . ."

"Harrison. Kate Harrison."

"Ms. Harrison—" by now he sounded downright forbidding "—there's obviously been a mistake—"

"Oh, no mistake," Kate said smoothly. "You haven't been abandoned, after all, Mr. Richards. Have a pleasant trip and we'll see you in a few hours."

She dropped the phone in the cradle. "Beast," she grumbled good-naturedly. Joanne had mentioned the guest was a lawyer from San Francisco. Normally Kate wasn't prone to judging by first impressions, but Mr.

Grant Richards struck her as stuffy and pompous and arrogant. She had a sudden vision of thinning hair and a belly that barely fit between his lapels.

Dismissing him from her mind, Kate spent the afternoon doing inventory of food and supplies, then turned to sprucing up the rooms upstairs.

In Joanne and Bill's room—the room Kate now occupied—she smoothed a wrinkle in the frayed patchwork quilt that covered the double bed. The quilt had been a wedding gift from one of Joanne's aunts. Over the years, the once-vivid hues had faded and yellowed, but the love Bill and Joanne shared had blossomed brighter than ever. Bill's romantic surprise was an eloquent testimony.

And yes, it struck a pang of envy within Kate.

Hugging a pillow to her breast, she sank down slowly, conscious of a sharp twinge in her chest. Joanne and Bill had the kind of marriage Kate had always wanted for herself—the kind of marriage she'd once been so certain she would someday have. But twelve years had passed since then. Twelve long and lonely years . . .

Kate couldn't help it. All at once she felt very old and very alone, and very much the spinster she was certain everyone thought her.

But she wasn't doomed for maidenhood after all, an insistent little voice reminded her. Derek was publisher of the weekly Gold Beach newspaper; he was dependable and reliable, responsible and respected. It simply wasn't like him to be impulsive or spontaneous. No, she thought with a dark stab of humor. Derek would never do what Ben had done. . . .

There was only one problem. She didn't love Derek the way she had once loved Ben.

CHARLIE'S JET BOAT roared in promptly at four o'clock. Standing on the boat dock, Kate caught the rope Charlie tossed her and wound it around the post. Charlie cut the engine and scrambled to the deck. His passenger followed with far more caution.

Kate took one look at Grant Richards and hastily revised her opinion. Oh, he still might prove to be stuffy and pompous and arrogant, but her prediction ended there. A square jawline, heavy jet brows, gray eyes and a jutting blade of a nose blended into a symmetry that was both elegant and rakishly handsome. Tailored slacks set off narrow hips; she suspected there was no need for padding in the shoulders of his jacket.

Her gaze skipped to her own worn jeans and the oversize plaid shirt she'd shrugged over her tank top and knotted around her waist. A rueful grin tugged at her lips. So Mr. Grant Richards was from San Francisco, eh, she thought. No doubt he'd decided he'd come to Hicksville, U.S.A.

She took a deep breath and stepped forward. "Mr. Richards. I'm Kate Harrison."

"Ms. Harrison."

His voice was low and faultlessly polite. Their handshake was brief and businesslike. Kate took note of the damp splotches on his snowy white shirtfront. "Hit a little rough water on the way, I see."

The newcomer shot a black look at Charlie. "Indeed we did."

Charlie let out a gusty laugh. "You know how it is when you hit a wave the wrong way, Kate. All you can do is duck—Mr. Richards here didn't always duck fast enough." Kate smothered a smile. She had an idea Charlie had had a little fun with Mr. Fancy Pants.

She watched as he transferred a leather suitcase and shiny black briefcase from the jet boat to the dock. He pushed his cap off his lined forehead and straightened. "I'd best be getting back 'fore it gets dark," he said cheerfully. "Anything you need next trip, Kate?"

She shook her head. "Not today, but I may have a list for you next week."

Charlie nodded. "Oh, before I forget, Ann asked me to tell you she's having your mail forwarded. I'll bring it up on my next run along with the other mail for the inn." He jumped into the boat. A flick of his wrist and the engine roared to life; seconds later the boat cut a powerful swath through the water.

Behind her the stranger cleared his throat. "Don't tell me," he intoned with frigid politeness. "He delivers the mail, too?"

"Yes, indeed," Kate said brightly. "Charlie is part mailman, chauffeur and deliveryman, too."

Dead silence greeted her pronouncement. Kate stole a look at his profile. His expression was dark as a thundercloud—it appeared Mr. Grant Richards was a snob on top of everything else. Determinedly ignoring him, Kate reached for his suitcase and briefcase.

She never got that far. Broad, wool-covered shoulders flashed into her line of vision. His hand brushed hers aside. "I'll get those," he muttered.

He straightened. Kate's brows rose at his rigid posture. A snob, she thought again, but at least a gentlemanly one.

Together they started up the grassy slope that led to the inn. Near the top, Grant halted so abruptly that Kate was several paces ahead before she realized he'd stopped. She turned inquiringly and followed the direction of his gaze.

He was staring with ill-concealed distaste at the stocky two-story structure built of massive logs.

Some tiny little devil leaped inside her. She inclined her head and smiled blandly. "Welcome to the Riverbend Inn, Mr. Richards."

He didn't appear to have heard. Indeed, he appeared to have forgotten her. "My God," he said finally, his tone pained. "I feel like I've stepped back a hundred years."

"Why, Mr. Richards, I'll admit the inn is a little rustic. But it has all the comforts of home."

"Is that a fact?" He swore under his breath. "This place is stuck out in the middle of nowhere!"

Her lips quirked. "We're a mere fifty miles from Gold Beach," she demurred.

"There's not even a road to this place!"

"If that bothers you," she told him lightly, "then try to think of it this way—the most direct route is by water." The humor of the situation was just beginning to strike her; not so with Grant Richards.

Inside she had him fill out the guest register, then showed him through the combination lobby, living room and dining room. He was singularly unimpressed by the massive stone fireplace, oak-planked floor and comfortable furnishings. Upstairs on the narrow landing, she told him he could have his pick of the four available bedrooms.

"It doesn't matter which one you put me in," he said grimly. "I may not be staying as long as I expected." Kate shrugged and opened the nearest door. Grant strode through and dropped his suitcase on the double bed, passing only a cursory glance around the room.

Kate wasn't about to linger. "Dinner will be ready in about an hour," she stated coolly.

She'd barely set foot into the kitchen when a clipped voice stating her name gave her a start.

"Ms. Harrison."

She turned slowly. He was leaning against the doorjamb, arms crossed over his chest.

This time he looked downright disapproving.

Kate gritted her teeth and assumed what she hoped was an expression of dutiful patience. "Yes, Mr. Richards."

He came straight to the point. "There's no bath adjoining my room," he pointed out darkly.

"There's no bath adjoining *any* of the rooms, Mr. Richards."

He didn't release her from his accusatory glare. Kate had the uneasy sensation he was counting to ten, maybe even twenty. "I sincerely hope," he remarked in an oh-so-pleasant tone that didn't fool her in the least, "that you're not suggesting there are no bathroom facilities here."

Kate couldn't resist. The devil was back and this time unstoppable.

"Not at all, Mr. Richards. Why, there's an outhouse in the back. But you have to be careful on the way out, because these woods are filled with animals—" her tone was innocence itself "—especially bears."

His stunned silence, brief though it was, was gratifying. But in the instant between one breath and the next, his expression became even more grimly forbidding.

Kate sighed. "Relax, Mr. Richards. The 'facilities' are through the next door on the left past your room."

His eyes narrowed. "Wait a minute," he said slowly. "Surely you aren't telling me what I think you are—"

Kate fought the urge to squirm like a guilty child. "I guess I am." Instead she offered a lopsided smile. "You see there's only one bathroom."

His muttered reply didn't reach her ears, thank heaven. A wealth of unlikely laughter welled in her chest as Kate watched him stalk up the stairs.

It seemed the beast had truly arrived.

Chapter Two

IT WASN'T LIKE GRANT to be so temperamental.

But if he was feeling rather peeved right now, he had a right to be. He paced around his room, finally flinging himself down on the bed.

It was his partner, Chris, who had badgered him into taking this vacation in the first place. He grimaced. As Chris had pointed out, he hadn't taken a vacation since they'd formed their partnership four years ago. Naturally there were reasons for that—they'd been busy courting clients and he'd wanted to make certain the partnership was firmly established. Grant had worked hard to get where he was, and he wasn't about to chuck it all for a few days of fun in the sun.

But Chris had managed to wear him down. According to Chris, he knew the perfect place for a little R&R; he'd even volunteered to take care of all the arrangements. "The Riverbend is the perfect place to get away from it all," Chris had said. "Work will be the last thing on your mind."

And wasn't that the truth, Grant affirmed sourly. Rustic, Kate Harrison had called the inn. He snorted. Hell, it was downright primitive!

He laced his fingers behind his head and glared at the ceiling. Maybe it wouldn't have rankled so if he hadn't actually begun to look forward to this little getaway. He had envisioned a sprawling coastal hotel, white-coated waiters, long hours of lounging beside gleaming sapphire waters of the heated pools, surrounded by a dozen bikini-clad females.

Instead, he'd had a taxi ride that compared to no other. The only pool within sight was the churning waters of the river outside his window—and he knew from experience that the chill of those waters was enough to take his breath away. The only female around was wearing an oversize shirt and faded jeans—and it appeared she was cook, maid and bellboy all rolled into one.

He should have known better, he acknowledged disgustedly. Chris and his wife had spent a week last summer backpacking in Yosemite. In August they'd planned a charter fishing trip in Alaska.

Oddly, it was the smell of something wonderfully aromatic that lured him downstairs again. He wandered into the dining room where Kate had just placed a steaming dish and basket of rolls on the table.

"You're just in time, Mr. Richards. Have a seat and I'll bring the rest in."

Her back was ramrod straight as she sailed by, her tone lukewarm at best. Grant didn't have to ask himself why. He hadn't exactly made a good impression with this pretty lady. And she *was* pretty, he realized suddenly, staring after her as she disappeared through a set of swinging doors into the kitchen. Her hair was the color of rich dark chocolate, waving gently to her shoulders. Her complexion was clear and golden, reminding him of a sun-ripened peach. Oh, yes, he decided when she reappeared. Kate Harrison was very pretty indeed....

All at once Grant wanted very much to rectify the damage he'd done.

"I hope you don't mind the informality," she was saying, "but meals are served family-style." She placed a yellow casserole dish and platter of sliced ham on the table. "Feel free to help yourself, Mr. Richards."

She turned to leave; he reached out and caught her hand. "Wait," he said softly.

Strong fingers curled firm and warm around her own. Kate turned, both confused and disturbed by his gesture. Even her voice was curiously unsteady. "Yes, Mr. Richards?"

His gaze slid to the single place setting at the head of the oak planked table. "Have you eaten yet?"

She shook her head. "I planned to wait until you were finished—"

"I'd feel rather awkward sitting here by myself. Won't you join me?"

If she was wary of his abrupt change in manner, she couldn't help it. She hesitated, wondering if she dared.

"Please."

His tone was very quiet. There was a subtle tightening of his fingers—or did she only imagine it? All at once Kate's nerves were unexpectedly aquiver.

Against all reason—against all instinct—Kate felt herself relenting. "I suppose it wouldn't hurt," she said slowly.

A few minutes later, Grant laid a slice of ham on her plate. A dry smile curled his mouth. "I assume I'm the only guest here."

She nodded. "Most of the inn's guests are white-water rafters. This is actually the first overnight stop just after the wild and scenic section of the river."

"'Wild and scenic'?" he echoed.

"Just a few miles upriver. No motorized craft are allowed," she explained. "Only rafts, canoes, kayaks and so on. The Rogue is actually one of the premier white-water rivers in the country, but it's still a little early in the season for many rafters to brave the rapids right now. Things will pick up in late July and August when the water level is lower. I think there's a party of guides coming through one day next week. The weekend, too, I think."

"Sounds a little adventurous for my taste. Charlie's jet boat ride was hair-raising enough, thank you very much."

Oddly, Kate found herself softening. It was possible, she decided cautiously, that she'd mistaken his shock for disdain. So far at least he hadn't pretended to be Mr. Macho.

"Let me guess—" a faint light appeared in her eyes "—golf is your sport, right?"

His laughter was strangely pleasing to her ears. He held up both hands in a conciliatory gesture. "Guilty as charged." He pushed his cup toward her when she reached for the coffeepot. "You must be pretty lonely if you don't have many guests until July," he remarked.

Kate bit back a smile, thinking of the blessed relief she'd felt at leaving her mother and Ann behind. "I'm afraid I won't be here long enough to find out," she said lightly.

Grant raised quizzical brows.

"The Riverbend belongs to friends of mine, Bill and Joanne Simms. They left yesterday for a trip to Mexico to celebrate their fifteenth anniversary, so I volunteered as temporary innkeeper while they're gone."

She propped her chin on her hand, deciding this was as good a time as any to say what was on her mind. "I have the feeling the inn isn't what you were expecting, Mr. Richards."

She chuckled when he nearly choked on his coffee. Clearly he hadn't expected her comment.

"It's not that it isn't nice," he said quickly. "It's just that in terms of lodging, I was expecting something a little more . . ." He gestured with his hands.

"Spacious, perhaps?"

"Exactly."

"And maybe classy and elegant?"

His sigh was eloquent.

The urge to tease was simply too good to pass up. "It's all a matter of outlook, Mr. Richards. Personally I find the inn rather cozy and homey."

He smiled weakly. "You have to admit, Ms. Harrison, the location is rather remote."

"Remote? Why, not at all! *Secluded* has a much better ring to it, don't you think? Oh, and by the way, in case you're thinking of booking early for next year, Bill and Joanne are planning a little remodeling later this summer to add a couple of bathrooms. That should ease your mind considerably, I expect."

She was laughing at him. Grant didn't mind, though. His gaze encompassed the timbered ceiling and pine paneling. It struck him that he had yet to see a television; he counted his blessings that there was even a phone! Maybe it was the fact that he'd just eaten the best meal he'd had in months, but he was feeling considerably less disillusioned right now.

And she was right—it *was* rather cozy. The overstuffed sofa in front of the fireplace looked like the perfect place to stretch out for an afternoon nap. His eyes returned to Kate, who had risen to take their plates into the kitchen. She bent to retrieve a fork that had fallen to the floor, presenting him with a view that no red-blooded male could ignore. He grinned to himself—the scenery wasn't so bad, either.

She returned with a fragrant wedge of apple pie that made his mouth water. "I can't help but wonder why you bothered to book two weeks here when it obviously wasn't what you wanted. It's usually only the dedicated outdoorsman who does that."

Grant grimaced and explained that his partner, Chris, had made the arrangements for him.

Kate listened quietly. So he hadn't taken any time off for four years. He was obviously very dedicated—or very ambitious. She decided to give him the benefit of the doubt and opt for the former.

"What kind of law do you practice?" she asked.

"Mostly business and corporate law. My partner is a tax attorney."

"I see. And are the two of you good at what you do?"

"The best." He didn't bat an eye.

Kate hailed his proclamation with raised brows. Had she been too quick to absolve him of arrogance? "I suppose everyone's entitled to their opinion," she stated rather coolly.

He was totally unrepentant. "Just being honest."

Obviously humility wasn't his strong suit. Kate's chin went up as her napkin dropped on her plate. Spying the flash in her eyes, he grinned unexpectedly. "That did sound pretty conceited, didn't it?"

Again Kate felt herself relax. "I think 'lofty' will suffice in this case." She chuckled.

He weighed her with a critical squint. "And you always seem to have just the right word tripping off your tongue. Are you an attorney, too?"

She shook her head.

He snapped his fingers. "Let me guess. A journalist."

"Afraid not," she said cheerfully, then smiled. "Although you might say I'm exceedingly well-read."

"I've got it! You're an English professor."

"You're getting warm." She confided that she worked as a librarian at the elementary school in Gold Beach.

Grant hid a smile. Despite the jeans she wore now, he had no trouble envisioning her, her hair swept up, all prim and proper and tucked into a lacy white blouse that buttoned clear to her chin. Nor was he surprised that she worked with children. She possessed a sweet natural honesty that youngsters would undoubtedly find encouraging and reassuring . . . for his part, he was finding it increasingly irresistible!

His second piece of apple pie was gone before she knew it; Kate made a mental note that he liked sweets. He dropped his napkin on his plate, his eyes seeking hers. "That was a great meal," he praised. Kate found his sheepish grin unexpectedly boyish . . . and utterly disarming. "Obviously I don't get fed like this very often. Most of the time I settle for frozen dinners and take-outs."

Kate flushed with pleasure. "Thank you. It's nice to have someone to cook for other than myself." Too late she could have bitten her tongue, certain the admission would make her appear lonely and rejected. . . . Perhaps she was being overly sensitive, but Kate couldn't help it.

Because that's exactly how she'd felt for a long, long time. Useless. Unworthy. And most of all—God, how she hated the word!—unwanted.

But Grant apparently thought nothing of it, and Kate felt the foolish ache in her chest ease.

Amid her protests, he helped her clear the table; he even helped load the dishwasher. It seemed perfectly natural when they ambled back toward the living room. But near the stairs, he paused, and all at once Kate experienced a twinge of disappointment. Tonight hadn't been nearly the ordeal she'd suspected it might be when he'd first arrived.... One thought led to another.... Nor did she want the evening to end so soon....

"I was rude to you earlier. I hope you'll believe me when I tell you how sorry I am."

Kate blinked. Somehow that wasn't what she'd expected him to say.

She shrugged. "It's understandable, considering the circumstances."

"Then all is forgotten? And forgiven?" A single step brought him within inches of her.

She had to tilt her head to be able to meet his eyes; in the back of her mind she compared him to Derek, who was a scant two inches taller than she. It gave her a jolt to note that she was eye level with the sensual curve of Grant's mouth.

She swallowed and jerked her chin upward once more. "I didn't take it as a personal affront, if that's what you're asking."

"Good." His gaze had yet to leave hers. "Because I think now would be the perfect time for me to make amends and start over."

She wasn't certain how to interpret his soft deliberation, or maybe she didn't dare. Consequently, her laugh was a little nervous. "Why, Mr. Richards. Don't tell me you've decided to stay, after all?"

"I have." The resolve in his tone startled her. His eyes delved straight into hers, a deep, searching look that inexplicably sent her heart atumble.

"Aha." She forced a light tone. "Because of the food, I'll bet."

His only response was a husky laugh that was oddly pleasing to the ear. Before she could stop him—before the possibility even crossed her mind—his hand stole upward. His lean fingers shaped themselves against her jawline; the pad of his thumb brushed slowly back and forth across her lower lip. The contact was fleeting and featherlight, almost a caress. Kate caught her breath, seized by a current of sizzling awareness.

"Good night, Ms. Harrison."

"Good night, Mr. Richards."

He withdrew quietly, leaving her standing at the foot of the stairs.

Kate swallowed, her pulse pounding wildly in her ears. Five minutes later, she was still there, conscious of her heart beating a ragged rhythm.

And her lips still tingled where he'd touched them.

SHE REMAINED oddly shaken when she slipped into bed a while later. Try as she might, she had the craziest sensation Grant had wanted to kiss her... crazier still, that she'd have *let* him.

The awareness made her cringe with guilt. She was engaged—not only was she engaged, but her wedding was only two weeks away!

Only to her everlasting shame, she couldn't stop thinking of Grant Richards. Her mind kept up a running commentary despite her best efforts to contain it. A part of her was relieved Grant wasn't the ogre she'd first thought. Still another wished almost desperately that he was, for it would have been so much easier to detest him.

He'd made it far too easy to like him instead.

Maybe, she rationalized cautiously, he'd been sweet and charming and attentive in order to make amends for his bad behavior earlier. Instinct told her he wasn't an insensitive clod; perhaps he'd felt honor bound. And it wasn't as if he'd gone above and beyond the call of duty, going so far as actually kissing her. In fact, maybe she'd been mistaken about that, as well. Kate seized on the notion. She was neither striking nor beautiful. Attractive enough, in a way some might define as cute, but hardly the type to turn heads. Feeling immensely relieved without quite knowing why, Kate thumped her pillow and went to sleep.

She awoke early, showered and went downstairs to put on some coffee. After restlessly pacing the kitchen for several minutes, she slipped out onto the deck. The day promised to be hot and scorching; she was glad she'd chosen shorts and a sleeveless top. Golden sunlight darted through the treetops; a bird issued a strident call to its mate, while the river lapped the rocky shore. Her face turned up to the sun, Kate breathed deeply and let the peace of the moment seep into her bones.

The coffee wasn't quite done when she stepped inside again. Her gaze lighted on a stack of bath towels she'd left in the laundry room; she'd better get them upstairs before Grant woke up. Her steps quick and unfaltering, she hastened to the bathroom and threw open the door.

There was a tall, starkly male form stationed in front of the mirror, outlined in far more detail than she cared to see. Kate's only thought was that the veneered sophisticate fell away with the absence of clothes. In the space of a heartbeat, her mind fleetingly recorded an impressive chest, densely matted with dark curly hair. His biceps looked hard and tight, glistening with tiny droplets of water; clearly Grant Richards didn't spend all of his time cloistered behind a desk. Nor did the bright pink towel wrapped around his hips detract from his presence in the least. He looked raw, sexy and very, very male.

"Ms. Harrison, I seem to have startled you. It must have slipped your mind that the inn only has one bathroom."

Her gaze jerked back to his face, half-obscured by shaving cream. His tone was mild, his eyes alight with dry humor. His calm aplomb only rattled her further. She buried her chin in a fluffy mound of towel and wished she could bury her head, as well.

"Excuse me," she muttered. "I didn't mean to barge in on you like this but I didn't think you'd be up yet.... I thought you might need a...a towel." Obviously he didn't need a towel—he was *wearing* a towel. All hope of dignity abandoned, Kate whirled and slammed the door shut.

It didn't help when he invaded the kitchen ten minutes later, all casual, lazy grace as he propped a shoulder in the doorway. He wore a torso-hugging white golf shirt tucked into perfectly pleated slacks. *Just the decorative touch I need*, she groaned inwardly. She suddenly felt like a limp dishrag and certain she looked it, too. Nevertheless, she directed a cursory glance over her shoulder.

"I hope you like pancakes, Mr. Richards."

"Oh, I think you'll find me relatively easy to please, Ms. Harrison. I'm not very choosy when it comes to food."

Maybe, she agreed silently. But his choice of a vacation getaway was a different story. The thought had no sooner chased through her mind than she felt unaccountably guilty.

"If you have any special likes or dislikes, you'll have to let me know."

He seemed to consider. "Actually," he murmured, "I do have one small request." He paused and went on, "With only one guest, surely there isn't enough to keep you busy the whole day. It might be nice if we kept each other company."

Kate froze. It took an instant for his speech to sink in. When it did, there was no mistaking the hint of suggestiveness in his voice. She whirled to find his gaze appraising the slim length of her legs, revealed by her denim shorts. While his regard wasn't precisely irreverent, there was an undisguised gleam of appreciation.

Her lips firmed. "I see," she murmured, her tone deceptively bland. "And I suppose we could get to know each other in the bargain?"

His eyes warmed. "Frankly, I'd like that. I'd like that very much."

Her jaw closed with a snap. She was suddenly angry with him, but just as furious with herself. Just when she'd decided he wasn't so bad ... She didn't know what was behind his decision to stay. But no matter what his reasons, she wasn't on the list of entertainment!

"I'm afraid I have a busy morning," she said smoothly. "But regardless of how it looked last night, there's plenty to keep the guests occupied."

"I'm all ears, Ms. Harrison."

Kate's gaze sharpened. His expression was mildly amused; she suspected he was mocking her and enjoying himself immensely.

"You may not have noticed, but there's a boathouse down by the dock, with dozens of fishing poles inside. And I know you haven't seen it yet, but there's a tennis court out behind the gazebo—"

He sighed. "There's not much challenge in playing tennis alone, Ms. Harrison."

Kate presented him with her back and jammed a whisk into the pancake batter. "There are also any number of hiking trails near here." She began whipping the batter furiously.

"As someone reminded me only last night, we're in the wilds of Oregon." The laughter in his voice was thinly disguised. "I could get lost."

"Please do," she muttered under her breath. Behind her there was silence. Kate gritted her teeth and turned, prepared to tell him in no uncertain terms that while he might be in the mood for fun and games, she definitely was not.

It gave her a start to find him standing almost directly behind her. A strange sensation trickled down her spine, not entirely pleasant, yet not unpleasant, either. Grant was studying her, not with teasing mockery, or with the infuriating confidence she'd expected to confront. Instead his eyes were unwaveringly direct.

"If I've done something to offend you," he said slowly, "I apologize."

Kate swallowed, painfully aware of their closeness and wishing she weren't. Yet all at once her defensiveness seemed petty and small. It wasn't like her to jump to conclusions—especially the wrong ones.

She had difficulty meeting his gaze. "I'm sorry," she said weakly. "It's just that I thought you were—"

"Making advances a man has no business making to a woman he met only last night?"

This time she didn't mind his teasing. "Yes," she agreed with a shaky laugh. "Especially when that woman happens to be . . ." All at once she faltered.

"What?" he prompted.

Kate glanced down at her hands. "Engaged."

Chapter Three

FOR THE SECOND TIME in less than a day, Grant sprawled on his bed, staring disgustedly at the ceiling.

She'd have been outraged if she'd known what was *really* on his mind.

Grant had never fancied himself a ladies' man; neither was he the type to let a pretty face go unnoticed. But some little-understood emotion deep inside had already recognized Kate as . . . different. He couldn't explain it, except to say she had dominated his thoughts since the moment they sat down to dinner last night.

But she'd thrown him one hell of a curve.

He'd been secretly pleased last night to note she didn't wear a wedding ring—and he'd been looking, no doubt about it. He didn't question that there had been other men in her life; he guessed her to be about his age, in her early thirties. He'd taken it for granted that she was divorced and single again. . . .

She was getting married. *Married.*

He joined her out on the boat dock a short time later. "So. Who's the lucky guy?" His casual tone implied an indifference he was far from feeling.

"His name is Derek," she murmured, watching him ease to a sitting position beside her. "Derek McCormick."

"Known each other long?"

Kate peeked at him from beneath her lashes. A curious shiver ran through her. For all the refined elegance of his features, there was something wholly masculine about him, something that made Kate uncomfortably aware of him as a man.

And just looking at him made her tingle in places she had no business thinking about.

But right now he was staring out at the rippling surface of the river, his jaw tight and clamped. Why did she have the uneasy sensation he was giving her the third degree?

She dipped a bare toe into the water, cautiously testing its coolness—and cautiously testing him. "I've known Derek just over five years. He used to be a sports reporter for the daily newspaper in Portland. We met just after he started up a weekly in Gold Beach."

Grant looked away with a grimace. Great. If her future husband was an ex-sports reporter, it stood to reason he was a jock. He probably pumped iron. Ran laps.

"And just when is this important event taking place?"

Kate's head whipped around once again. Her unease sharpened as she sensed an undercurrent of disapproval. Her eyes slid away, without her being fully aware of it. "The first Saturday in July."

It was Grant's turn to stare. He spoke unthinkingly. "That's only two weeks away! Good God, what on earth are you doing here? Why, I would think that you'd be running around like crazy, trying to make sure everything is done—"

She was on her feet in a flash, her eyes shooting fire. "I have a mother and sister who are determined to handle that, thank you very much. And not that it's any of your business, but Derek understands perfectly why I have to be here."

She was halfway down the dock before Grant caught up with her. He blocked her way, his hands on her upper arms. "Wait," he said quickly. "You're right. It's none of my business. I shouldn't have said anything. And I wasn't judging you, really."

He could feel her fragile bone structure beneath his fingers, the slender curve of her upper arms. The urge to crush her against him was overpowering—he'd do exactly that if he didn't drag himself from temptation's lure this second. He released her and stepped back.

"It's almost noon. I'd take you out for lunch if it were possible, but obviously I can't." A rueful smile tugged at his lips. "But if you don't mind me invading the kitchen, I do make a mean bologna sandwich. You won't have to lift a finger except to eat it, I promise."

A tremor shook her. Grant possessed a charm that eroded her anger as if it had never been. Hard as she tried, she simply couldn't hold on to it. His regret appeared genuine, his apology sincere.

An impish light danced in her eyes. "Not a finger, eh?"

"Not a one," he vowed.

"Well, then, Mr. Richards, lead the way. You just made me an offer I can't refuse."

They started up the grassy path toward the inn. Lunch, Grant thought grimly. He didn't want lunch.

What he wanted was Kate.

HE WAS MORE CERTAIN of it with every hour that passed.

He spent the next few mornings working, or trying to. One of his best clients had requested that the firm study the feasibility of acquiring a small company; his briefcase was stuffed with reports and documents. But Grant's mind wasn't inclined toward business for long.

It was just he and Kate most of the time, so the atmosphere was relaxed and informal. If he was restless, if there was something missing from his life, Grant hadn't admitted it—perhaps he hadn't even recognized it. But now that he'd finally taken some time out solely for himself, he realized he didn't miss the hectic pace of big-city living at all. If anything, it was a relief not to have to confront it.

He liked it here, he realized one lazy Wednesday morning. He liked waking up to the rustling of tree branches outside his window. He liked the quiet, the peaceful serenity, the incredible green of the forest framed by vivid blue sky.

Apparently he'd managed to convince Kate he wasn't the devil incarnate. She dragged him out of bed one morning to see a deer and her fawn daintily foraging just beyond the deck. Later they hiked along the path that paralleled the river, then ate a picnic lunch while a bald eagle held them in its steely stare from atop a lofty tree stump. From a nearby bluff, they held their breath while a daring soul in a kayak shot through a stretch of roaring, twisting white water.

Then there was Kate, his sole reason for staying on at the Riverbend in the first place.

He tried not to think about her upcoming marriage; he constantly reminded himself she belonged to another man. But he was attracted to her in spite of everything. He found her intelligent, witty, engaging—and with a mouth so immensely kissable he went a little crazy just thinking about it.

If he had an ounce of sense, he'd pack his bags and leave—now, while he could forget her. But Grant knew he wasn't going to be wise about this, not wise at all. . . .

But Kate's upcoming wedding wasn't the dream-come-true affair it should have been. Grant sensed it with every instinct he possessed. His younger sister had been walking on air for weeks before she'd been married several years ago. But Kate only talked about it when he persisted, and she was unusually calm and matter-of-fact, hardly bubbling over with joy and excitement the way Liz had been.

He found it odd . . . damned odd.

That very subject was on his mind one night as he sat on the stairs outside one evening, watching the stars appear one by one. Kate was curled up on a chair in the living room, reading. He glanced at her through the double doors that led inside. Her hair was twisted in a loose topknot on her crown. There was a pair of big-rimmed lenses perched on her nose. Both the glasses and her upswept hair lent her a prim, studious air.

The breath left his lungs in a rush. She was such a mass of contradictions. Loose tendrils escaped at her temples and nape, both innocent and sensual. She dangled a slim, bare leg over the arm of the chair, her expression thoughtfully severe. Every so often she popped a ripe strawberry into her mouth from the bowl at her side. Grant longed to pluck those glasses off her dainty little nose, rip the pins from her hair and plunge his fingers into it and let it flow over his hands. But most of all he wanted to plunder the sweetness of her mouth and claim it for his own.

His gut tightened as she intercepted his glance. A hint of a smile pulled at her mouth. She deposited the book and her glasses on the table and joined him outside. Grant eased sideways as if to make room for her; in reality it was simply so he could see her more fully.

"You know I'm still surprised you haven't migrated south by now."

Not a chance, he thought. Aloud he murmured, "Now why would I do that, especially when I'm booked for another week and a half?"

Her lips quirked. "Why else?" she said dryly. "Sheer boredom."

"Ah, but I'm not bored, Ms. Harrison."

She chuckled. "Oh, come on. You're sitting out here alone staring at the stars."

"But I'm not alone anymore." Nor was he staring at the stars any longer, he thought fuzzily. He was staring at her lips, now stained a deep rose. He lingered as long as he dared; reluctantly he lifted his eyes and slanted her a rueful smile. "How do you think I spend most of my evenings?"

"Oh, I don't know." Her pulse had picked up its pace, the way it always did when he was near. "I mean, you're a bachelor. And you know what they say about 'wine, women and—'"

"Kate."

By now Kate was secretly kicking herself. Why had she even said anything? She had no desire to hear about his female conquests, whether one or one hundred. She turned her head slightly and braved a peek at him.

He was smiling, his expression curiously warm and tender. A tingle raced across her skin; she felt all shivery inside.

"I'll admit I'm probably a workaholic. But I'm not a party animal."

"You lead a very mundane existence?"

"Exactly. I usually bring work home with me. And I'm usually in bed by eleven. My partner and his wife like to entertain, though. Of course I have to put in the obligatory appearance now and then. But for the most part, I leave the social scene to them."

Her brows shot up. "You don't strike me as a loner."
The observation slipped out before she could stop it.
"Are you saying you prefer your own company to some-
one else's?"

"Let me put it this way. There are times when I prefer
the company of two—" his eyes found hers through the
darkness "—to a crowd."

He saw her stiffen. The prim, disapproving set of her
jaw nearly set him off, but he didn't dare so much as a
smile. He wouldn't have called her old-fashioned, but he
suspected her morals were strongly rooted in traditional
values. Grant didn't mind. He liked that—he especially
liked it in her. But he had the feeling that just now she'd
mistaken his preference for companionship to be strictly
of the female variety.

"That doesn't mean I have an endless number of
women parading in and out of my home," he amended
quickly.

Unfortunately she detected an undercurrent of laughter and fixed him with a glare. "Then what does it
mean?"

"It means that right now I can't think of anywhere I'd
rather be than right here," he said softly. And then, softer
still, "With you, Kate."

His bluntness caught her off guard. He saw it in the
way her eyes widened. She hastily looked away.

Grant looked his fill.

Kate was disturbingly aware of his regard—she was
disturbingly aware of everything about this man, and in
a way she wasn't always comfortable with. Not for the
first time these past few days, she felt torn in two. Grant
wasn't the cool, cocky lawyer she'd first thought. He was
sweet and funny and surprisingly easy to talk to. And yes,
she was unwillingly drawn to him, but maybe it was be-

cause they'd been together almost constantly. His was the first face she glimpsed in the morning, the last at night. He scarcely set foot outside without asking her to come along, and somehow she always seemed to agree . . . and why, oh why, did her heart always clamor whenever he was near?

"I've embarrassed you, haven't I?"

Her eyes moved slowly back to his. "A little," she admitted. Silence reigned for several seconds before she spoke again. "Grant," she said slowly. "I'm flattered. Really. But you're a very attractive man and—"

"I suppose you think I'm on the rebound. No such luck, I'm afraid."

Kate hesitated. "Surely there must be someone—"

"Someone special?"

"Yes."

Not like you, Kate, he answered silently. *There's never been anyone like you.* His fervency came out of nowhere, but Grant knew his own mind too well to question it.

"I'm not involved in a current relationship, if that's what you're hinting at—" the amusement in his tone deepened "—which means I'm all yours, Kate."

Her glare returned, hotter than ever. "This isn't funny, Grant."

Lord, didn't he know it. "I was married once," he said after a moment.

"You were?" She darted him a surprised glance.

He nodded. "It was just after I graduated from college." He paused, then murmured almost as an afterthought, "We knew almost from the start that it was a mistake. I just didn't have the time to put into a serious relationship, let alone marriage."

"And now you have the time but not the inclination?"

He leaned over and tapped a reproving finger on her nose. "I didn't say that, pretty lady. I didn't say that at all. But I do think it's time we turn the tables on you. How is it Duane didn't have the sense to snap you up years ago?"

Kate sighed. "Derek. His name is Derek."

"Derek, then. How is it you've managed to elude dear old Derek all this time? Or was he the one determined to avoid the altar?"

Her eyes flashed. "As a matter of fact, this is the second time he's asked me to marry him," she informed him tartly. "The first time was nearly three years ago."

"Three years! And you left him dangling all this time? It certainly took you long enough to make up your mind."

He was teasing. Deep inside, she knew Grant didn't mean to hurt her. But that didn't stop the aching flutter of her heart as she heard herself say, "Of course I didn't. I just . . . I just wasn't ready for marriage."

And wasn't that the truth, she acknowledged bitterly. She wasn't one to repeat her mistake, and Ben had torn her self-confidence to shreds. Her wounded heart was far from eager for another bruising. It was years before she was willing to let any man close again. One by one she'd watched her friends get married and have babies; she envied them, resented them and then hated herself for feeling that way.

Oh, she laughed and pretended she was content with her solitary existence. But deep inside, her soul was still bleeding; she despaired that she'd been left behind. Didn't she deserve a chance at happiness, too? For Kate, that meant a home and family—most of all children. But the years had slipped by, and Kate watched her chances grow dimmer and dimmer, prospects fewer and fewer.

In a town as small as Gold Beach, eligible men were at a premium, she acknowledged dismally. She'd finally admitted she was lonely, that her biological clock was fast winding down and soon home and family might be forever beyond her grasp.

And so she'd accepted when Derek asked her to marry him again. He was dependable and safe and reliable, too staunch and upright to do what Ben had done.

Kate would never have consented to marry him if he weren't.

Beside her, Grant had gone very still. The ghostly shadows of the night rippled all around them, but he had no trouble interpreting the hunched tightness of her shoulders, the way she clasped her hands tightly in her lap. Had he inadvertently stumbled upon something here? "Uh-oh," he murmured. "I sense a messy divorce." He paused. "I can see where that might sour you on marriage again—"

"You think this is my second marriage?" She cut him off more sharply than she intended.

His hesitation was fractional. "If I had to guess, I'd say yes."

Her expression went carefully blank. Maybe she'd grown too sensitive through the years. It wasn't so much her age that she was touchy about. But the long absence of a husband in her life was another story. Why, just the day before school was out, Tommy Allison, the terror of the fourth grade, had asked her what a spinster was and then snickered.

She was on her feet without being aware of it. Her laugh was falsely bright, even as she wondered bitterly if Grant had ever been jilted. "I can see why you might think that. It must be my matronly air. After all, it's rare in this day

and age for a woman to reach the age of thirty-four without ever taking the plunge at least once."

He was on his feet, as well. Catching her wrists, he
pulled her before him. "You don't have to make excuses," he stated firmly. "And I wasn't putting you
down, Kate. I swear." The glimmer of reproach in his
eyes warmed; his tone grew low and husky. "Frankly, I
can't believe that you haven't broken your share of male
hearts. Look at me—mine has yet to recover. And when
it comes to marriage, why, I'll bet you've come a lot closer
than you realize."

Close? Her thoughts grew wild and disjointed. She
suspected Grant would be stunned to learn how very close
she'd come to tying the knot. But she couldn't tell him—
she couldn't bear to speak the words aloud. After all this
time, the humiliation was still too great.

She could look no higher than the base of his throat,
bronzed and covered with a bristly tangle of dark masculine hairs. Her bare feet were planted squarely between his. Her mouth had a tremulous set to it that made
her seem young and oddly vulnerable. Grant wanted
nothing more than to wrap his arms around her and
shelter her from any and all harm. Such protectiveness
was unfamiliar to Grant, but hardly unwelcome. Yet he
couldn't banish the niggling feeling that he'd wounded
her somehow.

He couldn't stand the thought.

"Kate," he whispered, and the contrition in his voice
made her throat ache all over again. "I'm sorry. I didn't
mean to hurt your feelings."

"I . . . it's all right."

But it wasn't. The tiny break in her voice wrenched at
his chest. He slipped his knuckles beneath her chin and
guided her eyes to his.

Everything inside him tightened into a knot. He stared at her lips, now stained a deep strawberry red, at the quiver she tried to subdue but couldn't. And he knew he'd just made a very grave mistake in touching her. . . .

Because he was about to do the unthinkable.

Chapter Four

IT DIDN'T MATTER that she was engaged. It didn't matter that they'd known each other only a few days. No force on earth could have stopped him from pulling her close and touching his mouth to hers.

Her lips still carried the taste of strawberries, sweet and fragrant. Her startled gasp echoed in the back of his throat. Grant's heart beat the frantic rhythm of a drum. A white-hot flame raced through him as he brought them together from chest to thigh; her body fitted his as if they'd been made for each other.

There was nothing tentative in his touch. His arm was hard and tight around her back, fingers splayed wide over the span of her waist. At first Kate was too shocked to protest, to even move. This was no sweet, gentle exchange, but the touch of a man who knew what he wanted—and how to get it. He explored her mouth with gentle but thorough demand, stealing her breath, then returning all that he sought in full measure. Kate's hands came up to his chest, as if to push him away. Only to her horror, her fingers slowly uncurled, registering the wiry rasp of body hair beneath the soft cotton of his shirt.

Grant, she thought helplessly. *Oh, Grant, what are you doing to me?*

The fusion of their mouths was unbearably sweet. A strange dark thrill ran through her. The quick, frantic pounding of her heart jolted her entire body. He kissed her long and endlessly deep, over and over. By the time he raised his head, her head was spinning.

There was a heated rush of silence. Grant heard her long, fractured breath and sensed she was grappling for control.

"Why," she asked, an unsteady catch in her voice, "did you do that?"

The hurt confusion in her wide-eyed gaze tore at him. The last thing he wanted was for her to feel guilty. It was better that she blame him rather than blame herself.

He ran a fingertip down her nose, calmed his breathing and forced a lightness he definitely didn't feel. "It was just a kiss, Kate. It's not as if I've taken anything away from dear old David."

It was a moment before the words sank in, but he knew the instant full-blown awareness returned. He braced himself for the storm he knew was about to come.

She didn't disappoint him. "His name is Derek, Mr. Richards. And as long as we're outside, may I suggest a midnight swim in the river? A refreshing little dip might cool you off." She stalked inside.

Kate wasn't just mad, she was steaming—her reverting to "Mr. Richards" from "Grant" was proof positive. *Lady*, he decided with a lazy smile, *that's where you're wrong.*

As far as he was concerned, things were just heating up.

KATE WOKE UP the next morning to the heavenly smell of bacon and coffee . . . and the uneasy sensation that she wasn't alone.

Her eyes flew open. She found herself gazing straight into gray eyes as cheery and bright as the morning sunshine pouring through the window.

"Grant!" she gasped. She frantically rescued the sheet from the tangle around her waist and jerked it to her chin. "What are you doing in here?"

"I would think," he commented dryly, "it's rather obvious."

She glanced at the tray he still held. "That it is. But what I'd like to know is why." She peered at him warily.

"Why does there have to be a reason?" he inquired mildly.

"In this case I think there is!"

"Kate." His sigh was eloquent. "Why are you so suspicious of me?"

Her eyes flashed mutinously. "After what you did last night, don't you think I have a right to be?"

The answer to that could be highly incriminating; wisely Grant kept his silence. Raising the tray slightly, he arched his brows. "If you don't appreciate my earnest efforts, I'll gladly dispose of the evidence myself. So if you don't mind . . ."

Kate eased up the headboard and obediently stretched out her legs so he could place the tray on her lap. She was careful to keep the sheet tucked firmly under her arm. Her T-shirt nightie was hardly provocative, but something inside warned she needed all the protection she could get from those knowingly amused gray eyes.

"You like your coffee black, don't you?"

She nodded, noting there was bacon, fluffy scrambled eggs and toast with raspberry jelly, just the way she liked it. But it was the ruby red rose whose stem was slipped inside a pop bottle that captured her attention the longest.

He smiled rather crookedly. "I'm afraid I couldn't find a vase."

Kate found herself softening. Breakfast in bed...it was impossible to hold on to her anger. And maybe this was Grant's way of apologizing.

Picking up the lime green bottle, she placed the rose on the bedside table, then reached for her fork. The mattress dipped as Grant sat down beside her. Kate ate while he talked, mentioning that Charlie planned to stay the afternoon and show him his favorite fishing hole. Kate bit her lip and struggled not to laugh. She suspected Grant didn't know one end of a fishing pole from the other.

Her breakfast quickly disappeared. Twice Grant reached for her coffee, his lips unerringly finding the spot hers had just vacated. Oddly, she didn't mind the casual intimacy of the action at all. But suddenly Kate was remembering all too vividly what it felt like to have that beautifully shaped mouth against hers. The bacon she was chewing suddenly tasted like dust.

She tried to ignore the peculiar tightness in her middle. So what if Grant had kissed her? It had happened once, but surely it wouldn't happen again.

His embrace last night had left her shaken—it was all she could think about for hours. He'd caught her wholly off guard. Kate didn't understand why she had allowed it to happen. But she couldn't deny there was a part of her that wanted his kiss to go on and on.

She'd never felt like that with Derek. She groaned inwardly. She had scarcely thought of Derek since Grant had arrived. Grant, on the other hand, was on her mind constantly.

Grant. He'd brought her breakfast in bed. It was sweet and touching and romantic, and Kate was suddenly heartstoppingly aware of their position...her *in* the bed...Grant *on* the bed...

He had shaved, she noticed, and smelled of some light, tangy scent. His dark hair was still damp where it blended with the tanned skin of his neck. Next to him, Kate felt tumbled and disheveled and longed to crawl back under the sheet.

"Tell me about this wedding of yours, Kate."

The question, out of the blue as it was, gave her a start. She blinked, her eyes flashing up to meet his. "My wedding? Why on earth would you want to hear about my wedding?"

He shrugged. "Just curious about what you and Dale have planned, I guess."

Kate suppressed a moan. "It's Derek."

"Derek, then." His smile was maddening. "So tell me, Kate. Have the two of you decided to break with tradition? Be married in a hot air balloon, maybe? Whisked away on your honeymoon on twin windsurfing boards?"

The idea of herself—let alone Derek, who was always so sensible and pragmatic—taking part in such an unconventional ceremony provoked a smile; unfortunately, Kate couldn't quite summon the courage to look at Grant when she spoke.

"No such luck," she said with a slight shake of her head. "I guess you could say it's all by the book, starting with a long engagement and ending with a traditional, old-fashioned church wedding."

A strange tightness crept around his chest, like a huge rubber band. "I see," he murmured after a moment. "The works, eh?"

Kate nodded. "As my mother has been telling me for the past six months, every couple deserves a wedding they'll always remember." Certainly *she* deserved it, especially after what Ben had done— She quieted the piping little voice and glanced up, only to find Grant gazing at her, his expression strangely intent.

He tipped his head to the side. "And what about you, Kate? What kind of wedding do *you* want?"

Kate inhaled slowly. "I want . . . the wedding I've dreamed about since I was a little girl." The wedding she'd been cheated of a dozen years earlier. "A big wedding party—a flower girl, bridesmaids wearing long, flowing dresses . . . a church crammed full of people and flowers everywhere . . . 'The Wedding March' playing . . . my dad beaming as we walk up the aisle, my mom holding back tears because she's thinking of her own wedding—because she knows it's the most precious moment of my life . . ."

She'd laid down her fork and was staring at the plate. Grant had the oddest sensation she was a million miles away. "I've waited a long time for this—" her tone was soft yet almost fierce "—and I can't let anything go wrong. I just *can't.*"

Strangely, Grant found her speech highly disturbing. He hadn't missed the wistful yearning in her voice, a yearning that had given way to a resolve that didn't quite reconcile with the woman who sat before him now. Kate had just described her dream wedding; in less than two weeks she would *have* that dream wedding.

So why wasn't she wildly ecstatic about her upcoming nuptials? Where was the radiant glow of a woman madly in love with her future husband? Instead, there was something almost pleading in the gaze that meshed slowly with his.

Embarrassment quickly followed. Grant had no trouble deciphering the dismay that flitted over her face—she had divulged too much . . . and realized it too late.

Something wasn't right. Grant was more certain of it than ever. Despite Kate's little-girl dreams, he couldn't shake the feeling that this wedding wasn't at all what she'd hoped for. Unfortunately, he decided, now was not the time to press her.

Nor, declared an insistent little voice inside that he despised, did he have the right.

Finished at last, she dropped her napkin on the tray. Her laugh was rather shaky as he set it aside. "You know, I've taken my parents plenty of breakfasts in bed on Sunday mornings, but this is the first time I've been on the receiving end—and it isn't even Sunday." Her fingers twisted in the sheet. Her eyes held his. "Thank you," she said softly.

Her lips were curved in a hint of a smile, a smile that sparked tiny golden lights in her eyes. Grant felt his control scatter to the winds. *Scruples be damned*, he thought. *Her wedding be damned*.

"I can think of a better way to thank me," he said huskily. Her eyes mutely questioned; he tapped a forefinger to his lips.

Dead silence followed. "I can't," she said at last, her tone very low. "Grant, please don't ask me to." Inside she winced. Good Lord, had he forgotten so quickly that they'd just been discussing her *wedding?* How could he torment her like this?

The naked distress he glimpsed on her face stabbed him. But Grant was a man who had always been true to his own heart; despite his best intentions, this was no exception.

"You're still upset about last night, aren't you?"

"No, but . . . it can't happen again, Grant."

He focused on the lovely curve of her mouth. "Why not?"

"You . . . you know why."

He picked up her hand where it lay on the sheet. His palm was warm and rough as he splayed his fingers against hers, palm to palm, fingertip to fingertip. The sight of his hand, so much bigger and darker than hers, made her feel small and fragile and unusually feminine.

"What I know is this, Kate." He spoke quietly, almost whimsically. "I see a classic case of boy meets girl. Boy likes girl—girl likes boy. They share the inevitable first kiss and—" he snapped his fingers "—there's this explosion of fireworks inside both of them. He knows she's different from any other woman he's met. She knows he's special like no other man." His tone deepened to huskiness. "I'd say they have no choice but to follow the logical sequence of events to its natural conclusion."

Kate trembled. How could he know it had been like that for her? He might have pulled that very thought from deep in her soul. But had it really been like that for him, too? She was both elated and disturbed. Whatever he was suggesting—and she wasn't sure she wanted to know—he made it sound so simple. Only it wasn't simple at all!

His gaze, both avid and tender, rested on her flushed cheeks. "Do you know what I'm thinking right now?" he asked softly.

She shook her head. Speech was impossible.

"I'm thinking the second kiss is bound to be even better than the first."

With that, his lips took possession of hers, gently persuasive, warmly tormenting. Deep within her, a slow curl of heat unfurled, unlike anything she'd ever experienced. She knew she should stop him. But Lord help her, no other man had ever affected her like this. Not Derek.

Not even Ben. Nothing, she thought dizzily, had ever felt so wonderfully right.

"You see?" He released her, his laugh as unsteady as her breath. "Each one better than the last. I think that's something to look forward to, don't you?"

Kate moaned. "Don't say that. Don't even think it!"

"Why not?"

"Grant, I—I like you." She expressed the only emotion she dared. "But I can't let this happen."

You can't stop it, either. He relived the sweet clinging of her lips against his. He hadn't mistaken her response, the stark pleasure, the soft hunger in her eyes. And he didn't bother hiding it in his.

Kate's heart beat raggedly. She resisted the urge to scramble back against the headboard. "Stop looking at me like that!" she cried.

The message in his eyes grew wantonly daring. And he was smiling—*smiling!* Was this only a game to him?

"Grant," she cried desperately. "I'm engaged. You may be unencumbered but I'm not!"

Unencumbered. Her choice of words made him smile. Only Kate would think to put it like that.

"You said it yourself, Kate." His tone was one of utter patience. "You're engaged. Correct me if I'm wrong, but that means you're not yet married."

He leaned forward. Kate reached out to stop him. The feel of his bare arms sent a jolt of pleasure through her. "That doesn't leave me fair game for you!" she managed to gasp.

He was totally unrepentant. "Oh, yes, it does. Innocent until proved guilty. Free and unencumbered," he stressed pleasantly, "until lawfully bound as husband and wife."

His expression, his entire demeanor, exuded satisfaction. Oh, he was so glib, so smooth. And only the mind of a lawyer could be so...so technical!

"Grant," she implored desperately, "why are you doing this? You don't really want me, you know you don't—"

"That's where you're wrong," he stated boldly. "I *do* want you. And I think if you're honest with yourself, you'll admit you want me, too."

"But this is so sudden," she blurted out.

His grin was disarmingly audacious, but there was something in his features that warned he was deadly serious. "I know," he said. "But I also know how I feel, Kate. And I've never been one to back down because of a few obstacles—in this case, only one."

He meant Derek. Kate didn't know whether to laugh or cry. Damn him, anyway, she fumed. Oh, how could he be so casual about this? He had no right to turn her world upside down, no right at all!

"You don't play by the rules," she accused, her gaze lifting as he rose lithely to his feet.

"No," he agreed. "I play to win."

He was whistling as he left her alone. He suspected he'd just thrown her a curve she hadn't expected. But it was just as he'd told her; it didn't matter that they'd known each other only a matter of days. Grant was more certain of his feelings for Kate than he'd been of anything in a long, long time. Call it crazy—call it outrageous.

Call it love.

FOUR DAYS LATER, Kate was thoroughly unnerved. Every time she turned around Grant was there, so ruggedly handsome that he took her breath away. They'd grown comfortably familiar with each other, though he teased her unmercifully about the single bathroom—more to the point, that there was no need for them to alternate who used the shower first in the morning. But beneath his teasing was a caring, sensitive man who was secure enough in himself and his masculinity not to be concerned that it showed.

With every day that passed, she discovered it harder and harder to balance her loyalty to Derek against her blossoming feelings for Grant. Was this a case of prewedding jitters? A nagging little voice inside whispered that she was marrying Derek for all the wrong reasons...or was she? Was it wrong to want someone to hold her? Someone to ease the loneliness of the endless nights she'd spent so alone all these years? Was it wrong to want someone to love her?

Her mind strayed often in this direction. But to her dismay, the face conjured up by her subconscious wasn't Derek's at all....

It was Grant's.

Kate was utterly mortified. And ashamed. Night after night she closed her eyes and tried to picture Derek. But all she could see was Grant—Grant laughing at the dinner table...his mouth, so smooth and hard, hovering over hers...

She could lie to herself no longer. Something was happening. Something she wasn't prepared for.

Something she couldn't stop.

Tuesday afternoon found her in the kitchen, stowing the last of the breakfast and lunch dishes in the cupboard. Several groups of white-water rafters had stayed at the inn the past two nights; she was a little surprised at how much work there was with the addition of only four people. But Grant was virtually her right hand, helping with everything from laundry to meals and cleanup, though Kate had told him that it wasn't necessary.

In the living room, she heard the sliding glass door open. Every nerve in her body quickened, pinpointing the exact moment Grant approached. He said nothing; he didn't have to. Quiveringly aware of his presence behind her, she closed the silverware drawer and turned to face him. He was leaning against the door frame, his pose nonchalant.

His smile made her heart turn over. "Just think, Kate. Everyone's finally gone." His eyes warmed to intimacy—and so did his tone. "It's just the two of us again."

Kate took a deep breath. "Grant," she pleaded, "you shouldn't say things like that."

He moved slower. "Why not, Kate? Oh, I see the warning in your eyes—I read it loud and clear. Hands off. No trespassing. But don't you know—" he stopped mere inches away "—it only makes me want you all the more?"

The air was suddenly close and heated. Kate wondered if he knew what that velvet tone did to her insides. A shiver traveled along warm, forbidden places. He touched her nowhere, but she felt as if he did.

She managed a shaky laugh. "Are we back to that unswerving honesty of yours again?"

He smiled crookedly. "Something like that," he murmured. His eyes snared hers, piercingly intent.

Kate did the only thing she could. She turned her back on him and grabbed the dishcloth, frantically swiping the counter, frantically praying he would go away.

He didn't. The graze of pleasantly rough fingertips slipped beneath the fall of her hair, baring her nape to the heat of his breath. Before Kate could whirl around, he kissed the back of her neck.

Kate moaned. "Grant! You can't go around kissing me all the time!"

His hands were on her shoulders; she was turned bodily into his embrace. "Then you kiss me," he stated brashly. "It's very simple, Kate. Here, I'll demonstrate." He caught her hands and dragged her arms up and around his neck. "There, now. All you have to do is lift your mouth, just a little, and touch your lips to mine."

"Grant—" She drew in a startled breath. There was no time for more. Her chin came up a fraction, the same instant his descended.

Their lips met and clung. Her limbs turned to butter. As if she had no will of her own, blatantly sensual images tumbled through her brain. Kate tried to close her mind against them—she tried desperately to close her mind against *him,* but it was no use. She needed no urging to keep her mouth fused to his, right where they both wanted it.

It was a long time later before his head finally lifted. "Nice," he whispered, his lips lingering. "Very nice."

Kate's thoughts were suddenly wild and disjointed. She wished he would leave. Now. Today. She wished he would pack up and take himself back to San Francisco where he belonged. His kiss aroused something she'd never before experienced. Passion and excitement and danger.

Danger. Alarm bells went off in her brain. She didn't want danger, she told herself frantically. She wanted safety and security, a man like Derek, reliable and solid as a rock. She shivered, suddenly almost frightened. In his own way, Grant Richards was the most dangerous man she had ever met.

But she knew if he left, she would miss him...miss him terribly.

She swallowed painfully. "This is wrong," she said jerkily. "Grant, I . . . you have to stop this . . . *we* have to stop it." She pushed herself back.

His hands released her, but not his eyes. "If it's wrong," he said gently, "why does it feel so right?"

Kate fell silent. Dear God, she thought bleakly. She'd been asking herself that very question for days already. And she had yet to find the answer.

Grant battled a surge of frustration. He wasn't a quitter, and he wasn't about to become a failure at this late date—especially not now, when there was so much at stake, more than ever before. Maybe, he decided grimly, it was time he began to fight harder for what he wanted.

But how did one woo and win a woman about to marry another man?

Kate felt something for him, he thought fiercely. She would never let him touch her if she didn't. And she was wearing down. He could feel it in the way her arms clung tightly to his neck, the way her lips trembled and yielded so sweetly beneath his.

There was only one problem. He had less than a week to win her over.

"You don't belong with him, you know."

Startled, Kate glanced up at him. She was stunned to note that all trace of teasing had fled his manner. For all that his voice held a note of something curiously like whimsy, his expression was utterly determined.

Her heart sank; she shifted uneasily. "I don't know what you—"

"Oh, yes, you do, Kate. You don't belong with Derek and you know it."

She wet her lips, wondering how she could possibly change the subject. "Well, well." Her laugh sounded high-pitched and nervous. "You finally got his name right." She decided to duck around him. "If you'll excuse me, I need to—"

His strong hands grabbed her shoulders. "Oh, no, Kate. You're not going anywhere until we hash this through once and for all." He pushed her into a chair near the table.

"Now," he said calmly. "Let's get on with this."

"Let's not," she snapped.

He leaned back against the counter and crossed his arms over his chest. Kate glared at him, feeling for all the world like a first-grader who'd just been sent to the principal's office.

"Kate, you don't have to pretend with me. If you loved Derek, you'd be in Gold Beach with him, not fifty miles away... and here with me."

She flinched at the pang of guilt that knifed through her. "I'm here because I'm doing a favor for a friend," she said evenly.

"No," he challenged flatly. "You're here because you want to be. You're here because you're running. And it doesn't take much to figure out you're running from Derek—probably because you don't love him."

"Of course I do!" she defended herself heatedly.

"Do you? Tell me, then, Kate. Tell me how much you love him."

The atmosphere was suddenly stifling. Grant saw too much, and at that moment, Kate bitterly resented him for it. She forced her lips to move, but the words she struggled to find simply wouldn't come. "I—I love Derek," she managed after what seemed an eternity. "I do!"

"Honey, you don't sound very sure of it—" his harsh laughter grated "—and that's supposed to convince me?"

Kate floundered. She was comfortable with Derek. It was true that professions of love had never come easily, but Derek didn't expect mushy sentimentality. And if he was not outwardly demonstrative, she had accepted it, because their relationship was founded on mutual friendship and respect. That was enough to build a marriage on . . . wasn't it? *Wasn't it?*

All of a sudden Kate was no longer certain at all. God help her, she wasn't. She had never considered she might be marrying the wrong man.

Until now.

"I suppose now you're going to tell me how much you've been pining away for him, how every day apart from him is an eternity."

Kate's spine went rigid. "There's no need to be sarcastic. And you don't know anything about it, Grant—you don't know *me*."

"Oh, no? Well, answer this for me, Kate. If it's Derek's arms you're so eager to have around you again, why is it you don't seem to mind being in mine?"

An icy wave of shock flooded her; hot shame quickly pursued. In some distant corner of her mind, she knew it was a low blow—and so did he. He cursed himself when her eyes, wide and stricken and betrayingly moist, locked with his.

"I didn't chase after you," she cried. "Grant, you know I didn't!"

He caught her when she would have charged past him. His arms came around her, engulfing her, bringing her shaking body tight against his. God, how he hated himself for doing this to her!

"I know you didn't." He buried his chin in the dark cloud of her hair. "Kate, I shouldn't have said that. I'm sorry. But I . . . oh, hell! Something's not right. I've known it since the day you told me you were engaged. You just don't look like a woman with stars in her eyes, who can't think of anything but love and marriage and the man she intends to share the rest of her life with—the man who's about to make her dreams come true."

She jammed a fist against his chest. "You told me yourself that your marriage was a mistake right from the start! What makes you such an authority?"

"I know." His eyes darkened. "Believe me, I know." He hooked his fingers beneath her chin so that she had no choice but to confront him.

But before he could say a word, someone knocked on the sliding glass door in the living room. Two pairs of eyes swiveled toward the sound. It came again, this time accompanied by a male voice.

"Kate? Kate, are you in there?"

A feeling akin to shock washed through her. "Oh, my God," she said faintly. "It's Derek."

Chapter Five

HE'D JUST STEPPED INSIDE when Kate rushed through the doorway. "Derek!" she cried. "Why didn't you let me know you were coming?" Too late she despaired the welcome of her greeting. Her face felt as if it would crack into a million pieces. She marveled that she was able to summon a smile at all.

He pressed a cool, brief kiss on her cheek. "Kate," he murmured. His gaze flickered past her to Grant.

Grant was busy sizing up the competition and wishing he hadn't. Kate's fiancé was blond, with even, attractive features. He was no giant, but his built was sturdy and trim.

Kate had stationed herself between the two men. She could feel Grant behind her, silently assessing, coldly disapproving. Would he make a scene? A hasty glance over her shoulder eased her fear, but only slightly. Grant's expression was impassive but she disliked the glitter in his eyes. Wishing she could disappear through the floorboards, she introduced the two men.

"Gr—Mr. Richards is vacationing here from California," she finished brightly.

Grant found his hand grasped into a loose handshake. The pleasantries were exchanged with Kate's anxious eyes bouncing between the two men. Grant found himself admitting that Derek appeared friendly and easygoing. He was, Grant decided grudgingly, probably one heck of a nice guy. No doubt Derek would probably make some woman a good husband.

But not Kate. *Please, not Kate.*

It was only after several pointedly directed glances from Kate that Grant could find it in himself to leave the two of them alone. He reluctantly excused himself and wandered outside.

Derek cleared his throat. "I won't be staying long," he said, stuffing his hands into his pockets. It struck Kate that he had yet to fully meet her gaze.

A vague flicker of unease ran over her skin. "Derek?" she murmured. "Is something wrong?"

Derek ran his fingers through his hair. "Oh, hell," he muttered. "There's no easy way to approach this, so I might as well just come out with it." He heaved a long sigh. "Kate, I don't know how else to say this. But I think we'd be making a big mistake if we go through with this wedding."

The world seemed to freeze. Kate couldn't move—she couldn't even breathe. She felt the way she had when she'd fallen off a swing when she was six, flat onto her back, the wind knocked from her lungs.

"What are you saying?" Her voice was scarcely audible; she had to struggle to force it past the constriction in her throat. "That you want to call it off?"

He nodded. "I've had a lot of time to think lately. Kate, we've known each other a long time. Maybe we've grown too complacent. Maybe we just felt we had to do what everyone expected. To tell you the truth, I've known for a while that something's missing...." His expression revealed his regret. "Kate, I don't mean to hurt you. But I think we're better off friends than husband and wife."

Kate sank down onto a chair. *This can't be happening*, she thought fuzzily. *Not again*.

She was dimly aware of Derek hovering. If only she could tell him she was secretly relieved. But all she could think was that this was her worst nightmare come true. *It's just like with Ben....* A wrenching pain ripped through her. *Just like with Ben*.

Her control was deceiving. Inside she felt he'd landed a blow at the very center of her heart. "It's all right," she said faintly. "I've had some doubts myself."

He looked vastly relieved. "Kate, I think you should know I've had a job offer from the *Oregonian* in Portland. I'm almost certain I'll take it but I need to leave to finalize the offer this weekend. I'll phone my side of the guest list, of course. But if you need any help with the rest of the cancellations, I'll be glad to—"

She rose to her feet without conscious volition. "Thank you, anyway, Derek, but there's no need. I'll manage." She sounded stilted and formal, nothing at all like herself. She winced at the fleeting guilt that crept into his eyes. She truly wasn't trying to shame him, but further understanding was beyond her right now.

She saw him to the door, her eyes so dry that they hurt. She even watched as he reached the dock, where Charlie still waited with the jet boat. The engine sounded very far away as it roared to life.

How long she stood there, she didn't know. Everything inside her seemed to shrivel up and die. The sunlight bathing the room in a golden haze was suddenly obscene. She shivered, cold to the marrow of her bones.

That was how Grant found her. The day was blazingly hot, but her arms were wrapped around herself, as if she were freezing. A tingle of foreboding inched up his spine.

He touched her shoulder. Her head jerked up. Their eyes collided for only a split second, but one look at her pinched, white features was like a fist to the gut.

He spoke her name sharply. "Kate. What is it? What did he say to you?" She shook her head and would have jerked away, but he caught her by the shoulders.

"Kate, talk to me! Tell me what's wrong!"

Her gaze moved slowly, inevitably, back to his. He saw the way her throat worked. Her voice emerged high pitched and quavering. "It looks like there isn't going to be a wedding on Saturday, after all."

"Good Lord! You mean he called it off?" Grant's fierce leap of joy died a swift death as Kate nodded miserably.

He blanketed both her hands firmly within his. "Kate," he said gently. "Maybe it's better this way."

Her eyes blazed. "Don't spout platitudes to me, Grant Richards! Oh, I know what you're going to say. You'll assure me it's not the end of the world. Or if I just wait a little longer, there's some wonderful guy out there just waiting to sweep me off my feet." She jammed her fists against his chest. "Well, I'm tired of waiting! Do you hear? And for God's sake, don't tell me it'll get easier. Because it doesn't. Believe me, I know. It doesn't get easier, it just gets harder and harder, day after day, year after year. So just . . . just don't say a word, because I've heard it all before!"

She'd stunned him by her outburst. She glimpsed it in his puzzled frown.

Her laugh was bitter. "I keep forgetting. You don't know all about Kate Harrison, spinster librarian of Gold Beach, do you?"

Grant's insides twisted into a sick, ugly knot. Snatches of memory paraded through his mind. He remembered how susceptible she'd seemed the night he mistakenly assumed she'd been divorced, her touchiness about the fact that she'd never been married. A crazy notion spun through his brain—no, not so crazy, after all. It made such perfect sense that he wondered how he'd been so blind.

"Kate," he said unevenly. "You don't have to do this—"

"You might as well know the whole sordid story, Grant. Everyone else does, so why not you, too?"

This time when she pulled back, he made no move to stop her.

Her voice came jerkily. "Remember the night you told me you'd been married? You said I must have come close. Well, you were right," she announced in a high, tight voice. "I *did* come close, nearly a dozen years ago. Why, I managed to get all the way into the church. But there's this tricky little catch when it comes to weddings, you see. There just can't be a ceremony without the groom, and this particular groom decided to head for parts unknown the morning of the wedding."

Grant couldn't hide his shock. "Good God. Don't tell me he—"

"Yes." The ragged breath Kate drew burned her lungs. "Dear old Ben neglected to tell me, his blushing bride-to-be, that he'd gotten cold feet. Right about the time the minister should have been saying 'Dearly beloved,' Ben was packing his bags and leaving town."

Grant swore silently. If "Dear old Ben" had been there before him, he'd have taken great pleasure in tearing him apart.

"I'll never forget standing in the back of the church, waiting, wondering what was keeping Ben. At first I thought there'd been an accident. My father and I waited . . . and waited. And then everyone kept looking back and staring." Her voice grew raw. "I kept trying not to panic, trying not to think what everyone else was thinking. But deep down inside, I already *knew* . . . God, it was awful. The church was packed. Half the town was there . . . all my friends . . . my parents' friends. . . ."

Grant had no trouble envisioning Kate as she must have been that long-ago day. For an instant he saw a young girl, yards and yards of satin and lace cascading around her, radiant and glowing and certain nothing could ever go wrong . . . and then later, humiliated and shamed, her hopes dashed like shattered glass.

Kate fought a valiant battle with runaway emotions and lost. "I could hardly look anyone in the eye for months afterward. I felt so useless and unworthy. Abandoned." She cried out her outrage and heartache. "I never understood how Ben could do that to me . . . what went wrong . . . I used to wonder if he didn't love me enough . . . if he *ever* loved me.

"It's easy for you to say it's better this way," she announced suddenly. "That it shouldn't matter what people say. But it does. Oh, I can just hear it now. 'There goes Kate Harrison. She's been jilted twice, you know— twice! The only way she'll get any man to the altar—and make him stay—is to slip a noose around his neck.' "

The anguish in her voice cut him to ribbons. "Kate," he said hoarsely. "Don't do this." He reached for her but she eluded his touch.

"No, Grant! You know this much, you might as well know the rest. Do you have any idea what my life has been like? How hard it is to run into old friends? Most of them have kids who are half-grown! Do you know how jealous I am when I see my sister and her husband together, how guilty I feel afterward? Do you know it tears me up inside to hold my two-year-old niece?"

She hauled in a deep shuddering breath. "My sister and I used to stage backyard weddings when we were kids. The neighbor kids played dress-up and came to watch. We lined up chairs on the patio and put dandelion chains over a dishtowel so my sister, Ann, could use it as a veil. Only I was older. Taller. So I always ended up playing the groom. I was never the bride...*never the bride*...I used to feel so cheated. God, I still feel that way!"

Her cry verged on anger. "All I ever wanted was a husband and family who loved me, children of my own— a baby of my own. If it doesn't happen soon, I'll be too...too old. I feel like I'm being punished—and I don't even know why!"

Tears were streaming down her face, tears he suspected she wasn't even aware of. Grant's chest grew achingly tight, knowing she was in so much pain.

And in that moment, her pain was his...it always would be.

He pulled her shaking body into his arms. She stiffened, palms against his chest. "Don't, Grant. Don't touch me. Don't be nice...not now."

"I want to. I have to."

"You only feel sorry for me."

He smiled at her teary-eyed defiance. "I'm sorry something so terrible happened to you, yes. But I'm not sorry that you told me. I'm not sorry that I'm here with you now." He dragged her palm against his cheek; his skin was pleasantly rough beneath her fingers. "Let me take care of you, Kate. Let me hold you. I want that— very much."

She felt she would break inside from the gentleness of his voice. "You don't. How could you? No one else does. Not Ben. Not Derek. Oh, God, Grant, what's wrong with me?" Her voice broke. "Why... why doesn't anyone want me?"

Her jagged sob tore into his heart. In that instant, Grant could no more deny his need than he could her stricken plea.

His arms tightened. "You're wrong," he whispered, a low rough catch in his voice. "Because I want you, Kate. And if you'll let me, I'll do more than just tell you." He pulled back to search her face. "I'll show you."

HIS QUIET INTENSITY penetrated where nothing else could have. They were tender, those arms, and strong and secure, a haven that offered sanctuary from both past and present.

His lips were unbelievably tender as he kissed her temple, the curve of her cheek, the quivering pink lips she couldn't withhold. At last he drew back and weaved their fingers together in a burning handclasp. His eyes never left hers as he brought their joined hands up between their bodies.

His lips brushed her knuckles. "Let me, Kate." His whisper betrayed a rough thread of hunger and need. "Let me show you how much I want you."

The tenderness in his eyes stole her breath. Kate didn't pretend to misunderstand what Grant was asking. He wanted to make love to her—to *her*. The very idea made her go all weak and fluttery inside. And all at once Kate didn't want to consider whether it was right or wrong. All the reasons why she shouldn't allow this to happen quickly fled her mind. Grant was here, with her. And right now, nothing else mattered.

Wordlessly, she gave him her answer. She wrapped her arms around him and clung as if she'd never let go.

She had little memory of Grant leading her up the stairs to his room. The next thing she knew she was standing beside his bed; sunlight dappled the spread. Awareness flitted in with the suddenness of a light switch going on at midnight.

She, Kate Harrison, was about to make love with a man for the very first time in her life. And it wasn't going to be as she'd always imagined, a breathless exchange half veiled in shadows and darkness, but in a room awash with golden streamers of sunshine. A flurry of panic gripped her mind. Would Grant know? Would he care? And ... oh, Lord, what if he decided he didn't want her, after all?

"Kate." His hands settled on her waist. He nibbled on the slender grace of her neck. "You haven't changed your mind, have you?"

She clung to him and shook her head; it was all she could manage.

His head came up. "Thank God," he whispered. Their lips almost touched but not quite. "Because I think I'd die if you did." His fervency shook her all over again. Her breath caught at the naked heat that flamed in his expression.

This time his kiss was long and deep, endlessly searching. He kissed her as if he were starved for the taste of her. The warmth of his hands and mouth drove out the cold emptiness in her soul. Her apprehension fled as if it had never been.

Her senses were spinning wildly when he finally released her mouth. He rested his forehead against hers, his laugh as unsteady as his breath. "Do you have any idea what you do to me? You've had me turned inside out since the day we met."

Kate bit her lip, her fingers absently toying with the top button on his shirt. "Grant." She swallowed, her tone very low. "You don't have to say that. Just because we're here—" her eyes grazed his, then flitted away "—like this, doesn't mean I expect to be showered with compliments."

"I'm not telling you what I think you want to hear, Kate. I'm telling you what I feel." He studied her. "You've been hurt—I know that. Maybe the timing for this is a little off. And maybe it's selfish of me, but so help me, I don't regret what happened today with Derek because it's brought you here—" he captured her hand and pressed a fervent kiss in her palm "—with me." His eyes darkened. "I want you, Kate. I want to make love to you, and I'm not ashamed to admit it."

Until that moment, Kate hadn't realized how desperately she longed for Grant to say those very words. For days she'd been fighting her feelings for Grant. But no more. *No more.*

For the second time in just a few short minutes, Kate clung to him, her throat achingly tight. Framing her face in his hands, he kissed her with tender gentleness. His hands coasted to the hem of her lightweight cotton top; a soft blush suffused her cheeks as he whisked it over her head, but she didn't turn away. And when he applied eager fingers to the buttons of his own shirt, hers were there to help.

He left no room for modesty or shyness. His fingers streaked over her bare skin, leaving heat and fire wherever he touched. When the last barrier of their clothing was no more, his fingers scaled the slopes of her shoulders. With a muffled groan, he brought her against him so they were welded together from chest to knees, her breasts nestled into the dark fur on his chest.

The scalding friction of skin against skin was almost
more than Kate could bear. Her heart beat high in her
throat as she felt the rigid heat of male arousal, pressed
heavy and tight against the hollow of her belly. Then all
thought scattered as he bore her gently to the bed.

He stretched out beside her, bringing her so they lay
face-to-face. His eyes were fiercely glowing. "God,
Kate." Her name was half laugh, half groan. "I've been
going slowly insane these last few days. I've been so
damned afraid...."

There was an odd catch in his voice. Her fingers traced
the hardness of his mouth, gently seeking. "Why?" she
asked softly.

"Because I didn't think you could possibly feel the
same way I did. Because I didn't think this would ever
happen. I was afraid you wouldn't *let* it happen. Lying
here night after night, knowing you were in the next room
with only that damned bathroom between us—Lord, it's
been driving me slowly crazy!"

The hungry heat tightening his features—the longing
he revealed so openly—both thrilled Kate to the tips of
her toes. For so long now she'd been empty and
alone... only half alive, half a woman. But Grant made
her yearn to experience all she had missed—all she had
longed for.

A blunted fingertip traced the length of her collar-
bone. "You're so pretty," he whispered. Kate trembled. Her soul rejoiced. He made her feel special.
Beautiful and cherished. Above all, so desirable that it
was as if she were the only woman on earth.

In some shadowy corner of her mind, she wondered if
this was why she'd held off making love with first Ben,
and then Derek. With Ben, she'd wanted everything to
be perfect, including their wedding night—she'd wanted

to come to her husband a virgin. Derek had been gently coaxing at times, but never insistent.

But with Grant . . . oh, Lord, it *was* perfect. Nothing had ever felt so right or so good. He'd opened the door to a world she'd thought forever barred to her. Being here in his arms was like coming home after a long, long journey.

His gaze swept the length of her; his fingers marked the path his eyes had taken. He slowly graced the peak of first one breast, and then the other, a tauntingly evocative rhythm. Her breath tumbled out in a rush. "So pretty," he murmured again.

His mouth slid with slow heat down her throat. Farther . . . even farther. Her nipples tightened, alive with a painful sensitivity that surpassed anything she'd ever known. Sharp needles of sensation pierced through her when the rough velvet of his tongue came out and touched the aching tip of one breast.

His touch was both bold and torrid, gentle and tender as he made the secrets of her body his own. He invited her exploration, as well, guiding her hands to the hair-roughened plane of his chest. At first Kate felt awkward and shy, but soon her hands grew even more daring. Hearing the ragged tremor of his breath, the pounding of his heart beneath her hand, Kate was filled with a heady sense of power, unaware that she tested the very limits of his control until he could stand it no longer.

Palms beneath her, he bound their hips together. "Look at me, Kate." He wanted her to see him. He wanted to make certain it was his face she saw in her dreams—that thoughts of no other man dared intrude on this moment.

His dark whisper compelled compliance. Helplessly, she met his gaze, knowing hers was glazed and smoky with desire. She was trembling, she realized, but so was he.

"You want me, don't you, Kate? I want to hear you say it—I need to hear you say it." His eyes shone with a fierce, possessive light, but the words were both a demand and a plea.

"I want you," she gasped. Her fingers dug into the binding of his arms. "Now Grant. *Please*."

His control shattered. He surged inside her, swift and deep. But the impact of his entry was a shock; though Kate bit back an involuntary cry, Grant's head jerked up.

"Kate—"

"It's all right. *I'm* all right." Above her his jaw was bunched tight with need. She sought to assure him, for already her body had accepted his filling heat; the slight sting was nearly gone. Her fingers weaved through his hair. Almost desperately she guided his mouth to hers.

Grant was lost. He initiated the sinuous dance of love, his tempo first slow and rhythmic, until the embers within them caught fire and raged out of control. Release came in a kaleidoscope of color that tipped the world upside down.

A long time later, he rolled to his side. Pushing himself up on an elbow, he brushed the tumbled hair from her flushed cheeks. "Are you okay?" he asked.

He loved the way her eyes shied away, only to return a second later. "I'm fine," she whispered. "Just fine."

He ran a finger down the tip of her nose. "You know you startled the hell out of me." He paused, then asked softly, "Why didn't you tell me?"

The question hung in the air. Kate hid her face against his shoulder.

"Tell me, Kate." His hand slid to the slope of her shoulder; his fingertips gauged the tension in her muscles.

Her gaze fell. She spoke quickly before she lost her nerve. "I—I don't know how to explain, Grant. Maybe I was afraid you wouldn't believe me. I don't doubt that thirty-four-year-old virgins are an endangered species these days." Her laugh was nervous and breathy. "Why, they may even be extinct as of the past hour."

All was silent for the span of a heartbeat. Another and another. Then strong fingers hooked beneath her chin, slowly guiding her eyes to his.

"Kate," he chided softly. "Don't you know it's nothing to be ashamed of? It only makes what happened here all the more special—" his tone went softer still "—all the more precious."

Precious. That was exactly how he'd made her feel, and all at once Kate couldn't look away. She longed to believe him but still wasn't sure she dared.

"You're not . . . angry because I didn't tell you?"

Not a chance, he thought fervently. Maybe he should have felt guilty—maybe later, he would. It had never crossed his mind that Kate would be a virgin; only now did he realize it should have.

He recalled the morning he'd brought her breakfast in bed, the morning she'd told him about her dream wedding—and the very traditional wedding she and Derek had planned. Oh, she was feisty and outspoken at times, but her morals were seated in staunch family values. To someone like Kate, there could be only one conclusion to such an event...making love with her husband for the very first time on their wedding night.

No, he thought again. There weren't many women left in the world like Kate. And maybe it was unforgivably conceited, but right now Grant was filled with a purely masculine pride and possessiveness. He, not Derek, had been Kate's first lover. Now Grant wanted nothing more than to be her last lover.

Her only lover.

The pressure on her chin tightened slightly. "I'm not angry," he affirmed. "I only wish I'd known before the moment of truth." His dry tone carried a twinge of regret. "I wouldn't have been quite so . . . zealous."

The thought of what they had shared made her feel all warm and glowing inside. She touched his cheek wonderingly. "You didn't hurt me," she whispered shyly. "Grant, it was perfect."

His husky laugh was as shaky as she felt inside. "So were you, lady. So were you."

"Really?" Kate held her breath, still afraid the words were only words.

"Really." He kissed her, his lips beguilingly tender. When he finally drew back, lean fingers splayed across the bareness of her belly. The possessiveness of the gesture, even more than the warm pressure of his mouth, went a long way in convincing her. He lowered his head as if to kiss her again, then drew back slightly.

His eyes searched hers. "The truth now, Kate. No regrets?" He posed the question very softly.

Her gaze clung to his. Wordlessly she shook her head.

"Looks like we have a consensus." Laughter flickered in his eyes. "In that case, I have a little proposition to make."

"What! Another one?" That she could tease after what had happened today was a miracle. Or perhaps a sign of how wonderfully complete Grant had just made her feel.

"Mmm." His lips lingered at the corner of her mouth. "We won't have to worry about who uses the shower first tomorrow morning, because I just had the nicest thought. What do you say we share and share alike?"

A little laugh escaped as Kate looped her arms around his neck. "I say it looks like we have another consensus."

Chapter Six

BUT MORNING came too soon, and with it all the uncertainties that had plagued Kate these past days. She lay huddled on her side, while daylight seeped through the curtains. Behind her, Grant still lay deeply asleep.

It was over with Derek. Kate was well aware of that, just as she accepted that Grant's words had been true—she didn't love Derek, not the way she should have. She had convinced herself she could be happy with Derek, but Kate knew now that could never have happened.

Not when she loved another man.

There was a painful heaviness in her chest. She'd been hiding from all the tumultuous feelings spinning around in her heart this past week; a part of her marveled that it had happened so fast. But yesterday's interlude—that wonderful, impossible time spent here in this very bed—had bared her soul.

She loved Grant. She loved him madly. Wildly. With all the pent-up passion hidden deep in her heart for so long now.

But that was exactly what it was—an interlude. If her thoughts were faintly textured with bitterness, Kate couldn't help it. Time and circumstances had taught her that it was far less painful to be a realist rather than a dreamer.

She forced herself to be pragmatic. Grant was returning to San Francisco on Friday. His reality was hardly hers. There would be no more sitting together on the deck, surrounded by midnight blue sky, and watching the stars come out. Grant's reality was white shirts, silk ties and suits in banker's blue.

No, she didn't dare believe it was the beginning for the two of them. She didn't dare to hope he felt the same.

Because Grant had the power to hurt her far more than she'd ever been hurt before.

She slipped from the bed, a hollow ache in her breast. Careful not to wake him, she gathered her clothes and crept from the room.

Grant was alone when he awoke a long time later. Judging by the sunlight gilding the room, it was late. A prickle of warning crept up his spine when he realized the pillow beside him was cold. A lump of dread sat like a stone in his stomach as he climbed from the bed.

He showered quickly—regrettably, alone.

He found Kate in the dining room, sitting at the table, staring listlessly out toward the river. He stood for a moment, the knot in his gut twisting and turning; there was a remoteness to her profile that hadn't been there last evening.

Finally he crossed to her. "You're up early this morning," he observed coolly.

Kate said nothing. He could feel her eyes on him as he poured himself some coffee and took the seat opposite her.

The silence was nerve grating. Kate's hands were suddenly as cold as her coffee. She clasped them tight around her mug to still their trembling.

"Well," he said at last. She was tense and on guard. He had no trouble reading that in the tautness of her posture. "It seems you spoke a little too hastily last night, doesn't it?"

Kate's gaze jumped to his. She wet her lips nervously. "What's that supposed to mean?"

"Oh, I think you know, Kate. The fact that we're sitting here like two strangers seems to say it all." His tone was cutting. "It isn't hard to figure out, you know. Obviously you're sorry about what happened yesterday. Because we—"

"No!" There was certainly no need for him to elaborate, she thought shakily. "That's not it, honestly."

"Then why the change of heart? You were perfectly willing to turn to me yesterday. Why are you so determined to turn away from me now?"

His eyes, as stormy as a thunderhead, pinned her remorselessly. Kate floundered, struggling for a reply and unable to find one.

"You said you had no regrets," he reminded her tightly.

"I didn't." Her shoulders lifted helplessly. "At least not then."

She faltered. Oh, how could she explain? She didn't want to examine what had happened too closely, afraid she might find that what had been the most precious moment of her life had probably been no more than a quick roll in the hay for him. Easy come, easy go. Didn't the fact that he'd remained a bachelor after his divorce prove he was hardly the marrying kind? She knew he hadn't taken advantage of her, but he hadn't had to make love to her, either. Maybe, she decided wildly, he considered that just a fringe benefit.

The urge to cry was suddenly overwhelming, the urge to flee even stronger. She jumped up and would have bolted but a hard arm snared her around the waist. He pulled her back against the unyielding breadth of his chest.

Her fingers dug into the crisp furring of his forearms. Suddenly she was babbling, all her confusion coming out in a rush.

"What do you expect me to say, Grant? I was…a mess after Derek left yesterday, I know. I apologize. I'm not usually so…so quick to fall apart. I'm grateful you were there, Grant. I—I guess I needed someone last night."

No, he wanted to shout. *You didn't just need someone. You needed me.*

He could see what she was doing. She was glossing over it, pretending it hadn't happened, trying to pass it off as an accident of fate. Anger stirred his temper; he was abruptly furious that she needed an excuse for making love with him. He didn't want to believe he'd been no more than a crutch, but she was making it damned difficult. Dammit, it wasn't her gratitude he was after—or her apologies, either!

"Grant, I—I don't know what else to say other than…maybe things went a little farther than either of us intended."

He whirled her around in his arms. "You're sorry it happened," he accused. "Dammit, Kate, you're sorry it happened!"

"Yes…no. Oh, Grant, don't do this to me. I—I don't know what to think right now!"

Their eyes met and held for the space of a heartbeat. His jaw was bunched and knotted. Time hung suspended for a never-ending moment. It was into this nerve-grating quiet that—for the second time in as many days—there was a knock on the glass door.

"Kate?" a female voice sang out. "Kate, we're back!"

Kate's head whipped around. Her eyes widened as a grinning Joanne stepped inside. "Joanne!" she gasped.

"I thought you and Bill weren't due back until tomorrow!"

Grant's hands fell to his side.

Kate fell into Joanne's arms and burst into tears.

AS IT TURNED OUT, the airline had notified Joanne and Bill that their Thursday-morning flight had been overbooked. Rather than taking a later flight, they'd decided to return a day early instead.

Joanne's heart went out to her friend when Kate haltingly confided that Derek had called off the wedding. Kate was heartily glad Joanne didn't notice the tension between Kate and Grant; of course it wouldn't be a problem much longer.

When Charlie delivered the afternoon mail, Kate intended to make the return trip to Gold Beach with him.

At two o'clock she lowered her suitcase to the deck. Joanne and Bill planned to take their boat out for some fishing later so they were down on the dock. Kate stepped outside, darting a wary glance in all directions. She hadn't seen Grant since shortly after lunch, and there was no sign of him now. To her horror, Kate couldn't figure out if she was relieved or disappointed. Heaving a sigh, she reached for her suitcase.

Her hand was peremptorily pushed aside. With a gasp, she confronted a pair of frosty gray eyes. "I'll take this down to the dock for you," came his stilted offer. "But before I do..."

Kate straightened slowly. Grant made no move to lift her suitcase. Instead it appeared he intended to speak his mind. "You know we still haven't finished our conversation from this morning."

She swallowed, unable to focus any higher than the hollow of his throat. "I think we have," she said faintly.

His gaze bored into her; his very silence was condemning.

"You know you had me fooled," he murmured, his tone almost conversational. "I didn't realize you were such a coward, Kate."

She inhaled sharply. Pride alone dictated her denial. "I'm not!"

His eyes narrowed. "You are," he stated baldly. "Because you're running again, Kate."

He was right. She *was* running. From him. From herself. And for an instant, she almost hated him for seeing through her so easily.

"What if I am?" she cried. "Why should you care?"

Grant cursed and came to an abrupt halt. "Dammit, Kate, how can you say that?" He reached for her.

She stepped back out of reach. Her control was fragile, slipping away like water through a sieve. "Don't, Grant! Don't touch me. Don't say anything. Just . . . just leave me alone."

She tried to march off; the weight of his hands came down on her shoulders, pulling her close. His expression was no less revealing than hers, but her anguish wouldn't allow her to see it.

Grant bitterly regretted that they hadn't had today alone, as he'd planned. There was so much he wanted—needed!—to say, if only Kate would give him the chance. But he was very much afraid she'd closed her heart against him as surely as a wall of stone.

"Kate." He ground out her name. "Just talk to me, will you? Is that asking so much . . . for you to just talk to me?"

She looked everywhere but at him—the endless stretch of sky, the fir trees looming on the horizon. Her tears were just a heartbeat away.

"Kate, look at me!" He was determined to tear down the barrier she'd flung up between them.

She did, through eyes that stung painfully. And in his she found all that she feared. Caring. Concern. And something else, some nameless emotion she didn't dare to label.

A hundred things crossed Grant's mind in that millisecond. He thought of pouring out every emotion that crowded his heart. But he realized bleakly that it was still too soon after Derek's betrayal—she would never believe him, and the knowledge speared his chest like a rusty blade.

His fingertips skimmed her cheek. "Why are you shutting me out, Kate? Don't you know I care for you?" Care, he echoed silently. That didn't even begin to describe what he felt for her.

But Kate couldn't place her faith in him just now. She couldn't put her faith in any man right now.

Not when she had so little faith in herself.

Her gaze grew chill, silently contesting his claim. "Do you? For how long, Grant? Until you're back in San Francisco, back where you belong? Until you board your plane?" Her laugh was short and harsh. "You know what they say—out of sight, out of mind."

His jaw clenched. "Dammit, Kate, that's not fair."

Something snapped inside her, a clear break that sent her tumbling over the edge. In her pain, she struck out blindly.

"What happened to me isn't fair, either. So do me a favor and don't make any token offers of help, because you can't! I'm doing a bang-up job of making a real mess of my life without any assistance from you or anyone else."

His hands deserted her shoulders. There would be no reasoning with her, he realized, not now. A stab of frustrated anger pierced the hurt.

"Just tell me one thing," he said roughly. "Are you leaving because of me—because of what happened yesterday? Or are you running back to try to talk Derek into changing his mind? To kiss and make up?"

Their eyes caught and held for what was surely the longest moment of her life. For one frantic instant, Kate felt as if she were coming apart inside. What did he expect her to do? Stay here with him? She'd been dealt a stinging blow to her pride—she'd been dumped not once, but twice! Did Grant really expect her to stick around and wait for the third time?

It was best this way—best for both of them. If she left now, there would be no need for him to let her down easily . . . because that was surely how this would end.

Somehow she managed to drag the tattered remnants of what little courage and dignity remained.

"I have a wedding to cancel," she said quietly. "So let's just leave it at that, shall we?"

She left five minutes later with Joanne's whisper of regret ringing in her ear . . . and Grant's eyes stabbing her in the back.

SEVERAL HOURS LATER, Kate found herself straggling up the sidewalk toward a weathered gray two-story house. She didn't wonder at what brought her here, to the home where she'd spent the first eighteen years of her life. She didn't want to be alone right now. Later there would be time to hide away, to lick her wounds in private and suffer in silence. But right now, like a child who'd stumbled and skinned her knee, instinct compelled her to seek comfort in the arms of her mother.

Rose Harrison was just hanging up the phone in the kitchen. "Kate!" she cried. "Thank heaven you're back, and just in time, too! The florist just phoned and he isn't sure he can get the lilies you wanted. Apparently there's some kind of little snag with his supplier."

Kate dropped her purse on the counter. "I don't think we need to worry about flowers just now—" she forced an evenness she was far from feeling "—not when we've hit a big snag with the whole wedding.

"A big snag," she repeated.

A troubled shadow crossed Rose's face. "Kate," she said faintly. "You can't be saying what I think you are."

"Oh, but I am, Mom." Kate's smile was as wobbly as her voice. "Your number-one daughter's been jilted all over again. Maybe," she tried to joke, "we should start keeping score."

There was an instant of shocked silence. Then her mother's arms slipped around her shoulders. A flash of movement in the doorway caught her eye; Kate saw her father and realized he'd heard, as well. Suddenly he was there, too, and Kate blindly gripped the hand he offered. She didn't cry, but clung to both her parents for a long, long time.

Ann stopped by later. A blessed numbness overtook Kate as she broke the news to her sister. But she wasn't prepared for the moisture glistening in her sister's eyes by the time she finished. It nearly sapped her precarious control.

It was Ann who raced from the florist to the caterer to the boutique to the photographer on Thursday. Her parents began the tedious task of calling those on the guest list. But it was her mother who fielded the calls when the inevitable curious questions began to filter in.

They didn't press her for more details than she was willing to give, bless them; Kate knew she'd never loved her family more than she did just then. But her heart was still bleeding too much to confess she'd fallen in love with Grant. Someday, perhaps, but not now.

Grant. The awful ache inside just wouldn't go away. She feared it never would. She struggled not to think of him—not to remember—but he was on her mind constantly. Never-endingly. How she regretted the way they had parted! She cringed inside whenever she recalled how she'd lashed out at him.

He'd said he cared.

But he hadn't claimed he loved her.

And why, oh, why, did the halfhearted hope that he might call—maybe even show up on her doorstep—continue to persist?

But soon even that meager hope shriveled and died. She chided herself for clinging to silly, childish dreams of happily-ever-after; she bemoaned her treacherous heart for betraying her so thoroughly.

Friday, the day Grant was due to return to San Francisco, was the worst. She spent the night fighting off tears . . . and not always succeeding.

At nine o'clock Saturday Kate dragged herself out of bed. The radio announcer cheerily predicted temperatures in the mid-seventies with only a hint of sea breeze. Still yawning, she peeked through the shutters. Bold, brilliant sunshine greeted her; the sky was an intense, vivid blue without a cloud in sight, the ocean gilded a dazzling silver.

It was a glorious day for a wedding.

But for Kate there would be no wedding, not today or any other day; neither marriage nor motherhood, husband or children. Kate longed to crawl back into bed, bury her head beneath her pillow and burrow away, never to be seen again. Instead, with a painful squeeze of her heart, she stepped into the shower.

An hour later she felt as if the walls were closing in on her. She knew there was no way she could stay here alone all day; with scarcely a break in her stride, she snatched up her purse and dug out her car keys. Maybe, she mused on the short drive to her parents' house, Ann would be there, too. Right about now their chatter would have been the most welcome sound on earth. A funny little pain knotted her chest—just a few weeks ago she'd actually been relieved at the chance to get away from it!

Her parents' house was locked up tight as a drum.

So was Ann's, Kate discovered several minutes later. And apparently Ann's husband and daughter were with her, as well.

Her shoulders slumped. *Wonderful,* she thought. Just when she needed them, neither was anywhere to be found. Kate drove home, feeling deflated, indignant and just a little hurt.

The phone was ringing when she walked through the back door. She dumped her purse on the counter and rushed across the floor to answer it.

It was Joanne. "Hi, Kate. Did I catch you on your way out the door?"

"No, I was outside at the mailbox. I almost didn't hear the phone." If her laugh was a little forced, her excuse a lame white lie, Kate couldn't help it. She simply couldn't bring herself to say her family had deserted her.

"Well, I'm glad you heard it because I thought I'd invite you up for the weekend."

There was a faint note of anxiety in Joanne's voice she couldn't quite disguise. Kate knew her friend well enough to know what she was up to.

"Joanne," she said gently. "You don't have to do this. I'm okay, really I am."

There was a sigh on the other end of the line. "Kate, I don't want you to be alone today. I'd rather you were here with someone."

"And I don't want to feel like a charity case."

"You aren't," Joanne insisted. There was a brief pause. "Actually, I have an ulterior motive for asking you. We're having an unexpected crowd this evening, and frankly, I can use all the help I can get."

Kate bit her lip. "Well," she murmured. "Since you put it that way...."

"You'll come, then?"

"I'll be there as soon as I can."

"Good. I already phoned Charlie and told him you might be tagging along on the mail run. He'll be waiting for you at the dock."

Kate smiled slightly. "Pretty sure of yourself, weren't you?"

"Kate," her friend teased, "if I had to bind and gag you and resort to kidnapping, I intended to see that you got here today."

It was only much, much later that Kate realized Joanne had hardly been joking.

As Joanne predicted, Charlie was waiting for her at the docks. Kate returned his toothy grin as best she could, but she was secretly glad the noise of the jet boat precluded much conversation on the trip upriver.

It was shortly after three before the Riverbend came into view. Kate was glad she'd worn a sundress rather than jeans and T-shirt; the temperature inland was considerably warmer than on the coast. A faint flush pinkened her cheeks by the time she entered the inn. She deposited her overnight case near the stairs.

"Joanne?" she called. She glanced around, but all was curiously still and quiet.

She was just about to head up the stairs when Joanne's voice hailed her. "I'm out on the deck, Kate!" Kate obligingly stepped outside.

Her body turned to stone. Her mouth went dry, her knees weak.

All she could do was stare.

Chapter Seven

THE PICNIC TABLES beneath the oak tree were draped in white. A wide arch decorated with a riot of yellow daisies was looped above the stairs leading from the grass onto the deck. In the middle of the deck was a small table with a vase of violets and two long white tapers.

Her mother and father were there. Joanne and Bill. Ann, her brother-in-law, Norm, and Stacy. The minister from the church... and Grant. *Grant!* He was still here—he hadn't left for San Francisco, after all!

All were gazing at her with silly, secret smiles.

Her heart lurched. Her eyes squeezed shut. She didn't dare hope. She didn't dare move for fear that if she did, this wonderful fantasy would disappear.

When they opened, Grant stood before her. His shoulders eclipsed her view of the others, but Kate didn't mind. His lean, dark features were all that filled her vision. Her soul. Her world.

Without a word, she stepped straight into his waiting embrace.

"Grant." His name was half laugh, half sob. "I thought you'd left already!"

He drew back, smiling crookedly. "I wasn't going anywhere without you, Kate."

She battled a stinging rush of tears. "I thought I'd never see you again. You... you should have told me!"

"I told you I cared," he chided gently. "But you wouldn't let me tell you how much, Kate. You weren't ready to listen, let alone believe me—" the timbre of his voice grew husky "—or believe *in* me."

"I am now," she whispered.

His hands slid down to grip hers. "I love you, Kate. I think I fell head over heels that very first night. And once I kissed you, well, I knew there wasn't a damn thing I could do to stop it—by then I didn't want to."

Tears stung her eyes. Too full of emotion to speak, Kate had to struggle to find her voice. She managed a shaky smile. Her nod encompassed the group surrounding them. "Grant, I'm almost afraid to ask . . . but is this what I think it is?"

A fleeting regret crossed his expression. "I'm sorry everything's so hasty and makeshift—but packing food and flowers fifty miles upriver poses a bit of a problem. Joanne and I had all we could handle trying to get your family here without you finding out."

His hands tightened around hers. "I know this isn't the grand wedding you've dreamed of since you were a little girl. I remember you said you wanted a big wedding party—a flower girl and bridesmaids with long, flowing dresses, a church crammed full of people and flowers everywhere, 'The Wedding March' playing. I wish I could have done all that for you. But I wanted to surprise you. Kate, I—I just wanted you to have your wedding day, after all."

Her heart fluttered, then began to soar, as if a pair of wings had taken flight inside her.

"I don't care where we live. In San Francisco, if you want. Although I've been thinking, I've come to like it here. I don't think I'd mind living in Gold Beach. It would be a change and . . . oh, hell, I don't care where I am as long as I'm with you."

He scanned her face anxiously. "Kate," he whispered, "in case you haven't guessed, I'm asking you to marry me." Every nerve in his body was tense as he waited. Waited an eternity, it seemed.

A melting tenderness flowed through her; a slow smile crept across her lips. "After all this, how could I say no?" she asked softly.

His laugh was as husky and shaky as she felt inside, but she sensed an unusual uncertainty in his manner. "I think I'd like to hear a very definite yes."

Their eyes locked. Uncaring that they had an audience Kate stepped closer. Her hands slid up his chest to wind around his neck. She pulled his head down so that her lips waited just below his.

"Kiss me," she murmured.

His hands dug into her waist. "Kate—"

"Just kiss me, Grant. Please."

He did, a kiss so breath-stealingly thorough that she felt herself spinning away to heaven and beyond. Her eyes opened, shining and dazzling.

"Now tell me what you see," she whispered.

He searched her face as if to memorize her features for all eternity. Aglow inside and out, Kate gazed at him, aware her expression bared every emotion pouring through her heart.

"Tell me, Grant." This time she was pleading.

His breath caught. His heart went wild. "I see—" a smile claimed his lips "—a woman with stars in her eyes."

"And I see a man who makes dreams come true, the man who's about to make my dreams come true." Her voice grew tremulous. "I love you, Grant. I *do.*"

"You can repeat those very words within the hour," he teased, then took her mouth in a long, binding kiss that earned a burst of applause from behind them.

When he finally allowed her up for air, a plump brunette who looked vaguely familiar had planted herself before them. Grant caught Kate's questioning look and winked.

"Kate, this is Mrs. Williams, the Curry County clerk. Joanne and I were able to convince her she could issue our marriage license just as well here as at the county courthouse. She very kindly consented to give up her Saturday to do exactly that." He grinned and went on with his familiar brashness. "Luckily, the waiting period can be waived at the time we apply for our license."

Kate's chuckle was rather unsteady. "Which is what we're doing now?" She accepted the pen Mrs. Williams handed her.

Grant presented his back for her to apply her signature. "Which is now done." His tone reflected his satisfaction. He handed the application back to Mrs. Williams with a flourish.

Kate's mother was suddenly there. "Honey, we never expected to meet our future son-in-law on your wedding day, but all we want is for you to be happy." She hugged her close. "And I didn't forget Grandma Allen's white lace handkerchief either, Kate. Grandpa gave it to her at the wedding, I carried it at mine and so did Ann." She was smiling but tears shone in her eyes. "Now it's your turn."

Ann scrambled for the necklace at her throat. "And I have my diamond necklace, Kate. I wanted you to wear it, remember?" She clasped it around Kate's throat.

Joanne clamped a hand over her mouth. "I almost forgot!" She raced inside, returning a minute later with a small package in her hands. She thrust it at Kate. Kate unwrapped it, lifting a delicately crafted gold bracelet from within.

"Oh, Joanne, how pretty!" Kate was radiant. As Joanne fastened the bracelet around her wrist, she quoted with a shaky laugh, "'Something old, something new, something borrowed—'" she bit her lip and glanced ruefully down at her sundress "—and it looks like I'm about to be married in something blue."

Grant pulled her close. "You look beautiful, Kate." His expression was so tender that she felt her heart turn over.

His look grew suddenly intent. "Are you sure you don't mind being married here? I didn't want anything to remind you of Derek or Ben," he added quickly. "And...well, I thought it was only fitting that we be married here at the inn since this is where it all happened."

Kate's gaze moved slowly from the daisies that lined the arch to the white sheet draping the impromptu altar; from the candles to the ribbon-tied bouquet of violets and pale pink azalea blossoms Joanne pressed into her hands.

Her hand crept into Grant's, her throat so clogged with tears that she could hardly speak. Did it really matter that she wasn't dressed in silk and satin, that her bridal bouquet was made up of violets and azaleas rather than snow-white roses? This was her wedding day. Her family and friends were here. Grant loved her...*he loved her*.

What more could she ask for?

Joy cascaded through her. "Grant," she said in a voice that shook. "It's perfect. Absolutely perfect."

Clapping and cheers burst all around them. The minister cleared his throat. "Will the couple please step forward?"

Beside her, Kate's father offered his arm. "I think it's high time I gave away the bride," he said with a wink.

Her father was beaming as he led her forward. Kate glanced over at her mother; she had no doubt her mother was thinking of her own wedding, just as she had no doubt that the tears in her mother's eyes were tears of pride and happiness, because she knew this was the most precious moment of Kate's life.

A radiant smile curved her lips. Suddenly this make-shift wedding seemed no different than the fairy-tale wedding she'd always envisioned. Kate couldn't imagine being happier than she was at this moment. There was no "Wedding March" as they took their place before the minister, but Kate didn't care, because there was music in her heart.

A rush of joy spilled through her as the minister finally spoke the words that made her Grant's wife. He turned to her, linking their hands together and tugging her close.

His eyes tenderly roved her features. "Remember the day I predicted each kiss would be better than the first?"

Her smile was misty. "I remember."

He lowered his head so that his lips hovered just above hers, almost touching but not quite. "I have another prediction for you," he whispered. "Each day of our marriage is going to be better than the last. I know it, Kate. I can feel it—" he raised their joined hands and splayed her fingers directly over his heart "—right here."

Kate opened her mouth to tell him she wholeheartedly agreed, but his lips came down on hers. And then it was a very long time before she was allowed to speak again at all.

Epilogue

"WELL, MRS. RICHARDS, how does it feel to join the ranks of the unemployed?"

Mrs. Richards. Although eight months had passed, Kate experienced a thrilling tingle whenever she heard those words, especially when they came from her husband's lips. As for his comment, Kate had just tendered her resignation to the local school board. The reason was obvious... and increasingly visible, as well, she decided, gently patting the swell of her abdomen.

Their baby was due in less than a month.

She marveled whenever she thought of how quickly summer had flown into winter, and winter into spring. Grant had indeed decided to pull up roots in San Francisco. Kate was not opposed to moving, but it was Grant who insisted he preferred they remain in Gold Beach. The general law practice he'd started was flourishing, so much that he was considering taking on a partner. And only last month, they'd moved into a new house, one they'd searched for and chosen together.

She watched as he tossed another log onto the fire. A sizzling hiss preceded a lick of flame that crackled up the chimney. Grant resettled himself on the couch next to Kate.

She slipped her hand through his arm and rubbed her cheek against his flannel-clad shoulder. "I'd rather be unemployed," she found herself teasing, "than unwanted."

"What! Is that a complaint I hear?" With a swift move he dragged her against him, then rose with her in his arms.

"Grant," she yelped. "I'm too heavy. You'll hurt yourself!"

He paid no heed to her feeble protests. "I wouldn't be much of a husband if my wife felt unwanted, now would I?" Seconds later he deposited her gently on the wide bed in their room.

Her arms remained locked around his neck. "You've never made me feel unwanted," she confided breathlessly. "Never."

"That's good—" his head lowered slowly "—because I aim to please." The kiss they shared was long and breathtakingly thorough. Grant released her mouth reluctantly and eased to his side, mindful of the burden she now carried. He propped himself on his elbow, one hand curled possessively on the hard swell of her abdomen. His eyes came to rest on the framed photograph that graced the nightstand near Kate's head.

Kate's gaze tracked his. The photo had been taken on their wedding day. Grant was gripping both her hands, his expression avid as he stared down into her upturned face, while hers was decidedly starry-eyed. Behind them in the center of the picnic table was a lopsided two-layered wedding cake Joanne had proudly claimed as her masterpiece.

A slight smile grazed Kate's lips. "I can't believe it's been almost a year," she murmured.

Grant's eyes lingered. "Kate," he said after a moment. "I've been thinking. Lots of people have their marriage vows renewed. If you wanted, we could do that, too. You know, go the whole route this time, with everything we didn't have the first time. We could have the ceremony in church. Invite everyone who wasn't there the first time. Maybe have a big reception afterward." He scanned her features anxiously. "What do you think?"

She eyed her mounding tummy. "I think they don't make wedding dresses my size," she said with a chuckle.

"It doesn't have to be on our first anniversary. We could wait until the baby's here and—"

"Grant," she said gently. "There's no need. Honestly."

"I know it's not *necessary*," he clarified. "But sometimes I feel bad because you didn't have the wedding you'd always wanted—"

"Oh, but I did." Even now, almost a year later, Kate felt a surge of joy when she thought of that day. She smiled when his eyes sought hers. "I told you once how my mother said a woman deserves a wedding she'll always remember. Well, you gave me that, Grant. I didn't need all the fanfare, after all, because you gave me the wedding I always dreamed of." Her hand came up to cradle his jaw. "I couldn't possibly feel any more married than I do right now."

Her confession kindled a rush of emotion unlike anything he'd ever felt before. He loved her more with every beat of his heart, his bride in blue. He buried his face in her hair and crushed her as close as the baby would allow. Her face was radiant when at last he drew back. He traced the smiling fullness of her mouth with his fingertips. "Are you sure?" he asked softly.

She nodded, her fingers tangling in the midnight darkness of his hair. "Remember you predicted each day would be better than the last?"

His laugh was husky. "I did say that, didn't I?"

She pulled his head down to hers. "You certainly did. And you know what?" She smiled against his lips. "You were right."

The First Man You Meet

DEBBIE MACOMBER

A Note from Debbie Macomber

Thinking about my wedding opens a floodgate of hilarious memories.

It all started with Wayne's bachelor party. My dad, Ted Adler, and my brother Terry joined Wayne and his friends. They were out half the night and returned to my parents' home, starving. My mother and several aunts had been cooking for days preparing for the dinner party that was to follow the wedding reception. My father fed the bachelor party what was supposed to have been the wedding dinner. My mother stood in the kitchen, dazed.

The next morning, a woman from the shop where we'd bought my wedding gown arrived to help me dress. To save money for the wedding, I'd given up eating lunch and the dress was too big. She ended up using safety pins to keep it from hanging on me. My poor mother kept circling me, mumbling in German.

Our wedding was set for noon, but the wedding scheduled before ours started late. Wayne, suffering the effects of his bachelor party, arrived late. He hurried into the church to find the ceremony in full swing. For a wild moment he was convinced my mother had persuaded me to marry someone else. He would have rushed up the aisle if his best man hadn't stopped him.

The wedding went without a hitch. There was plenty of food for the dinner that followed the reception. But it's taken nearly twenty-four years for my mother to forgive Wayne and my father for eating that ham.

Debbie

Chapter One

IT HAD BEEN one of those days.

One of those hellish, nightmarish days in which nothing had gone right. Nothing. Shelly Hansen told herself she should have seen the writing on the wall that morning when she tripped over the laces of her high-top purple tennis shoes as she hurried from the parking lot to her dinky office. She'd torn a hole in the knee of her brand-new balloon pants and limped ingloriously into her building. The day had gone steadily downhill from there.

By the time she returned to her apartment that evening she was in a black mood. All she needed to make her day complete was to have her mother pop in unannounced with a man in tow, convinced she'd found the perfect mate for Shelly.

That was exactly the kind of thing Shelly had come to expect from her dear, sweet *desperate* mother. Shelly was twenty-eight now and single, and her mother tended to view her unmarried status as something to be remedied.

Never mind that Shelly felt content with her life just the way it was. Never mind that she wasn't interested in marriage and children...at least not yet. That time would come, she was sure, not now, but someday soon—or rather, some *year* soon.

For the moment, Shelly was absorbed in her career. She was proud of her work as a video producer, although she continually suffered the cash-flow problems of the self-employed. Her relaxation videos—seascapes, mountain scenes, a flickering fire in a brick fireplace, all with a background of classical music—were selling well. Her cat-baby-sitting video had recently caught the attention of a major distributor, and she couldn't help believing she was on the brink of being discovered.

That was the good news.

Her mother hounding her to marry was the bad.

Tossing her woven Mexican bag and striped blue jacket onto the sofa, Shelly ventured into the kitchen and sorted through the packages in her freezer until she found something to strike her fancy for dinner. The frozen entrée was in the microwave when the doorbell chimed.

Her mother. The way her day was going, it *had* to be her mother. Groaning inwardly, she decided she'd be polite but insistent. Friendly but determined, and if her mother began talking about husbands, Shelly would simply change the subject.

But it wasn't Faith Hansen who stood outside her door. It was Elvira Livingston, the building manager, a warm, delightful but insatiably curious older woman.

"Good evening, dear," Mrs. Livingston greeted her. She wore heavy gold earrings and a billowing, bright yellow dress, quite typical attire. She clutched a large box protectively in both hands. "The postman dropped this off. He asked if I'd give it to you."

"For me, Mrs. L.?" Perhaps this day wasn't a total waste, after all.

Elvira nodded, holding the package as though she wasn't entirely sure she should surrender it until she got every bit of relevant data. "The return address is California. Know anyone by the name of Millicent Bannister?"

"Aunt Milly?" Shelly hadn't heard from her mother's aunt in years.

"The package is insured," Mrs. Livingston noted, shifting the box just enough to examine the label again.

Shelly held out her hands to receive the package, but her landlady apparently didn't notice.

"I had to sign for it." This, too, seemed to be of great importance. "And there's a letter attached," Mrs. Livingston added.

Shelly had the impression that the only way she'd ever get her hands on the parcel was to let Mrs. Livingston open it first.

"I certainly appreciate all the trouble you've gone to," Shelly said, gripping the sides of the box and giving a firm tug. Mrs. Livingston released the package reluctantly. "Uh, thanks, Mrs. L. I'll talk to you soon."

The older woman's face fell with disappointment as Shelly began to close the door. Obviously, she was hoping for an invitation to stay. But after such a frustrating day, Shelly wasn't in the mood for company, especially not the meddlesome, if well-meaning, Elvira Livingston.

Shelly sighed. This was what she got for renting an apartment with "character." She could be living in a modern town house with a sauna, pool and workout room in an upper-class yuppie neighborhood. Instead she'd opted for a brick two story apartment building in the heart of Seattle. The radiators hissed at all hours of the night in perfect harmony with the plumbing that groaned and creaked. But Shelly loved the polished hardwood floors, the high ceilings with their delicate crystal light fixtures and the bay windows that overlooked Puget Sound. She could live without the sauna and the other amenities, even if it meant occasionally dealing with an eccentric busybody like Mrs. Livingston.

Eagerly she carried the package into the kitchen and set it on her table. Although she wondered what Aunt Milly had sent her, she carefully peeled the letter free, then just as carefully removed the plain brown wrapper.

The box was an old one, she noted, the cardboard heavier than that currently used by stores. Shelly gently pried off the lid and set it aside. She found thick layers of tissue paper wrapped around...a dress. Shelly pushed aside the paper and painstakingly lifted the garment from its box. She gasped in surprise as the long white dress gracefully unfolded.

This wasn't just any dress. It was a wedding dress, an exquisitely sewn lace-and-satin wedding dress.

Surely it couldn't have been Aunt Milly's wedding dress... No, that couldn't be... It wasn't possible.

Anxious now, her heart racing, Shelly carefully refolded the dress and placed it back in the box. She reached for the letter and discovered that her hands were trembling as she tore open the envelope.

My Dearest Shelly,

I trust this letter finds you happy and well. You've frequently been in my thoughts the past few days. I suppose you could blame Mr. Donahue for that. Though now that I think about it, it may have been Oprah. As you'll have gathered, I often watch those talk shows these days. John would have disapproved, but he's been gone eight years now. Of course, if I wanted to, I'd watch them if he were still alive. John could disapprove all he wanted, but it wouldn't do him a damn bit of good. Never did. He knew it and loved me, anyway.

I imagine you're wondering why I'm mailing you my wedding dress. (Yes, that is indeed my infamous wedding dress.) I suspect the sight of it has put the fear of God in you. I wish I could be there to see your face when you realized what I was sending you. No doubt you're familiar with its story; everyone in the family's known about it for years. Since you're fated to marry the first man you meet once the dress is in your hands, your first instinct is probably to burn the thing!

Now that I reconsider, I'm almost certain it was Donahue. He had a show recently featuring pets as companions to the elderly, lifting their spirits and the like. The man being interviewed brought along a cute little Scottish terrier pup and that was when the old seamstress drifted into my mind. I must have fallen asleep, because the next thing I knew the six o'clock news was on.

While I slept I had a dream about you. This was no ordinary dream, either. I saw you plain as day, standing beside a tall young man, your blue eyes bright and shining. You were so happy, so truly in love. But what amazed me was the wedding dress you were wearing.

Mine.

The very dress the old Scottish woman sewed for me all those years ago. It seemed to me I was receiving a message of some sort and that I'd best not ignore it. Neither had you! You're about to embark on the grandest adventure of your life, my dear. Keep me informed!

Believe me, Shelly, I know what you're thinking. I well remember my own thoughts the day that Scottish seamstress handed me the wedding dress. Marriage was the last thing on my mind! I had a career, back in the days when it was rare for a woman to attend college, let alone graduate from law school.

You and I are a great deal alike, Shelly. We value our independence. It takes a special kind of man to be married to women like us. And you, my dear niece, are about to meet that one special man just the way I did.

All my love,
Aunt Milly

P.S. You're only the second person to wear this dress, my dear. Never before have I felt like this. Perhaps it's the beginning of a tradition!

With hands that trembled even more fiercely now, Shelly folded the letter and slid it into the envelope. Her heart was pounding loud and fast, and she could feel the sweat beading her forehead.

The phone rang then, and more from instinct than any desire to talk, Shelly reached for the receiver.

"Hello." It hadn't dawned on her until precisely that moment that the caller might well be her mother, wanting to bring over a man for her to meet. Any man her mother introduced would only add to the growing nightmare, but—

"Shelly, it's Jill. Are you all right? You sound . . . a bit strange."

"Jill." Shelly was so relieved that her knees went weak. "Thank heaven it's you."

"What's wrong?"

Shelly hardly knew where to begin. "My aunt Milly's wedding dress just arrived. I realize that won't mean anything to you unless you've heard the family legend about my aunt Milly and uncle John."

"I haven't."

"Of course you haven't, otherwise you'd understand what I'm going through," Shelly snapped. She immediately felt guilty for being short-tempered with her best friend. Making an effort to compose herself, she explained, "I've just been mailed a wedding dress—one that's been in my family for nearly fifty years—with the clear understanding that I'll be wearing it myself soon."

"I didn't even realize you were dating anyone special." Jill hadn't managed to disguise the hurt in her voice.

"I'm *not* getting married. If anyone should know that, it's you."

"Then your aunt simply intends you to wear it when you do get married."

"There's far more to it than that," Shelly cried. "Listen. Aunt Milly—who's really my mother's aunt, a few years younger than my grandmother—became an attorney just after the Second World War. She worked hard to earn her law degree and had decided to dedicate her life to her career."

"In other words, she'd planned never to marry."

"Precisely."

"But apparently she did."

"Yes, and the story of how that happened has been in the family for years. It seems that Aunt Milly had all her clothes professionally made. As the story goes, she took some lovely white material to an old Scottish woman who had a reputation as the best seamstress around. Milly needed an evening dress for some formal event that was coming up—business related, of course. The woman took her measurements and told her the dress would be finished within the week."

"And?" Jill prompted when Shelly hesitated.

This was the part of the tale that distressed her the most. "And...when Milly returned for the dress the old woman sat her down with a cup of tea."

"The dress wasn't ready?"

"Oh, it was ready, all right, only it wasn't the dress Aunt Milly had ordered. The Scottish woman explained she was gifted with the 'sight.' "

"She was clairvoyant?"

"So she claimed," Shelly said, breathing in deeply. "The old woman told my aunt that when she began the dress a vision came to her. A clear vision that involved Milly. This vision apparently showed Milly getting married. The old woman was so convinced of it that she turned what was supposed to be a simple evening dress into an elegant wedding gown, with layers of satin and lace and lots of pearls."

"It sounds beautiful," Jill said with a sigh.

"Of course it's beautiful—but don't you see?"

"See what?"

It was all Shelly could do not to groan with frustration. "The woman insisted that my aunt Milly, who'd dedicated herself to her career, would marry within the year. It happened, too, just the way the seamstress said it would, right down to the last detail."

Jill sighed again. "That's the most romantic story I've heard in ages."

"It isn't romance," Shelly argued, "it's fate interrupting one's life! It's being a...pawn in the game of life! I know that sounds crazy, but I've grown up hearing this story. It was as though my aunt Milly didn't have any choice in the matter."

"And your aunt Milly mailed you the dress?"

"Yes," Shelly wailed. "*Now* do you understand why I'm upset?"

"Frankly, no. Come on, Shelly, it's just an old dress. You're overreacting. You make it sound as if you're destined to marry the next man you meet."

Shelly gasped audibly. She couldn't help herself. "How'd you know?" she whispered.

"Know what?"

"That's exactly what happened to Aunt Milly. That's part of the legend. She tried to refuse the dress, but the seamstress wouldn't take it back, nor would she accept payment. When Aunt Milly left the dress shop, she had car problems and needed a mechanic. My uncle John was that mechanic. And Aunt Milly married him. She married *the first man she met,* just like the seamstress said."

Chapter Two

"SHELLY, THAT doesn't mean *you're* going to marry the next man you meet," Jill stated calmly, far too calmly to suit Shelly.

Perhaps Jill didn't recognize a crisis when she heard about one. They were talking about destiny here. Predestination. Fate. Okay, maybe, just maybe, she was being a bit melodramatic, but after the ghastly day she'd had, who could blame her?

"Aunt Milly came right out and said I'm going to get married soon," Shelly explained. "The family legend says that the first man you meet when you get the dress is the man you'll marry."

"It's just coincidence," Jill reassured her. "Your aunt probably would have met her husband *without* the dress. It would've happened anyway. And don't forget, she's an old woman now," Jill continued soothingly. "I know this wonderful old lady who comes into the pharmacy every few weeks and she always insists *I'm* going to get married soon. I smile and nod and fill her prescription. She means well, and I'm sure your aunt Milly does, too. She just wants you to be happy, the way she was. But I think it's a mistake for you to take any of this prediction nonsense seriously."

Shelly exhaled sharply. Jill was right; Aunt Milly was a sweetheart, who had Shelly's happiness at heart. She'd had a long, blissful marriage herself and wanted the same for her great-niece. But Shelly had a career. She had plans and goals, none of which included meeting and marrying a stranger.

The story of Aunt Milly's wedding dress had been handed down from one generation to the next. Shelly had first heard it as a child and had loved it. In her young romantic heart, she'd ranked the story of her aunt Milly and uncle John with her favorite fairy tales of Cinderella and Sleeping Beauty, barely able to distinguish truth from fantasy. However, she was an adult now. Her heart and her life weren't going to be ruled by something as whimsical as a "magical" wedding dress or a fanciful legend.

"You're absolutely right," Shelly announced emphatically. "This whole thing is ridiculous. Just because this wedding dress supposedly conjured up a husband for my aunt Milly fifty years ago doesn't mean it's going to do the same thing for me, no matter what she claims."

"Well, thank goodness you're finally being sensible about this."

"No one bothered to ask me what I thought before shipping off a so-called magic wedding gown. I don't want to marry just yet, so I certainly don't need the dress. It was a nice gesture, but unnecessary."

"Exactly," Jill agreed.

"I'm not interested in playing déjà voodoo." She paused to laugh at her own joke.

Jill chuckled, too. "I wouldn't be, either."

Shelly felt greatly relieved and sighed expressively. The tight muscles along the back of her neck began to relax. Jill was, as usual, full of sound, practical advice. Aunt Milly was a wonderful old lady, and the legend was a delightful bit of family lore, but it would be laughable to take any of this seriously.

"How about meeting me for lunch tomorrow?" Jill suggested. "It's been ages since we got together."

"That sounds good to me," Shelly said eagerly. Although they'd been good friends since college, it took some effort on both their parts these days to make time in their hectic lives to see each other. "When and where?"

"How about the mall?" Jill asked. "That would be easiest for me since I'm scheduled to work tomorrow. I can get off a few minutes before twelve."

"Great. I'll see you at noon at Patrick's," Shelly promised. Meeting her friend for lunch was just the antidote she needed after the terrible day she'd suffered through. But then what did she expect on Friday, April thirteenth?

SHELLY OVERSLEPT, then got caught in a traffic jam on her way to meet Jill the following morning. She detested being late, although she often was. Rather than fight for a convenient parking spot in the vast lot that surrounded the mall, she took the first available space and rushed toward the nearest entrance. Patrick's, a cozy, charming restaurant on the mall's upper level, was deservedly popular for business lunches. Shelly had eaten there often and especially enjoyed the spinach-and-shrimp salad.

A glance at her watch told her it was already after twelve, and not wanting to keep Jill waiting, she hurried toward the escalator. The shopping center was especially busy on weekends, she noted, as she weaved her way around several people.

Her mind must have been on the salad she intended to order for lunch instead of the escalator because the moment she placed her foot on the first tread, she lost her balance.

"Oh . . . oh!" Swinging her arms out at both sides in a futile effort to remain upright, she groped at thin air. She tried frantically to catch herself as she fell backward.

Landing in someone's arms shocked her as much as having lost her balance. Incredulous, she twisted around to thank her rescuer but this proved to be a mistake. Her action caught the man off guard, and before he could prevent it, they both went crashing to the floor. Once again Shelly expected to experience pain. Instead, her waist was surrounded by arms that were surprisingly strong. His grip was firm but gentle, protective. As they fell, he maneuvered himself to take the brunt of the impact when they landed. Sprawled as she was above him, Shelly found herself staring down at the most attractive man she'd ever seen. Her heart thrummed. Her breath caught. Her body froze.

For a moment neither of them spoke. A crowd had gathered around them before Shelly managed to speak. When she did, her voice was weak and breathless. "Are you all right? I'm so sorry. . ."

"I'm fine. What about you?"

"Fine. I think."

She lay cushioned by his solid chest, their faces scant inches apart. Shelly's long hair fell forward, framing his face. He smelled of mint and some clean-scented soap. Her gaze wandered curiously over his features; at such close range she could see the tiny lines that fanned out from the edges of his sapphire-blue eyes as well as deep grooves that bracketed his mouth. His nose was classically straight, his mouth full and sensuous. At least his lower lip was. It didn't take her long to recognize that this man was uncompromisingly male. His eyes held hers reluctantly, as if he, too, was caught in the same powerful trance.

Neither of them moved, and although Shelly was convinced the breathless sensation she felt was a result of the fall, she couldn't seem to breathe properly even now.

"Miss, are you hurt?"

Reluctantly Shelly glanced up to find a security guard standing over her.

"Um . . . I don't think so."

"Sir?"

"I'm fine."

The arms that were holding hers securely loosened.

"If we could have you both sit over here for a moment," the guard instructed, pointing at a bench. "We have an ambulance on the way."

"An ambulance? But I told you I'm not hurt," she objected.

The guard gently helped Shelly to her feet. Her legs were shaky and her breathing a bit uncertain, but otherwise she was unhurt.

"Officer, there's really no need—" the man who'd fallen with her protested.

"Mall policy," the guard interrupted. He hooked his thumbs into the wide leather belt and rocked gently back on his feet. "It's standard procedure to have all accident victims checked immediately."

"If you're worried about a lawsuit—"

"I don't make the rules," the guard interrupted her rescuer once again. "I just see that they're carried out. Now, if you'd both sit over here, the medical team will be here in a couple of minutes."

"I don't have time to wait," Shelly cried. "I'm meeting someone." She glanced longingly at the upper level, wondering how she could get word of her delay to Jill. It didn't reassure her to notice the number of people clus-

tered by the railing, staring down at her. Her little esca-
pade had attracted quite a bit of attention.

"I've got an appointment, as well," the man said,
looking pointedly at his watch.

The security guard ignored their protests. He removed a small notebook from his shirt pocket and flipped
it open. "Your names, please."

"Shelly Hansen."

"Mark Brady."

He wrote down the information and a brief account of
how they happened to fall.

"I won't have to go to the hospital, will I?" Shelly demanded.

"That depends," the guard answered.

This whole thing was ridiculous. She was perfectly
fine. A little shaken, true, but uninjured. She suddenly
realized that she hadn't thanked this man—Mark, was it?

"I'm terribly sorry about all this," she offered. "I can't
thank you enough for catching me."

"In the future, you might be more careful." Mark
glanced at his watch a second time.

"I will be. But if it ever happens again, might I suggest you just let me fall?" This delay was inconvenient
for her, too, but that wasn't any reason to be quick-
tempered. She studied her rescuer and shook her head
slightly, wondering why she'd been so impressed. He
looked as if he'd stepped off the Planet Square. Dark blue
suit and tie, crisp white shirt with gold cufflinks. This
guy was as original as cooked oatmeal. About as person-
able, too.

If she was giving him the once-over, she discovered he
was eyeing her, too. Apparently he was equally unimpressed. Her sweatshirt was a fluorescent orange and her
jeans as tight as a second skin. Her ankle-high boots were

black, her socks the same shade of orange as the sweat-shirt. Her hair cascaded about her shoulders in a layer of dark frothy curls. Mark was frowning in obvious disapproval.

The wide glass doors at the mall entrance opened, and two paramedics hurried inside. Seconds later, when the ambulance arrived, two more medical people entered the building. Shelly was mortified that such a minor accident would result in all this attention.

The first paramedic knelt down in front of her while the second concentrated on Mark. Before she completely understood what was happening, her shoe was off and the man was examining her ankle. Mark, too, was being examined, a stethoscope pressed over his heart. He didn't seem to appreciate the procedures any more than she did.

It wasn't until he stood up that she realized how tall he was. Close to six-five, she guessed. A good match for her own five feet ten inches, she thought automatically.

It hit her then. Bull's-eye. Aunt Milly's letter had mentioned her standing beside a tall young man. Mark Brady was tall. Very tall. Taller than just about any man she'd ever met.

Aunt Milly's letter had also said something about Shelly's blue eyes. She'd ignored it at the time, but her eyes weren't blue. They were hazel. Mark had blue eyes, though. The kind of vivid blue eyes women generally found striking... Nor could she forget her initial reaction to him. She'd been attracted. Highly attracted. It'd been a long while since a man had interested her this much. Until he stood, anyway. When she got one good look at him, she'd known immediately that they had nothing in common. Mark Brady probably didn't own a single article of clothing that wasn't blue, black or tan. Clearly the man had no imagination.

On a sudden thought, she glanced worriedly toward his left hand. No wedding ring. Closing her eyes, she sagged against the back of the bench and groaned.

"Miss?" The paramedic was studying her closely.

"Excuse me," she said, straightening. She jerked impatiently on Mark's suit jacket. He was involved in a conversation with the ambulance attendant who was interviewing him and didn't turn around.

"Excuse me," she said again, louder this time.

"Yes?" Mark turned to face her, his gaze impatient.

Now that she had his attention, she wasn't sure she should continue. "This may sound like a silly question, but, uh ... are you married?"

He frowned again. "No."

"Oh, no," Shelly moaned and slumped forward. "I was afraid of that."

"I beg your pardon."

"Surely you've got a girlfriend—I mean, you're a tall, handsome kind of guy. There's got to be someone important in your life. Anyone? Please, just think. Surely there's someone?" She knew she was beginning to sound desperate, but she couldn't help it. Aunt Milly's letter was echoing in her mind and all of last night's logic had disappeared.

The four paramedics, as well as Mark, were staring at her. "Are you sure you don't want to come to the hospital and talk to a doctor?" one of them asked gently.

Shelly nodded. "I'm sure." Then before she could stop herself, she blurted out, "What do you do for a living?"

"I'm a CPA," he answered wearily.

"An accountant," she muttered. She should have guessed. He was obviously as staid and dignified as he looked. And as boring. The type of man who'd probably never even heard of videos for entertaining bored house cats. He probably wouldn't be interested in purchasing one, either.

Surely her aunt Milly couldn't have seen Mark and Shelly together in her dream. Not Mark Brady. The two of them were completely ill-suited. A relationship between them wouldn't last five minutes! Abruptly she reminded herself that she wasn't supposed to be taking Aunt Milly's prediction seriously.

"May I go?" she asked the paramedic. "I'm not even bruised."

"Yes, but you'll need to sign here."

Shelly did so without bothering to read the statement. Mark, however, seemed to scrutinize every sentence. He would, of course.

"Uh, Mark . . ." Shelly hesitated, and Mark glanced in her direction.

"Thank you," she said simply.

"You're welcome."

Still she delayed leaving.

"You wanted something else?"

She didn't know quite how to say this, but she felt the need too strongly to ignore it. "Don't take offense at this—I'm sure you're a really great guy.... I just want you to know I'm not interested in marriage right now."

Chapter Three

JILL WAS SEATED at the table, doodling on the paper place mat, when Shelly arrived. "What kept you?" she asked. "I've been here for almost half an hour."

"I—I fell off the escalator."

Jill's eyes widened in alarm. "My goodness, are you all right?"

Shelly nodded a bit sheepishly. "I'm fine . . . I think."

"Shouldn't you see a doctor?"

"I already have," she explained, avoiding eye contact with her friend. "Well, sort of. The security guard called in the paramedics. A whole bunch of them."

"No wonder you're late."

"I would have been, anyway," Shelly admitted as she reached for a menu, though she'd decided an hour earlier what she intended to order.

"This has really got you flustered, hasn't it?"

"It's more than the fall that's unsettled me," Shelly explained, lowering the menu. "It's the man who caught me."

Jill arched her eyebrows jokingly. "Aha! I should have guessed there was a man involved."

"You might try to understand how I felt," Shelly said reproachfully. "Especially since I haven't recovered from receiving Aunt Milly's wedding dress yet."

"Don't tell me you're still worried about that first-man-you-meet nonsense."

"Of course not. That would be ridiculous. It's just . . . it's just I can't help feeling there might be something to that silly wedding dress."

"Then mail it back."

"I can't," Shelly said, slapping the menu down on the table. "Aunt Milly warned me not to—though not exactly in those words, mind you. She said I shouldn't ignore the dress. I mean, how can I? It's like an albatross hanging around my neck."

"I still think you're overreacting to this whole thing."

"That's the crazy part. I *know* I am, but I can't seem to stop myself. I grew up hearing the legend of that wedding dress, and now it's in my possession. I've got a piece of family history hanging in the back of my closet. Heaven forbid if my mother should hear about this." She shuddered at that thought.

"So you hung the dress in your closet."

"I couldn't very well keep it under my bed. I tried that, but I couldn't sleep, so I finally got up and stuck it in the back of the closet." She closed the menu and set it aside. "That bothered me, too. I tossed and turned half the night, then I remembered Aunt Milly had done the same thing when the seamstress gave her the dress."

"She stuck it under her bed?"

Shelly nodded slowly. "I seem to remember hearing something like that. She'd tried to refuse it, but the old woman insisted Aunt Milly take the gown home with her. By the time she arrived at her apartment she'd already met my uncle John although she still didn't know she was going to marry him."

Jill raised a skeptical eyebrow. "Then what? After she put it under her bed and couldn't sleep, I mean?"

"Well, she did the same thing I did," Shelly admitted. "She shoved it into her closet." Shelly felt as if she were confessing to a crime. "I didn't want the thing staring me in the face so I hung it in the back."

"Naturally." Jill was trying, unsuccessfully, to disguise a smile. Shelly could see how someone else might find her situation humorous, but she personally didn't think any of this was too amusing. Not when it was her life, her future, being tossed around like some cosmic football. At this rate, she'd be married and with child by nightfall!

"That's not the worst of it," Shelly added. She exhaled slowly, wondering why her heart was still beating so fiercely.

"You mean there's more?"

She nodded. The waitress arrived just then and took their orders, returning quickly with tall glasses of iced tea. Shelly breathed in deeply before she continued. "I literally fell into that man's—Mark Brady's—arms."

"How convenient."

"It's all very nice of him to have broken my fall," she said sternly, "but I wish he hadn't."

"Shelly!"

"I mean it," she insisted. She glanced around, as if to make sure no one was listening, then added, "The man's an accountant."

Jill reacted in mock horror, covering her mouth with both hands and widening her eyes. "No! An accountant?"

"Think about it. Could you honestly picture me married to an accountant?"

Jill took a moment or two to mull over the question. "Hmm, a CPA," she repeated slowly. "You still haven't memorized your multiplication tables, have you? You freeze up whenever you have to deal with numbers. No,

I guess you're right, I can't honestly see you with an accountant.''

Shelly raised both hands, palms up, in a dramatic gesture. "I rest my case."

Jill reached for some bread, carefully selecting a wholewheat roll. "Just because you fell into his arms doesn't mean you're going to marry him," she said in a matter-of-fact voice.

"I know that."

"Then what's the problem?"

"I can't make myself *believe* it," Shelly said. "I feel like one tiny pin fighting the force of a giant magnet."

"That's preposterous."

"I know," Shelly agreed readily. "I just wish I hadn't said anything to Mark."

Jill set the roll on her plate with exaggerated care. "You told him the story about your aunt Milly's wedding dress?"

"Of course not." Shelly was horrified her friend would suggest such a thing. "I just told him I couldn't marry him."

Jill's mouth dropped. "You didn't! Did you?"

Shelly nodded hesitantly. "I don't know what made me say anything so ludicrous. I honestly don't. I can't imagine what he must think of me. Not that I plan on seeing him again, of course. Unless—"

"Unless what?"

Their lunches were served. Jill had ordered a hot spinach salad with slices of chicken simmering in soy sauce sprinkled with sesame seeds. Shelly's spinach salad was piled high with shrimp, egg slices and black olives.

"Go on," Jill urged once the waitress had left the table. "You don't plan on seeing Mark again unless—"

"Unless it's unavoidable."

"I take it this means your aunt Milly's first encounter with your uncle John wasn't her last." Jill giggled. "Silly of me. Obviously it wasn't."

"No. Aunt Milly felt the same reluctance I do. My uncle was a wonderful man, don't get me wrong, and he was absolutely perfect for Aunt Milly, as it turned out, but the two of them were as different as night and day. Aunt Milly was a college graduate and Uncle John never completed high school."

Shelly sighed wistfully. At one time the story of their romance had been like her own personal fairy tale. But now Shelly didn't find it nearly as enthralling. "He helped Milly fix her car the night it broke down. The very next day she was in court defending a client in a lawsuit—"

"Let me guess," Jill interrupted, "your uncle John was the man suing her client."

Shelly nodded. "Yes, and that was only the beginning. Every time they turned around they were bumping into each other."

"How long after they met were they married?"

This was the question Shelly had dreaded most. She closed her eyes and whispered, "Ten days."

"Ten days," Jill echoed with an incredulous look.

"I know. It seems that once they kissed they both realized there wasn't any use fighting it."

"Did your aunt tell John about the seamstress and the wedding dress?"

Shelly shrugged. "I don't know, but my guess is she didn't . . . at least not at first." She hadn't touched her salad yet and paused long enough to savor a forkful of her favorite seafood. Then she said abruptly, "They eloped without telling anyone."

"Children?" Jill wanted to know.

"Three boys. My mother's cousins."

"What about granddaughters? You'd think your aunt Milly would want to hand the dress down to one of them."

"All three of her sons had boys themselves. I guess you could say I'm the closest thing she's got to a granddaughter."

"Ten days," Jill repeated. "That's really something."

Forking up another succulent shrimp, Shelly continued her story. "That old Scottish woman knew about the wedding even before the family did. When Aunt Milly and Uncle John returned from their honeymoon, there was a wedding card from the seamstress waiting for them at the house."

Jill propped her elbows on the table and gazed at Shelly. "Tell me what Mark Brady looks like."

Shelly frowned, trying to form her impressions of him into some kind of reasonably articulate description. He was compelling in ways she didn't quite understand. Principled and headstrong, but how she knew that, Shelly couldn't explain. "He's tall," she began slowly.

"How tall?"

"Basketball-player tall. He must be about six five."

"Brown hair?"

Shelly nodded. "With blue eyes. *Really* blue eyes. I can't remember the last time I met a man with eyes that precise color. They seemed to . . ." She hesitated, unsettled by the emotion that stirred within her when she thought about Mark. Although their encounter had been brief, Shelly was left feeling oddly certain that she could trust this man, trust him implicitly. It wasn't a sensation she could ever remember experiencing with any other man. She didn't like the feeling; it made her uncomfortable. Until Jill had started asking her about Mark, Shelly didn't realize she'd experienced any emotion toward him—except for embarrassment, of course.

"Why do you want to know?" she asked.

Jill gave her a silly, knowing grin. "Because if he's as tall as you say, with dark brown hair and deep blue eyes, then the man you described just walked into this restaurant."

"What?" Shelly felt her stomach sink. "Mark's here? Mark Brady?"

"That's not so amazing, is it? This is, after all, the same shopping mall in which you, uh, met—" Jill made a show of glancing at her watch "—thirty or so minutes ago."

"He's here." She reminded herself that Jill was right: Mark's choosing to have lunch at Patrick's was just a logical coincidence. Too bad she couldn't convince her racing heart to believe that.

"He's sitting on the other side of the room," Jill whispered.

"Has he seen me yet?"

"I don't think so."

Without being obvious—or at least Shelly hoped she wasn't being obvious—she turned to look in his direction. At that same instant, Mark happened to glance up. Their eyes met. Despite herself, she gasped. Her hands shook and she felt herself break out in a cold sweat.

Mark scowled and quickly looked away.

She couldn't blame him. He seemed surprised to see her there. Unpleasantly surprised.

"Well, is it him?" Jill demanded.

Shelly couldn't find her voice, so she answered with a quick nod.

"I thought it might be. What are you thinking?"

"That I've lost my appetite." Shelly doubted she'd be able to finish her lunch.

"You want my advice?" Jill asked, grinning broadly. "I don't have a lot of experience in the area of magic wedding dresses, but I recently read a fascinating book on home remedies."

"Sure." At this point Shelly was feeling reckless enough to try just about anything.

"Garlic," Jill said solemnly. "Wear a garlic rope around your neck. Not only does it deter vampires, but it just might ward off potential husbands conjured up by a magic wedding dress."

Chapter Four

HARD THOUGH SHE TRIED, Shelly had a difficult time ignoring Mark Brady. He sat there, stiff and unapproachable, at the other side of the small restaurant. Just as stiff and unapproachable as she was. Jill wanted to linger over her coffee before returning to her job at the PayRite Pharmacy in the mall, but Shelly was eager to be on her way. The sooner she left, the sooner she could put this bothersome encounter out of her mind.

"Don't forget Morgan's baby shower on Tuesday night," Jill said as Shelly reached for her purse.

Shelly had completely forgotten about their friend's party, which was understandable given her present state of mind. Most of their college friends were married and several were now having babies. Rather than admit how absentminded she'd suddenly become, Shelly asked, "Do you want to drive over together?"

"Sure," Jill agreed. "I have to go directly from work so I'll stop off at your place and we can leave from there."

"Sounds good to me." She tried to imagine their blond, scatterbrained classmate as a wife and mother. It was Morgan who'd gotten the entire dorm hooked on daytime soap operas. Before anyone could figure out how it had occurred, all the girls were obsessed with the characters and their lives. It became as important as mealtimes to learn if Jessie would ever find true love. To the best of Shelly's knowledge, she hadn't.

But then, Jessie didn't have an aunt Milly. The unexpected thought flashed through her mind.

Irritated with herself, Shelly dropped her share of the bill and a tip on the table. "I'll see you Tuesday, then."

"Right. And Shelly, don't look so worried. No enchanted wedding dress is going to disrupt your life unless you allow it to happen."

Easy for Jill to say, since it wasn't her life and her great-aunt's wedding dress. Nevertheless, her advice was sound. Aunt Milly might have had some fanciful dream about Shelly's marring a tall man with blue eyes, but that didn't mean it was going to happen, especially when Shelly was so determined that it wouldn't.

"You're absolutely right," she stated emphatically. "I know I keep saying that, but . . . well, I seem to need reminding. So, thanks. Again." With a final wave, she wandered out of the restaurant, barely noticing the colorful shop windows as she passed them. As Jill had pointed out, Aunt Milly meant well, but the letter and the wedding dress shouldn't be taken too seriously. Shelly was content with her life, and the last thing she needed right now was a man. Especially a staid, conventional man like Mark Brady.

Shelly knew exactly what kind of man she'd fall in love with. He'd be intelligent, and fervent about life, and as passionate as she was herself. Naturally, he'd appreciate her work and take pride in his own. He'd need to be a free spirit, like her. Unconventional. She'd like a man with gumption, too—someone who possessed a bit of initiative. It'd be nice if he was a little better at organizational skills than she was, but that wasn't absolutely necessary.

With thoughts of marriage so prominent in her mind, Shelly soon found herself standing in front of a jeweler's display window. A large assortment of wedding bands had captured her attention. Scanning the selection, she found one ring that stood out from the rest: three small rows of diamond chips, bracketed on each side by a thin band of gold. The ring was striking in its simplicity, its uncontrived beauty.

For the longest moment Shelly stared at the rings as her mind wove whimsical dreams around the happy bride and the tall groom. *Tall groom.* Her thoughts came to a skidding halt.

What on earth had come over her? She didn't know, but whatever it was, she didn't like it. Self-consciously she glanced around, fearful that someone was watching her. Well, a very specific someone, to be honest. Someone who definitely shouldn't see her gazing with open longing at a collection of absurdly high-priced wedding rings. Mark Brady.

With a sense of urgency, Shelly hurried toward the mall exit, her feet barely able to move fast enough. It was all she could do to keep from breaking into a run. No matter how fast she walked, however, she couldn't shake the feeling that *he* was there, watching her. Twice she whirled around, convinced she'd find Mark Brady strolling behind her, sneering and making contemptuous remarks.

He wasn't there.

Shelly felt herself relax as she neared her apartment. She parked her car, then stopped in the lobby to collect her mail. As soon as she opened the small box, Mrs. Livingston's head poked out her door.

"Good afternoon, Shelly," she chirped, gazing at her expectantly.

It took Shelly a moment to realize that Mrs. L. must have been waiting to hear about the contents of her package.

"It's a lovely day," Shelly said conversationally, sorting through her mail. Two bills, a flyer and something from the Internal Revenue Service. The way her luck had been going, it was probably an audit notice. A quick inspection revealed exactly that. She closed her eyes and groaned inwardly.

"A lovely day indeed," Mrs. Livingston echoed cheerfully.

Muttering under her breath, Shelly stuffed the IRS notice back inside the envelope. When she glanced up, she noticed that the older woman was now standing in the hallway, wearing another vividly colored outfit—turquoise and purple this time.

"I suppose you're wondering about the package," Shelly said resignedly, tucking her mail inside her purse. "It was a gift from my aunt Milly."

"Something from the past, I guess?" Mrs. Livingston asked.

"Why...yes, how'd you know?"

"I'd take whatever it was very, very seriously if I were you," Mrs. Livingston continued in a solemn voice. "Wizard wouldn't go anywhere near that box. Think what you want, but my cat has always had a sixth sense when it comes to this sort of thing."

"It's a dress, Mrs. L." Shelly explained, hiding behind a falsely bright smile. "How am I supposed to take a dress seriously?"

Mrs. Livingston opened her apartment door and scooped the large black-and-white cat into her arms. "That I wouldn't know," she returned, her eyes narrowed and mysterious. "All I can tell you is that Wizard felt skittish around that package. You don't suppose there's...magic in it, do you?"

Somehow Shelly managed a reply, although she felt certain it was unintelligible. Taking the stairs two at a time, she hurried into her apartment, leaning breathlessly against the door once she was inside. Even Mrs. Livingston's cat knew there was something strange about Aunt Milly's wedding dress!

WHEN JILL ARRIVED late Tuesday afternoon, Shelly was ready and waiting for her, brightly wrapped baby gift in hand. She was eager to get out and socialize—eager to get out, period. Anything to escape another phone call from her mother, who'd recently heard from Aunt Milly. Now Faith Hansen was calling daily for updates on the romantic prospects in her daughter's life.

"Well," Jill demanded as she entered the apartment. "Are you going to show it to me?"

"Show what to you?"

Jill gave her a look that seemed to question her friend's intelligence. "The wedding dress, of course."

For several hours Shelly had managed to put the dress out of her mind. "No," she said forcefully. "I want to forget about the whole thing."

"Met any tall blue-eyed men lately?" Jill couldn't resist asking.

"None," Shelly answered shortly. Checking her watch, she noted that they were early but suggested they leave, anyway. "Shouldn't we go now?"

"We've got lots of time," Jill countered, moving toward Shelly's bedroom. "Come on, it isn't going to hurt to let me look at the dress."

"Oh, all right," Shelly conceded ungraciously. Leading the way, she opened the closet door and reached into the back of the closet.

She brought out the lace-and-satin gown, holding it up for Jill's inspection. She'd barely looked at the dress the day she'd received it, and now she was almost shocked by how breathtakingly beautiful it actually was.

The laughter drained from Jill's dark brown eyes as she stared at the gown. "Oh, Shelly, it's ... lovely." She gently touched the Elizabethan sleeve and ran her finger along the delicate layer of pearls that decorated the cuff. The high neckline was also trimmed with an intricate design of pearls, so that it resembled a choke collar. "I don't know what I expected," Jill continued in an awed whisper, "but certainly nothing as beautiful as this."

Shelly nodded wordlessly. The dress was far more exquisite than she'd realized. Her heart swelled with unexpected emotion, and to her dismay, tears filled her eyes as she thought about the old Scottish woman who had so lovingly constructed the gown. Each pearl had been sewn into place by hand. She thought of her aunt Milly, as tall and statuesque as Shelly herself, wearing the dress. Then she recalled her uncle John, such a determined man. She imagined him, standing tall and proud beside Milly. Shelly thought fondly of those two, who'd been so completely different, yet had loved each other so well....

For a moment neither she nor Jill spoke. "Have you tried it on?" Jill asked finally.

Shelly shook her head adamantly, not wanting her friend to realize how emotional she'd become. "Heavens, no, but you can if you want."

"I don't think I could resist if I were you," Jill whispered, obviously affected by the dress, too. "Just seeing it ... makes me long to be a bride myself."

"There's always Ralph," Shelly teased. Jill had been dating Ralph, a computer programmer, for several months, but frankly she couldn't understand what her friend saw in him.

Jill tossed her an irritated look. "The dress is for you, not me."

"But I don't want it," Shelly insisted, though she was no longer sure what she felt. Not since she'd really examined the dress and allowed herself to remember the wonder of John and Milly's romance.

"You're sure you don't mind?" Jill asked, slipping off her shoes. "I mean, if you'd rather I didn't try it on, I'll understand."

"No, feel free." Shelly strove for a flippant air. "As far as I'm concerned the dress is nothing but bad luck. It arrived on Friday the thirteenth. The next day I had that minor accident on the mall escalator. Now I'm being audited by the IRS."

It was as if Jill didn't hear. "I doubt it'll fit," she said as she cautiously removed the gown from the padded hanger. "I'm a good five inches shorter than you and heavier on top."

"Maybe the dress was meant for you in the first place," Shelly ventured. Perhaps Aunt Milly had been confused and it was Jill she'd viewed in her dream. After all, Milly's eyes weren't what they used to be....

"Does your mother know?" Jill asked as she stepped into the dress. She raised it over her hips and turned around to let Shelly fasten the buttons that ran down the back.

"That's another thing," Shelly moaned. "Mom's been calling me every day since the dress arrived, wanting to know if I've met anyone special yet."

"What did you tell her?" Jill asked, looking at Shelly over her shoulder.

"What's there to tell?" she asked irritably.

"Well, you might have mentioned Mark."

"Mark," Shelly repeated. She shrugged elaborately. "I haven't given him a thought in days." Not strictly true, but she'd been *trying* not to think about him. Even if he was interested in her—and he'd made very clear that he wasn't—she couldn't imagine two more ill-suited people. "I haven't seen him since last Saturday and I doubt I'll ever see him again."

"You're sure of that?"

"Positive."

"Well, what do you think?" Jill asked next, pirouetting slowly in front of her. "My hair's a mess and I've got hardly any makeup on, but . . ."

Shelly looked at her friend and sighed audibly. Never had she seen Jill look lovelier. It was as if the dress had been made for her. "You look absolutely enchanting. It fits like a dream."

"I feel like I am dreaming," Jill admitted softly. "Here," she said, turning around, "undo me before I start longing for a husband and 2.5 children."

"Don't forget the house with the white picket fence," Shelly teased, unfastening the buttons.

Jill slipped out of the dress. "Your turn," she said as she laid it carefully across the bed. "If it fits me, then it can't possibly fit you. You've got the perfect excuse to mail it back to your aunt Milly."

"I . . . don't know." Shelly bit her lip. She felt an inexplicable urge to keep the dress, and at the same time she would've willingly express-mailed it back to her aunt. Even while she hesitated, Shelly found herself undressing. She couldn't explain her sudden eagerness to try on the wedding gown any more than she could fathom its growing emotional appeal.

The dress slid easily over her hips. She turned around so Jill could secure the back, then glanced toward the mirror, expecting to find the skirt miles too short. It would have to be in order to fit Jill as perfectly as it had.

"Shelly," Jill whispered, then cupped her hand over her mouth. "My goodness . . . you look beautiful . . . really beautiful."

The sentiment was what Shelly had felt when she'd viewed her friend in the dress. "Something's wrong," she said once she found her voice. "Something's very wrong."

"No," Jill countered, "it's very right. It's as if the dress was made for you."

"Then answer me this," Shelly whispered. "How is it possible for the same dress to fit two women who wear totally different sizes?"

Chapter Five

Shelly struggled to open the door of the Internal Revenue office, her arms weighted down with a huge box stuffed full of receipts and records she'd need for the audit. By bracing the box against the wall with her knee, she freed one hand to open the door. For the first time ever, she'd completed her tax return early—all by herself, too—and *this* was where it got her. She grumbled righteously and bit her lip, more in anxiety than annoyance.

She'd just managed to grasp the door handle, when the door unexpectedly opened and she staggered into the room, nearly colliding with an end table. She did a quick pirouette, convinced she'd ruined a new pair of panty hose. With a heartfelt sigh, she set her box of records on the floor and sank into the first available chair, neatly arranging her unaccustomed skirt around her knees. Only then did she bother to look around. There was one other person in the large reception area.

Shelly's heart did a nosedive, landing somewhere in the pit of her stomach. The man who'd opened the door for her, the man sitting in this very waiting room, was none other than Mark Brady—the man she'd hoped to avoid for the rest of her natural life. She gave an involuntary gasp.

Mark was leafing through the dog-eared pages of a magazine when he happened to glance her way. The automatic smile quickly faded from his face, and his gaze narrowed as if he strongly suspected Shelly had purposely arranged this meeting.

"What are you doing here?" Shelly demanded.

"I might ask you the same thing."

"I didn't follow you here, if that's what you're implying!"

"Listen, Ms. . . . Hansen, I really couldn't care less." With that he returned to his magazine as if he were reading the fine print in a million-dollar contract. "*You're* the person who blurted out to everyone within hearing distance that you weren't marrying me. As if I'd even asked! As if I even *knew* you!"

Shelly felt the heat rising up her neck and quickly offered the first excuse she could think of. "I . . . was distraught."

"Obviously," he muttered from behind his magazine.

A few minutes of strained silence passed. Shelly shifted uncomfortably in her chair, checking her watch every couple of minutes. For the first time in recent history she was early for an appointment, but if this was where promptness got you, she'd prefer to be late.

"All right, I apologize," Shelly said when she couldn't tolerate the silence any longer. "I realize it was utterly ridiculous and . . . and out of turn—"

"Out of turn," Mark echoed, slapping the magazine down on the table. "I repeat—I don't even know you."

"I realize that."

He inhaled deeply, which drew her attention to his broad, muscular chest. She noticed that he was as meticulously dressed as he'd been at their first encounter. His dark suit and silk tie, however conventional, added a touch of sophistication to his natural good looks.

"If there's anyone to blame for this it's Aunt Milly," Shelly said, more to herself than to him.

"Aunt Milly?" Mark repeated, sounding unsure. He eyed her warily.

She'd said this much; she might as well launch into the whole ridiculous tale.

"Actually, it has more to do with the wedding dress than with my aunt Milly, although by now the two of them are inseparable in my mind. I don't usually dabble in this sort of thing, but I'm beginning to believe there just might be something supernatural about that silly dress, after all."

"Supernatural?"

"Magic, if you prefer."

"Magic in a wedding dress?" Mark gazed hopefully at the door that led to the inner offices of Internal Revenue, as though he was anxious to be called away.

"It's unbelievable, but the dress fits both Jill and me— which is virtually impossible. You saw Jill—she's the friend I was having lunch with last Saturday. I know we were halfway across the room from you, but you couldn't help noticing how much shorter she is than I am. We're completely different sizes."

Mark hurriedly reached for the magazine as if he wanted to shut her out again before she said anything else.

"I know it sounds crazy. I don't like this any better than you do, but I'm honestly afraid it was you Aunt Milly mentioned in her letter." Well, it was only fair to tell him that.

Mark glanced in her direction again, blue eyes suspicious. "Your aunt Milly mentioned me in a letter?"

"Not by name—but she said she had a clear vision of me in the wedding dress and I was standing with a tall man. She also mentioned blue eyes. You're tall and you have blue eyes and the legend says I'm going to marry the first man I meet after receiving the dress."

"And I just happened to be that man?"

"Yes," Shelly cried. "Now do you understand why I was so disturbed when we met?"

"Not entirely," Mark said after a moment.

Shelly rolled her eyes. How obtuse could the man be? "You're tall, aren't you? And you have blue eyes."

He flipped intently through the magazine, not looking up at her as he spoke. "Actually, I really don't care what the letter said, nor am I concerned about this wedding dress you keep mentioning."

"Of course you don't care," Shelly said indignantly. "Why should you? It must all seem quite absurd to you. And I'm aware that I'm overreacting, but I do have a tendency to get emotional about things. If it helps any, I want you to know I'm content with my life just the way it is. I don't want to get married now—to anyone." When she'd finished, she sucked in a deep breath and began leafing idly through a magazine, doing her utmost to ignore him.

Silence returned. Silences had always bothered Shelly. It was as if she felt personally responsible for filling them. "If you want something to be grateful about, you can thank your lucky stars I didn't mention you to my mother."

"Your mother," Mark repeated, briefly glancing at her. "Does she know about Aunt Milly sending you this . . . dress?"

"Naturally she does," Shelly answered, closing the magazine. "She's phoned me every day since she heard, because she thinks I'm going to meet that special someone any minute."

"And you didn't mention me?"

"How could I? The instant I do that, she'll be contacting the caterers."

"I see." The edges of his mouth lifted as though he was beginning to find the situation amusing. "She believes in the power of this dress, too?"

"Unfortunately, yes. You have to understand where my mother stands on this marriage business," Shelly continued, undaunted.

"I'm not sure I want to," Mark muttered under his breath.

Shelly disregarded his comment. "By age twenty-eight—my age now, coincidentally—Mom had been married for eight years and already had three children. She's convinced I'm letting the best years of my life slip away. There's nothing I can say to make her believe differently."

"Then I'll add my gratitude that you didn't mention me."

Mollified, Shelly nodded, then glanced at her watch. Her meeting was in ten minutes and she was nervous, since this was the first time she'd done her own taxes. She should have known there'd be a problem.

"I take it you're here for an audit?" Mark asked.

She nodded again, studying her tax return, sure she'd be in jail by nightfall without even understanding what she'd done wrong.

"Relax."

"How can I?"

"Have you knowingly hidden something from the government? Lied about the income you received, or claimed expenditures you've never made?"

"Oh, no!"

"Then you don't have anything to worry about."

"I don't?" Shelly stared at him, soaking up his confidence. She'd been restless for days, worrying about this meeting. If it wasn't the wedding dress giving her nightmares, it was the audit.

"Don't volunteer any information unless they ask for it."

"All right."

"Did you prepare your own tax return?"

"Well, yes. It didn't seem that complicated, and well, I realize this sounds silly but Jill bet me I couldn't do it. So I did. Back in February. You see, usually numbers boggle my mind and I decided to accept the challenge, and . . ." She realized she was chattering, something she did when she was nervous. Forcing herself to stay quiet, she scanned her return for the hundredth time, wondering what she could have possibly done wrong.

"Do you want me to check it over for you?"

Shelly was surprised by his generosity. "If you wouldn't mind. Are you being audited yourself?"

Mark smiled and shook his head. "A client of mine is."

"Oh."

Mark crossed the room and sat next to her. When Shelly handed him her tax return, his gaze ran quietly down the row of figures, then he asked her several questions.

"I've got everything right here," she assured him, gesturing toward the carton she'd lugged in with her. "I really am careful about saving everything I should."

Mark glanced down at the large cardboard box. "This is all for one year?"

"No," she admitted sheepishly. "I brought along everything I had for the past six years. I mean, it made sense at the time."

"That really wasn't necessary."

"I'd rather be safe than sorry," Shelly said, managing a small grin. She watched Mark as he scrutinized her return. At such close range, she saw that his eyes were even bluer than she'd thought. Blue as the sky on a bright July afternoon, she told herself fancifully. Her heart felt heavy in her chest, and hard as she tried, she couldn't keep from staring.

Mark handed back her return. "Everything looks fine. I don't think you'll have a problem."

It was amazing how relieved she felt at hearing that. No, at hearing that from *him*. Mark smiled at her and Shelly found herself responding readily with a smile of her own. The fluttery sensation returned to her stomach. She knew her eyes were wide and questioning and although she tried to look away, she couldn't make herself do it.

A look of surprise mingled with gentleness came over Mark's features, as if he were seeing her for the first time, really seeing her. He liked what he saw—Shelly could read that in his eyes. Slowly his gaze traveled over her features, and she felt her pulse tripping into double time. The letter she'd received from Aunt Milly flitted across her mind, but instead of dismissing the memory, she wondered, *Could there really be something to all this?*

Mark was the one to break eye contact. He stood abruptly and hurried back to his seat. "I don't think you have much to be concerned about."

"Yes, you told me."

"I mean about your aunt Milly's wedding dress."

"I don't have anything to worry about?" Shelly wasn't sure she understood.

"Not with me, at any rate."

"I don't quite follow . . ." If he was even half-aware of the way her heart was clamoring as they gazed into each other's eyes, he wouldn't be nearly as confident.

"I'm engaged."

"Engaged?" Shelly felt as though someone had slugged her in the stomach. Her first reaction was anger. "You couldn't have mentioned this sooner?" she snapped.

"It's not official yet. Janice hasn't picked out a diamond. Nor have we discussed our plans with her family."

The irritation faded, swallowed by an overwhelming sense of relief. "Engaged," she repeated, reminding herself that she really had no interest in marriage. And this proved there was no such thing as a "magic" wedding dress. If Mark was involved with Janice, he wouldn't be free to marry her. It was that simple. Shelly leaped to her feet and started to pace.

"Are you all right?" Mark asked. "You're looking pale."

She nodded and pressed her hands to her cheeks, which suddenly felt hot. "I'm so relieved," she whispered hoarsely. "You have no idea how relieved I am. You're engaged... My goodness, I feel like I've got a new lease on life."

"As I explained," Mark said, frowning, "it isn't official yet."

"That doesn't matter. You're committed to someone else and that's all that matters. However—" she forced a smile "—you might have said something sooner and saved me all this anxiety."

"You did ask that day at the mall, but I was more concerned with avoiding a scene than revealing the personal details of my life."

"I'm sorry about that."

"No problem," Mark was quick to assure her.

Shelly settled back in the chair and crossed her legs, hoping to stroke a relaxed pose. She even managed to skim through a couple of magazines, although she barely knew what she was reading.

Finally, the receptionist opened the door and called her name. Eager to get this over with, Shelly stood, picking up the large box she'd brought in with her. She paused on her way out of the reception area and turned to Mark. "I wish you and Janice every happiness," she said formally.

"Thank you," he answered, then grinned. "The same to you and whomever the wedding dress finds for you to marry."

Chapter Six

SHE SHOULD BE HAPPY, Shelly told herself early the following morning. Not only had she survived the audit—in fact she'd come away with an unexpected refund—but she'd learned that Mark was practically engaged.

Yes, she should be dancing in the streets, singing in the aisles... Instead she'd been struggling with a strange melancholy ever since their last encounter. She seemed to have lost her usual vitality, her sense of fun.

And now it was Saturday, and for once she had no looming deadlines, no appointments, no pressing errands. Remembering the exhilaration and solace she'd experienced when she videotaped an ocean storm sequence recently, Shelly decided to see if she could recapture some of those feelings. She headed toward Long Beach, a resort town on the Washington coastline. The sky was clear and almost cloudless; the sun was bright and pleasantly warm—a perfect spring day. Once she drove onto the freeway, the miles sped past and two hours later she was standing on the sandy beach with the breeze riffling her long hair.

She walked around for a while, enjoying the sights and sounds about her, the chirping of the sea gulls, the salty spray of the Pacific Ocean and the scent of wind and sea. She was satisfied with the end product, her beach video, and started to work out plans for a whole series—the ocean in different seasons, different moods. That would be something special, she thought, something unique.

She wandered down the beach, kicking at the sand with the toe of her tennis shoes. Tucking her fingertips in the pockets of her jeans, she breathed in the vivid freshness around her. After an hour or so, she made her way back to the concession stands, where she bought a hot dog and a cold drink.

Then, just because it looked like such fun, she rented a moped.

She sped along the shore, thrilled with the sensation of freedom, reveling in the solitude and the roar of pounding surf.

The wind tossed her hair about her face until it was a confusion of curls. Shelly laughed aloud and listened as the galloping breeze carried off the sound.

Her motorized bike rushed forward, spitting sand in its wake. She felt reckless with exhilaration, as though there was nothing she couldn't do. It was that kind of afternoon. That kind of day.

When she least expected it, someone else on a moped raced past her. Shelly hadn't encountered anyone during her ride and this person took her by surprise. She glanced quickly over her shoulder, amazed by how far she'd traveled. The only other person she could see was the one who'd passed her.

To her surprise, the rider did an abrupt turnaround and headed back in her direction. With the sun in her eyes and the wind pelting against her, Shelly slowed to a crawl and she shaded her eyes with one hand.

It wasn't until he was nearly beside her that Shelly recognized the other rider.

Mark Brady.

She was so shocked that she allowed the engine to die, her feet dropping to the sand to maintain her balance. Mark appeared equally shocked. He braked abruptly.

"Shelly?" He seemed not to believe it was her.

Shelly shook her head and blinked a couple of times just to make sure she wasn't fantasizing. The last person she'd expected to encounter on a beach two hours out of Seattle was Mark Brady. Mr. Conservative on a moped! This time, though, he wasn't wearing a dark suit. He didn't have his briefcase with him, either. And he looked even handsomer than usual in worn jeans and a University of Washington sweatshirt.

"Mark?" She couldn't prevent the astonishment from creeping into her voice.

"What are you doing here?" She heard the hostility in his and answered him coolly.

"The same thing as you, apparently." She pushed the hair from her face, and the wind promptly blew it back.

Mark's blue gaze narrowed suspiciously. "You didn't happen to follow me, did you?"

"Follow you?" she repeated indignantly. She'd rarely been more insulted. "Follow you!" she repeated, starting her moped and revving the engine. "May I remind you that I was on the beach first? If anyone was doing any following, it was *you* following me." She was breathless by the time she finished. "In light of our previous encounters, you're the last person I'd seek out."

Mark scowled at her. "The feeling's mutual. I'm not in the mood for another story about your aunt Martha's damn wedding dress, either."

Shelly felt an unexpected flash of pain. "I was having a perfectly wonderful afternoon until you arrived," she said stiffly.

"I was having a good time myself," Mark muttered.

"Then I suggest we go our separate ways and forget we ever met."

Mark looked as if he were about to say something more, but Shelly was in no frame of mind to listen. She twisted the accelerator on the handlebar of her moped and took off down the beach. Although she knew it was unreasonable, she was furious. Furious at the surge of joy she'd felt when she recognized him. Furious at Mark, because he didn't seem even a little pleased to see her. She bit her lower lip, remembering the comment he'd made about not wanting to hear anything more about her "damn wedding dress." Now, that was just rude, she told herself righteously. She could *never* be interested in a man who was not only conventional but rude.

Squinting, Shelly hunched her shoulders against the wind, in a hurry now to return to the boardwalk area. She hadn't meant to go nearly this far.

The wet, compact sand made for smooth, fast riding and Shelly stayed close to the water's edge in an effort to outdistance Mark. Not that he was likely to chase her, but she wanted to avoid any possibility of another embarrassing encounter.

Then it happened.

A large wave came in, sneaking its way up the sand, creating a thin, glistening sheen. Shelly hardly noticed, as her front tire ripped through the water, spraying it out on both sides. Then the moped's front wheel dipped precariously. One minute she was sailing down the beach at breakneck speed and the next she was cartwheeling over her handlebars.

She landed heavily in a patch of wet sand, too paralyzed with shock to know if she was hurt or not.

Before she could move, Mark was crouching at her side. "Shelly? Are you all right?"

"I...don't know." Carefully she flexed one arm and then the other. Sitting up, she tested each leg and didn't feel pain there, either. Apparently she'd survived the experience unscathed.

"You crazy fool!" he yelled, leaping to his feet. "What are you trying to do, kill yourself?"

"Ah . . ." It was painful to breathe just yet, otherwise she would have answered him.

"Can you imagine what I thought when I saw you flying through the air like that?"

"Good riddance?" she suggested.

Mark closed his eyes and shook his head. "I'm in no mood for your jokes. Here, let me help you up." He moved behind her, sliding his arms around her waist and gently raising her up.

"I'm fine," she protested the instant his arms surrounded her. The blood rushed to her head, but Shelly didn't know if that was because of her tumble or because Mark was holding her as though he never intended to let go. Even when she was on her feet, he didn't release her.

"Are you sure you're not hurt?"

Shelly nodded, not trusting her voice. "I'm less confident about the moped, though." Her bike seemed to be in worse shape than she was.

"It doesn't look good to me, either," Mark said. He finally dropped his arms and retrieved the moped, which was lying on its side, the waves lapping over it. There were regular hissing sounds as the cold water splashed against the heated muffler. Steam rose from the engine.

Mark did his best to start the bike for her, but to no avail. "I'm afraid it's hopelessly wet. It won't start now until it's had a chance to dry. A mechanic should check it over to be sure nothing's wrong."

Shelly brushed the hair from her face and nodded. There was no help for it; she was going to have to walk the bike back to the rental shop. No small feat when she considered she was about three miles down the beach.

"Thank you very much for stopping," she said a bit primly. "But as you can see I'm not hurt. . . ."

"What do you think you're doing?" Mark asked as she began pushing the moped. It made for slow progress, the bulky machine was far more difficult to transport under her own power than she'd realized. At this rate, she'd be lucky to return it by nightfall.

"I'm taking the bike back to the place where I rented it."

"That's ridiculous."

"Do you have any better ideas?" she asked in a reasonable tone of voice. "I don't understand what you're doing here in the first place," she said, sounding far calmer than she felt. "You should be with Janet."

"Who?" he demanded. He tried to take the moped away from her and push it himself, but she wouldn't let go.

"The woman you're going to marry. Remember?"

"Her name is Janice and as I said before, the engagement's unofficial."

"That doesn't answer my question. You should be with her on a beautiful spring day like this."

Mark frowned again. "Janice couldn't get away. She had an important meeting with a client—she's a lawyer. Listen, quit being so stubborn, I'm stronger than you. Let me push the bike."

Shelly hesitated; his offer was tempting. She hadn't gone more than a few feet and already her side ached. She pressed one hand against her hip and straightened, her decision made. "Thanks, but no thanks," she answered flatly. "By the way, it's Aunt Milly who sent me the wedding dress, not Aunt Martha, so if we're going to get names straight, let's start there."

Mark rolled his eyes skyward, as though he'd reached the end of his limited reserve of patience. "Fine, I'll apologize for what I said back there. I didn't mean to insult you."

"I didn't follow you," she said.

"I know, but I didn't follow you, either."

Shelly nodded, finding that she believed him.

"Then how do you explain that we've inadvertently stumbled into each other twice in the last week?" Mark asked. "The odds of that happening have got to be phenomenal."

"I know it sounds crazy, but . . . I'm afraid it's the dress," Shelly mumbled.

"The wedding dress?" Mark repeated.

"I'm really embarrassed about all this. I'm not sure I believe any of it myself. And I do apologize, especially since there's been an apparent mix-up—"

"Why's that?" Mark asked.

"Well . . . because you're involved with Janice. I'm sure the two of you are a perfect match and you'll have a marvelous life together."

"What makes you assume that?"

His question caught her off guard. "Well, because . . . didn't you just tell me you're about to become officially engaged?"

"Yes," Mark muttered, frowning.

Although she was reluctant to admit it, Shelly found pushing the moped extremely taxing, so she stopped to rest for a moment. "Listen," she said a little breathlessly, "there's no need for you to walk with me. Why don't you just go on ahead?"

"There most definitely is a need," Mark answered sharply. He didn't seem too pleased with her suggestion. "I'm not going to desert you now."

"Oh, Mark, honestly, you don't have to be such a gentleman."

"You don't like gentlemen?"

"Of course I do—but it's one of the reasons you and I would never get along for any length of time. You're very sweet, don't get me wrong, but I don't need anyone to rescue me."

"Forgive me for saying so, but you *do* appear to need rescuing." The look he gave her implied that he was referring to more than the moped.

"I was the one foolish enough to get the engine wet," she said brightly, ignoring his comment. "So I should be the one to pay the consequences."

Mark waited a moment, as if debating whether to continue arguing. "Fine, if that's the way you feel," he said finally, straddling the moped and starting his engine, which roared to life with sickening ease. "I hope you don't tire out too quickly."

"I'll be okay," she said, hardly able to believe he was actually going to leave her.

"I hope you're right about that," he said, revving the engine.

"You . . . you could let someone know," she ventured, hoping the rental agency might send someone out with a truck to find her.

"I'll see what I can do," he agreed, then grinning broadly, took off at top speed down the beach.

Although she'd made the suggestion that he go on ahead without her, Shelly had assumed he wouldn't take it seriously. She'd said it more for the sake of dignity, of preserving her pride. She had actually been enjoying his company, enjoying the banter between them.

As he vanished into the distance, Shelly squared her shoulders, determined to manage on her own—particularly since she didn't have much choice in the matter. She'd been dragging the moped along for several minutes when she noticed a moped racing toward her. It didn't take her long to identify the rider, with his lithe, muscular build, as Mark. She picked up her pace, unreasonably pleased that he'd decided to return. He slowed as he approached her.

"Still eager to be rid of me?"

"No," she admitted, smiling half in relief, half in pleasure. "Can't you tell when a woman means something and when she's just being polite?"

"I guess not." He smiled back, apparently in a jovial mood. "Rest," he said, parking his own moped and taking hers. "A truck will be along any minute."

Shelly sank gratefully into the lush sand. Mark lowered himself onto the beach beside her. She picked several blades of grass and began weaving them industriously together. That way, she wouldn't have to look at him.

"Are you always this stubborn?" he asked.

"Yes," she said quietly, giving him a shy smile. Shelly couldn't remember being shy in her life. But something about Mark made her feel shaky inside, and oddly weak. An unfamiliar sensation, but she dared not analyze it, dared not examine it too closely. She turned away from him and closed her eyes, trying to picture Janice, the woman he was going to marry. Despite her usually creative imagination, Shelly couldn't seem to visualize her.

"Shelly, what's wrong?"

"Wrong?"

"It's not like you to be quiet."

She grinned. They were barely more than acquaintances, and he already knew her. "Nothing."

"I think there must be." His finger against the side of her face guided her eyes toward him. Their lips were so close. Shelly's breath seemed to be caught somewhere in her throat as she stared helplessly into the bluest eyes she'd ever seen....

His forehead touched hers, then he angled his face gently, brushing her cheek. Shelly knew she should break away, but she couldn't make herself do it. Gently, deliberately, he pressed his mouth to hers, his lips warm and moist.

Shelly moaned at the shock of sensation. Her eyes drifted shut as his mouth moved hungrily over hers, and soon their arms were wrapped tightly around each other, their bodies straining closer.

The sound of the approaching truck intruded into their private world and broke them apart. Mark's eyes met hers, then he scowled darkly and glanced away. But Shelly didn't know whether he was more angry with her or with himself. Probably her.

Chapter Seven

"HEY," SHELLY SAID reassuringly, "don't look so concerned. It was just an ordinary, run-of-the-mill kiss." She stood indignantly and brushed the wet sand from her jeans. "Besides, it didn't mean anything."

Mark's scowl darkened. "Didn't mean anything?" he echoed.

"Of course it didn't! I mean, we were both wondering what it would be like, don't you think? Good grief, we seem to be running into each other every other day and it only makes sense that we should want to, you know, experiment."

"In other words, you think the kiss was just a means of satisfying our mutual curiosity?"

"Sure. All this nonsense about the wedding dress overcame our normal good sense, and we succumbed to the temptation." Thank goodness Mark seemed to understand her rambling. Shelly's knees were shaking. It was a wonder she could still stand upright. Although she'd tried to minimize the effects of his kiss, it left her feeling as though she'd never been kissed before. Her entire body had been overwhelmed by a feeling of rightness. Now all she felt was the crushing weight of confusion. She shouldn't be feeling any of these things for Mark. A CPA! An almost-engaged CPA, to boot.

"And was your curiosity satisfied?" he demanded. His blue eyes probed and waited.

"Uh . . . yes. And yours?"

"Yes," he muttered, but he was frowning again.

The youth from the rental agency leaped out of the truck and loaded Shelly's moped into the back. "You're not supposed to get the engine wet," he scolded. "It's in the rental agreement. You'll have to pay a fine."

Shelly nodded. She didn't have an excuse; she doubted the agency would accept her trying to escape Mark as a legitimate reason for damaging one of their vehicles.

Mark hefted his own bike onto the truck as well, and the three of them got into the pickup's cab and rode silently down the long stretch of beach.

Shelly went to the office to deal with her fine and was surprised to find Mark waiting for her when she'd finished. "You hungry?" he asked in an offhand invitation.

"Uh . . ." She would have thought he'd be anxious to see the last of her.

"Good," he said immediately, not giving her a chance to reply. His hand grasped her elbow firmly as he led her to a nearby fish-and-chips stand. Shelly couldn't recall the last time a man had taken her elbow. Her first reaction was to object to what she considered an outdated gesture but she was surprised to find it oddly comfortable, even pleasant.

They ordered their fish and chips, then carried the small baskets to a picnic table.

"I should have paid for my own," she said once they were seated, vaguely guilty that he'd paid for both meals. Janice might be the jealous type, and Shelly didn't want her to hear about this.

His eyes met hers, steady and direct. "When I ask you to join me, I pick up the bill."

Any argument she had vanished before it reached her lips.

After that, Shelly concentrated on her fish and chips, which were fresh and absolutely delicious. Mark seemed preoccupied with his meal, as well.

"What brought you to the beach today?" Shelly asked, finishing the last few French fries in her basket. Perhaps if they could figure out what had brought them both to a lonely stretch of beach two hours out of Seattle, they might be able to make sense of how they'd happened upon each other a third time.

"I have a beach house here. After tax time I generally try to get away for a few days, to come down here and relax."

"I had no idea." She found it inordinately important that he understand she hadn't somehow managed to stalk him across the state. Their meeting was pure coincidence...again.

"Don't worry about it, Shelly. You couldn't possibly have known about the beach house or that I intended to be here today. I didn't know it myself until this morning."

Shelly suddenly wished that Mark hadn't kissed her. Everything was becoming far too complicated now.

"You're very talented," he told her out of the blue. "I bought one of your videos the other day."

"How did you know what I do?" Shelly felt flustered by his praise; she was at a complete loss to understand why it meant so much to her.

"I saw it on the income tax form and I was curious about your work."

"Curiosity seems to have gotten us both into a great deal of trouble," she said.

Mark grinned, a shameless irresistible grin. The kind of grin that makes a woman forget all sorts of things. Like the fact that he was practically engaged. And that he was

a tall, blue-eyed stranger who, according to Aunt Milly's letter, would soon become her husband....

Shelly scrambled to her feet, hurrying toward the
beach. Mark followed.

"You shouldn't look at me like that," she said, her
voice soft and bewildered.

"You said it was just a kiss. Was it?"

"Yes," she boldly lied. "How could it be anything
more?"

"You tell me."

Shelly had no answers to give him.

"While you're at it, explain why we keep bumping into
each other or why I can't stop thinking about you."

"You can't?" She hadn't been able to stop thinking
about him, either, but she wasn't ready to admit it.

"No." He stood behind her, his hands caressing her
shoulders. Leisurely he stroked the length of her arms.
His touch was so light that she thought she was imagin-
ing it, and she felt both excited and afraid.

He turned her around and gazed at her lips. "If that
was just a run-of-the-mill kiss, then why do I feel the need
to do it again?"

"I don't know."

His lips brushed hers. Briefly, with a whisper-soft
touch, as though he was testing her response. Shelly
closed her eyes and moaned. She didn't want to feel any
of this. They were so far apart, such different people.
Besides, *he* was involved with another woman and *she* was
involved with her career.

When the kiss ended and he slowly released her, it was
all Shelly could do to keep from sinking to the sand. "I
have ... to get back to Seattle," she managed to say,
backing away from him. She turned and took four or five

wobbly steps before she realized she was headed toward the Pacific Ocean.

"Shelly?"

"Yes?"

"Seattle is due north. If you continue going west, you'll eventually land in Hawaii."

"Oh, yeah, right," she mumbled, reversing her direction abruptly, eager now to escape.

THE FIRST PERSON Shelly called when she got home was Jill. "Can you come over?" Shelly asked without preamble. She could barely keep the panic out of her voice.

"Sure, what's wrong?"

"I saw Mark again."

"And?"

"Let me put it like this. We kissed and I haven't stopped trembling since."

Jill's romantic sigh came over the receiver as her breath softly caught. "This I've got to hear. I'll be there in ten minutes."

Actually it was closer to seven minutes. Shelly hadn't stopped pacing from the moment she got off the phone. She checked her watch repeatedly, waiting desperately for a dose of Jill's good sense.

"Shelly," Jill said, smiling as she breezed into the apartment, "what happened to your hair?"

Shelly smoothed down the errant curls. "I was at Long Beach."

"That's where you saw Mark? Good grief, that's something of a coincidence, isn't it?"

"I saw him earlier in the week, too.... Remember I told you I was being audited by the IRS? Lo and behold, guess who was in their waiting room when I arrived?"

"I don't need to be a rocket scientist to figure that one out. Mark Brady!"

"Right." Shelly rubbed her damp palms along her jeans in agitation. They, at least, had finally dried.

"And?"

Shelly groaned. "Can't you see what's happening? This is the third time we've been thrown together in the past few days. I'd never seen the man before, and all of a sudden he's around every corner. Then the wedding dress fit. It fit you . . . and it fits me."

"I agree that's all rather odd, but I wouldn't put too much stock in it, if I were you."

"Put too much stock in it . . . Listen, Jill, I've never had a man make me feel the way Mark does—all weak inside and, I don't know, special somehow. To be perfectly honest, I don't like it." She closed her eyes, hoping to chase away the memory of his touch, but it did no good. "You want to know the real kicker?" she asked abruptly, turning to face her friend. "He's engaged."

"Engaged," Jill echoed, her voice as startled as her expression.

"He keeps insisting it's not official yet. Nevertheless he's involved with someone else."

"But it was you he kissed," Jill pointed out.

"Don't remind me." Shelly covered her eyes with both hands. "I don't mind telling you, I find this whole thing unnerving.

"Obviously. Here," Jill said, directing Shelly toward the kitchen. "Now sit down. Let me make us some tea, then we can try to reason this out. Honestly, Shell, I don't think I've ever seen you so upset."

"I'm not upset," she cried. "I'm confused. There's a big difference. I'm . . . I'm trapped." Despite all logic to the contrary, she couldn't help fearing that the entire course of her life was about to change because her aunt Milly had fallen asleep watching "Donahue" one day and had some nonsensical dream.

"Trapped?" Jill repeated. "Don't you think you're being a bit dramatic?"

"I don't know anymore." Shelly rested her elbows on the table, buried her face in her hands and breathed in deeply. She had a tendency to become emotional, especially over family issues; she realized that. But this was different. This was scary.

"Calm down," Jill advised. "Once you think it through in a rational manner, you'll realize there's a perfectly ordinary explanation for everything."

Jill's serenity lent Shelly some badly needed confidence. "All right, you explain it."

"I can't," Jill admitted matter-of-factly, pouring boiling water into Shelly's teapot. "I'm not even going to try. My advice to you is to quit taking all this so seriously. If a relationship develops between you and Mark, just enjoy it—providing the other woman's out of the picture, of course! Just forget about that dress."

"Easy for you to say."

"That's true," Jill agreed readily. "But you're going to have to accept it for your own peace of mind."

Shelly knew good advice when she heard it. "You're right. I'm unnecessarily leaping into the deep end with this."

"A dress can't make you do anything you don't want to do. The same applies to Mark."

Shelly always counted on her friend's levelheadedness. Although Jill had given her basically the same advice several days earlier, Shelly needed to hear it again.

Jill prepared two cups of tea and carried them to the table. "Are you going to be all right now?"

Shelly nodded. "Of course. I just needed a friend to remind me that I was overreacting." She took a sip of the tea, surprised by how much it revived her. "You're still planning to see *Street Suite* with me tomorrow afternoon, aren't you?"

The recent Broadway hit was showing locally, and Shelly and Jill had purchased their tickets several weeks earlier.

"That's not tomorrow, is it?" Jill looked stricken, her teacup poised midway to her mouth.

"Jill . . ."

"I promised I'd work for Sharon Belmont. She's got some family thing she has to attend. She was desperate and I completely forgot about the play. Oh, dear, you'll just have to go without me."

"You're sure you can't get out of it?" Shelly couldn't help feeling disappointed.

"I'm sure. I'm really sorry, Shell."

Although frustrated that Jill couldn't come with her, Shelly decided to go to the theater alone. She wasn't pleased at the prospect and given her proclivity for running into Mark Brady, she didn't feel entirely convinced that this wasn't another attempt by the fates to regulate their lives.

However, if she stayed home, she'd be missing a wonderful play. Not only that, she'd be giving in to a nebulous and irrational fear, allowing it to take over her life.

The following afternoon, Shelly dressed carefully, in the type of conservative outfit her mother would have approved of. Mark, too, would approve of her rose-colored linen dress with its matching jacket.... The minute the thought flashed through her head, she rejected it.

She was on her way out the door when her phone rang. For a split second she toyed with the idea of not answering. More than likely it was her mother, checking in to see if Shelly had met a prospective husband yet. Her calls had become more frequent and more urgent since Aunt Milly's dress had arrived.

Years of habit prompted her to reach for the telephone.

"Shelly." Mark's voice came over the line. "I was about to leave for the afternoon's performance of *Street Suite*. Since we seem to have this tendency to run into each other everywhere we go, I thought I should probably clear it with you. If you're going to be there, I'll go another time."

Chapter Eight

"ACTUALLY I WAS PLANNING to see the play this afternoon myself," Shelly admitted hesitantly. "Jill had to cancel out at the last minute."

"It seems Janice can't attend, either."

Hearing the other woman's name, the woman Mark loved, had a curious and unexpected effect on Shelly. Her heart sank, and she felt a sharp pang of disappointment. She rebounded quickly, however, forcing a lightness into her voice, a blitheness she didn't feel. "Listen, there's no need for you to miss the play. I'll call the ticket office and see about an exchange."

"No, I will," Mark offered.

"That's ridiculous. Jill really wanted to see this play and—"

"Would it really be so terrible if we both decided to attend the same performance?"

"Uh..." The question caught Shelly unprepared. Mark was the one who'd suggested they avoid each other.

"What could it possibly hurt? You have your ticket and I have mine. It'd be absurd to let them go to waste because we're afraid of seeing each other again, don't you think?"

Forming a single, coherent thought seemed beyond Shelly at that moment. After her long talk with Jill the day before, followed by the pep talk she'd given herself, she'd recovered a degree of composure. Now, all of a sudden, she wasn't sure of anything.

"I don't think it should matter," she said finally, although it did matter, greatly.

"Good. Enjoy the play."

"You, too."

The theater was within walking distance of her apartment building, and Shelly left as soon as she'd finished talking to Mark. He was right. Just because they each had tickets to the same play was no reason for either of them to be penalized.

So Mark was going to see *Street Suite*. It wasn't the type of play she would have thought he'd enjoy. But the man was full of surprises. Riding mopeds on the beach, kissing so spectacularly, and now this . . .

Shelly's mind was full of Mark as she hurried down the steep hill on Cherry Street. The theater was only a block away when she saw him. Her pulse soared and she wasn't sure if she should smile and wave or simply ignore him.

She didn't need to do either. He stood on the sidewalk, waiting for her.

"You're late," he said, glancing at his watch. "But then you traditionally are." His grin was wide and welcoming. "I couldn't see any reason not to watch the play together," he went on. "What do you say?"

"You're sure?"

"Positive." He offered her his arm, and she reflected that it was the kind of old-fashioned courtesy, the kind of gentlemanly gesture, she'd expected from Mark.

The usher seated them and smiled constantly as if to say they were a handsome couple. Shelly was terribly tempted to explain that Mark was engaged to someone else; luckily she managed to hold her tongue. Minutes after they'd settled into their seats, the curtain rose.

The play, a clever satire about urban life, was as good as the reviews claimed, and Shelly enjoyed herself thoroughly. Throughout the performance, however, she was all too aware of Mark sitting next to her. She found herself wondering if he was equally aware of her. She also found herself wondering how long it would be before they "bumped" into each other again—and hoped it was soon.

By the end of the play Shelly felt inspired and full of enthusiasm, eager to start a new project of her own. As she and Mark left the theater, she talked excitedly about her idea for the "ocean moods" series. He asked a few questions and even suggested some shots. Before she realized it, they were several blocks past the theater, headed in the opposite direction from her apartment building. Shelly paused and glanced around.

"There's an excellent Chinese restaurant in this neighborhood," was all Mark said. Without giving her the opportunity to decline, he gently guided her toward the place he'd mentioned.

It was early for dinner, and they were seated immediately. Although they'd been talking comfortably during their walk, Shelly found herself suddenly self-conscious. She toyed with the linen napkin, smoothing it across her lap.

"I hadn't expected to like the play as much as I did," he said after a while.

Shelly thought it a bit off that he'd ordered tickets for this production, but perhaps he'd gotten them because Janice had wanted to see *Street Suite*.

"It's a little frightening the way we keep finding each other, isn't it?" she ventured.

"I can see how *you'd* find it disconcerting," Mark answered.

"You don't?"

Mark shrugged. "I haven't given it much thought."

"I'll admit all these...coincidences do throw me," she said, running her index finger along the outline of the fire-breathing dragon on the menu cover. Chancing a glance in his direction, she added, "But I'm learning to deal with it."

"So you feel you've been caught in something beyond your control?" Mark surprised her by asking.

Shelly lifted her gaze to his, amazed by the intensity she read in his eyes. "No, not really. Well...a little bit, maybe. Do you?"

"It wasn't *my* aunt Milly who had the dream."

Shelly smiled and dropped her gaze. "No, but as my friend Jill reminded me recently, no fifty-year-old dress is going to dictate my life. Or yours," she felt obliged to add. Then she realized why he'd asked the question. "You must feel overwhelmed by all of this. All of a sudden I've been thrust into your life. There's no escaping me, is there?" she said wryly. "Every time you turn around, there I am."

"Are you going to stand up and announce to everyone in the restaurant that you refuse to marry me?"

"No." Shelly was appalled at his remark until she remembered that she'd done exactly that the first time they met.

"If you can resist doing that, then I think I can bear up under pressure."

Shelly ignored his mild sarcasm. "I'm not interested in marriage yet," she told him seriously—just in case he'd forgotten. "I'm content with my life. And I'm too busy for a husband and family."

She hadn't noticed how forcefully she was speaking until she saw several of the people at other tables glancing in her direction. Instantly she lowered her voice. "Sorry, my views on marriage seem to be more fervent than I realized. But I'm not about to let either my mother or my dear aunt Milly determine when I decide to settle down and marry."

"Personally, I can't see you ever settling down," Mark said with a small grin. "You don't have to worry. When you're ready, you'll know it."

"Did you?" She hadn't meant to bring up Janice, but now seemed as good a time as any to remind him—and her—that there was someone else in his life.

Mark shrugged casually. "More or less. I took a good, long look at my life and discovered I'd already achieved several of my professional goals. It was time to invest my energy in developing the personal aspects of my life. Marriage, children and the like."

Mark made marriage sound as if it were the next chapter in a book he was reading or a connect-the-dots picture. Shelly couldn't stop herself from frowning.

"You have a problem with that?"

"Not a problem, exactly. I happen to think of marriage a bit differently, that's all."

"In what way?"

He seemed genuinely interested, otherwise she would have kept her opinions to herself. "People should fall in love," she said slowly. "I don't think it's necessary or even possible to plan for that to happen. Love can be unexpected—it can take a couple by surprise, knock them both off their feet."

"You make falling in love sound like a bad case of the flu."

Shelly smiled. "In some ways, I think that's exactly how it should be. Marriage is one of the most important decisions in anyone's life, so it should be a *deeply felt* decision. It should feel inevitable. It's the union of two lives, after all. So you can't simply check your watch and announce 'it's time.'" She was suddenly concerned that she'd spoken out of turn and might have offended him, but one quick glance assured her that wasn't the case.

"You surprise me," Mark said, leaning forward. "I would never have guessed it."

"Guessed what?" She was beginning to feel a little foolish now.

"That a woman who gives the impression of being a scatterbrain is really quite reflective. Beneath those glow-in-the-dark sweatshirts lies a very romantic heart."

"I seem to have a tendency to get emotional about certain things," she answered, studying the menu, eager to change the subject. "I've heard hot-and-sour soup is wonderful. Have you ever tried it?"

Their conversation over dinner remained light and amusing. Shelly noticed that Mark avoided any more discussion of a personal nature, as did she.

After they'd finished their dinner and Mark had paid the bill, they leisurely strolled back toward the theater. Mark offered to drive her home when they reached his parked car, but Shelly declined. Her apartment was only a couple of blocks north and she preferred to walk.

Walk and think. Their time together had given her plenty to think about.

"Thank you for dinner," she said as he unlocked the car.

"You're welcome," he answered. "Well, good night for now," he said, grinning. "I suspect I'll be seeing you soon."

She grinned back. "Probably within a day or two. Maybe we should synchronize our schedules," she teased.

"That wouldn't bother you, would it?"

"Oh, no. What about you?" She hated the way her voice rose expectantly with the question. She certainly wasn't bothered by the prospect of seeing him again. In fact, she was downright eager to see what tricks fate would play on them next.

Mark's eyes found hers then, and he slowly pocketed his car keys. His look was so potent, so full of emotion, that Shelly took a step in retreat. "I had a wonderful afternoon, a wonderful evening. Thanks again," she said nervously.

Mark didn't say a word as he continued to gaze at her.

"The play was great, wasn't it? And dinner... fabulous." Shelly's throat seemed to close as Mark stepped onto the curb and walked toward her.

The whole world seemed to come to a sudden, abrupt halt when she realized he intended to kiss her. *Not again*, her mind shouted. *Please hurry*, her heart sang.

Her heartbeat tripped wildly as Mark lowered his head, his mouth seeking hers. Despite the fierce battle inside her, Shelly was forced to admit how much she wanted this kiss. If for no other reason, she told herself, than to prove that the first time had been an accident, a fluke.

Only it happened again. But this kiss was a hundred times more compelling than the first one they'd shared. A hundred times more exciting.

Shelly wanted to cry out at the unfairness of it all. If a man's kiss was going to affect her this acutely, why did it have to be Mark Brady's?

He broke away from her reluctantly, his warm breath fanning her cheek. His eyes were filled with questions, filled with surprise. Shelly wasn't sure what her own eyes were saying to him. She didn't even want to know.

"Take care," he whispered as he turned away.

SHELLY STAYED home from work on Monday. She wasn't sick, just confused and puzzled. Nothing about her relationship with Mark seemed to make sense. He was everything she *didn't* want in a man—and everything she did.

Shelly didn't realize how despondent she was until she found herself standing barefoot in front of her closet, carrying on a conversation with Aunt Milly's wedding dress.

"I'll have you know I had a perfectly good life until you arrived," she muttered disparagingly. "Now it seems my whole world's been turned upside down." She slammed the door closed, then jerked it open. "No wonder Mrs. Livingston's cat wouldn't go near you. You're *dangerous*."

Chapter Nine

"THE PLAY WAS GREAT," Shelly told Jill over coffee Wednesday afternoon. She'd stopped off at PayRite, hoping Jill could get away for lunch. "Even Mark—"

"Mark?" Jill's coffee cup hit the saucer with a clang. "He was at the play?"

Shelly nodded sheepishly. "I guess I forgot to mention I ran into him, didn't I? Actually he called me first and since we both had plans to attend the same performance, we decided to go together."

"Is there anything else you haven't told me?" Jill's eyes narrowed astutely.

Shelly tried to hide her uneasiness behind a relaxed shrug, but how well she succeeded in fooling Jill remained to be seen. "We had dinner afterward...as friends. It didn't mean anything. I did tell you he's engaged, didn't I?"

"*Unofficially* engaged." Jill was studying her closely and Shelly felt distinctly uneasy under the scrutiny.

"We've been friends for a long time," Jill reminded her. "In some ways I know you as well as I do myself. There's something troubling you."

Shelly nodded, knowing it wouldn't do any good to hide the truth from Jill. Her need to confide in a sympathetic, understanding person was the very reason for her impromptu visit to Jill's workplace. Lunch had been a convenient excuse.

"You won't believe this," Shelly said, cradling the warm coffee cup in both hands and keeping her gaze lowered. "I can hardly believe it myself."

"You're falling in love with Mark."

Shelly's gaze shot upward. "It shows that much?"

"No," Jill said softly. "But you look like you're about to break into tears."

"If I wasn't so darn irritated I would. Good grief, think about it. Can you imagine two people less suited to each other? Mark is so . . . so responsible . . ."

"So are you."

"Not in the same way," Shelly argued. "He's so sincere and . . ."

"Shelly, so are you."

"Perhaps, but I'm such a scatterbrain. I'm disorganized and always late and I like to do things my own way. You know that better than most."

"I prefer to think of you as creative."

Shelly tossed Jill a smile of appreciation. "That's the reason you're my best friend. I don't mind telling you, Jill, I'm worried. Mark Brady may be the Rock of Gibraltar, but I sincerely doubt he's got an original thought in his head. Everything is done by the book or according to schedule."

"You need someone like Mark in your life," Jill returned kindly. "Don't look so shocked. It's true. The two of you balance each other. He needs you because you're fun and crazy and imaginative, and you need him because he knows his times tables by heart and will remind you when it's time for meals."

"The problem is, Mark's the type of man who would expect a woman to *cook* those meals."

Jill chuckled.

"If the fates are determined to match me up with someone," Shelly moaned, "couldn't it be with someone other than an accountant?"

"Apparently not."

"What really angers me about this is that I allowed it to happen. The first time he kissed me—"

"He *kissed* you?" Jill feigned a look of horror.

Shelly ignored it. "Yes. A couple of times. It's only natural—our being curious about each other, don't you think?"

"I suppose," Jill said quickly, no longer teasing. "So tell me what happened."

"Fireworks bigger than the Fourth of July. I've never experienced the feelings I do with Mark, and all because of a simple kiss. I can't even begin to imagine what would happen if we ever made love."

"And does Mark feel the same thing?"

"I—I can't speak for him, but I think it must be equally disturbing for him. He certainly looked as if he'd been taken by surprise."

"How do you get along with him otherwise?"

"Fine, I guess." Shelly paused long enough to take a sip of her coffee. "I'm sure I amuse him. But someone like Mark isn't looking for a woman to entertain him, any more than I'm looking for a man to balance my checkbook."

"His opinion of you has mellowed, hasn't it?" Jill asked, then answered her own question. "There was a time when he thought you were a little bizarre, remember?"

Shelly did, all too well. "At first I thought he was about as exciting as oatmeal, but I've altered my opinion of him, too."

"So what's the problem?"

"I don't *want* to fall in love," Shelly said pointedly. "I've got bigger plans for my life than to tie myself down to a committed relationship right now."

"Then don't. It shouldn't be that difficult. Decide what you want and ignore everything else. There's no law that says you have to fall in love this minute. For that matter, no one can regulate when and who you marry, either. Not even your aunt Milly."

Jill was saying everything Shelly wanted to hear. Everything she needed to hear. But it didn't make any difference; her heart was already involved. If she could forget she'd ever met Mark, she would. But it was too late. She was in love with him. With Mark, who was in love with someone else. Mark, who saw love and marriage as goals to be achieved within a certain time frame. He'd probably never done anything impulsive in his life.

A lasting relationship would never work between them. If he wasn't smart enough to figure that out, she was. Something had to be done and soon, and Shelly knew it would be up to her to do it.

SHELLY DIDN'T HAVE LONG to wait before she saw Mark again. They met at the main branch of the Seattle Public Library Wednesday evening. She was returning ten overdue books. Six months' overdue. The library had sent her three warnings, each one progressively less friendly.

She was half-afraid the buzzer just inside the library entrance would go off the moment she walked through the hallowed doors and armed officers would haul her away.

"I wondered how long it would take for us to find each other again," Mark said, strolling up to her at the counter. She'd seen him almost immediately and tried to pretend she hadn't.

Shelly acknowledged him with a quick nod and ordered her heart to be still. She managed a small smile. "Hello again," she said, drawing the checkbook out of her purse. The fine for the books was sure to be monstrous. It might be cheaper to buy them.

Mark set the two volumes he was borrowing on the counter. Shelly noted the titles—*Tools for Time Management* and *The State of the Language,* and groaned inwardly. To someone like her accountant friend, these books were probably easy reading. Her own tastes leaned more toward mystery and romance, with a little nonfiction.

"Have you got time for a cup of coffee?" Mark asked as she wrote out the check to pay her fine.

Her heart was gladdened by the invitation, but she knew she had to refuse it. Before he could say or do anything to change her mind, she shook her head. "Not tonight, thanks."

His smile faded as though her refusal took him by surprise. "You're busy?"

She nodded, smiling at the librarian as she tore the check free and handed it to the woman, who smiled pleasantly in return. It had been a civilized exchange, Shelly thought, and her library card had *not* been confiscated, despite her transgressions.

"A date's waiting for you?"

It took Shelly a second to understand that Mark was referring to her refusal to join him for coffee.

"Not exactly." She turned away from the counter and headed toward the exit. To her surprise Mark followed her outside.

"Something's wrong," he said, standing at the top of the steps. She stopped her descent and stood below him, looking up. Pretense had never suited Shelly; she was too innately honest to hide her feelings. "Mark, I think you're a very nice man—"

"But you don't want to marry me," he concluded for her. "I've heard that line before, remember? Actually half the mall heard it, too."

"I've already apologized for that. It's just that . . . all right, if you must know, I'm beginning to like you . . . really like you, and frankly that terrifies me." She stood facing him, two steps below.

Her candid response seemed to unnerve him. He frowned and rubbed the side of his jaw. "I know what you mean. I'm beginning to like you, too."

"See!" she cried, tossing her hands in the air. "If we don't take care of this problem now, heaven only knows what could happen. It has the potential of ruining both our lives. We're mature adults, aren't we?" At the moment, though, she felt singularly lacking in maturity.

All her senses were clamoring, telling her to enjoy their brief time together and damn the consequences. It was what her heart wanted, but she couldn't allow her life to be ruled by her heart. Not when it came to Mark.

"Liking each other doesn't have to be a federal crime," he said, advancing one step toward her.

"You're right, of course, but I know myself too well. I could easily fall in love with you, Mark." She didn't dare admit she already had. "Before we knew how it happened, we'd be spending more and more time with each other. We might even become seriously involved."

He remained suspiciously silent.

"You're a wonderful man. If my mother were to meet you she'd be shouting from the rooftops, she'd be so grateful. For a while I might convince myself that we could really make something of this relationship. I might even consider taking cooking classes because you're the kind of man who'd expect a woman to know how to make a roast and mashed potatoes."

"It'd probably come in handy someday," he admitted.

"That's what I thought," she murmured, disheartened. "I'm not a traditional woman. I never will be. The only time I ever baked a pie I ended up throwing it in the garbage disposal—and it broke the disposal."

"A pie ruined your garbage disposal?" Mark repeated, then shook his head. "Never mind, don't bother explaining how that happened. It seems to me you're getting ahead of yourself here. You're talking as though coffee together means a lifetime commitment."

Shelly wasn't listening. "What about Janice?" she demanded. "She's the one you should be inviting to coffee, not me."

"What's Janice got to do with this?" he asked impatiently.

"Janice," Shelly snapped, her own temper short. "The woman you've decided to marry. Remember her? The love of your life? The woman you're unofficially engaged to marry."

"It's not unofficial any longer," Mark explained evenly.

"Oh great, you're taking me out to dinner, kissing me and at the same time picking out engagement rings with another woman." She had to admit he'd never lied to her about his relationship with the faceless Janice. From the beginning he'd been forthright and honest about the other woman. But it hurt, really hurt, to learn that he was going ahead with his plans to marry Janice.

For a moment she'd been shocked into stillness. "Then..." She struggled to force some enthusiasm into her voice. "Congratulations are in order. I wish you both the very best." With that she turned and bounded down the stairs, taking them recklessly fast.

"Shelly!"

She could hear Mark calling after her, but she ignored him, desperate to get away before the lump in her throat made it impossible to breathe. Tears had formed in her eyes and she cursed herself for being so ridiculous, for caring so much. Her vision blurred and she wiped a hand across her face, furious with herself for the lack of control. This marriage was what she'd hoped would happen. What she wanted for Mark. *Wasn't it?*

"Shelly, for heaven's sake, will you wait?"

When she reached the bottom of the steps, Shelly moved quickly into a side street, hoping to disappear in the crowd, praying Mark wouldn't pursue her.

She thought she'd escaped until a hand on her shoulder whirled her around.

"Shelly, please listen," Mark pleaded breathlessly, his shoulders heaving with the effort of catching up with her. "The engagement isn't official, because there isn't an engagement. How could I possibly marry Janice after meeting you?"

Chapter Ten

"YOU BROKE OFF your engagement with Janice?" Shelly demanded furiously. Something inside, some reservoir of emotion, felt as if it had burst wide open. "You fool," she cried. "You idiot!" Her eyes brimmed over with tears and deep, deep inside her heart began its stirrings of glad excitement. "That was the worst thing you could have done!"

"No," he said. "It was the smartest move I've ever made."

"How can you say that?" she wailed.

"Shelly?"

He reached for her as though to offer comfort, but Shelly jerked her arms away and stepped back, freeing herself from his grasp. "Janice was perfect for you," she lamented.

"How do you know that?" he asked calmly, much too reasonably to suit Shelly. "You never met her."

"I didn't need to. I know she was right for you. You'd never have asked her to marry you if she wasn't."

"Janice is a wonderful woman and she'll make some lucky man a good wife, but it won't be me."

"You're crazy to break off your engagement. Crazy!"

"No, I'm not," Mark returned confidently. "I'm absolutely certain I did the right thing. Do you know why?"

Shelly could only shake her head, wiping away the tears with the back of her hand. She was ecstatic—and yet she was so frightened. She loved him, she was sure of it. Then why had everything become confused and difficult?

"What you said about love the other day changed my mind."

"You listened to me?" she cried in real horror. "Do I look like an expert on love? I've never been in love in my life!" Not counting what she felt for him, of course. She'd always thought love would clarify her life, not make it more complicated.

Mark ignored her outburst. "You helped me understand that I was marrying Janice for all the wrong reasons. I'd decided it was time to settle down. Janice had come to the same conclusion. She's thirty and figured if she was going to marry and have a family, the time was now. It wasn't a love match, and we both knew it."

"This is none of my business," Shelly said, frantically shaking her head as if to chase the words away. "I don't want to hear any of it."

"You are going to hear it," Mark insisted, gripping her elbows and gently drawing her closer to him. "You claimed people shouldn't plan love. It should take them by surprise, you said, and you were right. Janice and I are fond of each other, but—"

"There's nothing wrong with fond!"

His eyes widened in obvious surprise. "No, there isn't," he agreed, "but Janice isn't a zany video producer. I like spending time with you. I've come to realize there's a certain thrill in expecting the unexpected. Every minute with you is an adventure."

"A relationship between us would never last," Shelly insisted, drawing on the most sensible argument. "It would be fine for a while, but then we'd drift apart. We'd have to. In case you haven't noticed, we're nothing alike."

"Why wouldn't a relationship last?" Mark asked patiently.

"For all the reasons I listed before!" Mark was so endearing, and he was saying all the words she'd secretly longed to hear, but nothing could change the fundamental differences between them.

"So you aren't as adept in the kitchen as some women. I'm a fair cook."

"It's more than that."

"Of course it is," he concurred. "But there's nothing we can't overcome if we're willing to work together."

"You know what I think it is?" she said desperately, running her splayed fingers through her hair. "You're beginning to believe there's magic in Aunt Milly's wedding dress."

"Don't you?"

"No," she cried. "Not anymore. I did when I was a little girl . . . I loved the story of how Aunt Milly met Uncle John, but I'm not a child anymore, and what seemed so romantic then just seems unrealistic now."

"Shelly," Mark said in exasperation. "We don't need to do anything right away. All I'm suggesting is we give this thing between us a chance."

"There's nothing between us," she denied vehemently.

Mark's eyes narrowed. "You don't honestly believe that, do you?"

"Yes," she lied. "You're a nice guy, but—"

"If I hear any more of this nice-guy stuff I'm going to kiss you and we both know what will happen."

His gaze lowered to her mouth and she unconsciously moistened her lips with anticipation.

"I just might, anyway."

"No." The threat was real enough to cause her to retreat a couple of steps. If Mark kissed her, Shelly knew she'd be listening to her heart and not her head. And then *he'd* know . . . "That's what I thought." His grin was downright boyish.

"I think we should both forget we ever met," she suggested next, aware even as she said it how ludicrous she sounded. Mark Brady had indelibly marked her life and no matter how much she denied it, she'd never forget him.

"Are you forgetting you threw yourself into my arms? *You* can conveniently choose to overlook the obvious, but unfortunately that won't work for me. I'm falling in love with you, Shelly."

She opened her mouth to argue that he couldn't possibly love her . . . not yet, not on such short acquaintance, but he pressed his finger to her lips, silencing her.

"At first I wasn't keen on the idea," he admitted, "but it's sort of grown on me since. I can see us ten years in the future and you know what? It's a pleasant picture. We're going to be very happy together."

"I need to think," she cried, placing her hands on either side of her head. Everything was happening much too quickly; she actually felt dizzy. "We'll leave it to fate . . . how does that sound?" she offered excitedly. It seemed like the perfect solution to her. "The next time we bump into each other, I'll have more of a grasp on my feelings. I'll know what we should do." She might also take to hibernating inside her apartment for a month, but she wasn't mentioning that.

"Nope," Mark returned, slowly shaking his head. "That won't work."

"Why not?" she demanded. "We bump into each other practically every day."

"No, we don't."

He wasn't making any sense.

"*Street Suite* was a setup," he informed her. "I made sure we bumped into each other there."

"How? When?"

"The day at the beach I saw the play ticket sticking out of your purse. Our meeting at the theater wasn't any accident."

Mark couldn't have shocked her more if he'd announced he was an alien from outer space. For the first time in recent memory, she was left speechless. "Tonight?" she asked when she could get the words out. "The library?"

"I'd decided to stop off at your apartment. I was prepared to make up some story about the wedding dress luring me into your building, but when I drove past, I saw you coming down the front steps loaded down with library books. It didn't take a whole lot of figuring to know where you were headed. I found a parking space and waited for you inside."

"What about . . . the IRS office and the beach?" She didn't know how he'd managed those chance meetings.

Mark shook his head and grinned. "Coincidence, unless you had anything to do with those. You didn't, did you?"

"Absolutely not," she replied indignantly.

Still grinning, he said, "I didn't really think you had."

Shelly started walking, her destination unclear. She felt too restless to continue standing there; unfortunately the one action that truly appealed to her was leaping into his arms.

Mark matched his own steps to hers.

"It's Aunt Milly's wedding dress, I know it is," Shelly mumbled under her breath. She'd tried to bring up the subject earlier, but Mark had refused to listen. "You broke off an engagement because you believe fate has somehow thrown us together."

"No, Shelly, the dress doesn't have anything to do with how I feel," Mark responded calmly.

"But you'd already decided to marry someone else!"

"I'm choosing my own destiny, which is to spend the rest of my life with you."

"You might have consulted with me first. I have no intention of getting married . . . not for years and years."

"I'll wait."

"You can't do that," she cried. He didn't understand because he was too respectable and adorable and so much of a gentleman. The only thing that would work would be to heartlessly send him away before he wasted the better part of his life waiting for her.

She stopped and turned to face Mark. She was careful to wear just the right expression of remorse and regret. "This is all very flattering, but I don't love you. I'm sorry, Mark. You're the last person in the world I want to hurt."

For a moment Mark said nothing, then he slowly shrugged and looked away. "You can't be any more direct than that, can you? There's no chance you'll ever fall in love with me?"

"None." Her breath fell harshly, painfully, from her lips. It shouldn't hurt this much to do the right thing. It shouldn't hurt to be noble. "You're very nice, but . . ."

"So you've said before."

Falteringly, as though the movement caused him pain, he lifted his hand to her face, his fingers tenderly caressing the delicate curve of her jaw.

Until that moment, Shelly hadn't understood how fiercely proud Mark was. He could have dealt with every argument, calmed every doubt, answered every question, but there was nothing he could say when she denied all feeling for him.

"You mean it, don't you?" he asked huskily. He was standing so close that his breath warmed her face.

Shelly had schooled her features to reveal none of her clamoring emotions. His touch, so light, so potent, seemed to clog her throat with anguish, and she couldn't speak.

"If that's what you want—" he dropped his hand abruptly "—I won't trouble you again." With those words, he turned and walked away. Before she fully realized what he intended, Mark had disappeared around a corner.

"You let him go, you idiot!" she whispered to herself. A lone tear escaped and she smeared it across her cheek.

Mark meant what he said about not bothering her. He was a man of his word. He'd never try to see her again— and if they did happen upon each other, he'd pretend he didn't know her.

He might eventually decide to marry Janice. Hadn't he admitted he was fond of the other woman?

Shelly's heart clenched painfully inside her chest. Before she could stop herself, before she could question the wisdom of her actions, she ran after Mark.

She turned the corner and was halfway down the sidewalk when she realized he wasn't anywhere to be seen. She came to a skidding halt, then whirled around, wondering how he could possibly have gotten so far in so short a time.

Mark stepped out from the side of a building, hands on his hips, a cocky, jubilant smile on his face. "What took you so long, darlin'?" he asked, holding out his arms.

Shelly didn't need a second invitation to throw herself into his embrace. His mouth feasted on hers, his kiss hungry and demanding, filled with enough emotion to last a lifetime.

Shelly slid her arms around his neck and stood on her tiptoes, giving herself completely to his kiss, to his love. The only thing that mattered was being in his arms—where she was supposed to be.

"I take it this means you love me, too?" he whispered close to her ear. His voice was rough with emotion.

Shelly nodded. "I'm so afraid."

"Don't be. I'm confident enough for both of us."

"This is crazy," she said, but she wouldn't have moved out of his arms for the world. Breathing deeply, she buried her face in his chest.

"But it's a good kind of crazy."

"Aunt Milly saw us together in her dream. She wrote me about a tall, blue-eyed man."

"Who knows if it was me or not?" Mark whispered into her hair, and brushed his lips over her temple. "Who cares? If fate had anything to do with me finding you or if your aunt Milly's wedding dress is responsible, I can't say. Personally, I couldn't care less. I love you, Shelly, and I believe you love me, too."

She glanced up at this man who had altered the course of her life and smiled, her heart too full for words. "I do love you," she said when she could. "An accountant! In a suit! Hardly the husband I imagined for myself."

Mark chuckled. "I'd never have guessed I could find myself head over heels in love with a woman who wears the kind of clothes you do, but I am."

"I do love you," Shelly repeated and closed her eyes.

THE MORNING of her wedding day, Shelly, who was rarely nervous, couldn't sit still. Her mother was even worse, pacing in front of her, dabbing her eyes and sniffling.

"I can't believe my baby's getting married."

Shelly had to restrain herself from reminding her dear mother that less than a month before, she'd been desperate to marry her daughter off. Thank goodness Jill was around. Without her best friend there to reassure her, Shelly didn't know what she would have done. While her mother fussed with the caterers, complained to the florists and fretted about who had a key to the kitchen in the reception hall, Jill led Shelly upstairs to her childhood bedroom and helped her dress. When Shelly was finished, Jill stood back to examine her.

"Well?" Shelly asked, smoothing her hand down the antique dress, loving the feel of the satin and lace against her fingers. It was probably her imagination but now that she was wearing the dress, really wearing it, she could almost feel a magic quality.

Tears gathered in Jill's eyes as she stared at her friend.

"That bad?" Shelly teased.

Jill pressed her fingertips to her lips. "You're beautiful," she whispered. "Mark isn't going to believe his eyes when he sees you."

"Do you really think so?" Shelly hated sounding so insecure, but she wanted everything perfect for this day. She was crazy in love—and crazy enough to give her mother free rein planning her wedding. Crazy enough to go through with a formal wedding in the first place. If it had been up to her, they'd have eloped weeks ago. But Mark had wanted the wedding and her mother certainly wasn't going to be cheated out of this moment. So Shelly had gone along with it.

Mark and her mother had defeated the majority of her ideas. She'd wanted to hire clowns to entertain at the reception, but her mother didn't seem to think that was a good idea.

Shelly had never been that fond of white wedding cake, either. She wanted something a bit less traditional, like Cherries Jubilee, but Mark was afraid something might catch on fire and so in the interests of safety, Shelly had agreed to a traditional cake, decorated with pink roses.

A knock sounded on her bedroom door and Jill opened it. In walked Aunt Milly, looking absolutely delighted with herself.

She introduced herself to Jill, then turned to gaze lovingly at Shelly. "So I see the dress worked."

"It worked," Shelly agreed.

"You love him?"

Shelly nodded. "Enough to eat white wedding cake."

Milly laughed softly and sat on the edge of the bed. Her hair had faded to gray, but her eyes were still blue and clear. It was difficult to tell that she was a woman well into her seventies. She clasped both of Shelly's hands in her own.

"Nervous?"

Shelly nodded again.

"I was, too, although I knew to the very bottom of my heart that I'd made the right decision in marrying John."

"I feel the same way about Mark."

Aunt Milly hugged her tightly. "You're going to be very happy, my dear."

AN HOUR LATER Shelly and Mark stood at the front of a packed church with Pastor Johnson, who'd known her most of her life. He smiled warmly as he spoke a few words, then asked Shelly to repeat her vows.

Linking hands with Mark, she raised her eyes to his. Everyone else faded away. Aunt Milly. Jill. Her mother. There were only the two of them. She felt a jolt of pure joy at the love that radiated from Mark's eyes. He stood tall and proud, his gaze eagerly holding hers, the love shining through without doubt, without question, shining through for her to read. Shelly knew her eyes told him the same thing.

Later, Shelly couldn't remember speaking her vows aloud, although she was sure she did. The words came directly from her heart. Directly from Mark's.

They'd been drawn to this place and this time by forces neither fully understood. Shelly wasn't entirely sure she believed Aunt Milly's wedding dress was responsible, but it didn't matter. They were there out of love. She didn't know exactly when it had happened. Perhaps that day on the beach, when Mark first kissed her. Something had happened then, something that touched them both.

The love that began as a small spark had grown and flared to life until they'd been brought here, to stand before God and family, pledging their lives to one another.

To love. To cherish. All the days of their lives.

It was enough. More than enough.

HARLEQUIN

A Calendar of Romance

Be a part of American Romance's year-long celebration of love and the holidays of 1992. Celebrate those special times each month with your favorite authors.

Next month, we salute moms everywhere—with a tender Mother's Day romance.

MAY

S	M	T	W	T	F	S
					1	2
3						
10						16
	1		21	22	23	
24/31	25	26	27	28	29	30

**#437
CINDERELLA
MOM
by Anne Henry**

Read all the books in *A Calendar of Romance,* coming to you one per month, all year, only in American Romance.

Harlequin®

JANELLE TAYLOR

Valley of Fire

HARLEQUIN IS PROUD TO PRESENT *VALLEY OF FIRE* BY JANELLE TAYLOR—AUTHOR OF TWENTY-TWO BOOKS, INCLUDING SIX *NEW YORK TIMES* BESTSELLERS

VALLEY OF FIRE—the warm and passionate story of Kathy Alexander, a famous romance author, and Steven Winngate, entrepreneur and owner of the magazine that intended to expose the real Kathy "Brandy" Alexander to her fans.

Don't miss VALLEY OF FIRE, available in May.